SPIRIT WINGS

THE CAVE OF ABIGOR

BOOK TWO

BY

SANDY SOLIS

ILLUSTRATIONS BY SANDY SOLIS

SPIRIT WINGS PRODUCTIONS LLC
2013

This is a work of fiction. Names, characters, places, and incidents are either a work of the writer's imagination or are used fictionally. All resemblance to actual persons, living or dead, is coincidental or prophetic in nature.

ISBN-978-0615901640

Spirit Wings Productions LLC
10342 E 550 Rd
Colcord, OK 74338
Info@SpiritWingsOnline.com
www.SpiritWingsOnline.com

Cover and interior images by Sandy Solis

Library of Congress
TX 7-979-504

Pronouns referring to God are capitalized in the text for the sake of clarity.

Give ear, O my people, to my teaching;
incline your ears to the words of my mouth!
I will open my mouth in a parable;
I will utter dark sayings from of old,
things that we have heard and known,
that our fathers have told us.
We will not hide them from their children,
but tell to the coming generation
the glorious deeds of the Lord, and his might,
and the wonders that he has done.
Psalm 78:1-4

Acknowledgments:

Thanks to Brianne the "Grammar Queen"

Thanks to Ron for one more "spit polish"

NOTE FROM THE AUTHOR:
YOU MAY WANT TO CHECK OUT THE SPECIAL FEATURE IN THE BACK OF THE BOOK. IT IS CALLED "TYPES AND SHADOWS". SOME WILL WANT TO SEE IT AFTER THEY READ THE ENTIRE BOOK, WHILE OTHERS MAY WISH TO LOOK AFTER EACH CHAPTER THAT IS READ.
--- ENJOY GOING DEEPER . . .

CONTENTS

SPIRIT WINGS

THE CAVE OF ABIGOR

CHAPTER ONE

AWAKE, AWAKE, OH SLEEPER

Ruby and her dorm mates spill out into the commons area of Levi Lodge at the break of dawn. A commotion stirs everyone from their sleep. Whispers bounce off the expanse of stone and glass architecture. Someone cries out, "Do it now!" Confusion and panic fill the majestic Gothic space, with its vaulted ceilings and pointed arch windows. From her bed, Ruby recognizes Jesse's voice and rushes out to find him lying in the commons area just outside his doorway. Destiny runs out with her to see about him. All the young cadets quietly stand there, watching Jesse crying out and behaving strangely. Ruby kneels to see her dear friend collapsed and is breathing hard on the floor. Destiny bends down by his side.

"Night . . . is . . . coming . . . do it now . . ." Jesse says, as a warning whispered in the deep of night.

Ruby grabs his face in her hands.

"Are you okay, Jess?" she asks, ignoring his strange words.

Tears streak down his face; Ruby feels the moisture on her hands. She has never seen him with so much emotion. Destiny remains with her hand over her mouth, looking down at him.

The late July sun is starting to light up the eastern sky behind the Sangre de Cristo Mountain range in Colorado, but activity on the SWA campus has not yet begun. An exceptional young man broke the stillness of the early morning by waking up from his sleep, suddenly jumping from his bed, running into the commons area, and crying out.

"Night is coming when no man can work. What you are going to do for [1]Adonai, do it now, do it now . . ." His voice echoes off the massive carved rock walls like a monk's in a monastery. (See "Types and Shadows" 1)

By now, the rest of the students in Levi Lodge awaken to the commotion and open their large wooden double doors to see Jesse on the floor and people huddling around him. They hold lanterns to light the shadowy area in front of Jesse's doorway. For the last three months, the

---

[1] Adonai-Hebrew for Lord

entire country has been without electric service; lanterns are now the norm.

"Night is coming," Jesse gasps from the cold stone floor. Everyone questions each other, what does he mean? Concern and anxiety sweep through the commons area full of sleepy young warriors still in their robes.

Just three months ago, Jesse predicted the Great Crisis of April, calling it a time for survival and endurance. Now, he brings a new warning that causes everyone to brace for what is ahead.

The last few people in the Levi dorms spill out of their rooms and stand looking at the rumpled-haired young prophet. Jesse appears to be coming around. The seventeen-year-old boy with thin, straight, black hair in his eyes, in sweatpants and a t-shirt, seems to be coming to his senses. It is as if he was in a trance or walking in his sleep. Soon, the entire campus will repeat his words and speculate about what it is all about.

Melody, the girls' floor leader, runs out of Levi's Lodge past the Academic Towers and across the small bridge to the employees' residential area. She is heading to the Academy's Dean's home. He is somewhat of a mystery; his name is unknown, and he goes by "The General." He is greatly respected and admired by all the SWA community. His dwelling is unique — a two-story stone hunting lodge, humble and modest, with a curved stairway leading to the front door. Melody bangs on the thick wooden door.

“Something happened in the Levi Lodge!” Melody exclaims breathlessly to the face of the General, peering through the partially opened wood-planked door. His wife looks on from behind him, a cup of coffee halfway to her lips. The General is currently brushing his teeth.

Still in her fleece robe and terry cloth slippers, Melody looks alarmed from the other side of the door. Her short, brown hair is still disheveled from sleep.

“Okay, I will be right there!” the General tells her, removing his toothbrush from his mouth; he is barefoot but already dressed. Melody turns and rushes back to Levi Lodge. The General hops as he puts on his leather hiking sandals. He runs to spit out the toothpaste and heads for the front door. He is wearing his usual plaid shirt and jeans. His neatly trimmed beard has a thin line along his jaw. Depending on how much sun he gets that year, the General’s shoulder-length hair goes from light brown to blonde on the tips.

He tells his wife, Jennifer, “Levi Lodge, that’s Jesse’s dorm; I have a feeling he is the cause of this commotion!”

The General hurriedly exits his small stone fortress and runs across the campus toward the Levi dorm.

As Jennifer watches her husband go out into the early morning light, she expects he is right about Jesse. This young boy is a blessing and a handful all at the same time.

Still in his thirties, the General is always the voice of wisdom and clarity. He was everyone's pillar of strength during the terrorist crisis. Spirit Wings Academy is in survival mode, and the small community is frozen in their tracks by the words of an exceptional young man they know as Jesse.

The word spreads to everyone on campus — kitchen workers, groundskeepers, and one hundred cadets. Everyone remains in place, hushed, waiting to find out what to expect next. Jesse has had words from the Lord before; his reputation as a prophet is growing. He and Prophetess Ira had predicted the Great Crisis of April, and the General made the necessary arrangements. Now, what is coming? Will it be worse than the last crisis?

"**Night is coming, when no man can work**." **(John 9:4-6)** The phrase echoes throughout the campus. The General arrives at the commons area of Levi Lodge in time to see Jesse sitting on a couch near his dorm.

"Night is coming, General, night is coming," Jesse tells him with intensity and somberness.

"Is that all you heard?" the General asks, noting Jesse's troubled demeanor.

"No. Also, work while it is yet day, for night is coming when no man can work," Jesse says passionately, his voice still groggy from sleep.

"Night is coming . . . sounds like the latter part of the Tribulation. But I'm not sure. It's okay, Jesse, it's okay. Yahweh will show us what to do. I will go ask my mom if she has heard anything, and Jamie may know something."

The General's mom, Ira, the prophetess, is highly esteemed on campus. She often consults with several others on what the Lord is showing them. It is known as the "Gathering of Eagles," a phrase coined by Ruby. Jesse is the only student member of the group, which is quite an honor. Jamie, the groundskeeper, and the General make up the group, along with Ira, the Prophetess. This expression, "Night is coming," has never come up before now.

The General looks up at all the frazzled faces of the young members of the Levi tribe. Eric, Jacob, and Jesse's other roommates hover over him with expressions of concern. They stand ready as if to be sent off on an emergency errand at any minute.

"Tell everyone to meet in the sanctuary immediately," the General says to all in the commons area.

Eric and the guys nod their heads, still in a state of alertness.

The General leaves to find his mom and Jamie to see if they know what this is all about.

As the gang leaves Levi Lodge, Ruby opens the ornate wrought-iron cage door to release her young eagle. Hope has taken residence in the dorm's lobby. Ruby nursed the bird back to health in the spring. Professor Norman, with his knowledge of eagles, helps Ruby a great deal. The eaglet fell from her nest in March and broke a wing. As a result, she can't fly. Professor Norman's custom-built cage has an extensive round sculptured stone base about three feet high, with a large, tall wrought-iron cage on top, with decorative scrollwork.

Almost five months old, the eagle is maturing and changing colors. Her bright eyes look into Ruby's. Hope's feathers, eyes, and beak are shiny black at this age. The raptor is dipping her head into her stone water fountain that trickles through the lower part of her cage. She shakes her head, and her feathers are dry again. She leaves a trail of wet claw prints on the floor leading out to the front door. Ruby uses her socks to rub the water off the floor, leaving them damp and slightly dirty. There is no time for delays; they must get to the Shekinah Sanctuary. Ruby returns her wet feet to her leather mule shoes, and the gang leaves the dorm.

Ruby permits Hope to go outside to hunt her food — mostly mice, squirrels, and snakes. Hope rubs affectionately on Ruby's leg and then walks out to forage for nourishment.

By this time, nearly everyone on campus has heard that the General called for an assembly at the sanctuary. Any time uncertainty or crisis occurs, Spirit Wings Academy's response is prayer in the Shekinah Sanctuary. Jesse's early morning message sounded so urgent that everyone rushes to the ornate Gothic structure in robes and pajamas. The silent, peaceful interior streams with light as the massive wooden double doors open, and one hundred sleepy students, staff, and volunteers rush into the room. The noise of footsteps and whispering disrupts the silence of the serene sanctuary. Decorative candelabras that once sat unused are now the primary source of light. Everyone gathers in the Gothic-style structure. Jamie has lit all the candles, but the space is still shadowy in the dim morning light, and a little nippy.

Professor Norman has brought an emergency radio. He turns it on and adjusts the dial — no signal, just static. At first, everyone stands around, silent and anxious, listening for something, anything. Across the massive room with high ceilings, there is the sound of weeping. Prayer begins to fill the chamber. Young and old lift their voices to Adonai, who has proved Himself faithful.

Ruby's family is just now showing up. Ruby hugs them across the high-back pews as they come to join in the prayer time. Most professors sit in the front rows, along with floor leaders, volunteer families, and other staff. Ruby and the gang are sitting in the second row, back in the center. Most people are standing and seeking Adonai, speaking in hushed tones.

"What's going on?" her dad, Ruben (Professor Alvarez), whispers.

"Jesse woke us all up yelling, 'Night is coming, work while it is yet day.' Then he collapsed in his doorway!" Ruby whispers back.

"You alright, Jesse?" Professor Alvarez asks him.

"Um . . . yeah. I'm fine," answers Jesse, somewhat embarrassed.

Ruby's older brother looks half asleep, and her mom has no makeup. Ruby snickers when she sees that her brother Arlo's hair is sticking up in the back.

Soon, as the room settles and prayer subsides, the General asks Jesse to tell more of what happened to him at five in the morning. The vast room resonates with sound as everyone shuffles around, settling into the beautiful wooden pews.

Jesse's hair is still messy. He approaches the General and thinks back to what happened. The room gets quiet as Jesse prepares to speak.

"I guess I was dreaming, in the Spirit or something. I felt intense heat and had to close my eyes and turn my head away to bear it. There was a bright light, followed by a loud noise, and then darkness. That's when I heard a voice:

> **We must work the works of Him who sent Me while it is day; night is coming, when no one can work. As long as I am in the world, I am the Light of the world."**
>
> **John 9:4-5**

"It felt like it was urgent and for the whole world. I didn't consciously decide to run to the commons area. I just found myself there, yelling and all."

Jesse's face flushes as he thinks of the spectacle he must have been. His voice is unsteady and hoarse from his shouting earlier. He looks back at the General; he has nothing more to add.

The sun continues to stream intensely through the vast, long, beveled glass windows, starkly contrasting with the room's dimly lit, shadowy corners.

The General puts his hand on Jesse's shoulder and thanks him. "Jamie, Aurora, got anything?"

They shake their heads, but Ira stands up.

The prophetess walks up to address the group of apprehensive youth and the others. She is an early riser and is fully dressed. She has their full attention. Maybe she could bring some clarity to the day's events. Before the Great Terrorist Crisis of April, she lived alone as an intercessor near the summit of the mountain. She gave up her solitude to join the staff as a professor.

The Spirit of the Lord comes upon her, and she quotes:

> **"Do two walk together, unless they have agreed to meet? Does a lion roar in the forest, when he has no prey? Does a young lion cry out from his den, if he has taken nothing? Does a bird fall in a snare on the earth when there is no trap for it? Does a snare spring up from the ground, when it has taken nothing? Is a trumpet blown in a city, and the people are not afraid? Does disaster come to a city, unless the Lord has done it? "For the Lord God does nothing without revealing his secret to his servants the prophets. The lion has roared; who will not fear? The Lord God has spoken; who can but prophesy?"**
>
> **Amos 3:3-8**

The glory of Adonai lifts, and she catches her breath and continues, her distinct British accent articulating every syllable with clarity. "Adonai is preparing us for the difficult times ahead. The main question is — what does 'night is coming' mean to us? **Joel 2:1-2** shows us the meaning of Jesse's New Testament scripture in **John 9**."

She opens her tattered leather Bible and reads:

> **Blow a trumpet in Zion; sound an alarm on my holy mountain! Let all the inhabitants of the land tremble, for the day of the Lord is coming; it is near, a day of darkness and gloom, a day of clouds and thick darkness! Like blackness there is spread upon the mountains a great and powerful people; their like has never been before, nor will be again after them**
> **through the years of all generations.**

"The 'Night' is when Yahweh pours out judgment on the wicked and HaSatan.[2] and his army. How much time do we have? We don't know, but the urgency of the hour is clear!"

Everyone shifts in their seats; uncertainty always opens the door to potential unease. The young warriors feel the sting of fear trying to penetrate them.

Ira continues with strong emphasis, "Even now, a dark army is plotting against us, all the more reason we

---

[2] Hebrew for Satan

must not lose our focus. As the days grow closer, HaSatan's anger rages against us. Are we servants who wait for their master with swords on our sides and fire in our eyes? As Jesse quoted the words of our Lord: 'Work while it is yet day.' Times are changing; we have been in birth pains; next is the Great Tribulation. We must continue to cry out for justice on the Earth. We must remain resilient; [3]Adonai will sustain us! Darkness will not come upon us unaware. Yahweh is doing a new thing on the planet, and we have our part to play. Here is a scripture you should know; it speaks of a red moon!"

Ira reads **Joel 2:30-32**:

> **"And I will show wonders in the heavens and on the earth, blood and fire and columns of smoke. The sun shall be turned to darkness, and the moon to blood, before the great and terrible day of the Lord comes. And it shall come to pass that everyone who calls on the name of the Lord shall be saved. For in Mount Zion and in Jerusalem there shall be those who escape, as the Lord has said, and among the survivors shall be those whom the Lord calls.**

With no warning, she stops speaking and returns to her place.

---

[3] Yahweh – Hebrew, from YHWH; also, Jehovah, God

The room is engulfed with deep contemplation. Even the Angelic Guardians are more diligent; Anton and the others square their shoulders and stand ready.

The General tells the assembly:

"It is almost noon, and we have not even stopped to eat. Be dismissed for lunch. We will see later whether we need to pray more or go about our daily business. I call no official fast. For now, we need to build up our strength and shake off any fear that attempts to grip us. This darkness could be years away. We will need more revelation on the subject."

People stumble out into the bright daylight and wander back to their rooms to get dressed, still trying to grasp the full ramifications of the phrase: "Night is coming, work while it is yet day."

Jesse isn't leaving. He tells Destiny and Ruby, "I'm not going anywhere; I need to seek the Lord. We still have those hidden idols to find. I don't know if this 'night is coming' is connected."

Jesse secretly wants to pray about the darkness that might remain in his heart. He doesn't like the girls to push him on the subject.

"Yeah, we need to know more," Ruby settles on the altar floor. "The pressing issue of hidden idols and Jesse's monster of darkness are urgent, I think. It's only been a week since Baal manifested as a dragon. He laughed and mocked us for being idolaters, claiming that Jesse was harboring a monster of darkness within him. And that King

— Abigor, I think is his name — what should we do about him?"

Destiny straightens up Jesse's hair with her fingers and says, "We need the anointing of the [4]Sons of Issachar to understand the times and seasons. The Day of the Lord is when Yeshua comes down to judge the wicked and take HaSatan down, I'm pretty sure.

"Sometime during the last half of the Tribulation," Steven adds, having not gone to eat either.

Destiny nods in agreement.

Ruby, being anxious in nature, asks, "The [5]rapture comes first. Before the wrath comes down?"

Jamie is positioning himself on the floor, "What it comes down to is that the Great Tribulation is close, and we have our part to play."

Aurora walks over to add, "All I know is we will be safe under the shadow of His wings. As far as we understand, the seventh trumpet will blow just before the wrath (Seven Bowls of Wrath, **Revelations 19:21, Matthew 23:39**); I am not worried either way. Yahweh has got us covered."

Destiny has her Bible in her robe pocket; she opens it and reads for Ruby:

> **Now concerning the times and the seasons, brothers, you have no need to have anything**

---

[4] 1 **Chronicles** 12:32

[5] Raptured- to be caught up, **1 Thessalonians 4:17**

written to you. For you yourselves are fully aware that the day of the Lord will come like a thief in the night. While people are saying, "There is peace and security," then sudden destruction will come upon them as labor pains come upon a pregnant woman, and they will not escape. But you are not in darkness, brothers, for that day to surprise you like a thief. For you are all children of light, children of the day. We are not of the night or of the darkness. So then let us not sleep, as others do, but let us keep awake and be sober. For those who sleep, sleep at night, and those who get drunk, are drunk at night. But since we belong to the day, let us be sober, having put on the breastplate of faith and love, and for a helmet the hope of salvation. For God has not destined us for wrath, but to obtain salvation through our Lord Jesus Christ, who died for us so that whether we are awake or asleep we might live with him. Therefore encourage one another and build one another up, just as you are doing.

1 Thessalonians 5:1-10

Jesse marvels at Destiny's knowledge of the scriptures. *Urgent* . . . the word rolls around in Jesse's spirit like thunder.

"Wow, so sudden destruction may come, but not on us," Ruby realizes. "We are here to sound an alarm, warn of the coming darkness, bring into the Kingdom as many as we can."

Devin makes a statement that surprises everyone, "[6]He is coming for a pure bride."

Everyone looks at him. Destiny feels weeping rise up in her spirit-man; hearing the passage moved her.

Since when did he get so deep? Ruby wonders.

Jesse realizes there are more terms he doesn't know at all.

The Bride of Christ, wedding attendants, the Ecclesia . . . who is who? Jesse needs to learn more.

Steven and Devin watch the rest of the people leaving for lunch; they waver between being spiritual and just plain hungry. Hesitantly, they wave and leave to go eat. Ruby's mom and big brother also leave for lunch.

"You sure you want to skip lunch?" Yolanda, her mom, asks Ruby.

"I am sure, Mom. You guys go on," Ruby tells her. Ruby points at her hair and then looks at Arlo.

He feels his head and finds his hair sticking up. He attempts to brush it down with his fingers. He feels embarrassed as he and his mom walk off.

"Grab me something for later," Eric tells Jacob as he joins the others at the altar.

---

[6] **Ephesians 7:19-21**

Professor Alvarez says, “I need to shave off a few pounds.” He joins the rest who are staying to pray. Ruby is glad he is staying.

Destiny, Jesse, Ruby, Eric, and most of the Judah tribe set themselves to pray at the sanctuary's front altar. The tribe of Judah is known for its strength in fasting and prayer. The students who make up this tribe are worship leaders and musicians, ranging in age from about sixteen to eighteen. Currently, there are only about ten cadets per tribe, whereas the normal number is twenty-five. It remains uncertain whether SWA will receive any new students.

Aurora leads this little band of warriors. She is also known to move powerfully in the Spirit. Ruby and all the cadets look up to her.

“Here we are, Yahweh, reveal Your heart to us, that we may found doing Your will when You come. Give us the anointing of the sons of Issachar so we can discern the correct times, seasons, and ages,” says Aurora as she paces. She is a slender, twenty-something woman with an intense gaze and a defined jawline. Her expression is kind and gentle, a contrast to her forceful words and passion. She is a combination of compassion, and a militant warrior all rolled into one.

Ruby’s dad is like a father to the little group; he huddles over the kids as they pray. Jamie, a twenty-year-old staff member and close friend of Jesse and the gang, lies on the floor in prayerful travail. This group, comprising both young and old, as well as experienced and beginners, is a tight-knit band of believers. They have seen the Lord do great things in the last year at SWA — such as Jamie being saved from witchcraft last October.

In a cave near the campus, a gathering of dark creatures meets to prepare strategies for the coming year. The den is tucked into the mountainside and hidden behind scrub bushes and undergrowth. Inside is a ragtag cluster of fallen angels (also called watchers), demons (offspring of watchers who lost their bodies in the Great Flood), and one fallen principality (a fallen archangel) known as the Fire King, Abigor. He is their master. They are on the edge of breaking out into chaos; the only thing that holds them in check is the fear of their leader. Even though he is their champion, and they are under his protection, he does not hesitate to rain destruction on them at will.

The Fire King is the region's ruling strongman, and he is gathering information. A nasally voiced impish demon is reporting:

"Jesse Logan is still in the Levi tribe, the repulsive priestly tribe. He remains with the ever-annoying Steven, Devin, Eric, and Jacob. We still have a hook in Jesse that could put his light out once and for all! Time will tell if it grows to maturity and snuffs him out! Also, the young female humans Ruby, Destiny, Gloria, Faith, Kristen, Milagros, and Audrey remain faithful to 'you know who.'" He points skyward with disdain on his face.

"What of the Semitic youth?" the King interrupts with a foul expression. Just the mention of the word 'Semitic' caused him to be ill at ease.

"Yosef, the Israelite, remains for his second year also. It is disgusting, like springtime and sunshine. You failed . . . I mean, *we* failed . . . Master . . . to eliminate the trashy scum from our region."

The tiny green spy imp cowers in fear that the king will lash out in his wrath. The king holds his anger and motions with a gnarled finger for the spy to continue.

"Some of the young humans ran for home after the crisis when traveling was allowed. Those pathetic seeds of Adam, fearful, childish, repulsive . . ." The imp notices the king's anger surfacing and stops talking.

Abigor, the Fire King, scowls at his imp and motions with his hand for him to move on.

"Oh, yes okay then . . . let's see . . . one hundred and fifty little humans graduated last [7]Maia (May) and vacated in two separate groups earlier. They could be of great grief to us in the future."

All the hosts of Abigor's army groan and murmur among themselves in the clefts of the cavernous cave.

The imp ignores the moans as if they were unworthy of his consideration.

---

[7] Maia- the month of May is named after this goddess from Rome, her name means "increase"

"Fifty cadets don't stay for their second year but return to their pathetic little homes and putrid families. They abandoned their cause and retreated to the safety of their mothers' skirt-tails, sniveling, spineless, whiny children! Can we revel in our partial victory now?" The imp wants to celebrate.

"NO, YOU FOOL, WE ARE IN THE WORST POSITION WE HAVE EVER BEEN IN SINCE THE CRUCIFIXION," the Fire King Abigor bends down and glares in the imp's face. The imp's bony, long, clawed hands cover his head in fear. Then, he regains his composure and pride and continues.

"Okay, okay . . . I got it, King . . . I will continue regurgitating the facts. The youth who are overcoming and not retreating to their homes after the Great Terrorist Crisis of [8]Aprillis are a cohesive group . . . I could barely stand to look at them. The stench of their affection for each other, their patience, and long-suffering is still in my nose. I need a good roll in the mud," the imp reports with sarcastic flair and disdain.

King Abigor leans in and glares at his tiny, big-eared spy.

"What of the nation of Israel? Has she been done away with yet?" King Abigor disdains Israel's very existence. He wants her wiped off the earth along with all

---

[8] Aprillis – the month of April is named after the Latin word for fertility time.

followers of Yeshua. He drums his boney-pointed fingers on the mossy, carved stone throne as he leans in to ask his miniature company of demonic spies.

Another eavesdropper imp steps up to reveal his findings. He is minuscule, with large, hairy, pointed ears and a gold earring in one of them. He is full of arrogance and self-importance.

"Israel is in constant conflict to preserve its borders and survive as a nation. Jihad is on everyone's lips! The Great Eagle (U.S.) stopped helping Israel when the little 'inn-o-cent' planes crippled their homeland. (He uses "baby talk" and puts out his lower lip) The Arab Spring has happened . . . just as Baal promised, it is glor-i-ous!"

The imp pauses his report as the dark spirits shout and dance around, rejoicing over the terrorists' exploits and chanting, "Bab-y-lon, Bab-y-lon!"

"Huhum!" The imp doesn't like being interrupted. "The plot was to kill the Great Eagle's future by stopping the next generation of humans from being born. The chemical spray affected one out of every one hundred men, making it a dismal failure, really. The long-term effects will be a surprise. The arrogant Nephilim will not communicate with me on the matter. Just because they have bodies, they think they are better than us. There are rumors that soon, new Nephilim will be born — wondrous creatures. We will see how humans deal with that!"

"All I have seen of the new [9]seed of the Snake are failures — freakish, weak, and dying creatures," the King complains.

"Our time to dominate is at hand, I assure you, oh King," the imp bows half in jest. With smugness and conceit, the imp steps down from in front of the Fire King's throne, all the while showering insults at no one in particular.

The King groans. He rises and steps toward his army of evil spirits with his scepter in his right hand. Anger grows on him as the tongues of fire enlarge upon his body. His royal cape blows back in shifting hues of purple to orange, and his rage generates a blast of yellow air.

"Can anyone tell me," his voice growing louder, "a plan to shut down SWA before WE ALL END UP AS YESHUA'S FOOTSTOOL? This mountain range is our territory, and they are a real threat! I don't want to return to New Mexico in humiliation and defeat. DO YOU UNDERSTAND ME?"

His hoard leans backward at his rebuke. No one dares to open their mouths. A sharp wind flows from the evil king's mouth, forcing his army off their feet and blowing deep within the cave where a cavern of large eggs lies. Spider webs surround the eggs and make up the eggs' nest. The wind blows out of the mouth of the cave, and the

---

[9] Snake, serpent- reference of HaSatan, **Genesis 3:13-15**

vegetation flutters in the breeze. All the demon spies leave in haste, daring not to return without good news.

Inside the Shekinah Sanctuary, the group's diligent prayers continue. The concerned voices rise like incense up through the roof, into the sky, and eventually to the Most High's throne room. Angelic messengers carry the prayers in bowls and pour them out on the golden altar of incense in the heavenly temple. Those prayers are heard, mingled with thunder and lightning, and the voices of multiple worshippers in the throne room.

As the group continues praying in the sanctuary and the rest of the students eat lunch, the General walks around the campus seeking to hear from Adonai. The hum of generators on the campus is a constant reminder that times are different. He begins climbing the spiral metal staircase in Academic Tower West. The echo of his sandals fills the lonely tower. The General arrives at the roof, where rails circle the edge, and several stepped circular platforms provide places for people to pray when the weather is agreeable. He notes that no one else is up there to pray; they are all gathered in the sanctuary today. The view goes down the mountainside to the campus front entry. The clouds are bright and full of depth, spotting the blue sky and bringing dotted shadows on the land. He walks toward the railing and looks out over the campus.

I am closing the outdoor market just for today. We need to gather and get a hold of what You told Jesse about the night coming. Father, I thank You for the woodstoves in the kitchen; they are working well. All the tribes of the school have learned practical survival skills. They can cut firewood, build furniture, sew, make candles, and raise livestock, among other things. They really adjusted and took to the changes we made. Your grace made all the difference in these kids. The outdoor market brings me joy. We are certainly making a difference in people's lives. I need to reduce the market to only be open on Saturdays when classes resume soon. Training Your army must remain my focus . . . Yahweh . . . tell me what to do.

He looks at the personnel's cars sitting in the parking lot, unused for three months now.

Only buses and government vehicles use the highways until gasoline sources can replace the fuel that the terrorist countries now control. Yahweh, how long will I be able to train cadets for Your army? How much longer do I have? The General seeks the counsel of the Lord of Hosts.

After lunch, everyone on campus returns to the Shekinah Sanctuary. The massive Gothic stone and wood building, capable of seating five hundred, is situated between the dorms on the campus's top level. Hope wants to go inside with Ruby, but she is not allowed, so she hangs around by the door and naps in the sun.

The gang is done praying for the moment, and they watch as everyone else returns. Eric is glad to get a dinner roll full of lunchmeat from Jacob.

"Thanks, dude," Eric tells him.

"No prob, I dropped it on the floor; hope that's okay," jokes Jacob.

Eric smiles with his mouth full.

Ruby and the gang sit up front as usual; Jesse still wishes they would be off to the side or, better yet, sit in the back.

"Eric's roll smells good," notes Jesse. He wishes he had thought of asking for food, too.

Today, Devin carries a notebook to take notes; this is unusual. Now all eyes are on the General as he approaches the podium in the center of the stage.

The General refuses to give his name, always saying, "I must decrease that Adonai may enlarge." He told the school this, years ago, right at its inception.

He announces with a casual tone, "Ira offered her insight this morning; now Jamie has more of Yahweh's insight for us."

Jesse is amazed Jamie has prepared something; he just spent the morning with them in prayer.

It isn't the first time that Jamie speaks to the academy; as usual, Jamie has no notes. He knows the Bible better than anyone else on campus, as do most witchcraft followers of his former coven. The fierceness in Jamie's eyes is as intense as his expression as he approaches the front of the platform where the General stands. Just looking at Jamie stirs the fire of Yahweh in Jesse and the others. Jamie speaks with authority.

"This is what Adonai gave me as I lay praying on the floor all morning. As I speak to you, I would speak to the nation, the continent, and all the people of the earth. Urgently, I tell you, **Mark 13:35-37** shows us what we need to see:

> **Therefore stay awake—for you do not know when the master of the house will come, in the evening, or at midnight, or when the rooster crows, or in the morning— lest he come suddenly and find you asleep. And what I say to you I say to all: Stay awake."**

The drama and force of his words cause everyone to lean in and wait with anticipation. As Jamie continues, Jesse remembers the word URGENT from prayer time. The Lord has Jesse's attention.

"There should be an urgency in the air, but instead, complacency and dullness fill the atmosphere. It is just like the days of Noah. Noah received the word of the Lord that He was going to destroy all flesh. Noah began to prepare the place of deliverance and safety that the Lord had instructed him to build. For nearly one hundred and twenty years, the people watched him build the ark. They continued living as they had always done, marrying and giving in marriage, without altering their lifestyle. All men of the day were continually wicked before God. Only Noah's seed was not corrupted by the fallen sons of God.

I will not talk about the [10]Nephilim now, but they desire to corrupt men and fill the earth with violence. They will be a force in the future once again, attempting to rule the Earth. They lost their bodies in the flood and are the demonic servants of HaSatan to this day. Imps, demons, unclean spirits, apparitions, ghosts, are all the disembodied seed of HaSatan, through fallen angels referred to as 'sons of God' in **Genesis 6**."

The cadets look at each other; the idea is strange to them. Jamie knows many other scriptures will not make sense without this concept.

Jesse studies the General's expression; he seems comfortable with Jamie's mention of Nephilim.

I have so much to learn. I think I should have Jamie teach me some stuff, Jesse thinks.

Jamie continues with passion and expression in his voice.

"The people of Noah's day did not enter into the safety of the ark, only Noah and his family. God sees that iniquity has almost come to its fullness. He is looking for someone to cry out, 'Judgment is coming, escape His wrath and come into His covenant blessings.' Noah hammered on that ark, and the people did not change their ways. The wicked carried on with business as usual. They had never seen rain or heard thunder from the heavens.

---

[10] Nephilim- seed of the fallen ones, half human half angelic. Sons of God may refer to all those created or born of the Spirit as opposed to being born in the flesh. **Genesis 6:1-4**

"It's the same now . . ."

"Just as it was in the days of Noah, so will it be in the days of the Son of Man. They were eating and drinking and marrying and being given in marriage, until the day when Noah entered the ark, and the flood came and destroyed them all."

Luke 17:26-27

"What are we going to do when life as we know it ends? Will we seek intimacy with God during chaos and anarchy? Judgment is approaching; be prepared. We must give ourselves to seeking the face of Yeshua. The people did not change; they would not hear. They hardened their hearts from His ways. Then God released the floods He promised. I am here to affirm: Elohim needs a sound to be made on the earth, a wake-up call, a warning. Will we be silent at this hour and not give a warning to the people? Are we deaf and blind? There is an army Yeshua is equipping to rise up and announce, 'Everything is not okay.'

Jamie paces as he speaks, and everyone hangs on his words. It is reaching inside them and touching them all to the core. Jamie goes on, not stopping to catch his breath.

"We are in a country, a culture, that urgently needs stirring from its slumber. We need a wake-up call; we need an awareness of the times. We must awaken to the fact that Yahweh will pour His wrath out on the earth, but He has provided a way of escape.

"We are worthless servants if there's not a sense of urgency. If we walk around in our little circle of activities and purposes, we miss the high calling of Yeshua and become useless servants.

"Today is the day, people, we need to wake up and be about the Master's business. We pray for judgment of the wicked and forget how judgment begins in the house of God. The cares of this life consume us; now, we must mature and truly put our trust in Adonai. [11]Don't wait for darkness before you trim your lamps and buy oil. By this, I mean to confess your sins and be full of [12]Ruach HaKodesh. Night is coming . . . Jesse told us already.

> **"But watch yourselves lest your hearts be weighed down with dissipation and drunkenness and cares of this life, and that day come upon you suddenly like a trap. For it will come upon all who dwell on the face of the whole earth. But stay awake at all times, praying that you may have strength to escape all these things that are going to take place, and to stand before the Son of Man."**
>
> **Luke 21:34-36**

"The spirit of this age deludes men, deluded with our own plans to keep us safe, satisfied, and fulfilled. Great

---

[11] **Matthew 25:13**
[12] Ruach HaKodesh – Hebrew, Holy Spirit

Deception and [13]Strong Delusion are active on the earth. Our own devices consume our days. How can we know the heart of the Father when we are full of ourselves and our agendas?

"Adonai has called us to wake up. May He encounter us and break us out of our slumber and delusions of [14]peace and safety. We find confidence and security in our nation, our parents, our jobs, and our plans. How much are we genuinely relying on Yahweh? When was the last time we trusted Him for anything? Do we have any works of faith? Wake us up, Father! Yeshua did what He saw the Father do. Are we? Has His Kingdom manifested, and is [15]Has His Word been confirmed in our lives through signs and wonders? Are we in a position of prayer and watching for the Kingdom to manifest?

"**Matthew 25:29** says it all:

'For to everyone who has will more be given, and he will have an abundance. But from the one who has not, even what he has will be taken

---

[13] **2 Thessalonians 2:11**
Therefore God sends them a strong delusion, so that they may believe what is false,

[14] 1 Thessalonians 5:3
While people are saying, "There is peace and security," then sudden destruction will come upon them as labor pains come upon a pregnant woman, and they will not escape.

[15] **Act 14:3 So they remained for a long time, speaking boldly for the Lord, who bore witness to the word of his grace, granting signs and wonders to be done by their hands.**

away. And cast the worthless servant into the outer darkness. In that place there will be weeping and gnashing of teeth.'"

"Are we useless, faithless servants, eating at His table and not getting up to work in His fields? May Adonai break in on this generation and release us from business as usual. May eternity crash in on us, and we be found as [16]servants who wait for the Master, with [17]swords in our hands and praises on our lips.

"I pray we find the secret place of the Most High and live there, that we would be carriers of the glory of God. [18]We can't be seated with Yeshua in heavenly places and caught up in the cares of this world.

"Now Jesse has quoted Yeshua saying, '**Work while it is day, night is coming when no man can work**,' **John 9:4**. We are children of the day, and we will endeavor to bring the sound to wake up the masses; judgment is coming. Come to [19]Yeshua Ha'Mashiach, the place of peace and safety. So, I say to you, and I say to all,

---

[16] Luke 12:36- **and be like men who are waiting for their master to come home from the wedding feast, so that they may open the door to him at once when he comes and knocks.**

[17] **Psalm 149:6 Let the high praises of God be in their throats and two-edged swords in their hands,** (see rest of chapter)

[18] **Ephesians 2:6**

[19] Hebrew for Jesus the Christ, Salvation the Anointed One

watch and pray that you may be found [20]worthy to escape the wrath and stand before the Son of God.

"Check out these verses in **Joel 2:1-2**:

> **Blow a trumpet in Zion; sound an alarm on my holy mountain! Let all the inhabitants of the land tremble, for the day of the Lord is coming; it is near, a day of darkness and gloom, a day of clouds and thick darkness! Like blackness there is spread upon the mountains a great and powerful people; their like has never been before, nor will be again after them through the years of all generations.**

Jamie leaves the stage as everyone sits absorbing his message.

Jesse runs the words through his mind, *thick darkness . . . inner darkness, outer darkness.*

"Judgment begins in the house of God . . .," Ruby says, deep in thought.

Destiny evaluates, "Adonai is calling for carnal believers to wake up and be about the Master's business."

Jesse nods his head in deep contemplation; he can sense the massive numbers of people who have knowledge of God but never developed a genuine relationship with the Godhead. He knows his vision is the Father's heart to call

---

[20] Luke 21:36 **But stay awake at all times, praying that you may have strength to escape all these things that are going to take place, and to stand before the Son of Man."**

out to the earth and stir hearts to recognize the urgency of the hour.

He will spend many days pondering such things. The words grip him still, and he wonders if it affected everyone else as much as it did him.

Jesse tells the girls and the others, “We have got to find those hidden idols!”

The girls nod with stern expressions.

Ruby is captivated by the day's events and Jamie’s message and call to awaken a generation. She realizes it will be with her for a long time. *We need to address this idol issue!*

Destiny is also captured by the realization of the hour. Jesse and Jamie’s words bring change to SWA, with new perspectives and insight. Deep within their resolve, they purpose to be aware of the urgency of the hour they are living in and to find the hidden idols with the guidance of the Holy Spirit. She is enamored with Jesse and his encounters with Yeshua.

As Jamie steps down, the Judah tribe plays a gentle instrumental as Professor Ruben and others lead prayers. These are no ordinary times, nor are these ordinary teens. They excel in prayer and fasting and are not easily shaken in their faith. Fear will try to grip them, but they know how to fight it off. Worship is a powerful weapon to push back all the forces of darkness.

The praying dissolves into worship, and the band begins to play a new song. Aurora plays an intense piano melody that develops into a surging militant melody.

Acoustic guitars build the intensity of the music. They sing:

The Devil knows his time is short
He calls his fallen cohorts
The fight for the Earth has sides drawn
Awake My people, and come out of Babylon
Don't sleep through the war
Don't be blind and deaf on the floor
The enemy is full of fury
Why do people not worry?
Let us hear what the Spirit says to the [21]ecclesia
Let us see in the Spirit as the battles emerge

The power of God surges in the room; everyone stands with hands in the air. Worship resounds throughout the sanctuary. Unexpectedly, the electric power comes on in the massive stone structure, including lights, sound equipment, and everything else. Everyone yells with joy. To their amazement, the lights get dim when they stop worshiping. The stronger the worship, the brighter the lights grow. Ira walks to the microphones that are now working.

"This is God. No one else has power!" Ira yells in excitement. Her voice echoes through the sound system.

---

[21] Ecclesia – Called Out Ones, church,Strong's # G1537)

Worship continues unbroken for several hours, as everyone weeps under the Shekinah glory of the Lord. The sanctuary was named after this glory. How fitting it is that it now houses that brilliant, extraordinary glory of Yahweh.

Above the wood and stone rooftops, over the tall pines, past the mountain peaks, there is a sound of marching. Angels have been drawn in by the worship below. The angelic hosts march with fire in their eyes. Stirred by the worship emanating from SWA, to the sound of the drumbeats, they march to the campus and take up new stations.

The worship continues:

[22]**Blessed be the LORD, my rock, who trains my hands for war, and my fingers for battle;**

They point their swords up in the air, sparks and lightning flash across the blades. The beat of the SWA's drums is their cadence.

Just over the mountain range, a band of demons sleep. Like bats, they hang upside down off the cliffs of rocks. The greenish imps begin to stir as the sound of marching grows ever louder. The unclean demons start to panic, colliding with one another. They fight each other as chaos takes over. Brilliant light from the angels' swords blinds the evil horde. The demons can now hear the sound

---

22 **Psalm 144:1**

of the worship. They can do nothing now but hold their ears and moan in misery. As the angel troops approach the dark creatures, there is a sound of metal striking the rocks. A single lightning bolt from the hosts of angels shoots into the second heaven. As a result, the air clears of much of the darkness and evil. Anton and the other Guardians are overjoyed to welcome the added support. A holy warring angel now stands by Anton, sword drawn and in position.

"The worship drew us in, and we will stay," the eleven-foot warrior tells Anton without speaking out loud.

"Glad you are here; we can use the support," Anton replies. "Welcome to SWA."

The light-charged warrior swings his sword in the air, clearing any unseen darkness that might linger. Like gnats hitting an ultraviolet fly zapper, tiny demonic spies are taken out by the blue lightning on his sword.

The atmosphere over the entire nation clears of much of the gloom that the terrorist attack created. Strong resilience and hope fill hearts from coast to coast. Pockets of holy warring angels are now in place all over the country, as other groups of believers with their worship of Yahweh have also attracted them. Pockets of light burst through the fog in the second heaven.

As the worship in the majestic sanctuary mellows, the lights fade and eventually go out entirely. They all stand in silence and partial darkness again. Not a noise anywhere; they stand in awe of how Adonai had given them electricity during the worship.

And between the throne and the four living creatures and among the elders I saw a Lamb standing, as though it had been slain, with seven horns and with seven eyes, which are the seven spirits of God sent out into all the earth. And he went and took the scroll from the right hand of him who was seated on the throne. And when he had taken the scroll, the four living creatures and the twenty-four elders fell down before the Lamb, each holding a harp, and golden bowls full of incense, which are the prayers of the saints. And they sang a new song, saying, "Worthy are you to take the scroll and to open its seals, for you were slain, and by your blood you ransomed people for God from every tribe and language and people and nation,

Revelation 5:6-9

Father God is unfolding the battle plans to take back the title deed of the earth. HaSatan looks at humanity with more disdain than ever, knowing his time is short.

"Blessed be the Lord, my rock, who trains my hands for war, and my fingers for battle," echoes in the halls of heaven and the minds of everyone on campus.

At the sound of these words, the warring angels on campus, in unison, maneuver in a sword dance. They block, swing, step, and spin with their swords glowing with blue lightning. Ruby senses their activity, while

Aurora and Jamie see them distinctly. Jesse sees the lightning; Destiny sees orbs of blue light.

The General walks to the edge of the stage, visibly moved by the day's events.

"The call to get ready is clear. Darkness will not overtake us; we are children of the Light!" He adds, "Let us eat, and put on strength, for the Lord is our Rock."

Jesse shudders; the image of the lightning fades. *Darkness . . . I still have to deal with some stuff. I don't have the strength to look at my own failures. Why did You use me, of all people, to warn about darkness?*

Destiny notices Jesse's countenance and nudges Ruby. The girls know he is wrestling inside, and they wait for him to be ready to talk about it.

Everyone slowly wanders over to the dining hall for supper, as this is a day to remember. Jesse, Ruby, and Destiny are still in their pajamas, as are several others. Hope follows Ruby and the gang as they walk down the long stairway toward the campus's middle level.

"How ironic," mentions Destiny, "while we were still in our pajamas, we sang, 'I don't want to be sleeping, while the Devil is raging.'"

Ruby realizes Hope has been alone all day, and she brings her into the dining hall. Hope makes a perch of the bench next to Ruby. As the General approaches, Ruby worries that he will make Hope go outside.

"I see Hope has come in for some dining. Ruby, she is looking good. You really have been a good caretaker," the General compliments her.

Ruby smiles, relieved Hope can stay.

Jesse's concern over the darkness that may remain in his own heart grips him. He still longs to talk to the girls about it, but his pride restrains him. He hesitates to eat until the General comes over and urges him to. He doesn't realize how drained he is until he sits down to eat. His hands shake like they used to in the homeless days. He flashes back to days behind the mall, where he scavenged for food in the food court trash. He takes a big breath and thanks God for SWA and his friends here.

Professor Alvarez also tells Jesse, "You need your strength. Eat . . . Rocky."

As he walks by, he ruffles Jesse's hair with his hand.

Jesse jokes back, "Not the hair, man, not the hair!"

Destiny straightens his hair with her fingers again.

They are a close group, and kidding around is normal for them.

Ruby's Dad notices Hope and says to the young bald eagle, "You got lonely outside all by yourself, didn't you?"

Ruby is glad her dad understands, and he didn't make her take Hope outside either. Professor Alvarez goes on to the staff table and joins the adult conversations.

That evening, it's back to candles and lanterns. The miracle of the power coming on confirms to many that Jesse, Ira, and Jamie's words were from God. The campus is settling down from the turmoil of the day. The newly arrived holy warring angels find strategic points to occupy and settle in on their new assignment. These tall, armored angels with shields grace the rafters, rooftops, and outer walls of the campus.

In his dorm, Jesse reflects on how crazy the day was.

Is more chaos coming? Where are those hidden idols? Is there still some terrible darkness in me? Jesse asks Adonai. His conversation with the Lord is continual. In time, answers will come. For now, Jesse longs for deep sleep and rest. He casually but respectfully waves at the angels he knows are in the room. Eric glances over to see Jesse waving.

Eric thinks: *Boy . . . that guy is in a world of his own.* Eric smiles: he respects Jesse. He just doesn't understand all that Jesse experiences in the spirit realm.

Ruby puts Hope in her cage for the night and goes to her dorm. She brushes her long, red-brown hair and puts it back in a ponytail for bed. She can hear a guitar playing next door. Feeling close to her roommates is natural; they have been through a lot together. Ruby is grateful that her parents and brother are on campus this year, but she chooses to stay in her assigned dorm. She wants to be there for her friends. Before lights out, she prays for Jesse as she always does. Destiny joins her tonight. They agree that the enemy can't lash out against him because Yahweh used him today. Milagros, Gloria, Faith, and Audrey are already asleep. It has been a tiring day.

Aurora covers Jamie in prayer from Lion Lodge, praying that he, too, would not experience a backlash from the enemy. Along with being an instructor and worship leader, she serves as a floor leader for Lion Lodge, also known as Judah Lodge. She began at SWA as a student seven years ago.

It's a slow news day for the adults who linger in the dining hall to catch the nightly news. The battery-powered radio blares out the information on tiny speakers; everyone leans in to listen. Afterward, conversations around coffee and tea are sober.

"The world is going through change; it is in the air," Professor Alvarez comments, gazing out the glass ceiling to the stars.

"Yeah, there is a great unrest; people are looking for direction and not finding it," says Ira. "Many claim a one-world government is just a few years away. Anarchy is catching on with the college kids," Ira relates to her fellow staff members. "By the way, a new host of warring angels are assigned to us."

"That would indicate more demonic activity here in the future, I think," the General surmises.

"Hmmm. Yeah, I agree. Have you heard about pirates that are taking over ships and bands of thieves running across the country, terrorizing smaller cities?" asks Professor Norman, with his military voice.

"The news on the radio tonight makes it sound as though things are improving. They keep insisting the war on terrorism is over. Jesse and Jamie's messages from this morning, however, make it clear. We are about to be thrust into great conflict," Professor White, the dance teacher, notices.

"Watch and pray," Adonai whispers to the SWA community.

"He who has an ear, let him hear what the Spirit says to the churches"

Revelation 3: 13

But stay awake at all times, praying that you may have strength to escape all these things that are going to take place, and to stand before the Son of Man."

Luke 21:36

As it always does, the sun goes down that night, and darkness descends on the mountain. The long shadows of evening give way to complete nightfall. There is an absolute calm across the campus as their world is at rest. Tick tock goes the prophetic time clock; echoes and stirrings in the heavens occur unheard by humans below.

Time will reveal the unfolding plan of Yahweh to take back the title deed of planet Earth. The watch-spring winds up tightly as if only a minor impact could cause time itself to crash in on the planet and bring everything down. Yahweh holds time in its place, and it will continue to tick; all of heaven's creatures are watching the second hand now; time is running down. All the fallen also know that the time is late; they intensify their efforts, vowing to rule the universe and reign from the Earth. HaSatan, knowing his time is short, has a plan to bring as much destruction as he can before his time is up.

Life continues on the Colorado mountainside; it is a new day. There is a somber tone in the air after yesterday. Has the world changed by the announcement of darkness coming, or have only a few hearts been impacted today? A sense of expectancy mixed with awe over the miracle of electricity in the Shekinah Sanctuary. It is official, not just a rumor — wind turbines will soon supply SWA with power. However, until then, work continues as usual.

Bacon is on the breakfast plates for the first time in months. The Ruben tribe butchered their first hog. Several of the tribes' members remember the pig's name, and they pass on the bacon. The farming guild, led by the tribe of Rueben, is harvesting the remaining crops.

Before breakfast, Ruby gets Hope out of her cage and puts her outside.

"Happy hunting, Hope, and no eating on the steps; it's gross," Ruby instructs Hope as the bird pokes around for mice and the like.

In the dining hall, the gang sits down to eat at their tribal table as usual. The early morning light streams through the bent glass ceiling. It still takes Ruby's breath away — the beauty that surrounds her in the Rocky Mountains. The glass walls and ceiling expose the evergreen trees and mountains that hug the campus.

"Today seems dull in comparison to yesterday," Ruby comments.

"Fine with me," Jesse responds, digging into his food. "I am still getting used to God using me in these ways. I don't remember getting up and running to the commons area yesterday."

Jesse thinks *I've regained some self-esteem. I hope I can keep my newfound dignity. I have been saved for over a year now; I finally feel like this is home. I don't feel like street trash anymore . . . New York seems like a story, some faded nightmare.*

"You still worry that people will look at you like you are crazy, though," Ruby leans in to tell him.

Jesse swallows hard. He didn't remember telling her about that. He drifts off in his thoughts again, as he is known to do.

I am no longer homeless, scrounging for food in mall food courts. I am getting closer to Ruby and Destiny. It's a significant step for me to trust someone. That's good progress for one year, I think. We are to be a team after graduation. The world is so unstable, will we actually be able to graduate?

Jamie greets the group as he walks to the staff table.

"I hear you got a promotion, Jamie. Congrats," Jesse tells him.

"Yeah, feels good — Head of Maintenance," says Jamie, as he smiles and walks on.

Jamie and Jesse bonded last October. Jesse and Devin led Jamie to the Kingdom of Elohim on Halloween night. Jamie lost his position as a councilor after he confessed to being part of a witch's coven and plotting against SWA with spells. Most people accepted Jamie after he accepted Christ. A few, however, never stop watching him for signs of betrayal.

In the past, Jesse used to put extra bacon in his pocket, a habit he developed while being homeless. The gang used to smell the bacon and didn't know why.

"Strawberries and real whipped cream on pancakes today!" Jesse is still grateful for good food.

Strawberry pancakes are a campus favorite. The kitchen staff painstakingly makes a ring of strawberries around the edge of each pancake. Jesse is halfway through eating when he gets dizzy, the room spins, and voices are muffled. He feels like he used to when he couldn't find food for days. But this is different somehow.

Destiny and Ruby look at each other. They felt the enemy would lash out at Jesse, but prayed against it the night before.

Jesse feels a cool sensation, and then a light, floating feeling sweeps over him. He sees people's mouths move but doesn't hear the sounds. Then Jesse passes out cold. He slumps over on Eric, and Eric guides him down to the floor behind the bench where they had sat. Eric holds Jesse's head so that it doesn't hit the floor. Professor Norman is the first to get to Jesse; he is quick to respond to emergencies as an ex-marine. The nurse sets down her coffee and rushes over. She and Professor Norman huddle over Jesse. Everyone around Jesse stands up in alarm; the rest of the room looks on in alarm.

The nurse checks Jesse's pulse and breathing and finds them stable. Then she tells Professor Norman, "You and Jamie take Jesse to the clinic."

They jump into action and lift his arms over their shoulders. Everyone at their tribal tables watches as they carry Jesse out of the dining hall. The clinic is in the administration building. They take Jesse down the ramp that leads to the lower level by the front gate. Ruby and all of the Levi dorm members follow them.

The receptionist stands up from her office chair with concern as they carry Jesse past her desk to the clinic. She watches as around ten students stream in behind him. She goes to locate Doctor Luz. They set Jesse down in the waiting room; he is starting to come around. Professor Norman sits with him, as he is slumped over on a chair; Jamie sits on Jesse's other side. The professor shoos all the gang out.

"Give him some air," he tells them with concern on his face.

The gang settles on the main lobby floor, looking in through the clinic's open door. The receptionist has returned and invites them to wait over by her in the lobby's couches, but they want to see what's going on and choose a spot just outside the clinic door. The receptionist smiles as she returns to her desk by the front door. The gang begins to pray quietly on the cold stone floors. The large windows in the front and back of the administration building bathe it with light. Bent lumber columns run up the corners of the ceiling, and stucco walls are bright white.

Inside the clinic, the rooms are sterile with white walls and grey floor tiles. Doctor Luz is due to arrive any second. Jesse comes around but still isn't himself.

As the word spreads that Jesse is ill, the campus comes to a halt, and prayer rings out in the mountain air. As a result, Jesse's two angels get authorized to minister to him. A dark spirit has drained Jesse's energy and left him dehydrated. It is also trying to attach a disease to Jesse's body, but cannot because of the girls' prayers yesterday. The dark spirit floats around Jesse like a slow whirlpool of sinister smoke.

Anton and his new partner, a warring angel, fight the dark spirit over the top of Jesse. Jesse is aware of the dark entity's presence, but his mind is cloudy, and he can't form clear thoughts. It is as if the shadowy spirit has covered Jesse in thick mud in the spirit realm. Ruby and Destiny cast off the Spirit of Babylon (confusion) and command it to go. Jamie releases healing and protection to

Jesse and begins quoting scriptures about Calvary and the power of Christ's blood.

The dark imp screams a horrid, “NOOOO!” that only the angels and Jesse hear, and it is gone like a candle flame in the wind. The mud-like heaviness lifts off Jesse and dissipates into the air. Jesse’s two angels linger over him with their wings wrapped around him in protection. Nothing can get to him now. Father God nods to his agents from his throne; another battle is over. His nod to them reminds them of the vital importance of their assignment, and they become even more diligent.

With his eyes closed, Jesse can see white orbs floating. Jesse opens his eyes and sits up, scratching his head.

“I wasn’t through eating . . .” He looks around and gets his bearings.

“You gave us quite a scare, young man,” the nurse tells him in her kind, casual voice.

She puts her hand on Jesse’s forehead, checking it for fever and chills.

“Can I go finish eating now?” Jesse asks her, looking out the door at everyone peeking in from the main room.

“Not just yet; Doctor Luz wants to examine you first, just to be safe. We need to run some blood work also.”

Ruby and Destiny wave; he motions his hand with embarrassment, realizing his predicament.

Jamie, hearing the nurse's comment, says, "The Blood of Jesus did its work."

Jesse hears him and nods. *Blood work . . ..*

"Yes, Jesus, I remember what You did on that cross." *I wonder if I said that out loud. It doesn't really matter.*

Doctor Luz steps into the clinic. He and the nurse discuss Jesse's condition. Doctor Luz looks Jesse over. Jesse remains pale, with dark circles around his eyes.

"Jesse, let's go into the exam room and check you out," Doctor Luz gently tells him.

A look of pure dread washes over Jesse's face of all remaining color. Ruby and Destiny get up and watch as Jesse stumbles into the exam room. Eric and Jacob know how Jesse hates it when anyone sees his scars. They know he is upset, but they don't feel they can tell the girls about it, though. That is up to Jesse to share when he is ready. They promised to keep it confidential.

The nurse smiles at the nervous group on the floor just outside the clinic as she shuts the exam room door.

Doctor Luz sees the anxiety on Jesse's face as he washes his hands in the sink and dries them.

"Let's just start by removing your shirt, shall we?" The doctor lights a large lantern that hangs down over the exam table. It is an antique bought from a vintage store. Because there are small windows in the room, it gives off additional needed light.

Jesse's hands are visibly shaking now. He sits at the exam table, but he has not taken off his shirt. The nurse and the doctor guess he suffered trauma in the past and proceed more slowly.

"I am just going to lift your shirt and listen with my stethoscope." Doctor Luz slowly lifts the back of Jesse's t-shirt. He sees scars across his back, starting on the waistline and going across his shoulders. He forgets to use his stethoscope. Jesse looks down at the floor and wishes to be somewhere else. The nurse tries to hide her shock as the doctor steps back behind Jesse and gathers his composure. He can tell the scars are not fresh and that they are lashes from being whipped.

"I am . . . sorry, son. I am going to have to take pictures of these scars and send them to the authorities. Can you tell me who did this?"

The doctor doesn't press the issue and continues with the exam. The tension in the room builds as Jesse hesitantly pulls his t-shirt over his head and clutches it in his lap.

The doctor also observes odd scars on his abdomen, short, evenly spaced scars, clustered in one area just above the beltline and to the side.

Now Jesse's face gets even paler, and then he throws up in the exam room's sink.

Outside, the gang hears vomiting.

"OOOU!" They all make faces of disgust. Ruby is anxious about Jesse now. She stands up and begins to pace the floor. Destiny whispers prayers.

Jesse sits back down on the exam table. They give him some water and a damp towel. He wipes his face; he is sweating now and still shaking.

The nurse hands the doctor an old instant Polaroid.

"Let's see if this old thing still works," says the doctor, aiming the camera at Jesse's back.

Please don't work; please don't work, Jesse silently begs.

There is a flash and the sound of a picture ejecting from the old camera. The nurse takes it and waves it in the air so that it can be processed. Then she puts it in Jesse's medical file.

Finally, the doctor has Jesse lie back and he checks his abdomen for tenderness. There is some pain on one side. He has Jesse put his shirt back on.

"Jesse, I will have to tell the General about your scars, but as a doctor, your privacy is also my concern. Don't worry about that," the doctor tells him while he makes notes on Jesse's medical folder.

Jesse knows the General's office is just up the stairs to the balcony on the building's far end. He hopes the General doesn't come and see his scars for himself. It would be too humiliating.

Several minutes pass as the nurse collects blood samples from Jesse's arm, and they finally exit the exam room.

Destiny bolts from the main room and hugs Jesse; he returns the hug, pressing his face into her neck.

"I was . . . we were . . . so worried about you," Destiny blushes and steps back in the lobby as Professor Norman glares at her from the waiting room.

Jesse sits down in a chair by the door; he looks out into the main room and smiles a feeble smile. Ruby feels a little better about his condition, seeing him alert and stable. Destiny is still blushing over their tender embrace.

The doctor tells the small gang, "Jesse is okay for now; you all can go on with your day."

Everyone gets up to leave, but Ruby, Destiny, Eric, and Jamie stay behind, waiting for Jesse.

Doctor Luz sends the nurse to the General's office with some paperwork, and then he talks to Jesse.

"You can go now, Jesse, but no work for you today. I want Eric or Jamie with you all day today," the doctor instructs firmly. "Come back in the morning after the lab work results are in, and we will go from there."

He sympathetically pats Jesse on the shoulder.

Jesse gets up to leave with Jamie and Eric. Ruby, however, sees that he is upset. Eric knows how secretive Jesse is about his scars, being his roommate. He wants to be there for Jesse, but doesn't know how.

"You okay?" Ruby puts her hand on his shoulder.

"Yeah, sure, it's just a stomach thing, nothing to worry about," Jesse says weakly.

The woman at the front desk tells Jesse, "You take care of yourself."

They step out into the courtyard; the sun, beating down on the cobblestones, gives off a comforting heat.

Ruby notes Jesse's head is covered in sweat and recognizes that more is going on than Jesse is letting on.

They walk up the ramp back to the dining hall level. As they begin to walk up the long steps to the top level of campus, everyone realizes Jesse is not in a talking mood. So, the girls leave him with Jamie and Eric. Ruby expects he will probably be quiet for a day or two. She is accustomed to it, but she hates it when he becomes distant. One of Jamie's workers comes to get him to help with a maintenance issue. Jesse and Eric walk silently toward Levi Lodge.

The sight of Jesse up and walking around gets everyone else back to the business of the day. The marketplace is opening, and local people are arriving by horse and carriage. The gardening is the responsibility of the two tribes, but Destiny and others help out. Steven and Ruby go to the garden to pull weeds when she realizes she forgot to put Hope up after breakfast.

"Oh no, where is Hope?" Ruby surveys the campus.

Ruby and Steven rush out to the garden. Hope is spotted over at the dorm doors, waiting for Ruby. She is a creature of habit and doesn't like Ruby forgetting her.

"I'm sorry, girl. Let's get you back where you belong."

Hope follows Ruby up the stairs and into the dorm's grand entrance, where her beautiful wrought iron cage sits off to one side in the massive entryway. Ruby lifts

Hope in, and the eagle starts throwing hay around and fluffing up her nest.

Jesse and Eric walk into the entrance of Levi Lodge and pass by Hope. Hope stops fluffing her nest and spreads out her wings as straight as she can, her piercing eyes looking seriously at Jesse. She doesn't move but stands sternly with her wings outstretched. Ruby looks at the wing cocked downward, where it broke after falling as an eaglet. She often feels sad that this majestic bird is earth-bound.

Jesse's angels see the bird and tell her, "Don't worry, we got him. We got him, Hope."

The young eagle relaxes and sits looking contentedly at Ruby.

"Why did you act that way, Hope? You silly bird," says Ruby, with a voice only pet lovers use. Recently, Professor Norman added a fountain to Hope's cage where she can wash and drink. It is made of rocks and adds a great sound of water to the entrance of the Levi dorms. Hope ducks her head in the water, shakes her head off, and is content.

Ruby and Steven return to the garden located behind the dining hall because the weeds are choking out the carrots and strawberry beds. Jesse and Eric are in their dorm room.

Jesse is desperate to ditch Eric and escape somewhere, releasing the heaviness he feels inside.

"I am gonna take a shower, man. I'll feel better with a hot shower."

"Okay, I will be right out here if you need me," says Eric, taking his assignment seriously.

Eric rifles through his armoire, looking for a candy bar he stashed there earlier. Candy bars are rare treats these days, and Eric is stress-eating.

Jesse closes the door to the shower room. He looks around; *no one is here — good.*

The idea that the authorities and the General are now aware of his scars grieves Jesse. He fears they will make him see a therapist, or even worse, remove him from school. Jesse gets in the shower, turns the water on full blast, and weeps as he leans on the shower wall with his arms cradling his head.

Outside in the heat of the noonday sun, the mayor of Eastcliffe takes the horse and carriage shuttle to the campus market. The General shows the mayor the new expansion of the community marketplace sprawled across from the dining hall and around Ox Lodge. White canvas tents are bright in the full sun. In his crisp brown suit, the mayor follows the General as they walk into the open-air market.

The General brings the mayor over to the new tents.

"There is a new activity I want you to see. The marketplace is only a few months old, as you know. We have gathered for business here ever since the crisis. The students joined guilds with the leadership of the academy. Metalworks, farmers' markets, sewing, and embroidery are thriving crafts. Candle making and furniture making have taken over some classrooms. Canned fruit and vegetables are being put away for winter. Under the direction of Ira, new tents go up today."

The General is glowing with satisfaction. The kids really excelled during the summer.

The mayor frowns as he reads the new signs that say: "Healing, Dream Interpretation, and Prophesy." "No charge" is also on every new sign. In other towns, fortune-telling and other dark arts are popping up all over. There is also increased looting, and police utilize citizen patrols to maintain safety on the streets at night. The pinging of hammers on metal tent pegs stops once all the new tents are up.

The General puts his hands on his hips and admires the marketplace.

"I feel this is one of the most important things we have ever done, offering God's signs and wonders to confirm His word. We are looking outward to the world. People are hurting, and we can make a difference."

The mayor sees many people from town doing business, and they greet him. Twenty or so locals meander in the market, taking the horse and buggy shuttle.

The General sounds as if he's giving a speech, Devin thinks to himself as he comes to inspect the new area himself.

He respects the General. Many spiritual leaders come to SWA to meet with the General and consult with him. Travel is still somewhat limited in the country, but the leaders find ways to get there.

"The students are trained and ready to work in the new tents," the General explains to the mayor.

"Have you trained anyone to deal with wildfires and emergency drills?" the mayor inquires, looking over the tents.

"Professor Norman is on top of it. He does evacuation drills on occasion," the General replies, wondering why the mayor always seems to talk about the possibility of wildfires when he sees him.

"That will have to do, for the time being, I suppose," the mayor answers back. "Are you getting new students this fall?"

"It's a wait-and-see kinda thing. It all hinges on the wind turbines getting attached to the grid. If things don't improve by August, we will not add any new cadets," the General tells him.

"Glenn Johnson owns a wind turbine business right here in Eastcliffe, but he is as slow as mud to put any up around here," complains the mayor.

"Hmmm, I'm sure he has his reasons," the General responds. "There is concern that the turbines might negatively impact the local bird population."

A flock of crows lands in the evergreens at the edge of the market area. They begin to caw and carry on, flapping their wings in the trees. Everyone stops what they are doing to see what the noise is. The noisy crows hop from their perches and fly off. Ruby and the gang look up from their gardening.

Destiny observes, “The crows are mocking us.”

Ruby nods in agreement. She wonders, *Where are all the bald eagles today?*

Jesse only wants to hang out in the dorm and read his Bible, so Eric settles in with him and tries to read a book he found among the reference books that are in every dorm room library. It is called *Binding the Strongman*. Eric quickly drifts to sleep. Jesse sits in front of the large window on the top level, lost in thought.

The crowds of city dwellers look curiously at the new tents in the marketplace, but no one goes inside them. They don’t know what to make of the out-of-the-ordinary services offered and at no charge.

The popular tents have the grass worn out in front of them, handmade shirts, candles, and jelly being the top sellers. The Levi tribe makes up the Sewing and Embroidery guild. With Professor Adora’s guidance, they made a beautiful wedding dress for a local bride. Their hand embroidery work is most popular. They make repairs on clothing and embellish them with embroidery. Jeans are the most common items to be brought in for repairs. Colorful, unique patches cover holes. Apparel is a valuable commodity, as the Great Crisis of April had shut down shipping routes and disrupted the power grid. The artwork and skill of this guild are highly regarded and commands premium prices. Bartering is commonplace in the market. Food, clothing, fuel, batteries, and candles are top items. Devin and Jacob have started several thriving enterprises — battery charging by stationary bike and a wall for posting want ads, to name a few.

As the sun draws down to the west, the tents shut down for the day. The students and staff at SWA gather for supper. The General wonders what to do about the new tents — no one is going inside them.

Jesse is hungry and looking forward to a good night's sleep. Destiny and Ruby plan to cover Jesse in prayer again tonight. Ruby spots her mom, dad, and big brother Arlo eating with the staff. She looks at all the kids around her, far from their homes.

I wonder if I could be brave and live without my parents at sixteen years old? I am excited to turn seventeen next month. I gotta pray more for my classmates every day, not just once in a while. Destiny and Jesse talk a lot these days; I know they are meant for each other. SWA doesn't allow students to date or hold hands and stuff. Destiny has her brother Jacob with her here at school. She is the oldest. Kristen seems to have mellowed in the past year, not so self-centered. Jacob is still as cocky as ever, but really funny. Devin dropped his attitude and acts as though he feels accepted, and he knows he belongs here now. I love my friends!

Somehow, the General managed to find oil streetlamps and placed them in the courtyards, allowing people to get around after dark without electricity. Jamie's crew has the job of lighting them and putting them out each day.

Ox Lodge is across from the dining hall; they get teased that they eat more than the other dorms.

In Levi Lodge, situated next to Shekinah Sanctuary, Ruby and the girls are getting ready for bed. Audrey has kept a journal all year; she is making a new entry:

Another summer day has passed, and life seems okay for now. A cool breeze is so refreshing after the heat of the day. SWA is holding on, making it through the hard times together. Devin has candy bars ... I WANT ONE!

She shuts her journal and settles in for the night.

Destiny and Ruby are praying for Jesse. Milagros, Gloria, Audrey, and Faith are already settled under their covers.

The two girls pray **Psalm 91** over the campus and especially for Jesse.

"Father, we speak protection and peace. We declare that the enemy cannot come against Jesse or us," prays Destiny. "Let the angels be empowered to conquer and be victorious in battle."

They are surprised how tired they feel and head off to bed. Ruby looks for angels but doesn't see any. She is aware that Destiny, Jesse, and Gloria have all seen demons and angels.

Father, let the world know: "Night is coming where no man can work." Don't let us be sleeping; let us be aware. Don't let Jesse's darkness overtake him. Please show us the hidden idols; we don't want to have anything in common with the enemy. I can't wait till we graduate and become a real team, going on missions!

Ruby then reflects on the day; *Jesse seems to be back to talking a lot again at supper. I'm happy he's opening up, just like old times. The guy still hasn't shared with us what the darkness is. I wish he would; it's dangerous to let things fester. If the hour is urgent, we should really deal with it.*

She lies back on her bed, content with things at the moment. The song begins to ramble in her head: [23]**"Blessed be the Lord our rock, who trains our hands for battle, trains our fingers for war . . ."**

Destiny prays quietly again from her bed, "Father, help Jesse get the darkness out of his heart, help him let us in and not keep it to himself. He is so special and gifted. I like him so much."

Her eyelids grow too heavy, and she falls asleep.

---

[23] **Psalm 144:1**

Eric wants to gather the guys in the dorm room for prayer.

"I just feel like something is going to happen, I don't know what exactly," he tells Jesse, Devin, Steven, Yosef, and Jacob.

All of them are still together for their second year of school. Most of them haven't seen their parents in a year now. Jesse, of course, does not even know where his parents are. They travel around singing in bars. They left Jesse at twelve years old with an uncle. After that, he had three years of unspeakable trouble, most of which carries too much shame to reveal what happened. From his bed, Jesse looks around the dorm at his friends. Armoires and beds are located on the lower level; above is the living room, featuring a fireplace and a study area. Beautiful pointed arched windows adorn the Levi Lodge, just like the sanctuary.

Jesse thinks *Yosef is the farthest from home, Israel. He still talks with a heavy accent, and he used to be hard to understand. Everyone at SWA loves Israel, God's chosen. A lot of prayer time focuses on them around here. Devin throws himself into music as a means of coping with stress; he is more spiritual than he realizes. His bicycle rig is an excellent gadget for charging batteries. Eric is a guy you count on to always be in a good mood, and he knows how to pray. I am impressed with him.*

Eric calls from above, "Hey, you guys, we need to pray! Get up here."

All six guys gather on the rug in front of the big window at the top level.

Eric starts praying first, "Father, we agree together that the blood of Jesus covers this campus and our families. No evil influence can come near our families or us. Let people know that night is coming, and to work while it is yet day."

All the boys pray and agree together; it is an emotional and heartfelt experience. They feel the heaviness leaving the room; instead, peace and calmness drift down like a blanket in the space. The guys go off to bed. Jesse sees his two angels outside in the pine trees. They are just bright spots glowing, but Jesse knows it is his angels, Anton, and the new angel. Jesse has yet to learn the latest angel's name.

Later that night, around three o'clock in the morning, a flock of crows lit on the roof of Shekinah Sanctuary. As they land, each one turns into a dark imp, with one larger imp in the center of them. They are bony thin with long, spindly arms and legs. The largest one looks around and begins to send them to specific dorm rooms. The dark bodiless spirits stumble over each other and bump into one another. They are spirits of confusion. In just a few minutes, over half the imps return, saying they can't get in. Several forgot where they were supposed to go. The larger imp is furious with his subordinates, kicking them and yelling at them. They see several angels coming towards them. They turn back into crows and leave the area. Only a few of them manage to remain on campus.

Jamie stirs from his sleep and looks at his old-fashioned windup clock; "3:15 a.m.," the face reads. He feels Yeshua calling him to pray. Dropping to the floor, Jamie opens his Bible and begins to pray. He is still praying when daylight comes. He gets up and gets ready to go to work.

Deep in the cave of the Fire King, one of the eggs shows signs of hatching soon. An orange glow emanates from the center of the eggs. The king's laughter causes a slight breeze, making the spider webs vibrate.

Speakers around campus buzz as the words come forth, "Last week of the marketplace, kiddos. Next week it will only be on Saturday. Back to school soon, everyone!" Jennifer announces with her usual cheerfulness just before the generator to the dorms is turned off for the morning. She still manages to wear her heels all summer; it is her way of staying optimistic.

The General wants the newly opened tents to do better today. Around noon, a group of transients comes into the marketplace. They have colorful horse-drawn wagons that are well-traveled. They are gypsies with thick Slavic accents. The tribes of Gad and Benjamin are the guilds of combat and security. They are watching the group just in case they are thieves. The first thing SWA does is offer them a free meal and talk with them. But this group does not accept the tribes' kindness. They dress in homemade, patchwork clothing that is very ethnic and colorful. A heavyset woman with long, bleached blonde hair seems to be the leader; she heads for a particular tent. She walks straight to the Dream Interpretation tent and stomps right in, leaving her group of men, women, and a few children outside. They look hostile as they stand outside the tent.

Inside, Ira the prophetess, Milagros, Gloria, Faith, and Audrey are staffing the tent. The heavy-set woman sits down at the table, throws her hair back out of her face, gold bracelets rattling on her arms. She begins to share with the group what is on her mind, speaking in her thick accent.

"I don't like you all putting up this tent for dream interpretations. You have some nerve; we have done this in my family for generations, and who are you to cut into our action?"

She waits to see their reaction, gloating on the chance that they are upset at her words, her Slavic accent weighty in the room.

Milagros looks over to Ira. She nods back.

Milagros leans over the table, looks her in the eye, and says, "What we do, we do by the unction of the Holy Spirit. What you do is by devils and deception. The Lord has told me you were mistreated by an ecclesia when you were a child. And your mother also beat you when you told the future."

Milagros stops talking as the woman begins wailing and weeping loudly.

Ira takes over; a gentle weeping came over her as she comforts the woman. Ira prophesies:

"Wanda, you are Slavic. You were born a prophetess, but your people only knew dark arts and witchcraft. They thought you were cursed. They didn't know any better. Forgive them for their cruelty and be free of your own."

As the woman continues to weep, she takes off several necklaces from around her neck and lays them on the table.

"We have been so wicked. God forgive us," Wanda, the gypsy cries out. "These are for incantations and spells; they repulse me now. I don't want them."

She takes off several gold rings and bracelets as well.

"What must we do to serve God?"

Ira and Milagros's words move the proud lady in colorful quilted clothes; tears run down her heavy makeup.

Just then, Jamie and the General come in. Jamie, being saved from witchcraft, recognizes the items on the table.

He says, "I know what to do with these. Burn them."

Everyone in the tent spills out into the bright daylight. The woman's tears mystify her group as she speaks to them in a Russian gypsy dialect. They all agree they will follow her in whatever she says to do. The

General leads them all to Christ, telling them of the virgin birth, Jesus' death on the cross, and His resurrection from the dead.

Many of them weep openly, most of all Wanda. The town's people gather around the spectacle. The gypsies' repentance is whole-hearted. Many of them take valuables out of their pockets, all the things they had stolen. Several townspeople recognize their lost items and, with relief, retrieve them. Afterward, the gypsies accept food in the dining hall. Ira and her crew return to their booth, only to find a line of people waiting for them. At the Healing and Prophesy booths, there are also people anxiously waiting in line.

In the dining hall, Jesse goes over to the gypsies.

"Have you seen an old white van with stickers all over it in your travels?" Jesse asks Wanda.

Her band of gypsies don't know of his parents. Ruby sees the sadness in Jesse's eyes that he tries so hard to hide. They are close again, and Ruby knows he is hurting.

Wanda calls back to Jesse, "I know your parents will love you someday. They missed out on a special boy; you didn't deserve to be abandoned. Neither did . . . I, neither did I."

Jesse smiles back at her, but he keeps walking. He and Ruby sit down on the steps outside the dining hall that looks down to the front entry and gate tower. Suddenly, Jesse puts his head on Ruby's shoulder and starts to cry. Ruby doesn't know what to do, so she just puts her hand on the back of his head. Eric comes and puts his arms around Jesse. Ruby is so glad. Her heart is pounding, and now she can comfort Jesse better. Jesse's shoulders heave as he sobs — the three huddle on the steps. Jesse sits up and stops crying, wiping his face with his t-shirt.

"I feel better now."

I can't believe I just broke down in front of my friends. This outburst of emotion took me by surprise. I thought I had it stuffed deep inside and that if I didn't think about my parents, I wouldn't miss them. But I am glad that I have friends who care and are there for me, Jesse thinks.

A few eagles fly overhead and screech. Destiny looks for crows . . . there are none. She sees Jesse and the others on the steps. As she gets closer, she can tell something has happened, but she doesn't dare ask. She will grill Ruby later.

Another summer day in the Rocky Mountains has ended. Twenty Slavic souls have been born into the Kingdom. Five gypsy wagons camp on campus, not wanting to wander away from this special place. Jesse drops some heaviness off on his friends. His step will be lighter, his smile brighter. They have made a difference in the world. What kind of world will they wake up to tomorrow?

> **There are many who say, "Who will show us some good? Lift up the light of your face upon us, O Lord!" You have put more joy in my heart than they have when their grain and wine**

abound. In peace I will both lie down and sleep; for you alone, O Lord, make me dwell in safety.

Psalm 4:6-8

CHAPTER TWO

POWER PLAY

There is a buzzing sound in the dorms. "12:00 a.m." blinks on the digital alarm clock display. A hum, a buzz, and suddenly the lights come on. Alarm clocks and air conditioners hum with the flow of electrical power. Jesse opens his eyes and stares at the light bulb glowing on the ceiling. He questions how this all fits in with what the Lord told him — impending darkness and trouble.

Ruby's dorm erupts with cheering as the girls rejoice over the returning power.

Destiny mentions, "I hope no one will deny how God Himself powered the sanctuary two days ago. It was a sign and a wonder."

"Yeah," Ruby nods in agreement.

With the electricity back on, everything seems different. Rooms light up, and the hum of electrical equipment fills the air. The General is out checking on everything with Jamie and his crew. Everyone is jumping and excited; life is getting back to normal. Wind turbines on the plains of Kansas brought help during the crisis in the Sangre de Cristo Mountains. (See "Types and Shadows" 2)

Kristen is hugging her curling iron.

"Oh, how I have missed using you!" She moves from one item to another, greeting each one like a long-lost relative.

"No more hand-washing clothes!" Kristen grins at the rest of the girls who are plugging in devices and charging cell phones.

On the way to breakfast, Jesse and Eric see the two guys who stay very distant and cold from the rest of their classmates. The boys have spiked hair and look hardened and worldly. They never seem to fit in at SWA, yet they have stayed for the whole year so far. Steven is the only one they talk to, for the most part. The oldest guy surprisingly speaks to Jesse before they arrive at the dining hall.

"Hey, dude. You got guts, man. I think you're crazy, but I still admire your drive," he says as he kicks the dirt under his foot.

Jesse smiles and starts to respond, but then he suddenly feels lightheaded.

Oh, Lord, don't let me faint in front of the toughest guys in school . . .

Jesse slumps right over on the guy's chest. He manages to catch Jesse and lets him slide gently to the ground. Eric takes off for the clinic while the two guys stay with Jesse, laid out on the grass in front of the dining hall doors.

Once again, Jesse finds himself waking up on the clinic's exam table. This time, it is just the nurse and the General in the room. Eric and the two guys sit anxiously in the waiting room.

The nurse makes sure Jesse doesn't get up too soon.

"You were to come and see me, Jesse, but I didn't intend to see you passed out again. I have the results of the tests we took. You have a stomach infection caused by H. pylori. You probably had this condition for a while. You need a regimen of antibiotics for over a month. Just come by here before every meal to take your pills. And don't skip any meals. You are also anemic. That means you are low in iron, so I have a supplement of that for you, as well."

She looks into his eyes with her light and checks his blood pressure.

"Here, take these two pills and go eat," she smiles at Jesse.

The General steps over and puts his arm around Jesse, playfully wrestling him back and forth. He wants to explain why Jesse might be having these health problems.

"Considering you were homeless in the past and had a terrible diet, this is small in comparison. It could be a lot worse, Jesse," the General says.

Jesse isn't happy about the medical report. He has had stomachaches for over a year and just tried to ignore them.

"I know, but it is not a good witness to people to be weak and sickly," Jesse says as he looks at the pill bottles the nurse has with his name on them.

"Rock Man, we all go through seasons of weakness at some time in our lives. We just learn to lean more heavily on the Lord. **2 Corinthians 12:9** says:

> **But he said to me, "My grace is sufficient for you, for my power is made perfect in weakness." Therefore I will boast all the more gladly of my weaknesses, so that the power of Christ may rest upon me."**

Jesse looks at the General in amazement. *How can he remember Bible verses so well? I will have to reflect on that verse. But for now, my stomach is grumbling.*

As Jesse leaves the exam room, he sees Eric and the two rowdy guys who were there when he fainted. Jesse feels his face blushing in embarrassment. *Oh man, my pride is hurt; I thought I was so spiritual, but my pride can still get the best of me at times.*

Jesse smiles awkwardly at them. The boys are seriously concerned; seeing him go out cold upset them, and they feel a connection to Jesse and Eric through the incident. The oldest guy speaks up as they walk up the ramp to the dining hall.

"Hey, you guys, can we come to your prayer thingy this week?"

"Sure," Jesse responds, surprised by the two guys warming up to him. Jesse hasn't had prayer rock since the Great Terrorist Crisis of April, but they don't want to miss this chance to help the two guys. Jesse and Eric will have a prayer rock just for these two.

"I am Ray, and this is Gabriel."

"Jesse and Eric," Jesse responds, pointing to himself and his good friend.

"We know who you are, Jesse. You're the Rock Man, and you're different than anyone we know," says the older boy, Ray, with a grin.

Jamie and his crew spend the remainder of the day getting electrical systems up and working, testing phones, and the like. They are amazed at how fast TV and radio stations get online. Rumors suggest that fuel is returning to normal levels, but for now, only government and emergency vehicles are on the roads.

Tonight, most people linger in the dining hall to hear the nightly news. The headline announces the president's advice to Israel to partition some land and make room for the Palestinians.

In the nearby cave, the Fire King is also getting the news. He sits on his rocky throne in the cavern as a single dark scout comes to inform him of the state of things. This particular spy tends to mock even more than his fellow spies. His voice is annoying at best, but the King must endure the imp to be informed.

"All the press can talk about is the President. The President gets credit for the wind turbines with glowing comments from the press. It made me ill to hear it! The Secretary of State held a press conference. He announced a new holiday on July twenty-fifth, as 'Christmas in July,' to celebrate the President's achievements with a festival of lights. Everyone is to put up lights, similar to those at Christmas, in honor of the President. They plan to give gifts and not go to work. The media is all abuzz with it. It is disgusting, my lord. Arrogant, self-centered, pathetic humans, they repulse me."

Back at SWA, everyone feels a coldness in the room, hearing of Christmas in July on the news. Is the President taking Christ's place in the nation?

"We are not going to celebrate this new festival," the General tells everyone, feeling a check in his spirit. Everyone agrees.

Back at the hollow of the mountain, the imp is getting his second wind.

"Now, this gives me some pleasure to report. Governments are toppling from the economic crisis, and riots are arising among the youth, mostly in Eastern countries. I am so happy . . . A few small Asian countries are also unstable. Floods, tornadoes, volcanic eruptions, and severe weather patterns torment the earth! Also, famines and pestilences! Shipping in the Great Eagle (U.S.) is in full force, and gasoline supplies are too. This nauseating nation we are stuck in just bounces back, no matter what the catastrophe. How the President managed all these breakthroughs remains a mystery. It seems the people only care for the results, not the price."

The imp said all he has to say, and the king dismisses him with a quick wave of his hand.

"Begone, you are a horrible stench," the King releases him with disgust. "I am not pleased . . . there are no calamities in my area. The other kings will look at me with disdain. Something must change around here," the Fire King broods in his dark domain; his generals are seated around him.

A hoarse female voice echoes in the cave, "They are hatching, they are hatching!"

The king stands up from his throne, half-way delighted and half-way in fear for his wellbeing. Wind now blows out of the cave, causing spiders to tumble out into the night air.

In the dining hall, Ira stands up and interrupts the TV broadcast.

"Today, we see a fracture in our society. Today, we pull away from this world and stick out like sore thumbs.

Our nation is splintering, and sides are forming — a great division between the true believers and the religious. But don't let your heart be heavy, for Messiah told us these things must take place before His return. We see iniquity growing to maturity. Let us look to the harvest and then to the sky and His coming; and don't let the times and season take your joy."

Ira reaches for her Bible resting on the table, opening to a marked place, she reads:

> **See that you do not refuse him who is speaking. For if they did not escape when they refused him who warned them on earth, much less will we escape if we reject him who warns from heaven. At that time his voice shook the earth, but now he has promised, "Yet once more I will shake not only the earth but also the heavens."**
>
> **This phrase, "Yet once more," indicates the removal of things that are shaken—that is, things that have been made—in order that the things that cannot be shaken may remain. Therefore let us be grateful for receiving a kingdom that cannot be shaken, and thus let us offer to God acceptable worship, with reverence and awe, for our God is a consuming fire.**
>
> **Hebrews 12:25-29**

Ira sits back down, and the General stands to conclude the night.

"Let's get some rest. Tomorrow is another day, and Adonai will need us to be at our best. The darker it gets, the more we need to be salt and light; this is our finest hour," he tells the SWA community.

The General looks over the group as they trail out of the building. He wonders if he has prepared them as Yahweh wanted. *Are they ready to be the last days' army?*

Jesse feels that his warning of dark times remains on target. He hears kids talking as though everything is going to be fine from now on. Ruby and Destiny agree to fast every Wednesday. Some of the girls say they will try to fast, but they never manage to give up more than two meals before they quit.

Everyone at the academy goes to bed with an uneasy feeling. Times are changing, and the heart of the country is changing. Slowly, the late-night TV viewers leave to go to their quarters quietly and somberly. Everyone faces their night alone, deep in thought.

Jesse lies looking up at the bunk bed above him. He thinks about fainting in front of the cool kids and what the General said about glory in infirmities.

I am surprised my pride hit me so sharply. I assumed time on the streets had stripped me of egotism, but there it is again.

Jesse is aware that the flesh and the spirit often clash inside him.

Maybe . . . I'm not as spiritual as I thought. Maybe . . . humility is not that easy, Jesse decides.

Destiny and Ruby pray alone in their beds, covering Jesse with protection and healing scriptures. The other girls are talking about how weird it is to have a new holiday all of a sudden and about having the power back on.

By invitation, the gypsies settle into West Gate dorms (Ox Lodge); they learn the Lord's ways very fast. Wanda sits up suddenly in her bed, feeling a quickening in her spirit. "I must talk to Ira tomorrow," she tells herself.

Sleep settles on the campus on the hot July night. The birds are also silent; no owls, nothing, just the breeze in the pines.

CHAPTER THREE

SHAKE, RATTLE AND ROLL

Ruby glances at the alarm clock, now glowing after months of having no power. At six o'clock in the morning, she yawns and stretches. The electricity seems to be on for good. She can hear Hope screeching down in the lobby. Ruby yawns and puts her feet on the floor.

Hope stayed in her large, wrought-iron cage all night.

Faith wakes up, too. "What is Hope carrying on about?"

Faith's voice is scratchy from sleep.

Suddenly, Ruby's alarm starts to vibrate and falls off the nightstand. Water pipes in the walls rattle, and a low rumble is on the ground. Ruby runs down to the lobby to let Hope out, in case there is an emergency. The shaking stops, and it is all quiet. Then it starts again. Everyone comes rushing out of their dorms and then outside to see what's going on. It is a tremor. The earth rumbles beneath them. (See "Types and Shadows" 3)

The General runs out of the dining hall to listen for more rumbling.

Professor Norman runs up to him and says, "The news said there was an earthquake in Illinois, Indiana, Missouri, and Arkansas. Memphis, Tennessee, was flooded when the river changed course. We are experiencing some aftershocks locally. They said there is great damage to roads, cities, and rural farms; as if the nation split in half!"

The General is surprised, "Some prophets had mentioned earthquakes, but few truly expected it to happen on U.S. soil. California, maybe, but not here in the Midwest and central plains."

"Birth pains, I suppose," adds Professor Norman.

"I suppose," responds the General, deep in thought.

During breakfast, the news plays over the loudspeaker. "Large openings in the earth have opened, and gas is spewing out. There is a potential risk of explosions, necessitating evacuations. Hot Springs, Arkansas, is the worst hit. The Missouri River changed course and flooded many areas. Roads are impassable in many areas. The country, in many respects, is severed into two parts. Power grid disruptions, gas and water lines break. Due to the significant danger and the necessity of keeping roads open for emergency vehicles and evacuations, people are required to shelter in place. A crevasse as large as twenty feet across has opened in four different locations, emitting noxious gas. With fuel available once again, everyone seems to want to drive around; this could be a dangerous situation. Some experts predict the ocean will begin to fill the crevasse, and it will be necessary to make new maps."

Everyone gasps and stops eating as they listen. The familiar news anchorwoman's voice continues.

"While scientists focused on California's seismic activity, a major earthquake occurred on the New Madrid Fault line in the center of the U.S. Aftershocks are happening all over the country. Authorities fear that a major earthquake will occur at Yellowstone National Park, where hot springs are also present. The quake was only a seven on the Richter scale, but it was most destructive in the Missouri River area. One thousand homes are destroyed. The Government has declared over twenty disaster areas. We have gone from a terrorist crisis to a natural crisis."

"Shaking in the Heartland" is coined by the media and newly operating TV and radio stations.

Destiny worries about her family in North Dakota.

"I wonder if my family has power and water and stuff. Cell phone connections are overloaded, and many cell towers are down. I can't get calls through to check," Destiny says, looking at the "no service available" on her phone.

"Yeah, cell phone service has only been up and working for two days now. The General and Ira have family in Arkansas. I'm sure many others are from areas in the earthquake zone," Eric says.

"Yeah, my family is in Kansas; is Kansas affected?" Devin asks.

Wanda, the gypsy, is talking to Ira at their table, tears running down her face as she recounts the dream she had.

"It was a month ago. I dreamed of a U.S. map, and two hands came and tore the map right down the middle. I didn't know what it meant. I thought it was political or something."

Wanda speaks softly, but it seems the whole school hangs on her every word. Several students also dreamt about earthquakes.

Ira stands up and turns off the news with a remote. She has the strength of the Lord on her as she steps out to the middle of the dining hall and speaks to everyone.

"There is a plan of the enemy to divide this nation. The ecclesia has been a sleeping giant. Now is the time for the army of Elohim to arise and fight in the Spirit. There is war in the heavens. This earthquake is a physical manifestation of a spiritual condition. We must cry out for justice. Fight for the soul of this nation."

In all the morning excitement, Jesse forgot to go to the nurse's office for his pill. The nurse walks into the dining hall and heads straight to Jesse, holding two white capsules in a tiny plastic cup. Jesse's face turns red. Now the whole school knows that Jesse is taking iron pills and antibiotics. Ira stops talking for a minute. She has an odd look on her face, as though she wants to laugh or something.

"Rock Man is low in iron, it seems. I'm sorry, Jesse. I can't help myself. It's silly, really — but I feel laughter — welling up inside me." Ira's dignified Brit voice begins to turn to giggles.

The room begins to snicker and then breaks out into full-blown laughter.

Jesse looks at all the faces. He smiles. God is using him again, in a strange way, to bring laughter in a crisis. The laughter is filled with power from the Holy Spirit, like a victor rejoicing after a battle.

Ira comes and squeezes Jesse around his shoulders.

"I apologize, Jesse," she says.

"It's okay," Jesse responds, still holding the pills in his hand.

An aftershock makes the plates and glasses vibrate on the tables. Everyone gets quiet. Then laughter breaks out again, only louder this time. The power of Adonai sweeps through the campus, and the spirit of fear subsides. Yet it remains in the shadows, waiting for new opportunities. Destiny sees Fear. He looks so harmless now, but a few minutes ago, he was a towering giant. The cloaked figure, with a forlorn face, cowers in the corner and then disappears completely. Destiny looks to see if Jesse saw him, but apparently, he did not.

The angels stand on the roof, their swords facing outward, their eyes blazing with intensity on the horizon. The opening of the Earth's crust had released a pocket of demons onto the surface.

Aurora motions Jamie over from the other side of the staff's table.

He comes and sits next to her.

"Did you see anything about what is going on in your prayer time?" she asks with a serious tone.

"Well, yes. I saw a deep crevasse and crows flying out, along with bats and all kinds of dark-winged creatures. It was noisy, and they came out in waves," Jamie articulates to her, looking into her eyes.

"Hmmm, you should tell the General," Aurora says, dropping his gaze.

Jamie feels his face flush as he leaves to talk to the General. He definitely has a crush on her.

Hope is outside the dining hall on the lawn; she has crow for breakfast.

Jesse manages to swallow his pills and his pride.

The flesh is an unpredictable animal. You never know when it will flare up, Jesse thinks to himself.

He wants to make sure his natural man doesn't sit on the throne of his will. Jesse reaches into his pocket. Instead of bacon, he has a folded paper; he pulls it out and reads it:

> **But he said to me, "My grace is sufficient for you, for my power is made perfect in weakness."**

Therefore I will boast all the more gladly of my weaknesses, so that the power of Christ may rest upon me. For the sake of Christ, then, I am content with weaknesses, insults, hardships, persecutions, and calamities. For when I am weak, then I am strong.

2 Corinthians 12:9-10

"When I am weak, then I am strong . . ." Jesse still can't fully understand . . . *At least now, I keep spiritual food in my pocket, and I don't smell like bacon in the mornings!* Jesse smiles widely, and his friends look on curiously.

"Don't ask!" Ruby knows Jesse will not share his inside joke with them.

She shakes her head and smiles back at him. Destiny looks at Jesse in genuine fascination; this guy is getting to her. Faith elbows Milagros, motioning toward Destiny's dove eyes over Jesse.

Fall is coming, and classes will start soon. SWA must go about the business of life. And that is getting more complicated by the day. The assumption that life will go on as usual is thrown out the window for this group. The mind can conceive a host of potential tragedies, and the news continually blares of possible gloomy scenarios. Yet some people walk around in a fog of apathy, caught up in their own world. Having electricity back on makes life more comfortable, but concerns over the earthquake dampen their rejoicing.

In the dark king's cave, a small party is going on. "The president encourages Israel to give up land to make peace. Many nations have broken off being allies with Israel for fear of terrorism," the king announces to his minions. "Babylon must be abuzz with optimism."

The evil horde is drunk with violence.

One of the king's sons sits off to the side. He is not in the celebrating mood, and he speaks to his brothers, "So far, Israel remains firm and holds her ground, only sacrificing a few acres at a time. Plus, Israel has also found oil in the wastelands. They are now self-sufficient in fuel and heating. Great wealth is gained from the oil finds. What are these fools celebrating? Baal is sure to come and pour out his wrath on us," the prince mumbles in disgust. His brothers agree.

The king leaves the celebration to check on the eggs, deep inside the cave. A one-horned snake hatches. He is so big that he breaks rocks off the cavern walls as he writhes around. The king backs away silently and returns to his throne, watching his army dance. Soon, he will have some amusement of his own.

Back on the side of the mountain at SWA, people are looking forward. They have food for the year stored in their corrals with cattle and hogs. Many others are not so prepared. The earthquake breached truck routes that were just starting up again. In the heartland, many airport runways are declared unsafe and in need of repair. The nation has new challenges.

Considering the earthquake, the new holiday, the Festival of Lights on July twenty-fifth, doesn't gain much popular support. In the center of the nation, power lines are down, and repairs will take more than a month to complete. News footage showing the destruction in the country's heartland is broadcast day and night on the news channels. Expert guests discuss potential seismic future events that could bring more changes to elevations along the fault line. They present catastrophic scenarios, including a map showing a crevasse filled with ocean water that is one hundred miles wide, potentially running up to the Great Lakes. Uncertainty and speculation rule the airwaves.

Ruby gazes at Jesse and the rest of her friends at lunchtime. She wonders . . . *How will our young lives play out? Will we graduate, marry, and work at jobs? I know one thing for sure: signs and wonders are in God's plan for us. Isn't this the God we serve? And some kids might get offended when their world crashes in on them. It is all through the Old and New Testaments. God makes provision for His people in every situation. All I know is that we need to graduate and fulfill our destinies together, as the prophecies said.*

Ruby smiles like Jesse does when he and God are having an inside joke. It feels good to connect to God's heart. It is on the voice of the Father that Ruby has learned to hang all her confidence.

"*Ruby, My warrior, when the hidden idols come down, unbelief will break off this body of believers, and great signs and wonders will break out among you. The hidden idols are found throughout your nation, not just in you,*" Adonai tells her.

Ruby relates what the Lord told her to Jesse and Destiny.

"He didn't say anything about what the idols are. We are clueless at this point," Destiny responds.

"I . . . think . . . like . . . well, I heard the name Nimrod just now. Maybe Jamie knows who that is," Jesse says.

"We will have to ask him about it," Ruby suggests.

As they eat lunch, Ruby tells the gang about the new program.

"The Levi tribe is a priestly tribe, as you know, so we are to be servants to the other tribes. I have been working with the General to create a mentoring program for first-year students."

"You mean newbies?" Jesse says, with a joking smile. Knowing she always insists that the term 'newbies' is rude.

"We set it up so that all second-year students will be assigned a first-year student to help them in their first year. I am proud of the program, at the time, I didn't know if we will even get any new students due to the Crisis of April, and now the earthquake," Ruby tells her friends, frowning at Jesse for using the term "newbie."

"So, we *have to* spend time with an underclassman and show them the ropes?" Steven asks.

He is not sure he likes the idea. Gloria sits there, but her mind is miles away. The earthquake has shaken her up. She breaks into the conversation abruptly.

"I watched the scenes of homes falling off into a sinkhole, roadways broken into chunks, and bridges half gone, and no river flowing below it. It's crazy! I feel as though I have been sleepwalking all this time, and I am just waking up. Ruach HaKodesh is rushing through me like a wind right now. There is heat on the palms of my hands, look! For the first time, I see what is important," says Gloria, feeling changed somehow.

"I was so self-centered and miserable. I spent more time and money on my hair than on the things of the Lord. Now I have changed all of a sudden. I am filled with the compassion of Yahweh to touch the lives of others more than ever before."

Gloria feels stirred and walks over to Wanda, putting her hand on Wanda's shoulder. There is a puff of wind, and Wanda makes a sound of surprise. Everyone around Wanda is in awe and talks in muffled voices. Instantly, she has lost thirty pounds, and her clothes hang on her like a child playing dress-up with their parents' clothes.

"Avoid eating anything with sugar in it, and the weight will stay off."

Gloria speaks in her casual voice, even though her mind is racing to process what has just happened.

Wanda's voice is loud on a typical day, but now her voice booms through the room.

"You are worthy to receive glory, honor, and power, Oh Lord," Wanda says, jumping around with her hands in the air. Well, one hand holds up the skirt that is now too big for her. The rest of her clan joins her, and soon they are singing and dancing to the Lord as only a saved Slavic clan can. It is quite a spectacle. Gloria lives up to her name, bringing glory to God and walking in that glory.

Devin leans over to Eric and says, "**Revelation 4:11**."

"What?" Eric questions.

"Wanda quoted the book of Revelation just now."

Devin has been reading the book of Revelation for several months and cannot seem to get enough of it.

Eric nods his head. Today is a day of surprises. He always worries that Devin is too caught up in his business and not very "spiritual."

Holy awe fills the hearts of SWA. God is doing a new thing, just as in **Isaiah 43:15-19**:

> **I am the Lord, your Holy One, the Creator of Israel, your King." Thus says the Lord, who makes a way in the sea, a path in the mighty waters, who brings forth chariot and horse, army and warrior; they lie down, they cannot rise, they are extinguished, quenched like a wick: "Remember not the former things, nor consider the things of old. Behold, I am doing a new thing now it springs forth, do you not**

> **perceive it? I will make a way in the wilderness and rivers in the desert.**

Breakfast on this late summer's day in the Rocky Mountains is eventful. The SWA campus recognizes that a new era has arrived, bringing greater joy and more significant challenges in the world. Chaos can break out at any moment, but the Spirit of the Lord causes this band of believers to have peace and even joy in the midst of it. Ruby feels the presence of Elohim sweep over her as she digs into her now cold peach oatmeal and sausage. She finds herself smiling with a sense of empowerment. At this moment, she can take on the world. Jesse's voice echoes through her thoughts, "work while it is yet day."

"May we be found faithful and worthy to escape the wrath to come," Ruby whispers under her breath.

Jesse leans over and says, "Amen." Destiny and Faith nod in agreement.

Devin flips open his notebook, filled with business transactions and plans for future inventions. He flips to the back page and begins to read to the group.

> **In this you rejoice, though now for a little while, if necessary, you have been grieved by various trials, so that the tested genuineness of your faith—more precious than gold that perishes though it is tested by fire—may be found to result in praise and glory and honor at the revelation of Jesus Christ. Though you have not seen him, you love him. Though you do not now**

see him, you believe in him and rejoice with joy that is inexpressible and filled with glory, obtaining the outcome of your faith, the salvation of your souls.

1 Peter 1:6-9

Devin closes the notebook and returns to his breakfast. The rest of the group stares at him in surprise. It appears that Devin is a force all by himself. He, like Gloria, has been sleepwalking in his faith, but now is fully awake and sober. Everyone is thoughtful, and the only sound filling the air is the tinkling of silverware.

Jesse realizes: *so, even among my close friends, there can be the need to shake out of slumber. I didn't think any of us were . . . lukewarm!*

Eric breaks the silence.

"We need each other, like what Devin wrote in his notebook. We needed to hear that. God has put us together, and we need to protect and value what we have as a group."

Jesse feels a cold chill run down his back.

I know what Eric said is true, but emotionally, I still don't want to trust people. Not even good people like Ruby, Destiny, and the General. I feel You dealing with me, to look at my weaknesses and face them head-on. I need to discuss this with Ruby later. She can always say just the right thing.

The Spirit Wings Academy marketplace, which launched in April, remains strong. Everyone has places to go and things to accomplish, all the while talking about the earthquake and the restoration of the power grid.

Ruby and most of the Levi Tribe are becoming skilled in sewing and embroidery. They are becoming very accomplished in the few months since the General started the guilds. They are known chiefly for putting lion faces on jackets with the words "Lion of Judah." They use various hues of gold thread. It is very impressive needlework. Destiny moved to the Ruben guild because she loves to garden. Kristen joined the Benjamin Guild — security and combat.

However, Jesse did some artwork for the sewing guild; mainly, he works in the Naphtali guild. He even drew a family portrait for the mayor of the local town. Devin is a guild unto himself, rigging up a bicycle to charge household batteries and inventing many other devices that have gained him some distinction. Jacob is the man to see to make a deal or find a hard-to-get item.

Tents in the marketplace that flourish the most are now the Healing Tent, Dream Interpretation, and Prophesy booths, where Wanda and her gypsy clan came into the Kingdom.

Everyone goes to their duties for the day, earthquake or not. Jesse specializes in portraits and has orders waiting for him. School starts next week; then the marketplace will only be open on Saturdays and will do business on a limited basis.

Many cadets find new confidence in working with their hands, learning real survival skills that they can take with them for the rest of their lives.

Jesse makes an excuse to go over to the sewing room in the dance classroom in the East Academic Tower. He finds Ruby tracing a lion pattern onto a jacket.

"Hey Jesse, decided to come back to the sewing guild?" Ruby asks as she looks up from her work.

"No, I just wanted to talk, okay?" Jesse says, sitting down next to her at the worktable.

"Okay, Jesse, shoot," Ruby sets her fabric pencil down and leans in towards him.

"I don't trust you. I have trouble trusting anyone. I don't even trust my parents," Jesse states with a note of shame and detachment in his voice.

Ruby tries not to take it personally.

"When you accepted Jesus, you had to let Him in, risk being vulnerable, and open up to Him. Now you are learning to open up to us and risk being vulnerable. You have good reasons not to trust your parents. But we haven't done anything to cause distrust, have we?" Ruby gathers her thoughts again. "The enemy wants to separate you from us, get you by yourself, and have you for lunch. We need each other, just as Eric said. You can't shake that monster of darkness on your own; this is no time to draw back and be alone."

Ruby leans in closer as she finishes talking.

Jesse feels Ruach HaKodesh coursing through him. He smiles and leans back.

"Ruby, you see things so clearly, and sometimes I have confusion and this dark cloud . . ." Jesse's voice trails off. Then he tells Ruby, "I need you, and you need me. Destiny is very sharp in the Word; she is deep. I like her. But I don't think I can ever have a girlfriend or anything. She is so good, and I was so bad in my past."

Ruby changes expressions and points her finger at Jesse.

"You can have everything good and pure and holy. You're a child of the Living God. He has made you worthy, and don't you forget it."

"Okay. Okay . . ." Jesse smiles and leans back in his chair. "We have some really good talks, don't we? Destiny and I are . . . talking.

Jesse's face lights up.

"Manuel prophesied 'my destiny', so maybe she will be mine? And not just a team partner, so our purpose or destiny was found here at SWA," blushes Jesse, realizing what he just admitted.

"Okay, there you go," responds Ruby with a smile.

"How is the mentoring program going with the General?" Jesse asks, feeling a load off his shoulders.

"We finished; it is ready to go. I just don't know if we will get any new students to mentor," Ruby says as she leans back over her lion pattern. It is a lion face in a full roar; she plans on using bronze, copper, and gold metallic threads to embroider it.

"I think we are done here," Ruby tells him.

"Yeah, I feel lots better. I still need ask Jamie about that Nimrod guy," says Jesse, as he gets up to go to the dorms.

The cool evening air comes quickly to the campus of SWA. Hope doesn't want to get in her cage for the night. She flaps her wings; her broken wing will not extend up, but she tries to get away from Ruby.

"Hope, you come in here this instant!" Ruby's patience is getting short. Gloria has to come up from behind and grab Hope. The young Eagle is a handful when she wants to be. Finally, Hope is in her colossal cage in the dorm entry. She paces in her full-sized fancy birdcage, looking anxious.

"That's odd," says Ruby, "I haven't seen Hope this upset since I first started taking care of her. Maybe she is sensing another earthquake," says Ruby, with worry.

Hope is not cuddly like a kitten, but she still has her expressions that melt Ruby's heart. Ruby decides to leave her in her cage. If there are tremors, she will let her out then.

As evening falls on the SWA campus, people are reflecting on the earthquake. How can something like that happen here, right in the middle of the country? What else might happen?

Jamie feels the need to pray in the middle of the night. He prays:

And as for all who walk by this rule, peace and

mercy be upon them, and upon the Israel of God.

Galatians 6:16

Hope sits awake also, her piercing eyes watching.

Ruby and her roommates are tired and fall asleep fairly quickly, considering the commotion the earthquake caused. Some people drift off listening to the twenty-four-hour news on the radio. The beautiful nation had suffered a rending that would cause maps to be recharted. Patriots everywhere shed a tear.

The guys in Jesse's dorm room are sleeping soundly — except Jesse. He lies there, staring at the bunk above him. He has mixed emotions. He loves who he is in Christ, but hates the part of him that is scared and lonely. He knows his feelings are still a powder keg that could explode and be beyond his control; on top of all that, a spirit of urgency still grips him. He doesn't know what to do with the sense of urgency other than stay alert and seek the Lord.

The lamp on Jesse's bedside table begins to vibrate. It falls on the floor with a bang. The rumble stops; everyone sits up and looks around. Devin turns on the lights.

"Wow, another aftershock!" says Devin, his eyes squinting in the sudden light. He opens the dorm doors. Others are also looking in the commons area.

The floor leader, Benny, tells everyone from his doorway, “Don’t worry, it’s just tiny aftershocks. Try to get some sleep.”

All the boys’ doors shut, and the rooms are dark again, as are the girls' rooms.

Hope screeches in her bird condo; she is restless, and she wants out. Ruby hears her and comes to see her.

Jesse tells her from his doorway, “Hope is keeping everyone awake.”

She nods to him in passing. Her slippers echo through the large, deserted commons area. She decides to let Hope go to her room for the night since she keeps everyone awake with her squawking.

CHAPTER FOUR

IDENTITY CRISIS

Jesse is tired as he gets up this morning. He looks in the bathroom mirror at his face, focusing on the scars. Every scar is a reminder of bad times and abuse. The latest is a gash on his upper lip; his dad had backhanded him last October. He sticks out his tongue and makes a face.

Eric comes out of the shower, wrapped in a towel, and sees Jesse.

"What are you doing?"

Jesse pulls his tongue back in.

"Oh, nothing," Jesse says in his monotone voice. Eric knows not to push the issue.

During breakfast, everyone discusses the president's comments, noting that the nation is no longer an 'Ecclesial' nation, and the devastation caused by the earthquake. Ira, Wanda, and the General are very displeased at the president's assessment of the nation's spiritual identity.

Later, Jesse shows up at Ruby's worktable again. He sits down and starts playing with the fabric pins. Ruby looks at him, studying his face for clues about his mood. Destiny brings her embroidery work over and sits with them; gardening is mostly over for the year.

Ruby looks at Jesse's face again.

"What?" Jesse reacts.

Ruby sits back and asks, "How do you see yourself, Jesse?" Ruby holds her gaze.

Jesse looks surprised by the blunt question.

"When I look in the mirror sometimes, I see street trash; that's what they called me."

Jesse lowers his eyes to the pins on the cushion.

"I know God sees me as a victorious warrior, and I get that. It's just my past. It still has a hold on me. My parents don't think enough of me to keep me."

Jesse hears his voice crack.

Destiny puts her hand on Jesse's shoulder.

"You have an orphan spirit. You still feel like a reject, but you're not," says Destiny, her eyes flashing with fire. (See "Types and Shadows" 4)

Ruby leans forward.

"Father, we come against this orphan spirit, and we break it off Jesse and replace it with the Spirit of Adoption whereby we are Yahweh's children, and we can cry Abba, Father. Let the new creature in Christ that Jesse has become rise up and take its place. Old things have passed away. Behold, all things are made new," Ruby says with strength in her voice.

Destiny takes her Bible from her book bag, opens it, and shows Jesse:

> **But if Christ is in you, although the body is dead because of sin, the Spirit is alive because of righteousness. If the Spirit of him who raised Jesus from the dead dwells in you, he who raised Christ Jesus from the dead will also give life to your mortal bodies through his Spirit who dwells in you. So then, brethren, we are debtors, not to the flesh, to live according to the flesh. For if you live according to the flesh, you will die; but if by the Spirit you put to death the deeds of the body, you will live. For all who are led by the Spirit of God are sons of God. For you did not receive the spirit of slavery to fall back into fear, but you have received the Spirit of adoption as sons, by whom we cry, "Abba! Father!" The Spirit himself bears witness with our spirit that we are children of God,**
>
> **Romans 8:10-16**

Destiny asks Jesse, "Who are you going to let lead you, your flesh or your spirit? Live after the Spirit, Jesse. Now, look at these verses."

> **From now on, therefore, we regard no one according to the flesh. Even though we once regarded Christ according to the flesh, we regard him thus no longer. Therefore, if anyone is in Christ, he is a new creation. The old has passed away; behold, the new has come. All this is from God, who through Christ reconciled us to himself and gave us the ministry of reconciliation; that is, in Christ God was reconciling the world to himself, not counting their trespasses against them, and entrusting to us the message of reconciliation. Therefore, we are ambassadors for Christ, God making his appeal through us. We implore you on behalf of Christ, be reconciled to God.**
>
> **For our sake he made him to be sin who knew no sin, so that in him we might become the righteousness of God.**
>
> **2 Corinthians 5:16-21**

Jesse realizes that he still has a way to go before he is rooted and grounded in Adonai.

"Sometimes, I am strong in the Lord, but at times I feel cold inside."

Jesse knows he is moody at times, especially with his roommates. He experiences flashes of dark images at times. Scenes of him locked in a dark cave where screams of torture echo off the rock walls. He doesn't tell the girls about the images or the terrible grief the visions create in him.

"You need to control your thought life. Think about good things, don't dwell on the past," Ruby interjects. "Hope is the anchor of the soul, you know. Then you can control your emotions. Look and see where you feel hopeless, then you can master it!"

"I know . . . my identity is in Christ."

Jesse is still playing with the pins, wandering off into his own thoughts.

The rest of the day seems typical for the most part. Everyone goes about their work while discussing the earthquake.

As sunset comes, Jesse goes behind the campus, past the caution sign, and sits on the rocky cliffs; this is his prayer rock. Everyone knows he goes back there. The granite boulders are still warm from the sun. Jesse reflects on the world events, and a wave of excitement washes over him. The Lord has told him in dreams about the last days' adventures and how He will do many signs and wonders. Jesse also knows the enemy will show false signs to deceive the world.

"I thank you, Lord, that You have drawn me so close. I pray that we will all be found faithful and worthy to escape the wrath to come," Jesse prays. A hot tear runs down his cheek. "Don't forget my parents, Lord. Reveal yourself to them. Forgive them for how they treated me."

"Do you forgive them?" The Lord invites Jesse to look inward.

I have interceded on behalf of my wayward parents. At least that's a step in the right direction; Jesse consoles himself.

Four years ago, Jesse's parents left him because they wanted to travel with a rock band. They dropped him off to live with an alcoholic uncle. Jesse's life was harsh after that until Manuel gave him a candy cane at Christmas time, and Manuel's family, the Perezes, took Jesse in and led him to the Lord. It was the Perez's fellowship that saved up the money for Jesse's tuition to SWA. Jesse can still see his father's angry eyes and hear his harsh criticisms. His father, Allen, is not pleased with Jesse's newfound walk with God. He said it had made Jesse soft. Jesse hasn't heard from his parents in months. All these memories often cause Jesse to wrestle with anger and depression.

Dark clouds . . . Anton the Guardian knows all too well the dark clouds that are plaguing Jesse. The angel wishes he could disperse the dark energy, but Jesse's thoughts are generating them. There are laws in the spirit world, just like gravity in the natural world. Anton remains vigilant and ready to do his part in bringing Jesse freedom from the murky clouds. But Jesse, for now, needs to face the darkness. Anton urges him to do so; Jesse feels the urging but dismisses it. He is waiting for more strength; he is fearful of what lurks inside his very soul.

It is time to go inside. Jesse leaves the prayer spot and heads to his dorm room. Another day and still no breakthrough on the idols . . . His thoughts take a positive turn. He used to have great prayer meetings at SWA. Up to fifty people came at a time. During the Great Terrorist Crisis of April, everyone was busy praying, working, lighting lanterns, and doing many other necessary things without the benefit of electricity. *It is time to start the "Prayer Rock" up again. Ray and Gabe are counting on it.*

Jesse sees Hope at the entry of the dorms; her king-size cage graces the lobby. She follows Jesse with her eyes as he lumbers down the commons area toward his dorm.

As darkness falls deep in the Rocky Mountains, the weary believers on campus find their rest. Up on the rooftop, Asher, the warring Principality Angel, has returned to serve the SWA campus. He is standing in the air, holding his staff in his hand, waiting for something. His eyes are like fire as he watches the horizon.

Aurora stirs from her sleep. She is twenty-five and serves as a floor leader for the Judah tribe, having a private room. She sits down at her electric piano and begins to sing; her open Bible sits on the music stand. She sings out of **Psalm 18:1-3:**

> **I love you, O Lord, my strength. The Lord is my rock and my fortress and my deliverer, my God, my rock, in whom I take refuge, my shield, and the horn of my salvation, my stronghold. I call**

upon the Lord, who is worthy to be praised, and I am saved from my enemies.

Asher's staff begins to glow in hues of blue. His face lights up from the power flowing out from his majestic rod. Small lightning bolts shoot from it. A fallen angel with a rod of authority, as well, manifests before Asher to resist him.

Aurora sings more from **Psalm 18:4-12:**

The cords of death encompassed me; the torrents of destruction assailed me; the cords of Sheol entangled me; the snares of death confronted me. In my distress I called upon the Lord; to my God I cried for help. From his temple he heard my voice, and my cry to him reached his ears. Then the earth reeled and rocked; the foundations also of the mountains trembled and quaked, because he was angry Smoke went up from his nostrils, and devouring fire from his mouth; glowing coals flamed forth from him. He bowed the heavens and came down; thick darkness was under his feet. He rode on a cherub and flew; he came swiftly on the wings of the wind. He made darkness his covering, his canopy around him, thick clouds dark with water. Out of the brightness before him hailstones and coals of fire broke through his clouds.

Asher begins to spin his staff; the lightning wraps around the fallen angel. At that moment, an Angel of Light occupies the fallen angel's throne. Many angels are now ascending and descending from heaven. They are carrying revelation from the throne to pour out on the people of the area who have "ears to hear." It causes vibrations in the spirit world. Two massive silver angels come to take the fallen angel away.

"My brothers are many, and we grow stronger; you will not be able to bind us all, Asher! Baal and Asherah are all over this land," the bound fallen angel screams and thrashes. His last words are, "Wait till Great Deception comes, just wait!"

Great Deception is indeed approaching, and he has many dark creatures under his command. For miles around, demons hide out in the forest trees. They scatter out of their perches and find themselves banished from the area by Asher's power and authority. The pines rustle as the imps of darkness are cast into desolate places unknown to man. The Fire King shrinks back in his cave, hoping Baal will keep him covered and safe from Asher.

Aurora continues:

> **The Lord also thundered in the heavens, and the Most High uttered his voice, hailstones and coals of fire. And he sent out his arrows and scattered them; he flashed forth lightnings and routed them. Then the channels of the sea were seen, and the foundations of the world were laid bare at your rebuke, O Lord, at the blast of the breath of your nostrils. He sent from on high, he took me; he drew me out of many waters. He**

rescued me from my strong enemy and from those who hated me, for they were too mighty for me. They confronted me in the day of my calamity, but the Lord was my support. He brought me out into a broad place; he rescued me, because he delighted in me.

Psalm 18:13-19

Aurora's eyes grow heavy, and weariness pulls on her. She is invigorated by the song's anointing, but she doesn't fully sense what just occurred. However, she does know that the heaven above the school is open, and Adonai is pouring out His glory on them. She knows angels are involved and that Yahweh has prevailed over darkness. Her sleep will be sweet as the Heavenly Father sings love songs over her.

As the Angel of Light sits in the high place where darkness once reigned, his staff radiates waves of light. His clothing is so brilliant that his image is blurred, and only the shape of his body is visible. The glory of Yahweh begins to increase in the body of believers in the area. They begin to cry out even more to the Lord for Israel's salvation and justice on the earth.

Before returning to Israel, Asher stops in Jesse's room. Anton greets him with a respectful bow. Asher smiles and places his hand on Jesse's forehead. Jesse doesn't wake, but he sees Asher in the Spirit. Asher tells Jesse, "Be of good cheer; Adonai is pleased with you. See yourself as the Father sees you, a warrior. Someday, your father will call you blessed and accept who you are. Listen to the Heavenly Father for your identity. You won't receive it from the world. Remember the chainmail armor that Adonai gave you in the spring? Now see the whole armor you have on."

Asher waves over Jesse's eyes, now Jesse can see in the spirit a silver shield, intricate in design, decorated with silver braid work. It flashes with light.

Jesse looks around. He is caught up in the second heaven, seeing the universe of stars all out before him. Asher touches Jesse on the shoulder, and Jesse is back in his bed.

"Don't forget Adonai's chosen people," Asher whispers in Jesse's ear as he leaves.

Jesse opens his eyes, and the dorm room is back. He drifts off to sleep while Devin's snoring echoes in his head.

A nation changes from being the ecclesia to secular in what seems like an overnight transformation. However, it is an insidiously slow transformation from worshipping God to following after the lusts of the flesh. The public now sees the ecclesia as separated from the rest of the nation, labels them as intolerant, and declares it to be a religion of hate. The president, thinking that kind words will change the terrorist agenda, is wooing the radical terrorists who plot to destroy the nation and Israel.

The earth is the Lord's and the fullness thereof, the world and those who dwell therein, for he has founded it upon the seas and established it

upon the rivers. Who shall ascend the hill of the Lord? And who shall stand in his holy place? He who has clean hands and a pure heart, who does not lift up his soul to what is false and does not swear deceitfully. He will receive blessing from the Lord and righteousness from the God of his salvation. Such is the generation of those who seek him, who seek the face of the God of Jacob. ***Selah***

Psalm 24:1-6

Now, a nation that once shone as a beacon must find its role in the final days. Will the country be the [24]Land of the free, Home of the brave? The nation's identity has changed. Is there any going back?

Terrorists continue to wreak havoc with random acts of terrorism in the U.S. and abroad.

Jamie rose early to pray. It is three a.m., also known as the fourth watch.

"Father, remember the nation's good works and revisit us with favor and protection. Judge the wicked in high places and give us Godly leadership. Turn the hearts of the fathers to the children, and the children's hearts to the fathers lest you come and smite the earth with a curse." Jamie prays from **Malachi 4:1-6:**

"For behold, the day is coming, burning like an

---

24 Star Spangled Banner, Francis Scott Key 1814

oven, when all the arrogant and all evildoers will be stubble. The day that is coming shall set them ablaze, says the Lord of hosts, so that it will leave them neither root nor branch.
But for you who fear my name, the sun of righteousness shall rise with healing in its wings. You shall go out leaping like calves from the stall. And you shall tread down the wicked, for they will be ashes under the soles of your feet, on the day when I act, says the Lord of hosts. "Remember the law of my servant Moses, the statutes and rules that I commanded him at Horeb for all Israel. "Behold, I will send you Elijah the prophet before the great and awesome day of the Lord comes. And he will turn the hearts of fathers to their children and the hearts of children to their fathers, lest I come and strike the land with a decree of utter destruction."

The Lord speaks to Jamie, "This is to be your finest hour. Soon you will expose the hidden enemy to this body, revealing the hidden idols."

Jamie says, "[25]According to Your Word, be it unto your servant."

---

[25] **Luke 1:38 And Mary said, "Behold, I am the servant[f] of the Lord; let it be to me according to your word." And the angel departed from her.**

Nonetheless, he realizes this may upset many, and once again, he could risk having to leave SWA.

Ruby, Ira, Destiny, and Aurora all awaken to the call from Ruach HaKodesh to pray for Israel this morning. They kneel at their beds and begin to cry out to the Lord, as many others join them in the call to pray all across the land.

"Redeem Israel out of his troubles," Ruby weeps (**Psalm 25:22**). Destiny is in travail next to Ruby, rocking on the floor and weeping. The other girls go on to breakfast without them.

"Peace within your walls and prosperity within your palaces," Ira prays from her quarters (**Psalm 127:7**).

CHAPTER FIVE

WRAP ME IN YOUR ARMS

As Jesse wakes up, the sun is streaming through the long, tall, slender windows of the dorm. The sunlight warms the stone floor. Devin and the rest of his roommates have already headed off to breakfast. Jesse walks over to the window and sits on the floor. He feels the warmth of the sunshine on his face.

Closing his eyes, he whispers, "I should be excited about Asher's visit last night, so why does sadness so easily grip me? Father, the breach of the nation grieves my heart. I feel like I am torn in two, like the earthquake did to the heart of our great country." Jesse feels a hot tear stream down his cheek.

The Lord is silent, so Jesse reaches for his Bible. He randomly opens it.

> **Sell your possessions, and give to the needy. Provide yourselves with moneybags that do not grow old, with a treasure in the heavens that does not fail, where no thief approaches and no moth destroys. For where your treasure is, there will your heart be also. "Stay dressed for action and keep your lamps burning, and be like men who are waiting for their master to come home from the wedding feast, so that they may open the door to him at once when he comes and knocks."**
>
> **Luke 12:33-36**

The Lord speaks to Jesse, "You have trusted the wisdom of leaders of this nation to keep you safe, instead of Me. My children often mistakenly rely on the world's systems and the wisdom of men. It is the godless "Babylon system" ruled by the Evil One, or My Kingdom, reigned over by My Son. You are in one or the other."

Jesse's eyes go up to the verses in front of what he just read:

> **And he said to his disciples, "Therefore I tell you, do not be anxious about your life, what you will eat, nor about your body, what you will put on. For life is more than food, and the body more than clothing. Consider the ravens: they neither sow nor reap, they have neither storehouse nor barn, and yet God feeds them.**

Of how much more value are you than the birds! And which of you by being anxious can add a single hour to his span of life? If then you are not able to do as small a thing as that, why are you anxious about the rest?

Consider the lilies, how they grow: they neither toil nor spin, yet I tell you, even Solomon in all his glory was not arrayed like one of these. But if God so clothes the grass, which is alive in the field today, and tomorrow is thrown into the oven, how much more will he clothe you, O you of little faith!

And do not seek what you are to eat and what you are to drink, nor be worried. For all the nations of the world seek after these things and your Father knows that you need them."

Luke 12:22-30

"*I have you wrapped in My arms, Jesse. This world is in constant change, but I change not. Keep your eyes on Me, and the world will not shake you. It is time for your iron pill. I have put iron in your spirit man. Through Me, you can overcome this world.*

"I have said these things to you, that in me you may have peace. In the world you will have tribulation. But take heart; I have overcome the world."

John 16:33

The words of Asher run across Jesse's mind: "Don't forget Adonai's chosen people."

Israel, Lord, I bless Your people, save Yosef's family.

Jesse closes his Bible and goes to breakfast, leaving the real intercession for the girls.

All that crying and stuff, the girls are better suited for it. I don't feel much connection with Israel yet, like everyone else; I guess it will grow in time . . . the Lord spoke of tribulation. . ..

It is July 25th, and the nation is holding its first Festival of Lights to celebrate the president's restoration of the power grid after the Great Crisis in April. Most terrorist threats get shut down before their plans are executed.

As Jesse sits down to eat, he sees that Ruby and Destiny aren't there yet. The TV in the dining hall shows footage of celebrations put on the network channels. Parades in a few large cities and homes with light displays flash on the screen. However, most families did not celebrate the new holiday. In the heartland, many are dealing with earthquake damage.

Yosef thinks about the real Festival of Lights, a Jewish holiday called Hanukkah, which is celebrated in November or December. Being from Israel, Yosef feels the "Christmas in July" holiday is an insult to Jews and Called Out Ones alike. He is glad the school isn't celebrating this government-inspired holiday that the president proclaimed.

Yosef looks over at Jesse and the gang. They are in a good mood, eating and joking. He feels the twinge of missing home. Just the thought of Hanukkah brings his mother's face to his mind. Eric notices Yosef's intense expression and puts his hand on his shoulder.

"Hey, why the somber face?"

"Oh, you know . . . thinking of home."

Even after being in the States for a year, Yosef's accent remains thick, but everyone is accustomed to it now.

Eric nods knowingly. He misses his mom, too, even though his mom is just a few hours away.

Wanda has woven a tapestry showing hands holding the earth. The hands have nail scars. She and her band of gypsies have many skills. Wanda and Ira have become close. The two women are hanging the tapestry at the entrance of the dining hall. It has a scripture on it:

> **"To him who sits on the throne and to the Lamb be blessing and honor and glory and might forever and ever!"**
>
> **Revelation 5:13b**

As the women and the gypsies work on their project, they are laughing and quite loud. The happy sounds echo into the dining room. The adults in the entry drown out the sounds of the TV. The General gets up and turns it off.

"I think we have had enough of the New Holiday of Lights," he says, returning to his heavily sugared tea.

One of the cooks runs in to tell the General what she just heard on the radio. He gets up and turns the TV back on.

"News alert. Live footage of Israel, where they have installed a new set of missiles. They call it Jericho IV. Normally, very secretive about their artillery program, they are making a show of force, seeking to intimidate their enemies who are breathing down Israel's neck with threats by land and sea."

Israel is making a show of arms, and the Middle East is a hotbed of war and strife.

Eric glances over at Yosef. He is hanging on every word of the broadcast, his hands tightly gripping his silverware. Eric tries to think of something to say to Yosef, but nothing comes. He goes over to Yosef and just sits with him, wrapping his arm around his shoulder.

"We won't let your people down this time; just you wait and see," Devin tells him, sitting a few seats down.

A hot tear rolls down Yosef's face, but his expression doesn't change. There is a mature, strong look in Yosef's eyes. He grew up living with bombs and death in his homeland.

"A reported range of eleven thousand kilometers," the news reporter states, "has many surrounding countries calling for a UN inspection."

"This is not legal to have such capabilities," a leader from a neighboring country exclaims with rage on the TV screen. The broadcast returns to a parade in Boston, featuring ornate floats with patriotic themes, lights, and girls in gowns waving. Businesses are hoping to achieve as many sales as they do during the Christmas holidays.

Click. The TV goes off again.

Yosef has lost his appetite. He ambles to the prayer tower for some time alone with Yeshua.

Jesse has a family portrait to do. It is of Wanda and her clan of gypsies. Ira and the General ordered the artwork as a surprise. Jesse sees the girls as he prepares to work on the family portraits.

"Ruby and I are staffing the healing booth at the market today. Ray and Gabriel are supposed to help, but we know they tend to be standoffish," Destiny tells Jesse in the courtyard of the dining hall.

"I expect they will just goof off in the back. I have never seen them do anything 'spiritual.' They are members of the guild of Gad; combat and metal-working suit them well," Ruby comments as Hope trails behind her.

"We had a prayer rock meeting with them just a few days ago; they seem to be seeking. They may surprise you today," Jesse tells the girls.

Jesse waves bye as they go their separate ways for the day.

Jesse finds Jamie in the dining hall's courtyard, repairing the masonry where some stones are loose.

"Hey, little bro!" Jesse calls out to Jamie. "What can you tell me about Nimrod?"

"Nimrod? He is responsible for the Tower of Babel, the King of Shinar, a mighty hunter of men, and the first person to be worshipped as a god. His name means rebel; he is the beginning of all witchcraft and idolatry. **Genesis 10**. . ..”

Jesse looks at him blankly. “Okay . . . information overload!”

“Why are you asking?” Jamie says, adjusting the freshly cemented stones on a retaining wall next to the dining hall.

“Oh, it’s a long story . . . hidden idols, Baal, a dragon thing.”

Jesse doesn’t want Jamie to know he may have ties to the stronghold somehow.

“Well, I have more to tell you about this dude, but now is not the time . . .” Jamie continues dealing with a loose stone.

“Okay, thanks, well, we can talk about it some other time,” Jesse suggests.

“Yes, when the time is right,” Jamie says.

The phrase “when the time is right” reminds Jesse that they first saw the Fire King manifest himself over the cliff, and Destiny, as she uses this expression the most.

Jesse waves goodbye as he goes to work on the gypsy portrait. Jamie knows it’s up to him to expose the idols when the Lord is ready.

He still worries . . . *this could get me kicked out this time. People may not like what I have to tell them. Jesse can handle the truth; it is everyone else I agonize over.*

Ruby, Destiny, Gabriel, and Ray meet Doctor Luz, the Healing tent leader, inside the tent. The white canvas tent lets the light shine through, and the area feels charged with energy. A refreshing breeze keeps the tent cool. Hope pokes around outside in the grass.

"Let's pray before everyone arrives," Doctor Luz says as he slips on his white physician's coat. Ray and Gabriel look nervous. The doctor has a dignified appearance, with grey hair at the temples and wire-framed glasses. He always wears a shirt and tie.

"Ruby, lead us," the doctor instructs.

Ruby takes a deep breath.

"Father, we pray for eyes to be opened, ears to hear You, and hearts to be softened by Your touch. Make us Your instruments and use us. Confirm your Word with signs and wonders!"

"And *please*, let someone come inside today!" Doctor Luz adds.

Ray and Gabriel nod their heads in agreement as the first visitor of the day breaks daylight into the booth. An overweight woman shyly walks in and sits in a chair. She looks at Dr. Luz and begins to cry. Wrapping her face in a bandana, she tries to explain her condition. Ray and Gabriel's eyes widen, unsure of how to deal with the crying woman. Her words are impossible to make out. Ruby and Destiny look to Doctor Luz. He kneels to look at the sobbing woman's face.

"You are dying of neglect, my dear woman. You are desperate for your husband's affection and have lost hope of getting it," Doctor Luz tells her softly.

Immediately, she stops sobbing and looks at the doctor.

"Yes, I guess you are right," she replies, surprised by his comment.

The doctor continues.

"You need healing from a broken heart, and then you will stop comforting yourself with food. No matter how much you eat, you are never satisfied because of your hunger for affection."

Doctor Luz and his team tell her about Yeshua and begin to minister to her needs.

"I would like to believe, if I could know for sure, He is real," she tells them.

Just then, Gloria drops by the booth to see if they have enough help. She sees the lady in the chair and lays her hands on her, just as she did with Wanda. The woman lets out a loud "Whoa! My waist is smaller!" She pulls at her waistband.

The lady is thinner; her face looks even skinnier.

"This is a sign and wonder for you and your husband also; that he may know God has touched you and receive salvation," Gloria tells the ecstatic woman.

"Thank you, thank you!" she breathlessly responds as she hurries off to find her husband.

She runs out, yelling, "He's real! He's real."

Ray and Gabriel stand wide-eyed throughout the day, watching people whom Elohim touches. They still wonder how they are qualified for the Healing Booth. They prefer to walk the market's perimeters, watching for the rumored group of thieves victimizing Eastcliffe.

The booth is quiet again. Doctor Luz looks over at the boys; they look at him sheepishly.

"You guys think you don't belong in this booth?" Doctor Luz asks the boys. They look at his name on his lab coat: "DR. L. LUZ, Dept. of Science SWA," and feel intimidated. They have no answer; they just stand there in their low self-esteem.

The doctor puts them in arm locks and wrestles them to the ground. Everyone is giggling and joking. Just then, a frail man steps in, looking for healing. He sits down with a grunt, looking at all the guys on the grass. He doesn't seem amused by their playfulness as he leans on his cane and glares at them. Doctor Luz and the boys get up and brush off the grass. Ray and Gabriel stare at the man as if they know him.

"Look at my arms. They are wasting away to nothing, and no one knows what is wrong with me."

The older man holds out his arms. They are thin and emaciated.

"And why the cane?" Doctor Luz asks.

"I use it for defensive purposes. I'm quite wealthy. You may have heard of me, Glenn Johnson of Wind Turbine Technologies? I also own the Eastcliffe Department Store. I might get mugged for my gold ring and watch. I see you have gypsies around here."

The man's eyes are steely blue and cold and locked on Gabe and Ray.

Destiny sits down next to the gentleman.

"Tell us about your sons," she requests, led by the Holy Spirit.

The man's face grows stern.

"My sons are good-for-nothing bums. We don't speak — haven't for two years." He leans back in the chair, glaring at Gabriel. He points to Gabriel with his cane. "He is my son. Enough chitchat, I am ready for you to heal me; I paid his tuition, so it is reasonable that I benefit from something," he demands. "I heard about the lady who lost thirty pounds earlier."

Gabriel's face turns pale, and Ray steps close to Gabriel as if to hold him up.

Destiny opens her Bible to:

> **"Behold, I will send you Elijah the prophet before the great and awesome day of the Lord comes. And he will turn the hearts of fathers to their children and the hearts of children to their fathers, lest I come and strike the land with a decree of utter destruction."**
>
> **Malachi 4:5-6**

She reads it to the man. Next, Ruby tells him, "Wrap your arms around your sons, and the Lord will heal you."

"So, you say; I have cursed myself. It's that simple?" Glenn sees a tear run down Gabe's face.

Gabe is upset to see how frail his dad has become and his cold, indifferent treatment after two years of estrangement.

"Perhaps it is time to reassess the situation," Glenn says, gazing downward.

He holds his arms in front of him, looking at the atrophied muscle. His hands tremble with weakness.

Glenn rises from his seat. He turns to Gabriel and looks him in the face. Gabe is shaking with emotion, not knowing what to expect. Glenn, moved by the emotions on his son's face, raises his arms and hugs both boys, pulling them in close to him. The boys' eyes show their surprise.

"I am sorry I was so harsh. I thought tough love would cause you to shape up. Gabriel, my son, I hear you have been clean and sober for a year now, and you didn't quit SWA like I thought you would. I guess I have been slow to come around. Ray, you were like a son to me until you boys got into drugs. You have always stuck close to Gabriel. Your loyalty is commendable."

He put his hands on Gabriel's face.

"You are not the same snot-nosed boy who stole my gold coins and pawned them for drugs. I see that now; I am weary of being angry. I feel all the anger and resentment have left me. It is as if a wind had come and blown it all away. What is in this tent? I feel so — different!"

By now, Gabe's face is wet with tears. The three cling together in a reunion.

"Dad, what about Michael?" Gabriel questions his dad.

"Your brother joined the Army and ran off to Afghanistan, just to avoid being in the family business. I can't hug him now, can I?" his voice returns to coldness.

"Didn't Mom tell you about the ambush? A land mine hit his Hummer. He is in Denver, getting fitted with an artificial limb. Mom must have been afraid to tell you. He lost his arm, Dad," Gabriel's voice gave way with emotion.

Gabriel's father crumples to the grass.

"He was hurt? Oh, my little Mikey! I'll go to Denver immediately and see him."

Gabriel's mother peeks into the booth.

"Oh, there you are, Glenn. What are you doing on the ground?"

She stops and sees him with their son Gabriel. Gabriel's face is wet with tears.

Glenn rises and dusts off his suit.

"Mother, we will take the plane to Denver. Call the pilot. I must see Michael right away. Woman, you have been keeping secrets . . . there is some angel in this tent, I tell you, I have never experienced such freedom. Gabe, keep up the good work! Ray, you too! What a day this has been! I tell you what a day!"

Glenn gives a gentle smile to his wife, who freezes in the doorway of the tent. She has named both their boys after angels; she loves the notion of them and has angel figurines in big glass displays in their lavish home.

Gabe's dad kisses him on the forehead and leads his wife by the hand out of the booth. Gabe's mother blows him a kiss.

Gabe drops to the grass. His dad has left his cane in the tent; Gabe picks it up and looks at it.

"But what about his arms; did he get a healing?" Gabe says, thinking it all went down so fast.

"I believe his strength will grow daily, now that he is free to love again," Doctor Luz tells him.

"What if I didn't come to help today, what if I . . ." Gabe stops, deep in thought.

Ray sits down next to him.

"But we did show up, Gabe. We are where God wants us for a change."

The boys bump knuckles and grin. Ruby finds a deeper understanding of the boys and regrets being so judgmental toward them. Last fall, the boys chose SWA over going to Juvenile detention. SWA takes a few troubled kids each year. Steven also came the same way two years ago at Christmas.

The morning flies by fast. Jesse is ready for a break. Drawing twenty Slavic gypsies in one family portrait is a challenge. He is halfway to the dining hall when Ray and Gabriel come running up to him. Their fast approach takes Jesse aback, and he braces himself for the unknown. Flashbacks to street fights fill his head. The two boys embrace him and begin weeping, telling him about

Gabriel's dad and the reunion. Jesse slowly put his arms around the two "toughest" guys in school.

"We just prayed at your prayer meeting last week, and now look what happened. God is awesome, Jesse," Gabriel is talking fast.

He has a tear on his face and is carrying his dad's cane in his hand. His best friend, Ray, is moved by the miracle, knowing full well how Gabriel's dad had sent him off to school, demanding Gabe never contact him or his mom again.

"He was the richest and meanest man I ever met. We were scared of him. His temper was awful. Now he is all nice and kind and stuff," Ray tells Jesse, as he tries to get a grip on his emotions.

The three boys look around to see who has seen them and begin walking toward the dining hall as casually as possible. Jesse is trying hard not to crack a smile. He doesn't know what normal is for a guy. His dad only has two emotions: mad and furious. It was just a while back when he cried all over Ruby's shoulder. He can hold his head a little higher now. Gabe and Ray have never smiled so much. Their faces glow with the essence of Yahweh's presence on them.

The Angel of Light and his troop of angels have brought a breakthrough into the humble canvas tent. It is a gateway for the power of Adonai to be released. The Father's good pleasure is poured out and received by those who have "an eye to see."

CHAPTER SIX

MOVING FORWARD

This week is the last full week of SWA's outdoor market. Soon it will close due to the winter weather. August brings a shift in the focus of SWA along with the changing color of foliage. Yellow, orange, and red leaves contrast against the dark green of the evergreen trees. It is a beautiful time of year. Attention is again turning to the training of leaders for the latter-day work of the Kingdom of Light.

At breakfast, the General and Professor Norman chat about current affairs over coffee in the dining hall. The sunlight filters through the evergreen trees, creating scattered shadows in the room.

The General takes a sip of his coffee and tells Professor Norman, "The power seems to be on for good. Internet and cell phones are up and operational."

The General pulls out his cell phone and sets it on the table. "We are getting new cadets after all!"

"This is good news. The terrorist threat seems to be under control at the moment, and no more major earthquakes yet," Professor Norman comments.

Ira joins the men at their table and adds to the conversation.

"The earth is in birth pains, yeah? Earthquake aftershocks continue, and road construction is attempting to restore transportation across the center of the country. Many people must relocate, including entire towns. Pockets of spewing gas from the earthquake are still making some areas dangerous. It is a wild world out there these days. Jamie has seen demonic birds flying out of the great crevasse in Missouri. We must warn the earth of the coming darkness; judgment begins in the House of God."

Professor Norman adds, "It sure does. I hope we have our 'house' in order! The country is cautiously moving on past the Great Crisis of April. Israel continues to gain wealth, and surrounding nations continue to threaten its existence. What is next? Have you heard anything, Ira? We have new kids coming in a few days."

She shakes her head. "No. I have, however, had the strangest sensation of spider webs on my face as I pray at night; it is the strangest thing," she adds.

"Hmm," the General responds. He has no idea what spider webs might mean.

He looks around at the young warriors sitting at their tribal tables.

Are they prepared for what is to come? Will they overcome and be part of Yahweh's army?

Ruby and the gang sit in their usual places. It seems quite bright with the lights back on.

Ruby sees Hope out the big windows as she pokes in the grass for food. The young eagle is growing and changing her feather colors. She loves to follow Ruby around, which is very unusual for an eagle to care for human company.

Jennifer announces over the loudspeaker: "Due to the power restoration and public transportation, SWA will welcome the usual first-year students after all."

The room breaks out in applause.

"As a result, kiddos, first-year students arrive in just two days. Please ensure you receive your mentor packet at lunch today and familiarize yourself with your new student's information. Remember how you felt on your first day. Thanks go out to Miss Alvarez of the Levi tribe for all her efforts with the mentor program."

Jennifer, the British voice on the speaker, is the General's wife. Her mothering ways amuse everyone. She is sincere with her affection for the students and is known for her flashy high-heeled shoes.

Jesse drifts off into his thoughts as the gang talks around him at the table.

Over a year ago, I was living in New York with Manuel and his family. They took me off the street. I hope Manuel will be able to come this year. I can't believe they sent me over their own son to SWA. Manuel was so good about it. He led me to the Lord; I owe him a lot.

Jesse is excited about the prospect that Manuel might come to SWA this year.

I should have stayed more in touch and written more often; then, I would have known if Manuel was coming or not. They paid my way; I owe them so much. I'd better start writing more often. Now I feel guilty. . ..

Ruby looks over at Jesse and wonders: *What is on his mind now?*

During lunch, the students get their mentor packets. In two days, the newbies will get the support they need. Ruby wishes there had been a mentor program last year; she could have used a mentor in her first year. She feels fulfilled in working on the program with the General. *He is so down-to-earth and easy to talk with,* she thinks. *Dad and Mom said they are proud of my contribution and vision for the program. Arlo still sees me as a kid, but I am growing up. I hope he will stop treating me like a child.*

Jesse is dreading mentorship. He doesn't want anyone taking up his alone time with God. The girls never stop talking about how they are going to make the new girls feel at home. Devin and Eric seem curious about who their newbies are. Ruby's envelope has the name Alexandria.

"Blonde, sixteen years old, guitar player . . . Sweet!" Ruby imagines hours of sitting and singing with her.

Destiny's assignment is a girl named Trisha. She is a newborn in the Kingdom; she is from Scotland!" (Newborn – expression for just being saved)

"I got a tweaker," Steven exclaims with concern.

"A what?" Ruby doesn't know drug slang.

"He's a Meth user, fresh out of rehab. Why did they assign him to me? I am barely clean myself."

Jesse stands, looking at his packet. The name on it says, "Manuel." Jesse's palms begin to sweat.

What if this is my Manuel? I don't want to get my hopes up. It would be great if we could be together again.

"Open it already," Ruby says as she nudges Jesse in the side.

Sure enough, it is his friend. Jesse feels a lump in his throat.

"*Oh, Lord, this is super fantastic. I know I prayed that he could come, but I really didn't expect this. Thank You, Lord.*"

Jesse looks up at the gang. *What can I tell them?*

"I got Manuel, the very guy I told you about, who led me to the Lord two Christmases ago." Jesse continues staring at the paperwork.

"Are you gonna cry?" Devin jokingly teases Jesse. Jesse and Devin wrestle. Eric joins in.

"Boys!" says Destiny, as she and Ruby leave the guys rolling on the grass.

Eric's envelope catches the wind. All efforts to catch up with it are in vain. The three boys watch as it blows off out of sight.

"Better tell the floor leader what happened," Devin advises.

"Nah, I'll just wing it." Eric tends to be too casual about such things.

Aurora Oliver, the song leader, is a "[26]Pillar in the temple." She will continue for another year. It is her eighth year as a worship leader (she started at seventeen years old). This year is Jamie's second year at SWA. (See "Types and Shadows" 5)

The General will soon give his annual speech to the new recruits.

Ruby reflects on how fast the year went.

It was a very eventful year, even without the Great Crisis of April. This year, my mom will be around and Arlo! I will be more relaxed having her close. Ira, the

---

26 **Psalm 144:12 May our sons in their youth be like plants full grown, our daughters like corner pillars cut for the structure of a palace;**

prophetess, has never lived on campus before. Incredibly, she left her sanctuary on the mountain to join us on campus. She is so powerful in the Spirit, and she is going to teach some. I hope I get a class with her.

This year, Ira has formed a good friendship with Wanda and feels at home at SWA. She plans to return to her mountain cabin in the spring for the prophetic work during the summit hike. The gypsies make their mark on the school with their tapestries, loud laughter, and colorful clothes. They will take positions in maintenance and as kitchen staff, and help with the farm animals. Now that new students are arriving, the gypsies perfectly fill the need for additional staff.

Jesse looks over his mentoring packet.

I still can't believe Manuel will be at SWA in two days. I wonder if Papa and Ana will bring him or if he is taking the bus? Are the roads in the earthquake zone fixed? I have matured a lot, but I hope that Manuel and I will still feel as close as when I was in Spanish Harlem.

It is August, alright. The air is crisp, and the leaves rustle in the breeze. Classes will start on Monday, and the market will now be open only on Saturdays. Jesse finishes the gypsies' clan portrait, and Ruby and Destiny finish with their embroidery work.

Floor leaders review a list of ways students can make the newbies feel at home. Jesse can't wait. Steven, however, feels the weight of his assignment and is dreading facing his new student. Ruby and the girls make welcome posters and are all "perky," as Steven calls them.

Ruby stares at Jesse; he is going to be quiet today. She wishes she knew what was on his mind.

Is he in a crisis? I'm worried about him.

Jesse is deep in his own thoughts.

To think, last year, I hitchhiked from New York City. A lot has happened since then. Jamie was saved from witchcraft, then the Great Crisis of April, and most recently, the earthquakes in the heartland. I am considered a prophet! Jamie is giving profound speeches, and Ruby has developed a mentoring program with the General. Everyone respects Destiny as a student leader and seer due to her pointing out the red lightning last October. Man, we have changed . . . Thank You, God. Now. . . to just graduate and fulfill our callings as a team.

Friday around noon, Faith announces, "The first bus is here!"

Faith and Milagros have been waiting on the dorm steps. Like last year, floor leaders with clipboards meet the students and show them to their dorms.

Destiny is the first to find her newbie Trisha getting out of one of the buses.

"Welcome to SWA; I am Destiny. We are in the same dorm," Destiny tells the new cadet.

"Thanks, Destiny; I don't know anyone here," Trisha confides.

"Don't worry. I will introduce you to the gang. But first, let's get your stuff to the dorms," Destiny tells her as they walk up the long steps to the upper level of the campus.

Jesse finds the gang is busy with their new cadets. Manuel doesn't arrive on any of the scheduled buses. Jesse walks over to Jamie, who is placing signs all over the campus for the new cadets.

"Wow, I can't believe it was a year ago you were a floor leader, casting spells as a warlock."

"Yeah, if it weren't for you and Devin leading me to the Lord, I would be long gone. I owe much to Commander Alvey, too, of course. I am content to learn the ways of Adonai and be a groundskeeper."

"And now you are Head of Maintenance, a very dedicated and insightful servant of Yeshua. You even give speeches and anointed messages from the Lord," Jesse remarks, smiling.

They look across the campus at the new cadets, their luggage in hand.

Eric sees a kid standing with no mentor. He looks lost.

"Are you assigned to Levi Lodge?" he asks the nervous guy.

"Um . . . yeah, my name is Jorge, I am from Mexico. This is my first time in the U.S."

"Cool, I'm Eric; I'll show you around." Eric hopes he hasn't got the wrong guy, since he let his newbie packet blow away.

They walk up to the upper level, and Eric shows Levi Lodge to him. All the gang is there in the commons area with their newbies, except Jesse.

One hundred and fifty new students will arrive in the next few hours. It became possible because the power and fuel situation has dramatically improved since early summer.

Jesse stands on the grass, watching as all the parents carry in luggage and kiss their children goodbye. Jesse feels a twinge of pain, missing his parents again. He realizes his hands are clenched and stops himself by opening them. Jesse looks down at his palms to check the scars that came from clenching them so hard that his nails cut into his palms. He shakes off the dark emotions and focuses on Manuel, his special friend, who is nowhere. He asks all the floor leaders, but Manuel hasn't checked in yet. All the buses have come and gone.

It is now six o'clock in the evening. All the benches are full; the new kids take their places according to tribal assignments at supper.

Ruby thinks about graduating next spring.

I can't think of anywhere else as exciting as SWA, but I want to graduate and move on with Jesse and Destiny as a team. However, I worry about how this will happen with things so chaotic; we have to stay together, no matter what!

"So, supper is here, and no Manuel," Jesse tells Destiny and Ruby.

"I hope he was able to get across the Great Breach. Helicopters are the main means, and I have heard some kids say you have to pay bribes to get across," Ruby tells him. (See "Types and Shadows" 11)

"You can always find something to worry about, can't you?" Jesse says, wishing for encouragement, not more anxiety.

"It's a gift!" Ruby says jokingly, wishing she had been more positive.

"I am sure he will show up, Jess. Did you ask the General?" she asks.

He shakes his head to indicate he did not. He doesn't want to bother the General about it just yet. He looks swamped today. Jesse is too nervous to eat. He just sits there looking at the dining hall doors. Jesse finally gets up and goes outside. Ruby and Destiny are worried too. Jesse sits alone on the steps that lead down to the lower level and the entrance.

It is getting too cold to hang around outside in the evenings, but I want some quiet time to hear from the Lord. Manuel has already missed Tribal Assignments and the General's speech. I see two people coming out of Levi Lodge; it looks like Jamie and somebody.

Jesse gets up and walks toward them.

Maybe Jamie has gotten a word from the Lord about Manuel.

As he gets closer, he sees that it is Manuel with Jamie. Manuel is limping and has a bruised eyebrow and scratches on his face.

"Manuel! What happened to you?" Jesse runs to him. They embrace like brothers.

"Ouch." Manuel smiles in embarrassment about his condition. "I don't think the enemy wanted me to get here."

"Manuel, you look like you got hit by a truck!" Jesse says, trying to bring a bit of humor to the situation.

Ruach HaKodesh comes down, and Jamie gives them both a message.

"Iron sharpens iron," Jamie tells them both. (**Proverbs 12:17**) He continues, "Although you will have separate ministries, you will always be close and give each other good counsel."

Jamie gets a call on the walkie-talkie and has to leave.

"Wow! Who was that?" Manuel asks.

"Oh, that's just the groundskeeper!" says Jesse playfully as Jamie heads off. Jamie waves as he rushes to his crew.

"If that's a groundskeeper, I'd love to meet the leaders around here!"

Manuel is impressed with Jamie.

"Are you hungry?" Jesse feels his stomach churning.

"Yeah, really hungry; I missed lunch. I will tell you later what happened on my way here."

The boys walk into the dining hall to see the General walking toward them. The General looks over Manuel's condition — his banged-up face, his dirty clothes. It seems as though he had trouble getting here.

"You gave us quite a scare, Manuel. The last time we had a student lost in transit was well . . . Jesse here. We will talk about that in the morning. Glad you are here and safe. We were just praying for your safe arrival!"

Manuel's face changes expressions. He forgets about his injuries.

"God has given me a message for this school," says Manuel as the power of God begins to fall on him.

Manuel is full of the anointing. The General discerns the influence of Ruach HaKodesh all over him.

The General gets the kids' attention, "We just prayed for Manuel, and now here he is!"

Everyone claps and yells. The General quiets them down.

"Now listen, he has a word for us from the Lord. Manuel, speak your heart," the General tells him.

Jesse couldn't help but smile.

Just like old times. . ..

"I have to speak the Lord's heart to this body. You think . . . you think a lot has changed." Manuel's voice carries through the dining hall. "The Father would say . . .

it has just begun, the birth pains. The earth reels to and fro. I am preparing to judge the earth, even as you have called out for justice. Remember, judgment begins in the [27]house of the Lord. I will cover you with My wings and with My angels. Hold not back from your intercessions; We have a great adventure ahead. At this moment, preparations for the wedding supper are going on."

Manuel's body bends under the power of the anointing.

The room fills with weeping. Many kids under the power of Ruach HaKodesh are lying on the floor wailing. The new students are getting a taste of the move of the Holy Spirit in the place.

"He led you to the Lord, eh, Jesse?" the General asks.

Jesse nods his head.

"I should have known," the General smiles and pats Jesse on the shoulder. "I can feel our anointing has gone up a level, Manuel. You and Jesse have a powerful connection. Don't let the enemy pull you apart," the General warns them.

The room settles, and the boys go to get warm plates of food. Everyone returns to their meals.

"Wow," Destiny says as she looks at Jesse and Manuel; she feels the anointing they have together. Ruby

---

[27] **I Peter 4:17**

smiles at Manuel with a silly grin; she is already quite taken with him.

"ATTENTION: There has been a break-in in the nurse's office. Anyone who can offer any information, please come to the main office." Jennifer's voice sounds very official.

Lee, the new student, and Steven's mentor assignment slinks down in his chair. He is of Asian descent with sharp features and clean-cut, black hair. The girls find him quite handsome. Steven's eyes get big.

"Lee . . . what have you done?" whispers Steven.

Lee grins back at him. Just then, Jamie walks up and is standing behind them both. "You two . . . stand up."

Jamie pats down Lee and finds a bottle of pills in his pocket. He hands them to the General. The General reads the bottle and tries not to burst out laughing. Steven is very puzzled now.

"Lee, why did you feel the need to break into the medicine cabinet?" the General leans down to get on his level.

"Well, just in case I . . . I had more withdrawals, I just . . ." Lee's voice wavers, embarrassed by the public exposure to his crime.

Steven is thinking . . . *How typical. Just luck, trying to keep my nose clean, and now my newbie is a criminal.*

"Did you know you stole — iron pills?" The General cracks a smile.

Just then, Ira breaks out in laughter, in holy laughter. She tells the school, "Just as Jesse needs iron for his body, the Lord is putting iron in our spirits so that we can stand in the last days."

Ira, feeling the power of the Spirit, continues to laugh between sentences.

"Lee's actions are a shadow of the Lord's. Lee will stay — HAH — and receive strength. Build him up — tee hee — don't pull him down. He is a diamond in the rough, and the Lord wants him here."

Ira is now giggling on the floor.

Steven looks around the room; holy laughter is getting a grip on him. He drops to the ground, slapping the floor with his hands, yielding to the influence. Lee, too, is getting a dose of the Holy Spirit.

The General declares over the dining room, "The joy of the Lord is our strength."

And he, too, can't stand for laughing. Ruby and Destiny try to maintain their dignity. They snicker, and soon they join in holy laughter. Jesse marvels at how, every time iron pills are mentioned, holy laughter appears.

It is an excellent start to a new school year. Lee and Steven both experience profound healings through the holy laughter that night. Manuel has delivered his message, and now he can relax.

Jamie is turning out to be an effective watchman. There is a new job at SWA. The General gives Jamie a new title: "Watchman on the wall." It is a spiritual position for which Jamie is well suited and carries some honor with it.

Jamie remains Head of Maintenance because it allows him to be present throughout the school and strategically places him in the heart of the action. He gathers with the leaders to pray every week.

Steven and Lee sit on the floor, laughing. It turns out to be very exhausting.

"Hey, Lee," Steven gets his attention.

"Yeah, Steven?" Lee is too tired to raise his arms.

"Why did you steal iron pills, of all things?"

"I couldn't find anything good, and I didn't want to go empty-handed. I think I'm going to be okay here. I think I can trust Yeshua. It's not easy letting Him have control, but I think I am beginning to feel He really cares for me; you know?"

Steven nods.

"Yeah, I know. I used to think no one cared . . ."

Steven can see how they will be right for each other, and that maybe it wasn't a mistake putting them together.

As Friday night ends, the campus of SWA settles in for the night. The new cadets have the events of supper to reflect on as they settle into their dorms. The student body is just two hundred and fifty this year. The gypsies take up some room, as they number over twenty. Many second-year students mentor two newbies each to make up the difference.

Ruby can hear Alex playing her guitar next door. *Not bad . . .* Ruby thinks. *Not bad.*

Jesse realizes that Manuel didn't tell them how he got so beat up. Manuel is next door, and they aren't allowed to leave the dorm after ten o'clock at night except for emergencies. It will have to keep till tomorrow. Jesse looks at his hands again. There is one small cut with the shape of his nail on his palm.

"Sorry, Lord, I can be so faithless," Jesse whispers as he drifts into a deep, restful sleep.

Thank you, Lord, for bringing Manuel here.

Jesse feels a cool breeze across his face. He opens his eyes to see a bright light about three feet above his bed. He sees a tall angel in shimmering raiment pointing to his Bible, which is open, and the words on the pages glow.

"Come, Jesse, and I will show you what heaven is preparing for those who are found faithful and who will be overcomers."

The angel's hand points to the book of **Revelation,** chapter **19**. Suddenly, the room changes to a lavish stone palace. Large open-air windows reveal the beauty of rolling hills and deep blue skies. The villa has white marble walls and floors adorned with white flowers, and flowing luminescent fabric drapes the windows. The atmosphere is filled with stars, with an occasional light cloud sprinkled overhead in a deep blue expanse of space. Cherubim and other creatures stand on the sides of the banqueting hall. Jesse hears a multitude of people, thundering, and the voice of many waters, all saying,

> **"Hallelujah! For the Lord our God the Almighty reigns. Let us rejoice and exult and give him the glory, for the marriage of the Lamb has come, and his Bride has made herself ready;**
>
> **Revelation 19:6b-7**

All the people are clothed in wedding garments, except for the people who are serving. The servants' robes are plain — no gold or silver or jewels. The wedding garments are fabulous, sparkling silver and gold embellishments on white linen. Many wear multiple crowns with jewels. Laughter fills the space, and great joy is evident on everyone's face. All the cultures of the world are there from every tribe, tongue, and nation. They are in white ethnic garments with jewels and gold and silver embellishments. Ornate, elegant crowns with jewels and engravings flash in the light.

The angel brings Jesse outside the mansion to the large front doors. [28]Five virgins with unlit lamps stand sadly on the steps with a few people who didn't have wedding garments on. Jesse remembers the parable in the New Testament about them.

The angel waves his hand, and the scene changes. The sound of the wedding has turned to hooves pounding and metal clanging. Jesse sees a white horse; Christ is

---

[28] Matthew 25:1-13

seated on it. Engraved on his thigh are the words "Faithful" and "True." The bride dissolves into millions of individual people. They are on horseback, wielding weapons, primarily swords. The armies of Heaven follow on white horses. The holy military, clothed in fine linen, white and clean, follows Yeshua Ha'Mashiach (Jesus, the Anointed One, Messiah, Christ). The saints have new bodies that can't die. A banner drops down over the sky, saying, "-[29]**and in righteousness he judges and makes war**."

Jesse feels himself falling. The scene fades above him as he loses altitude with the angel remaining by his side. They both stand on a barren hill. Now they are on the Earth, looking over the mountains of Colorado. The wind is picking up and getting cold.

Jesse's eyes burn from the wind. The angel tells Jesse, "It's because of the level of revelation that you are under the mantle of Paul and Daniel."

Jesse studies the angel's face, trying to understand. "What do you mean . . . because of the level of revelation?"

The angel smiled. "Your iron deficiency, your fainting spells. Paul had a thorn in the flesh. Daniel had

---

[29] Revelation 11:19 Then I saw heaven opened, and behold, a white horse! The one sitting on it is called Faithful and True, and in righteousness he judges and makes war.

•

persecution. Pride desires to ruin you. (**2 Corinthians 12:7**)

> **But he said to me, "My grace is sufficient for you, for my power is made perfect in weakness." Therefore I will boast all the more gladly of my weaknesses, so that the power of Christ may rest upon me.**
>
> **2 Corinthians 12:9**

Jesse nods. Although he doesn't think of himself as equal to Paul or Daniel in any way, it makes some sense to him. The angel waves his hand again, and Jesse finds himself in his bed. Without any warning or goodbye, the angel leaves. Jesse isn't sure whether he was dreaming or if he had actually moved from his bed. He pulls the covers up to warm his cold face and sleeps the rest of the night.

Ira is wiping cobwebs off her face in her sleep. When she wakes, she remembers and begins to seek the Lord for its meaning.

That morning, Jesse is looking forward to seeing Manuel at breakfast. He doesn't see him in the dorm's commons area or on the way to the dining hall. Once again, Jesse sits, waiting for Manuel, while everyone else eats. All the newbies are sitting with their mentors. It's quite a contrast to last year, when the second-year students checked out the newbies from across the room. Jesse leaves his plate on the table and heads back to the dorms. He knocks on Manual's door. Manuel pushes the door open. "Rocky, is that you?" Manuel hides behind one of the oversized arched double doors.

"Yeah, it's just me."

By now, Jesse is wondering what is going on. As he steps inside the dorm room, he can now see Manuel. His eye became swollen overnight, and his bruises have darkened and become more pronounced. Manuel is upset by his appearance and dreads going down for breakfast.

"Have you had some powerful encounters with God recently?" Jesse leans in to ask while examining Manuel's swollen eye.

"Well, yeah. Why do you ask?"

Jesse smiles, "It must have been pretty big to get the enemy to beat on you like this. What happened to you, anyway?" Jesse asks, remembering he had forgotten to go to the nurse for his pill. As they walk out of the dorms, Manuel asks Jesse about the large empty cage in the lobby.

"That's the cage for Hope, the eagle. Didn't I tell you?" Jesse is impatient to hear about his trip to SWA. Jesse didn't write Manuel about the eagle. He hated writing letters and would often give brief reports back to Manuel.

"You didn't tell me you guys have an eagle. Cool!"

"Yeah, it took too many words in a letter. I'll tell you later — just tell me what happened to you," Jesse demands.

As the boys start the descent down the long steps to the middle level of campus, Manuel attempts to tell him about the last three days.

"I started on the bus knowing the earthquake damage would only let the bus get me to Illinois. On the second day, the bus broke down in the middle of nowhere. And we are stranded on the side of the road. I have never seen the sight of just land as far as you can see. I felt so helpless because I didn't have control over anything. I couldn't call a cab or order a pizza. I had to trust God for everything. Being from Spanish Harlem, this was an eye-opener."

"Yeah, I know how ya feel," says Jesse.

"So, after a repairman fixed the engine, we made it to the earthquake zone, and things changed. Heavy equipment was moving dirt everywhere. Police checked everybody looking for looters. The bus route ended, so I was supposed to take a helicopter ride across the earthquake zone into Illinois. However, a rich individual had chartered it for the rest of the day, leaving me and six others stranded. I had no money for a hotel. I didn't want to sit around. I don't know if it was fear or God driving me, but I took off on foot by myself! I pulled my backpack off the bus, and I decided to see how far I could get before nightfall. Barricades blocked off the fault line. I slipped past the police checkpoints and headed toward the 'Great Breach' as they call it. I slept that night in an old hollowed-out tree that had fallen over. I could see where they had set some flammable vapor sites on fire. It lit up the night. I thought about you, Jesse, when you lived on the streets, homeless."

Jesse nods his head; being homeless seemed like a distant nightmare to him now.

Jesse stops by the nurse's office to pick up his iron pill. Then they head for breakfast.

Manuel continues, "My tuition was quite a stretch for our little fellowship. I just had tortillas to eat the last few days."

Jesse remembers the ecclesia where he first learned about God's presence and the power of the fellowship of saints.

To the boys' disappointment, breakfast has cleared out, and there is no more food available. Jamie sees their predicament and takes them to the kitchen for leftover bacon and biscuits. Jamie goes back to replacing light bulbs in the dining hall as the boys go outside.

Ruby is taking Hope out for some fresh air and sunlight. She finds Manuel handsome and is always nervous and giggly around him. Jesse finds her actions strange. *She was so serious and well-centered before Manuel came around.* Manuel and Jesse sit on the dining hall steps where the sun can warm them, and Manuel finishes telling his story.

"There is a temporary bridge erected over a broken highway, for emergency use only. To get to it from where I was in the hollow tree, I had to get through a bunch of underbrush bulldozed to clear the road. The branches scratched up my hands and face. One limb popped back and slapped me across the face. I sat in the middle of the thicket holding my face and checked to see if there was blood. I felt like the enemy had slapped me."

Jesse can see the scratches on Manual's hands and face. It upset him to see his friend banged up.

"I heard voices that were telling me to turn back and give up. The more I sensed them, the more determined I got."

Ruby is trying to steer Hope toward the boys, but the eagle does not cooperate.

Manuel continues.

"It was sad to see the damage from the earthquake, our great country with such devastation. At one point, I became overwhelmed, and I sat and bawled. No one was around for miles, just fallen trees, toppled buildings, and crumbled roadways. I felt like I was in a movie; it wasn't real to me. The Lord comforted me, speaking about how these things must come to pass before the end can arrive. And that He had a message for me to give to the school. So, I pressed on even more determined."

"So . . . how did you get that shiner above your eye?" Jesse needs answers faster.

"I had to leave New York to get mugged!" Manuel finds humor in his trauma and laughs easily. "I got across the bridge and hitched a ride to the nearest town. It was a little town with just a post office and a truck stop. These two guys looked like they were our age and didn't like what they called 'dirty Mexicans.' They laid into me and went through my stuff. They laughed at me for having a Bible and threw it in the dirt. It was a cowboy boot that left the shiner. I thought the Lord should have struck them with lightning or something, but He showed me they were afraid and driven by the enemy."

By now, Ruby and Hope meander over to join the two boys.

"Alright if we join you?" Ruby included her eagle Hope in the "we."

Manuel just now noticed the great raptor and is taken aback that Ruby is the caregiver of her very own eagle. Jesse, seeing the amazement on his face, tells him, "That's another story altogether."

"So . . . is this Destiny or Ruby?" Manuel asks with a smile.

"Ruby," Jesse says impatiently. "Okay, so what happened next? Where did you sleep that night?" Jesse wants to know more.

"In jail!" Manuel says, cracking a smile. It is embarrassing to him.

"No way!" Jesse leans in, and so does Ruby. Manuel's blushing made Ruby crush even more on him.

"After I got mugged, the people at the truck stop called the cops. I lost my driver's permit to those two cowboys, so the police thought I was an illegal alien. They cuffed me and called immigration. They didn't call my parents till the next morning. The cool thing was that I got to introduce a family to Jesus. They had to go back to El

Salvador, all fourteen of them. So, I kinda feel like Paul in the New Testament."

Just then, Manuel sees the General out of the corner of his eye. He is walking toward them with a stern look on his face.

"Manuel, I need you and Jesse in my office now."

The General is serious; no one speaks until they are in his office. Jesse looks at his friend's beat-up face. He wishes he could help him not feel the stress of the moment.

Ruby and Hope watch them leave. She can't wait to hear what is going on. She finds Manuel very handsome despite the shiner on his eye.

Jesse has never seen the General's office before, just the wooden stairs that lead up to a balcony office. On the walls are pictures of all two hundred and fifty or so students, high-back leather wing chairs, and bookcases filled with books. The end wall features a floor-to-ceiling window with curved wood accents, overlooking the campus.

The boys sit down in the chairs and watch the General lean back in his leather chair.

"Manuel, your hitchhiking really gave us a scare. Anything could have happened to you, and your parents could have spent their lives wondering about your fate."

The General's face shows genuine concern, "I . . . had to assure the authorities I would put you on strict restrictions. They wanted to ship you back to New York. You are under strict supervision and are not permitted to leave the campus for field trips. You need to call your parents. When they heard you didn't take the Great Breach flight, they reported you missing. And then, when immigration released you, they lost track of you again!"

Manual's eyes well up as the gravity of his little adventure grips him — the General dials and hands the phone to Manuel.

Manuel speaks in Spanish to his dad. Jesse can't make out much of the conversation.

Meanwhile, outside, Eric and Devin saw the boys go to the General's office.

"Man, Jesse is taking this newbie assignment seriously." Devin is feeling a little jealous of Jesse's devotion to Manuel.

"Didn't you know? They are best friends. That guy led Jesse to the Lord in New York."

"Oh, he's THAT Manuel." Devin feels silly for not putting it together.

Manuel has tears running down his face when he hangs up. Jesse almost cries too, feeling his pain. Manuel pulls the end of his shirt up to wipe the tears off his face.

The General's countenance turns softer, "Manuel, what do you need in the way of clothes?"

"I need everything," Manuel replies with a hint of sadness still lingering in his voice.

"You know Jesse arrived last year with no luggage to speak of, also. Anyway, I have to declare you are officially on detention and stripped of all your privileges. I know you are very anointed, bold, and gutsy, but you need to learn some things. Your actions have consequences; you affect others, not just yourself."

Manuel nods his head.

"Adonai Himself said you are to stay, and I am happy with that. However, as part of your detention, you are assigned clean-up duty with Jamie when you are not in class. Detention is for a month. We must keep the officials happy so you can remain at SWA."

"Can I join Manuel in detention?" Jesse asks.

"Why? Do you think it is unfair?" the General asks.

"No, I just want to be there for him any way I can."

Jesse truly wants to show his appreciation to Manuel for leading him to the Lord.

"Okay, that is fine. Both of you can now report to Jamie. He is working on a water leak behind the kitchen. He is expecting you. Well, at least one of you anyway."

The General grabs both boys and bear hugs them.

"Please, you two — don't run off and do anything crazy without talking to me first. God requires accountability, you know. You're both exceptional, but I don't know how much more I can handle!"

The boys step out into the sunlight. Most of the students are sitting around, laughing, and getting to know their newbies.

Ruby, Hope, Eric, and the rest of the crew watch from afar as the boys disappear behind the dining hall.

The two friends find Jamie up to his hips in a muddy hole.

"Oh, there you are . . . Hand me that pipe wrench right there."

Jamie's tool belt is lying just beyond his reach from the hole.

"I just . . . can't get this loose," he grunts from the muddy pit. Jamie is getting frustrated with the rusty, leaky water fitting.

Jesse grabs a handful of mud and begins dripping little drops down the back of Jamie's neck while Manuel hands him the wrench. Jamie strains with the tool and grunts. He stops and feels the back of his neck, looks at the mud on his fingertips, and turns to see Jesse's hand dripping mud over him. Manuel's eyes get big; Jamie is well built. Manuel recognizes a fellow weightlifter. Jamie drops his head and takes a long breath. Before Jesse knows what hit him, Jamie grabs his leg and pulls him down into the muddy pit. Manuel begins to back away, laughing, when Jamie grabs him with a messy hand and pulls him in, too.

"Oh, no, you are not getting away clean," Jamie says, laughing.

Jamie playfully wrestles both boys down into the hole. They are laughing and squishing each other with mud when they hear someone walk up. Wiping the dirt from their eyes, they look up to see Professor Alvarez standing with his hands on his hips. The three in the mud stand motionless, out of breath from playing.

"How is the repair coming along, Jamie?" the professor inquires, looking over the scene.

"Um, well . . . I have some help, but the fitting is too rusty to turn." Jamie gets his "back to business" voice back.

The General just promoted Jamie to a spiritual office of "Watcher on the Wall," and he thinks perhaps he just lost all credibility.

Professor Alvey cracks a smile as he turns back and calls out, "Carry on!"

The three muddy guys go back to their mud fight.

Ruby is waiting for her dad to come back so she can grill him on what is going on with Jesse and Manuel. She looks at him as he walks past her. He only shakes his head slowly. He knows it is torture for Ruby, but the look on her face is priceless.

"DAD!" Ruby complains.

The professor simply raises his hand and continues walking. Ruby will have to wait to ask the boys herself. She goes off to find Destiny and the girls, maybe look up her newbie, and see how she is getting along.

She finds her newbie, Alex, in the commons area playing her guitar. Ruby tries to strike up a conversation, but Alex tells her she is in the middle of writing a song, so Ruby leaves her alone.

Destiny and Trisha are pressing flowers for their scrapbooks. They laugh about finding a three-leaf clover.

"Now, you should know the four-leaved clover represents faith, hope, love, and luck. I don't believe in luck, do you?"

Trisha's charming Scottish accent makes the conversation even more enjoyable for Destiny.

"Yeah, luck is superstition," says Destiny, examining a little plant she pulled up. "Even my name Destiny means something inevitable . . . like you have no choice. I think we have a choice in our lives, don't you?

"Yeah, for sure, I think God's plan for us could be a destiny, though," says Trisha.

"For sure, I don't want to miss my destiny. What does Trisha mean, do you know?" asks Destiny.

"It means noble; it is Latin."

"Cool!" responds Destiny.

The girls put their flowers in the largest books they had — a dictionary — and places them in their big wooden armoires.

SWA classes start on Monday. Steven shows Lee the location of all his classrooms. He wants to fill him in on Doctor Luz's leaded glass window with sunlight shining through the beveled glass, about how we are the glass, and the Holy Spirit is the sun. But he doesn't want to ruin the surprise. All the girls think Lee's Asian features are very attractive.

Jamie hoses off Jesse and Manuel to get them clean enough to go inside the Levi dorms and shower. Jesse and Manuel come into the dining hall at noon with wet hair. It is too nippy out for them to be that wet. They shiver a little till they warm up. Manuel is self-conscious, with his lip still swollen and bruised, as well as his eyebrow. Jesse feels comfortable and confident. He decides to introduce Manuel to the gang officially; last night was too eventful to do it then.

"This is Eric; he is rich. And this is his coat I'm wearing. Next to him is Devin. He is a genius. Ruby, you met, she can pray like nobody's business. And Destiny is beaut—." Jesse stops himself.

He feels a flush of heat on his face. Manuel is grinning, seeing his embarrassment.

"I mean . . . she is well versed in the scriptures." Jesse sits back down. All his confidence drains down his chair to the floor. Destiny looks down at her plate, a little flushed herself, but rather pleased to see some affection out of Jesse.

CHAPTER SEVEN

HEARTS OF STONE

The first day of classes at Spirit Wings Academy is going smoothly. The only hitch is Eric's newbie, Jorge. People keep calling him "George."

"It's Jorge, like 'hoar-hay.' The J is an H sound," Eric tells people.

During lunch, the General comes and tells Jesse to go to his office. Ruby and Destiny are concerned. Ruby goes straight to the prayer tower, skipping class and the rest of her meal. She lies down on the carpet at the altar area and begins to travail in prayer for Jesse. They call it 'lying between the porch and altar' at SWA. Two prayer leaders sit on the floor and pray with her. Destiny feels at peace about the situation and goes on to class.

As the General and Jesse enter his office, Jesse realizes his dad is sitting in a chair next to the General's desk. Jesse's hands go into fists as he looks at his father with cold eyes.

"Have you come to take me away again?" Jesse asks as the panic begins to take hold of him. "Where have you been for the last nine months?"

"No, boy, we just —" Jesse's dad, Allen, is cut off from talking.

"DON'T CALL ME BOY!" Jesse is in full rage. The General closes the office door. He has never seen Jesse like this.

"We got saved, me and your mom, last week. We are clean and sober," Allen blurts out, trying to redeem the situation.

He puts out his arms for a hug.

By now, Jesse is pacing wildly about the room, like a caged lion.

"You think you can show up, and everything's fine? You abandoned me for three years, and I haven't heard from you since last November. And now you want me to be all lovey-dovey?"

Jesse's face flushes. He is silently begging God to prevent him from slugging his dad. He feels love and hate at the same time. It is chaos in his mind and heart.

"They're saved, Jesse!" The General wants Jesse to focus on the good news.

"You don't know what you put me through. You have no idea," says Jesse, still yelling, his whole body shaking at this point.

He feels like his heart is going to beat out of his chest.

"Tell me, Jesse, what was so bad? I am sorry for backhanding you across the mouth last year. Is this what it is all about?" Allen sits down, giving up on the hug.

"One split lip? No, it's not about that. It was three years of hell on earth. I was like trash thrown out in the street. I cannot say it. It is too horrible."

Jesse sees a notepad on the desk, so he writes a few words on the paper. Allen leans over to read it. His face turns to horror. He, too, begins to shake.

"You're right . . . it is unforgivable."

Allen gazes at the floor, visibly shaken.

"Did my brother do all this to you? I will make him pay!"

"Bill is a mean drunk, but it got worse on the streets. I didn't know if you were dead or alive! I had no one."

Jesse collapses in one of the oversized leather chairs, his energy drained by his emotions.

The General rubs his forehead with his hand; this situation is getting over his head. He calls his assistant, Ruby's mom, Yolanda.

"I need Jamie, your husband, and Ruby in my office now!" the General speaks in hushed tones, looking at Jesse and his dad. "Yes, your daughter Ruby; Jesse needs her."

Jesse and his dad sit in silent devastation. Jesse thought he was above all this anger. Instead, he had only pushed it back and hid it. Allen is feeling the cold, hard consequences of neglecting his son. He is free of the numbness of drugs and is experiencing being present in the moment, not high or drunk.

Jamie is easy to find when the walkie-talkie on his tool belt buzzes with a message. Ruby is in the prayer tower. Aurora taps Ruby on the shoulder. Ruby's body is heaving with tears and sobs.

"Jesse needs you in the General's office," Aurora whispers.

Aurora hates to interrupt her intercession. Ruby doesn't mind; she is off like a shot.

Now I can release all this anointing; she runs from the prayer tower, tears still fresh on her cheek.

Jamie and Ruby hear Jesse yelling all the way up the stairs. They look at each other with raised eyebrows. Jamie takes a deep breath, and they open the office door. Ruben runs up the steps into the office, also.

Jesse is breathing heavily, hands clenched. Pacing again, he looks over at Ruby with a look of "Help me!" in his eyes.

No one says anything. Ruby walks over and lays her hand on Jesse's chest. Jamie stands behind Jesse. Jesse feels a warm heat sweep over him, then heaviness. He is falling backward, but he doesn't care, knowing it is Ruach

HaKodesh. He closes his eyes and gets prepared for the ride.

Allen stands up.

"What did she do to him? Call 911!"

Seeing Jesse on the floor, eyes closed and not moving, alarms him. He pulls out his cell phone, but when he sees that the General recognizes it as the one he gave Jesse last year, he blushes and places it on the desk.

"He has fallen under the Holy Spirit, Allen. He's fine," the General assures him, handing back the phone.

Jesse can hear Ruby's voice, something about rejection and an orphan spirit. Her voice fades, and Jesse wraps up in the Father's love. He feels like spiritual surgery is going on. The pain is leaving, and peace once again floods his heart. Lights are floating above him in gentle, rhythmic patterns. The grief and anger are lifting . . ..

Ruby's dad and the General take this opportunity to minister to Allen. The room is full of prayer. They help Allen begin to forgive himself for abandoning Jesse.

Jesse begins to cry; his chest heaves, and he sobs. His heart is being tenderized after years of walls erected from an abusive life in New York. His heart did soften some at his salvation, but bitterness and hatred towards his dad and uncle kept him from being completely free of bondage. (See "Types and Shadows" 6)

Jesse comes back to his senses. His face is wet from sweat and tears. The first thing he sees is his father's hand outstretched to pull him up. He isn't sure he is ready to stand; he grabs his father's hand and gets his bearings, leaning forward but not yet getting up. Jesse pulls on his dad's hand and stands up. They embrace and cry together. Jesse's face presses into his father's chest. His knees start to buckle, so they sit down on the couch by the big windows. Ruben and Jamie decide to leave the room so they can have some privacy. Jamie gives Jesse a knuckle bump as he leaves the room.

"I'll have you know your son saved me from suicide and helped lead me to the Lord. I owe him everything," Jamie says, his voice failing him due to emotion.

Yolanda comes in with drinks and sandwiches; Ruby grabs a soda gratefully. It is two o'clock in the afternoon. She had been praying for Jesse for two hours and is exhausted. Jesse is also exhausted. He turns down the food; his stomach feels queasy from being so upset.

Yolanda insists. "Jess, you need to eat something. We don't want you passing out."

Ruby's mom is like a second mother since she moved to campus. He takes a few bites and lays his head back to rest.

"Jesse, your palm is bleeding," Allen notices.

Jesse has fallen asleep. Allen gets a napkin and puts it in Jesse's palm as a bandage. He has clinched his hands so tightly that his nails cut into his palms again. Jesse's scarred hands are a result of doing this a lot when he was homeless. Allen opens Jesse's hands and sees the scars. He bites his lip and looks at the scars on his young face.

I had never noticed the scar on his lip or the gash above his eye before. There is one on his cheek and another on his nose, too.

"Hello, Dana," says the General, as he sees Jesse's mom slip in quietly.

She goes over and sits on the other side of Jesse.

"I heard you had a rough go at it," she says, looking over at her sleeping boy.

Jesse stirs.

"Mom, where have you been all this time?" Jesse asks, his voice hoarse from yelling.

"I was just below listening to your yelling. Ira and Wanda are my new best friends," says Dana, winking at the General.

"No . . . where were you the last four years?" Jesse's voice fades.

Jesse drifts back to sleep; he has never felt this safe before. All the people he loves are in one room, except Destiny, and he isn't quite ready to accept that he loves her yet. He also feels Yahweh's love in a fresh and real way.

"Thank you . . . Jesus," slips from his lips.

Dana, who has been weeping over Jesse's question, becomes relieved.

Everyone else feels moved, and worship sweeps over the General's office. Even Jesse's parents lift their hands toward heaven and worship. Ruby wishes Jesse were awake to see them now.

Then everyone sits down.

"Ruby, is that your name? Could you tell me about my son, please? I want to know everything." Allen holds Jesse's hand, and his mom takes hold of the other.

Ruby, still tired, remains in her place on the floor, where she is comfortable.

"I knew Jesse was special when I first saw him. He is moody and has a bad temper, but that will probably change now. He loves very deeply and is loyal, even to a fault. The Lord has given him many revelations. He sometimes gives messages to the whole school, without getting nervous till it is over. I greatly respect him and esteem him as my friend."

Ruby wishes Jesse could hear how she feels about him.

The General adds, "Rock Man, that's our nickname for him. He is a born leader with great devotion. He and Ruby both are exceptional students, along with Destiny, of course."

Ruby smiles.

"Ouch!" Jesse jumps and grabs his side. He looks around. "How long have I been out?" he rubs his eyes.

"What is wrong with your side, Jesse?" his mom asks with worry in her voice.

"Remember I told you of his stomach infection?" the General answers.

"I have just the thing to make you feel better," Dana says as she starts digging in the large messenger bag she uses for a purse for an herbal supplement.

Allen sternly shakes his head at her.

"I am sure they have it under control," Allen says, as he pats her hand.

Allen takes the little note from off the desk and puts it in his pocket, not wanting Dana to see it and fall apart.

With sad eyes, she says softly to Jesse, "I saw the doctor's file on you." Her face fills with sorrow, and her voice strains with grief. "I thought I was keeping you away from violence. I thought you were safe. . .."

She touches Jesse's face near the scar on his cheek and wipes her eyes with a tissue.

"It's not your fault, Mom. I never blamed you."

Jesse always kept an idealized image of his mom. It was his dad that he blamed, and his uncle.

"Jesse, how would you feel about your parents staying on campus?" the General leans in to ask.

Jesse looks at his mom and dad.

"Well, that sounds good. Just don't smother me cuz I need to go slow. I have trust issues — just ask Ruby."

Jesse searches his feelings, not exactly knowing how he feels. He looks at Ruby, wishing he could tell her how much he appreciates her. She nods as if she read it in his eyes.

"Well, I will leave you guys alone to get to know one another," Ruby says, getting up.

"No!" Jesse finds that his voice is too loud. He puts his hand back down. "Don't go."

She is glad he wants her to stay.

Everyone sits and reflects on the day's events.

Yolanda comes in with some gauze and, without a word, cleans and wraps Jesse's hand.

"I'm sorry, Allen," Jesse says weakly, not ready to address him as his dad.

"For what?" his dad says with surprise, not blinking at his son calling him by his first name, Allen.

"For all the times I cursed you out in my anger. Anything bad that would happen, I would yell at the sky, as if my words could reach you." Jesse reflects on his past desperation.

"I'm the one who should say I'm sorry, boy. I mean, Jesse, I am so sorry."

Allen put his hands on Jesse's face and kisses his forehead.

Ruby is surprised that Jesse doesn't shrink back. He hates to be touched and is just getting used to Jamie and others hugging him.

Jesse looks at his mom. She has a polished appearance. In the past, she wore plain clothes, no makeup, and long, unkempt hair. He remembers his vision last Christmas; it has come true.

Allen puts his hand on Jesse's shoulders and tells him, "Jesse, we foolishly thought we didn't have to grow up, and if we became parents, our dream to become rock stars would be over. The drugs demanded all our resources, and we let them. We wasted all those years. Now we want to learn how to use music to minister to the Lord, maybe even here at SWA. Last year, when I hit you, your mother went ballistic. She threatened to leave me if I didn't send you back to school. She saw my violence toward you and wouldn't put up with it."

Dana looks for a reaction from Jesse, but there is none.

"One day at a time," the General interjects.

Ruby feels the anointing and begins to speak to Jesse's parents.

"Mr. Logan, your battle will be to overcome shame and condemnation, as Jesse had to do the same. Mrs. Logan, you will grieve over the loss of raising your son. Try not to smother him now."

Ruby speaks with compassion and wisdom beyond her years.

The Logans nod and give it some thought.

"Well," the General says, rising from his high-backed chair, "let's head to the dining hall for supper."

Manuel is so glad to see a familiar face. Jesse takes his place at the Levi table. Destiny questions Ruby about why they missed the afternoon classes. Ruby tilts her head toward Jesse's parents, who are sitting down across the room.

They sit at the volunteer table with the rest of the resident parents. His mom waves to him repeatedly during the meal. Destiny asks Jesse when he is going to introduce her to his parents. He doesn't answer. Jesse still has no appetite, and his stomach hurts. She notices he looks drained and feeble. She feels compassion for him, but doesn't know what to say to him.

Manuel and Jorge have met and begin to talk away in Spanish, laughing way more than anyone else at the table. Jesse explains that Manuel laughs very easily. Destiny is glad to see Jesse lighten up.

The General advises the Logans not to interrupt Jesse's routine and let him stay in the dorms. He is connecting well with his friends, and they, perhaps, shouldn't bring any chaos into the mix. After the meal, Jesse's mom kisses him on the cheek several times as they say goodnight. Destiny comes up and introduces herself as a good friend of Jesse's.

"Is this your girlfriend, Jess?" Allen asks.

Jesse turns red.

"We are not allowed to date here, Allen."

"Oh," Allen replies, with a wink to Destiny.

"Ruby, did you tell them?" Jesse asks, red-faced.

She shrugs her shoulders innocently, and Destiny beams with joy, being thrilled, as this is as close as he has ever been to admitting that he likes her.

Ruby's parents help the Logans settle in at the resident parent cabins. Back at the dorms, Jesse doesn't even change clothes. He crashes on the bed and doesn't stir till morning. Eric pulls the covers over his weary friend.

Ruby is also exhausted and jumps into her pajamas and goes to sleep without praying.

Destiny covers her tired friend in prayer and then goes to bed herself. Thinking of the expression on Jesse's face today at supper, she feels excited about her relationship with him, now more than ever.

The next morning, when Jesse shows up for his iron pill, the nurse examines him. She has him lie down on the exam table and feels his stomach. "Does that hurt?" she pokes around for sore spots.

"Ahh!" Jesse pulls his knees up and grips his side.

"Looks like you need stronger antibiotics. I want you to go back to bed for today."

The nurse feels his forehead for a fever.

"Yep, you have a fever. No classes for you today." She helps him sit up.

He doesn't argue. He is feeling rough, and sleep sounds like a good idea to him.

At breakfast, he goes up to his parents and hugs them, telling them he is going back to bed. His mom talks him into lying down in their cabin for the day, and the General gives them the "Okay."

Jesse waves at the gang as his parents take him to their cabin. Ruby worries that they will be separated from him. However, Destiny doesn't think so.

Manuel's heart sinks, another day alone. His face is improving, but he is feeling homesick and lonely. Jorge catches up with him, and his spirits lift somewhat.

Jesse crashes into the queen-sized bed at his parents' one-room cabin. The cabins are nice but compact. The fireplace, Indian blankets, and log furniture add charm to the space. Jesse's mom pulls up a chair and sits next to him. Jesse sees an open Bible on the nightstand. She holds his hand, and he closes his eyes, longing for rest. The fever makes him ache, and his side is hurting. He pulls his hand in to change positions, trying to reduce his pain. He thinks about asking her to pray, but he doubts if she knows anything about prayer. Allen is filling out paperwork at the table while Jesse's mom strokes Jesse's face with the back of her hand. Jesse remembers getting backhanded by his uncle and his dad. The flashbacks don't have their usual sting. Jesse is pleased with the change.

"It's our fault, you know, Allen, this infection. Jesse didn't eat right for more than two months," she laments.

His mom is taking it all in. Allen walks over and puts his arms around his wife.

"Maybe he can use some cayenne pepper for his stomach," Dana suggests.

"No, mom, please, none of your herbal stuff, it tastes awful," Jesse says, remembering that her natural medicines were always hard to swallow or smelled weird.

"We will spend some time repenting, and then we must look forward," Allen says as he kisses her on the cheek.

Jesse has never seen his dad be affectionate to her before. Jesse rolls over toward the wall. He draws his knees in and holds his side tighter, pressing his face into the pillow. The sharp pain in his side is getting worse. Sleeping is impossible at this point. He wants to be with his parents; conversely, he resents being away from people who know how to pray. Dana puts her hand on her son's shoulder.

"Lord, please send someone who knows how to pray to come pray for Jesse."

A few seconds later, they hear a knock at the door.

"That was fast," says Allen, as he heads to the door.

Jamie steps in from the bright outdoors to the dimly lit room where Jesse is lying. He gives hugs to the Logans and heads toward Jesse.

"I heard you are not feeling well," Jamie says as he sits on the edge of the bed, as Jesse rolls over, holding his side.

"When you got so upset yesterday, it caused your immune system to be vulnerable to an attack," Jamie tells him.

"My side is pinching like crazy," Jesse tells Jamie. Jesse's face is full of pain.

Jamie puts his hand on Jesse, where he is holding his side.

"Ah," Jesse grimaces.

Jamie prays, rebuking the fever, infection, and the cause of the side ache.

Another knock, and the nurse steps in to drop off some antibiotics for Jesse, which he promptly takes.

"Drink plenty of water, Jesse. Nice to meet you, Mr. and Mrs. Logan, welcome to SWA," the nurse says all in one sentence as she keeps her hand on the door to leave. Jesse lies back down as the nurse leaves.

Jamie sits with Allen and talks casually. Dana sits next to Jesse and reads from her Bible.

"Read out loud, Mom. It is more powerful," Jesse tells her, closing his eyes.

His pain is almost all gone. He can finally get some rest.

Dana reads:

The Lord is my chosen portion and my cup; you hold my lot. The lines have fallen for me
in pleasant places; indeed, I have a beautiful inheritance. I bless the Lord who gives me counsel; in the night also my heart instructs me. I have set the Lord always before me; because he is at my right hand, I shall not be shaken. Therefore my heart is glad, and my whole being rejoices; my flesh also dwells secure. For you will not abandon my soul to Sheol, or let your holy one see corruption. You make known to me the path of life; in your presence there is fullness of joy; at your right hand are pleasures forevermore.

Psalm 16:5-11

Her voice fades, and Jesse is at rest. Jesse recalls images of the cave vision and thinks of the phrase his mom read. **"For you will not abandon my soul to Sheol**." He finds comfort in it and hopes his sleep will not take him to dark places. Jesse lets himself fall asleep, listening to the conversation in the room, and feeling content.

Allen is happy for the company. He and Jamie talk about Jesse for hours. They also have a shared interest in music and songwriting.

Jesse wakes up that evening, ready to eat, but the nurse has left strict instructions for Jesse not to be in public for twenty-four hours after his fever is gone. Allen brings his wife and son plates of food from the dining hall. Jesse, feeling much better, gulps down the food. He kisses his mom on the cheek, hugs his dad, and heads for the dorms. They stand in their cabin, watching him walk away. Dana leans her head on her husband's shoulder. They are so proud of their boy.

As Jesse enters Levi Lodge, he says to Hope, "Aren't you a pretty bird?" and heads towards the girls' room.

Knocking quietly at their door, he waits for an answer. Ruby peeks her head out.

"Jesse, is everything okay?" Ruby whispers, not wanting to get in trouble.

"Yes, everything is good. I just wanted you guys to know I am okay. I know how you worry. Do you think the monster inside me is gone now? I dealt with some heavy stuff, and you helped me — big time," Jesse hastily whispers, glancing around for Destiny. Destiny is leaning around the corner with her toothbrush in her mouth. She is not showing herself in her pajamas to Jesse.

Ruby looks at Jesse and asks the Lord.

"There is still more darkness inside you, Jesse, but you are halfway there. Now get out of here before Melody sees you," whispers Ruby with a smile.

Jesse waves and quietly heads for his dorm across the commons area. He wishes she said he is free. The pain of dealing with the past takes a great deal of strength, so he doesn't know if he can handle any more.

Everything is almost perfect now. Nothing can mess this up, Jesse thinks.

Manuel meets Jesse at the door.

"Jess, I want to go home," Manuel tells him with not so much as a "Hello."

Jesse pulls him to the big picture window, opens the curtain, and shows him the beautiful view, pushing Manuel down in front of it.

"Look at where you are, Manuel. You went all 'commando' to get here. Now you're just going to go home?" Jesse isn't giving him a break. He lays his hand on Manuel's chest.

"Dark forces, I bind you in the name of Jesus. Spirit of fear, I release you from Manuel. Grace and peace be multiplied," says Jesse, with authority. "Now go to your room before we get in trouble," commands Jesse.

"Okay, but tomorrow I want to hear about your parents and stuff," says Manuel.

Manuel does feel better. Manuel smiles a big smile without another word, punches Jesse in the arm, and leaves for his room. Jesse sits on the edge of his bed.

"I thought your mom might hold you captive overnight," says Eric, while brushing his teeth.

Jesse smirks.

"It was great spending the day with them, but my home is with you guys."

Jesse lies back on his bunk, hands behind his head.

"You think Manuel will stay?" Devin asks from a top bunk.

"Sure, he's just homesick. Everyone else went through it too, except me," says Jesse, matter-of-factly.

"You look different, Rock Man. I can't explain it." Eric looks closely at Jesse.

"I can; I got some deliverance from rejection and an orphan spirit. Ruby walloped me in the Spirit and laid me out on the floor yesterday. It was awesome. My dad wanted to call 911. That's about all I remember. I wanted to slug my dad when I went out, but then I wanted to hug him when I got up. I never felt so much love from the Father before that moment. He melted my heart, as it says in **Ezekiel 36**. I am sorry if I have been hard to live with, guys."

Jesse remembers the last time he apologized to them when he lied about his past.

"They don't call you 'Rock Man' for nothing. Are we going to have to find you a new nickname?" Yosef asks jokingly.

"Nah, the New Testament talks about Peter and the rock of revelation that He builds His ecclesia on; I want to carry *that* rock," Jesse answers.

There is a knock at the door; it is the floor leader, Benny, with Jesse's nightly antibiotics. Jesse swallows them without water and crawls into bed.

"Jesse, you have to see the nurse before you can return to class in the morning," says Benny through the cracked door before he leaves and shuts it.

Jesse is asleep as soon as his head hits the pillow.

CHAPTER EIGHT

ANNIVERSARY SPIRIT

August and September pass quickly. The Logans and the newbies are getting settled into life at SWA. Ruby turns sixteen in September. Jesse is happy to have his family around, even though he still calls his dad Allen. Manuel finds SWA comfortable now; he just had to give himself time to adjust. He is no longer in detention.

Ruby and Destiny still need to find anything that might be considered idols in their lives. They come up empty. Jesse's information from Jamie about Nimrod has raised more questions than it has answered. Jamie has still not told anyone about the hidden idols, and Jesse hasn't mentioned it. Adonai tells Jamie it is for an appointed time. (See "Types and Shadows" 7)

Jesse, Jamie, Ira, Wanda, and the General all meet to see if anyone has a prophetic word from the Lord in mid-October. It is chilly outside, so they meet in the General's office. Ira begins the discussion.

"The earthquake zone is still in cleanup mode. Tremors occasionally shake things up, and Yellowstone Park is experiencing an increase in volcanic activity. But I haven't heard anything more than '[30] He will shake everything that can be shaken,'" Ira tells the others. "It's ironic; we all expected California to have all the seismic activity."

"Yeah, and now the president's popularity has waned, and the nation's mood is nervous at best. Terrorist threats and small attacks are also increasing. The whole earth seems in an uproar, politically, and in the weather. All I am hearing is — 'watch and pray,'" Jamie tells the group.

The General feels uneasy but doesn't bring it up. Ira recognizes her son is tense, but she doesn't know why.

Jesse brings up an old topic: "Did anyone figure out why Ira was feeling spider webs during prayer?"

Jamie has an idea, "What comes to mind is **Isaiah 59:5-6**

---

[30] **Hebrews 12:27**

They hatch adders' eggs; they weave the spider's web; he who eats their eggs dies, and from one that is crushed a viper is hatched. Their webs will not serve as clothing; men will not cover themselves with what they make. Their works are works of iniquity, and deeds of violence are in their hands.

"Hmmm, divination is the root. Well, we better ask the Lord for insight on this; is it local or for the whole earth?" the General tells the group as they get up and go on about the day. Jesse wants to ask them about the hidden idols, but he can't find the words, and his pride restrains him from pursuing it further.

The Logans are taking volunteer orientation classes at SWA in the evenings, so Jesse just sees them at meals. That is fine with him. He needs time to adjust to them being around. Manuel has settled in. Although he misses his parents, he matures and focuses on his studies.

Alex is like an island, the only newbie who doesn't connect with anyone. As much as Ruby and Destiny try, the girl has walls up. Gloria has a burden for her and determines to talk to her if she gets the chance. Lee is doing well, and with Destiny's help, Trisha is learning fast the ways of the Lord. Jorge is thriving at SWA; he and Manuel are fast friends. Jorge used to be very lonely back home in a small, isolated town.

The mountain air is crisp and breezy. Allen and Dana practice with the worship band and instruct the musicians and vocalists, but they will not play in worship for three months till they can learn the spiritual side of things. That is fine with them. They have much to learn from the youth on ministering to the Lord through music. Jamie comes over to their cabin, and they jam together, writing songs and singing. Jesse is finally off the antibiotics and only takes iron pills.

Jamie has invited Jesse, Professor Alvey, and Devin to a picnic on the thirty-first to celebrate his first anniversary of being saved. Jesse asks to bring Manuel along. Jesse thinks back to a past Halloween when he ran away from his uncle's house. He is glad to have something to do that night to keep him from getting lost in dark memories from the past trauma. Jamie has special permission to take the boys off-campus. The weather is crisp but not too cold as Jamie squeezes the three boys into his little VW Beetle. It is getting dark by the time they unpack the food at the small campground, the very spot where he found Yeshua.

"Guys . . . soon as I get this fire going and Professor Alvey gets here, I have something vital to reveal to you," says Jamie as he squats down in front of the fire pit with a can of lighter fluid in his hand.

Jamie has cooked a meal for them himself. He loves to cook, but doesn't get many chances. He is working on the fire. It won't catch, so he adds a squirt of charcoal starter. Whoosh, it takes off. Jamie has to fall back to avoid the flames.

“I think you got it, Jamie,” jokes Devin, putting his hands out to warm them. A car pulls up to the campsite; it is Professor Alvey; he, too, was there when Jamie's whole life changed.

“Did I miss anything?” the professor asks.

“Only Jamie singeing his eyebrows!” Jesse calls out.

“Just call me Ruben tonight; we are off campus,” the professor tells them all.

The flames are reaching higher and almost getting too big for the fire pit.

Everyone hears a hiss coming from the bushes. Ruben tells everyone to get a stick and light it.

Jamie is still on the ground, and he does not get up. He lies there looking up. He is having a hard time talking. A demon appears over the fire with red eyes and a threatening voice.

“He is mine; you can’t have him anymore. Leave this place.” The unclean spirit wants to strike fear into their hearts.

Jamie struggles: something is holding him down. Manuel’s eyes are big; he has never seen a demon manifest itself before. Jesse and Devin start rebuking and pleading the blood of Jesus. Ruben, however, has another strategy:

“Father, I thank you for the redemption power of the cross that broke Jamie’s covenant with hell.” Ruben offers up worship, and Manuel joins him.

Jesse and Devin drop to their knees and also sing.

"[31]**Worthy is the Lamb who was slain, to receive power and wealth and wisdom, and might and honor and glory and blessing!**"

A mountain lion type creature manifests. It leaps at Jamie and scratches his chest. Jamie cries out. Everyone circles around Jamie. The demon takes one more swing at Jamie. As he swoops over Jesse, the demon's claws get Jesse in the shoulder, cutting through the expensive ski coat.

"Ahhh!" Jesse grabs his shoulder and falls back.

Ruben stands and declares:

"[32]Bless the Lord, O you his angels, you mighty ones who do his word, obeying the voice of his word!

Bless the Lord, all his hosts, his ministers, who do his will! Bless the Lord, all his works, in all places of his dominion. Bless the Lord, O my soul!"

"YES!" agrees Jesse, wincing in pain.

Anton draws his sword and swings. There are thunderclaps and a flash of light.

The demon yells out as he flees, "See you next year, Jamie." The dark spirit threatens him. Jesse is unsure whether it was a real animal or some demonic creature.

---

[31] **Revelation 5:12**

[32] **Psalm 103:20-22**

Peace returns as the apparition or animal is gone. Ruben checks Jamie. Devin and Manuel pull back Jesse's coat to see his shoulder wound.

"I didn't know demons could do that," says Manuel as he puts paper towels on Jesse's cut, adrenaline coursing through his own body.

Jamie's cuts are not deep, but he has long gashes on his chest. Ruben explains that demons can possess animals to use their bodies; shapeshifters are also a possibility.

"Let's put out the fire and head to the nurse's office for stitches," Ruben tells the stunned group.

"Wait," Jamie says breathlessly, "I came to offer God praise, and this just makes me more determined."

Jamie gets on his knees and raises his hands to the sky.

"Father, I thank you . . . for Your servants, Jesse, Devin, and Ruben. All I have, I commit to You. I ask that You keep us in fellowship . . . till your Son's return. Let the angels of the Lord sweep through SWA and purge the area of evil spirits. Help me tell the guys about the hidden idols," Jamie prays. Jamie knows this night is a high holy day for pagans and witches.

Jamie drops his arms as his shirt gets bloodier. Several flashes of light are seen over toward the campus. They know the angels have completed their assignments. The evil king's cave, however, is just out of reach of the angels' dominion.

The paper towel on Jesse's cuts is getting soaked with blood, and Jamie's chest is still bleeding too much.

"Eric's ski coat got trashed," says Jesse, feeling bad about it.

"We will have to finish this picnic later, Jamie; you guys are bleeding too much," says Ruben, as he opens his car door.

"But Jamie is going to reveal something to us, Ruben," protests Jesse.

"It's okay, Jesse, this is a lot of information, and I will need a while to show you everything. I think I got ahead of Adonai on this. It will keep," Jamie assures Jesse.

Devin rides with Jamie in his car while the others ride with Professor Alvey.

Jesse thinks . . . *It has been three months since we began searching for these hidden idols. It appears we will have to wait a bit longer.*

Back at the nurse's office, the nurse washes Jamie's chest and puts bandages on his cuts. "No need for stitches, Jamie, just some butterfly strips."

The nurse takes Jesse into the examination room and shuts the door. She knows he has trouble showing his scars. Doctor Luz joins them.

"Two stitches for you, Jesse; that's all," the doctor says, putting on rubber gloves and then getting out a syringe to numb the site.

Jesse is pleased that he remains calm this time with his shirt off. He is starting to feel the pain, however, as the adrenaline fades out of his system.

The syringe hurts, but soon the effects of the painkiller take over, and his pain subsides.

The nurse covers the newly sutured cut with a bandage. Jesse puts on the bloody shirt, and they go back to the front of the office.

"They're good to go, Ruben," says Doctor Luz.

Ruben tells the boys to go to the dorms.

"It is late; we will get together soon, I promise," Professor Alvey tells the guys.

"Okay, I must explain some things when the time is right," Jamie says, still anxious to talk.

"The Lord will arrange everything according to His plan and purpose, Jamie, it will keep," says Professor Alvey.

Jesse, Manuel, and Devin walk to their dorms in silence. It is a strange night. Manuel is jittery and glares out into the darkness as though something will jump out at them. He walks to his dorm room in a state of shock. As Jesse and Devin step into their dorm room, the other guys see Jesse's bloody shirt and a bandaged shoulder.

"Eric, I'm sorry about your coat."

Jesse holds it up for him to see.

"Whoa! What happened? It's all bloody!" Eric wrinkles his nose.

Devin speaks up.

"A demon did it!"

"No way!" Eric grabs the coat for closer inspection. "Are you okay, Jess?"

"Yeah, just a little gash. It got Jamie, too, on the chest," Jesse says. "Let me wash the coat. Maybe it can be fixed."

Jesse rinses and rinses, but it is useless.

"Looks like it is beyond repair, Eric. I know it was expensive," says Jesse, holding it up.

"Just chuck it in the trash, Jesse. It was an extra. I am just glad you're okay," says Eric, not wanting Jesse to stress over the coat.

"It's late. Lights out will be any second." Jesse hurries to change clothes.

"Lights out!" Benny yells from the hall.

In the dorm room next to Jesse's, Manuel lies in his bed, his heart pounding, freaking out from what happened at the campground.

"Did you hear that?" He keeps hearing things. "Can I sleep with you, Lee?" Manuel asks, giving up all his dignity.

"NO WAY!" Lee responds. "Go to sleep."

Manuel whispers, "[33]**Worthy is the Lamb who was slain."**

An angel appears at the end of his feet. The angel puts his finger to his lips.

"Shush," the angel cautions Manuel.

"Are you Jesse's angel?" Manuel asks, leaning up to see him better.

---

33 **Revelation 5:12**

"No, I am yours. I have been with you since birth," the angel whispers, somewhat annoyed.

"My birth or yours?" Manuel feels dumb for asking.

"Yours," the angel is losing his patience. "Please remember to use me. I could have been a great help on your travels, but I just had to watch you stumble around. Even tonight, you did not invoke my aid."

"How do I get your help, exactly?" By now, Manuel knows the angel is not pleased with him.

The angel adjusts his sheath that holds his sword.

"Simple, just use the scriptures, like **Psalm 91** or **Psalm 7:1-2.** There are many verses."

Lee calls down to Manuel, "Manny, turn the light out. People are trying to sleep."

Instantly, the room goes dark, and the angel is out of sight.

Manuel realizes that the angel is still in the room. It wasn't a vision. He grins from his bunk.

"Okay, angel. Father, thanks for the angels that watched over us tonight," whispers Manuel.

He lies back down and watches a white feather drift down and rest on his chest. Manuel puts the feather under his pillow for safekeeping, remembering Jesse's angel feathers back in New York. He can sleep now.

"God, You are awesome," Manuel whispers. "Sorry, I had such little faith. You deserve better. **Psalm 7:1-2, Psalm 7:1-2** . . . got to remember what he said . . ."

The next morning, Lee wakes everyone up. "There are feathers everywhere. Did someone's pillow blow up?" asks Lee, laughing.

Manuel sits up and looks around. Feathers as tiny as a coin to a foot long are all over.

"Do angels shed?" Manuel asks.

Everyone turns and looks at him. He isn't joking. They all gather up the feathers and keep them. There is a holy stillness in the room.

Jesse wakes and moves his shoulder. It hurts.

It wasn't a dream, he realizes.

At breakfast, there is a buzz of talk. The Logans are waiting for Jesse at the entrance of the dining hall. As soon as he steps through the door, they ask to see his wound.

"It's no big deal. It's almost healed up. Who told you what happened?" Jesse pulls the neck of his shirt so that they can see his bandage.

"Everyone is talking about the demon manifestation. Some families are talking about leaving SWA," Allen whispers and pulls Jesse over to a wall. "Now, take off your bandage so that we can see for ourselves how bad it is." Allen is stern but gentle.

Jesse did not want to do it. He pulls his shirt collar to the side and peels back the bandage to reveal his cut.

"Oh, Jesse. It is worse than any cut you got when you were . . . well you know . . . homeless," says Dana putting her hand to her mouth.

Jesse is about to put his bandage back on when someone yells, "Let us see it for ourselves if this scratch is real."

Many people agree. Jesse turns around to see everyone staring at him. His cut is about three inches long, with two stitches in the center. The room grows louder with anxious discussion. Jamie is nowhere around. Jesse wants to leave and look for him, but the General silences the voices to say something.

"There will be an assembly right after breakfast. Attendance is mandatory for all students, staff, and volunteers.

The General's voice reverberates throughout the hall. He motions for Jesse to come over. Jesse and his parents walk over to the head table.

"Jesse, I want you to stay by my side till after the assembly, please. Allen and Dana have a seat. Let's eat."

The General seems undaunted by the unrest that is stirring. Ruby and the gang see Jesse up with the General; they feel the tension in the room. They eat their meals with some anxiety, wondering what is going to happen next.

After breakfast, everyone goes to the sanctuary. The General takes Jesse up on the platform and begins talking to the assembly. Many local people are there — parents of some of the students. The General reads:

For we do not wrestle against flesh and blood, but against the rulers, against the authorities, against the cosmic powers over this present

darkness, against the spiritual forces of evil in the heavenly places.

Ephesians 6:12

Someone yells out, "It is not safe here for our kids!" The crowd murmurs.

"Send Jamie away, and the problem is solved!" another man in the back yells.

The General leans into the microphone. "I will not send Jamie away. He is a watchman on the wall. The enemy desires to keep us blind and undefended."

The General looks over at Jesse.

"You have something to say, Rock Man."

I do?

Jesse steps up to the podium. He sees his friends in the front. He doesn't know what to say, so he stalls by flipping pages of the Bible. *What do I tell them, Lord?*

His eyes fall on a passage, and he reads:

...There are some things in them that are hard to understand, which the ignorant and unstable twist to their own destruction, as they do the other Scriptures. You therefore, beloved, knowing this beforehand, take care that you are not carried away with the error of lawless people and lose your own stability. But grow in the grace and knowledge of our Lord and Savior Jesus Christ. To him be the glory both now and to the day of eternity. Amen.

2 Peter 3:16b-18

The man in the back yells, "Who are you calling unlearned and unstable, kid?"

The General steps up.

"If you feel the need to break from our fellowship and follow a different path, now is the time to decide. There will be no more debate. We know our calling is to pray and fast. Nothing has changed. We must be one, as Ruach HaKodesh, the Son and the Father, are one. Dismissed!"

Loud talking ensues. A few people almost get into fistfights. Jesse's dad steps up to the General and explains that he was told in a dream last night not to leave SWA.

"I saw Jesse's wound in a dream last night; only it was not bleeding. It was jewel incrusted in my dream," explains Allen.

Jesse can't take it anymore. He runs out to find Jamie and knocks on his door. Jamie opens the door for Jesse.

"How are your cuts?" Jesse opens the conversation.

"Not bad. I don't see what the big deal is. The General won't let me resign. I would for the good of the academy, you know?" Jamie seems sad and disheartened.

"Remember last year, I cast a spell to break the unity of SWA. Now it seems, I am the cause of some breaking the ranks and leaving," remarks Jamie solemnly.

Jesse feels a wave of the Spirit.

"Jamie:

But we ought always to give thanks to God for

you, brothers beloved by the Lord, because God chose you as the first fruits to be saved, through sanctification by the Spirit and belief in the truth. To this he called you through our gospel, so that you may obtain the glory of our Lord Jesus Christ. So then, brothers, stand firm and hold to the traditions that you were taught by us, either by our spoken word or by our letter. Now may our Lord Jesus Christ himself, and God our Father, who loved us and gave us eternal comfort and good hope through grace, comfort your hearts and establish them in every good work and word.

I think it is from **2 Thessalonians 13-17.** It is just a call for you to stand fast in the truth. Commander Alvey had us memorize tons of scriptures a year ago."

Jamie opens his Bible and reads:

2 Thessalonians 2:1-3

Now concerning the coming of our Lord Jesus Christ and our being gathered together to him, we ask you, brothers, not to be quickly shaken in mind or alarmed, either by a spirit or a spoken word, or a letter seeming to be from us, to the effect that the day of the Lord has come. Let no one deceive you in any way. For that day will not come, unless the rebellion comes first, and the man of lawlessness is revealed, the son of destruction,

"That's what the Lord gave me to contemplate. It's the reference to rebellion, I guess, that is going on now. I feel it is my fault people are falling away . . ." Jamie's voice trails off.

He is trembling — bang, bang. Someone is banging on his door.

"Who is it?" Jamie calls out, alarmed by the high pitch of his voice.

"It's me, Ruben," Ruben says, shivering at the door, looking around.

Jamie opens it.

"Well, we lost a third of the student body, staff, and family volunteers," Ruben calmly tells Jamie.

"Aren't you upset?" Jamie asks.

"Nah, the General was told a month ago by a prophet in California that this was coming. He said, 'God chooses those that remain, and nothing will separate us.'"

Jamie has heard the phrase "chosen by God" twice now. He is getting reassured. Jamie sits down and tries to sort it all out.

"I think the enemy is pleased with last night. He managed to do more damage than just a few physical cuts." Jamie is still distraught.

"Yes, it would appear so. **And we know that for those who love God all things work together for good, for those who are called according to his purpose. Romans —"** Ruben is interrupted.

"**Romans 8:28,** I know." Jamie nods his head.

"The 'called' Jamie. Don't lose sight of your calling. The same thing happened last year, remember? It's an Anniversary Spirit, and we need to break it," Ruben tells them both.

Jesse feels the anointing confirming Ruben's words.

"Remember it said, 'see you next year' as it left?" remarks Jesse.

The three rebuke the Anniversary Spirit, calling the angels to chase it. (**Psalm 35:6-7**). Jamie's oppression leaves, and his peace returns.

"I'm not allowed out today, not until most of the angry people have packed up and left. The General said a few men had plotted to beat me up and push me into leaving. For being a watchman, I sure didn't see this coming."

Jamie peeks through his front window. The cabin next door has a car backed up with people loading up their belongings.

"What smells so good?" Rubin walks over to the kitchenette.

"Oh, that's the food I made for our picnic yesterday. Shall we eat? Just wish Devin was here."

Jamie pulls out several items from his fridge.

"Hey, let me in!"

They hear Devin's voice outside.

The fellowship is bittersweet as the four guys sit down together. Outside, several cars leave the campus, never to return. A few will have a change of heart and return, but SWA numbers will reduce by one-third. An entire dorm will be closed, and everyone will move out of Ox Lodge and move to Eagle Lodge or Levi Lodge.

After lunch, Jesse and Devin must report to their floor leader. Spirit Wings Academy takes roll to see who chose to stay. Classes are, of course, canceled for the day.

On the way, Jesse stops by his parents' cabin. He wants to see if they still have peace with being there. Allen meets Jesse at the door.

"Son, you are blessed of the Lord. I can now accept who you have become."

Allen puts his hand on Jesse's shoulder.

Some time ago, the Principality angel, Asher, had told Jesse that his dad would say these exact words.

"Thank God you have come to know Christ. I still need assurance that you won't leave me again. I still . . . don't know if you . . . *really* love me."

Jesse hates to bring up something that will cause his parents pain, but he wants to be honest and not put on a pretense.

"Well, my boy, my special boy; that will take time — time that I am willing to put in."

Allen can't help kissing his son on the forehead.

"Okay, I gotta go!" Jesse hurries off to the dorms.

In the commons area of Levi Lodge, the gang gathers.

"Who did we lose?" Devin asks Benny.

"We lost about eighty cadets from other tribes, nobody from Levi. Many of the local kids pulled out of SWA, but Ray and Gabe are still here. But overall, we are down to under one hundred and seventy kids on campus."

Jesse catches up with Manuel in his room. "Do you think your parents will be alarmed by what happened today?" asks Jesse.

"I doubt it; my uncle Ramón worked in Honduras. They had demonic activity all the time there. My mom always said, 'If you don't have any trouble with the devil, you're not doing anything worth upsetting him,'" Manuel comments as he folds his laundry.

He reaches under his pillow and pulls out the feather that he put there that morning.

"Angel feather, huh?" Jesse says, looking at it. "Just like the one I got at your house, remember? Only mine had gold dust. It was lost last year when I hitchhiked here. I had forgotten how everyone called me a Chosen One, like Jamie is today." Jesse's memories of Manuel's home are precious to him.

"Jess, I always thought that your encounters with God were special, that I would never have experiences like you. But now I know, God meets us according to our desire for Him."

Manuel shakes the feather to see if any gold dust will fall off.

Jesse changes the subject altogether.

"If I don't trust my parents, does that mean I still have bondage to an orphan spirit? I feel free, but am I?"

Manuel stops and looks into Jesse's eyes.

"It all stems back to your identity. Do you see yourself as the beloved of God or street trash? So, which is it? Also, your parents need to earn your trust."

Manuel and Jesse are accustomed to being blunt with each other. They like it that way.

Jesse examines his feelings.

"I feel I am the beloved of God for the most part. The enemy tries to pull me into the pit, but I don't fall for that much anymore. I think that I let go of the past hurts in the General's office that day my parents came. I feel lighter and more grounded since then. Ruby has rebuked an orphan spirit off me twice. I think I let it come back. I don't want to make that mistake again. And there are these weird images of me stuck in a cave. Creepy sounds, snakes, and spiders cover the walls. I don't know why I keep seeing this stuff."

Jesse pulls the bandage off his shoulder to look at it.

"Yeah, spirits are usually worse if they come back," Manuel says, putting his clothes away. He comes to look at Jesse's wound.

"Did you see the demon? Because I sure didn't. Don't know if there was a mountain lion either. It was just a shadow, you know?"

Manuel lightly touches Jesse's cut.

"Ouch! Watch it!" Jesse winces and pulls back. "I didn't see anything either; I just heard it! You know, I have been neglecting the girls. I should go find them."

Jesse presses the bandage back, but it has lost its stickiness.

"Okay, see ya," says Manuel.

Manuel stays to clean up his dorm room. He is somewhat of a neat freak.

Ruby, Destiny, and Gloria are now in the commons area with Hope. Jesse comes down the stairs and sits on the comfy leather couch. The girls gather around him.

"We couldn't find you; are you alright?" Ruby asks with an anxious tone.

"Jess, there is blood on your shirt, and it looks fresh," Destiny notices with a hint of alarm.

"Oh, yeah, the bandage won't stick," Jesse tells them casually. "I need to check on Jamie; he is upset."

He pulls the fallen bandage out of his shirt. Gloria has a package of tissues; she hands them to him. He places them against the wound, wincing slightly.

"Aren't you going to the nurse for a new bandage?" Ruby asks.

"Nope, tired of being in her office. It will stop in a second. I pulled the bandage off, and the scab came off with it." Jesse says, wanting to talk about something else.

"So . . . how have you been?" Destiny asks, half-joking, half flirting.

"Good . . . *real* good," Jesse nods his head up and down, making a smirk.

There is silence. It seems the two are somewhat out of touch.

Ruby blurts out with optimism. "Aurora might accept me into the worship team, and your parents might play, too. Quite a few members left today; Aurora didn't leave, of course."

"That will be good if you get on the worship team. I know you always wanted to be part of the Judah tribe. It will be a trip to see my parents up there after all their rock and roll days. Jamie and my parents are writing songs together. It's wild, my parents being here and all."

Jesse is having a hard time expressing himself.

By now, the blood starts trickling down between Jesse's fingers, where he is pressing on his wound with the tissues.

"Ew!" the girls all say in unison.

"Okay. . . okay. I'm going." Jesse gets up and heads to the nurse's office. By the time he gets there, blood is dripping off his hand.

"Jesse! What did you do? Did you take off your bandage, pulling off the scab?"

The nurse sets him down on the exam table. "This is going to sting," she tells him as she puts salve on the cut. "Be still!"

Jesse can't help but pull back.

"You have to leave this alone; you hear me?"

She reprimands him tenderly, adding a few butterfly strips to pull the skin back together.

"Now wash that blood off your hands and stay away from my office for a while!" she says, smiling.

Jamie steps into the office; his shirt is also bloody.

"What happened to *you*?" the nurse exclaims.

"Some angry dad jumped me when I went to get some firewood for the cabin."

Jamie has a split lip, and he holds his ribs.

"We should call the police and file a complaint!" the nurse tells Jamie.

She is angry that someone attacked him.

"NO! I mean, no, he was just upset. I think he broke my rib, though. It hurts to breathe," Jamie says, holding his side.

Jamie is self-conscious about getting beaten up. He gets X-rays, and she wraps his broken rib. His previous cuts had opened and look worse than when he got them. The General runs into the office, out of breath.

"Jamie . . . are you . . . alright? I thought I told you not to leave . . . your cabin?" The General is quite upset, seeing Jamie's condition.

He sits down to catch his breath. Then he pulls out his cell phone.

"Mom, Jamie is in the nurse's office. Some angry dad got a hold of him." He hangs up. "We saw blood on your porch. Is the other guy okay?" The General is still in worry mode.

"Yeah, he hurt his hand on my face, but he isn't bleeding or anything," Jamie says, still breathing shallow so as not to hurt as much.

Jesse comes out from washing his hands in the exam room.

"Didn't you defend yourself?" Jesse is getting alarmed at Jamie's attitude.

"No, I just felt sorry for him. He was so confused and scared. I just stood there, taking it." Jamie is mourning the people who left. "I felt the Father's heart. He mourns for those who don't know Him, those who are just religious followers. The people who have only head knowledge and no connection with the Father's heart. I felt His concern for them." Jamie lets a tear roll down his face.

The General puts his head down. Jesse feels the urgency again that came over him after the encounter that warned . . . night is coming when no man can work.

"I feel sadness also, but we can't let it overtake us. The Lord doesn't want us to focus on the loss. We must look ahead and pull together that which remains. Judgment begins in the House of God. These things should not take us unaware. I wish he had beaten *me* up, not you. I would gladly take your place."

It hurts the General just to look at Jamie.

"I want you to stay at my hunting lodge tonight, Jamie. I won't sleep unless I can keep an eye on you."

Ira runs from Jamie's cabin all the way to the nurse's office. She comes rushing in.

"Jamie, let me take a look at you, you dear boy."

Ira bites her lip and weeps.

"Mom, stop, or we all will be crying."

The General didn't want to show weakness.

"Sorry, son, but Jamie is so dear to us. Jesse, your shirt is bloodied. Did you get beat up, too?" Ira runs over to him.

"Oh, no, I just took my bandage off too soon." Jesse feels dumb for doing it.

"I feel we should have a lock-in tonight. Let's gather together. I want us all to be together tonight."

The General makes a phone call, and soon Jennifer is announcing it.

"Everyone is to sleep in the sanctuary tonight. Bring your own pillows," Jennifer announces.

The General takes Jamie and Jesse with him straight to the sanctuary. Jamie is given the couch from the lobby to use as a bed. Jesse flashes back to the great ice storm last year when they used a generator for power. Everyone slept in the dining hall then.

"Boys sleep on one side, girls on the other. Get your sleeping bag as you come in," says Professor Norman, as he organizes the event. The Logans think this will be great fun until they see Jamie beaten up and lying on the couch.

Dana makes some lavender tea for Jamie.

"This is a calming tea; it relieves stress," Dana says as she gives it to him.

Allen has grown close to Jamie as they sing and write songs together. Allen tells Jamie, "Oh, man. I used to get in bar fights and get banged up all the time. But this isn't cool. It's my fault. I should have stayed with you. I should have been there for you. I am a bad friend."

Allen is going on and on about it.

"Will you stop it?" Jamie grabs his arm. "What's done is done. I know you are there for me. It's just one broken rib. I used to get in fights all the time back in the day, fights over drugs or girls, or nothing at all."

Jamie tries to keep the mood light and sips his tea.

"Me too," Jesse confesses. Dana looks tenderly at her son; she can't imagine him fighting. She sees he has bloodied another shirt.

Jamie tells the General, "Ever since yesterday, I was trying to tell everyone . . . about these hidden idols." Jamie is in pain, and talking doesn't help.

"Jamie, it will have to wait; you need to lie still. We will talk first thing in the morning, I promise," the General assures him. "The nurse gave you breathing exercises, focus on that for now.

Jesse is becoming curious about the hidden idols again; it is undoubtedly what the Fire King was referring to *three months ago. I know the enemy doesn't want to be exposed. I feel anxious to find out what Jamie knows. But for now, Jamie needs to get better; it will have to wait.*

"I'm off to bed, looking forward to some sleep," Jesse says, hoping Eric won't talk a lot like last year in the storm.

Eric shows up with a clean shirt for Jesse.

Alex and some of the girls play guitar and sing softly. Ruby and Destiny are happy to see Alex taking part.

"Lights out in an hour," Professor Norman yells out.

Some kids are afraid of Hope, so she has to go in her wire dog cage for the night.

Jesse waves to the girls on the other side and slips into his sleeping bag. He closes his eyes. The lights are dim, so he doesn't have to cover his eyes.

"Hey, Jess, are you sleeping?" It is Eric.

Oh, no, Jesse groans silently.

Eric sits next to Jesse, talking away. Finally, Manuel gets into his sleeping bag, and Eric talks to him. Jesse lets the voices fade. The girls' singing is calming, and the room seems peaceful. The General sits by Jamie, looking out at the remaining members of SWA. His heart is full.

The General thinks: *This is a new day, even a new age, more than a season of change, a new era.*

The General, Ira, Professor Norman, and the Logans sleep close to Jamie. The General comes and gets Jesse.

"I want you to be over here with us tonight. Humor me, okay?" The General wakes him up to move him.

Jesse, still groggy, carries his pillow and sleeping bag; he steps over his buddies and follows the General up to the lobby. Jesse once again lies down. His mom and dad kiss him goodnight. Jesse wants to tell them he is too old for that, but he doesn't. He kind of likes it. He is still longing for their love. Allen puts his hand on Jesse's head while lying next to him. Jesse falls asleep fast.

It is about midnight, the room is quiet, except for the snores. The General looks over at Jamie; he sees that Jamie is awake. He is lying there, weeping.

That's what I was afraid of, the General tells himself. "Jamie, this sorrow is not good. You can intercede for them when you are better. The anointing will keep."

The General is considering asking the nurse for a sedative. "Maybe you should take a pain pill." He pauses, "Tomorrow, we will gather, and we will all pray for those who departed, okay?" The General knows Jamie is devoted, but this impresses him.

Jamie swallows hard and says, "Okay . . . but we must deal with the idols —"

"Not another word till morning, please, Jamie," the General urges him to rest.

Jesse is awake enough to hear them. The General looks over at Jamie and back at Jesse.

Oh, great. Now I am burdened with Jamie's burden, Jesse realizes. He feels sorrow swell up in him. Jesse rolls over and cries into his pillow for a moment, hoping no one will see his chest heave. He feels the travail of the Holy Spirit that Ruby gets.

Oh, no, Lord, not now. Save it till morning, please. I thought only girls travailed.

The travail lifts to Jesse's relief, and he can sleep.

It is now November second, and soft, gentle snow is beginning to fall. There is no wind, so the snow piles straight up on the buildings and trees. Big snowflakes fall silently to the ground, covering it in a matter of minutes.

At sunrise, Jesse sees the light coming through the leaded glass windows of the sanctuary. He hears something; it is the sound of travail. Jesse knows it comes from Ruby and Aurora. Now, more voices join in. The whole room awakens to the spirit of travail. Jamie lies on the couch, holding his pillow, weeping. It hurt his ribs, but he doesn't let it stop him. Jesse feels the travail hit him. He rolls on his stomach and cries into his pillow. There are few words spoken. Just calls for mercy, mostly — most people travail on their knees or flat on the floor. The General, Ira, everyone, weeps. It continues for more than an hour, building up and dropping off in intensity. Wanda and the gypsies are the loudest. Their passion runs strong.

Jesse looks at Jamie crying, and it hits him all over again. Allen's heart melts at the sight of Jesse weeping, and he begins to weep. The nurse and Jennifer go around, distributing water bottles and tissues to people.

As the intercession for those who had left comes to an end, the weeping lifts. Everyone goes to their dorms to get ready for breakfast. The kitchen workers go straight to work. Most are not dressed for the heavy snow. Everyone returns to their domiciles and puts on warmer clothing.

The nurse is worried about Jamie. Intercession is exhausting, and Jamie has a broken rib. He drifts back to sleep on the couch. The General assigns a few people to sit with him and pray over him.

It was just like last year; Ruby realizes, looking at Jamie.

She tells Jesse outside, "After that ice storm last year, Jamie got sick and lay on a cot in the dining hall just like yesterday, with people wanting Jamie to leave SWA, so it was exactly a year ago. Someone even threw his staff picture down and broke it last year. Remember?" Ruby says.

"Yeah, but we rebuked the Anniversary Spirit already. I think Jamie is safe now," Jesse tells her confidently.

"I feel something sinister is hatching, Jesse," Ruby warns him. "It's cold, see you later."

In the Fire King Abigor's cave, there is a rumble coming from the cavern of hatching eggs during the night. The massive horned snake has matured and is leaving the nest. All the other dark creatures scamper to clear its path. Rocks and dirt fall around the mammoth horned snake as it approaches the cave's mouth, and soon it is gone out into the early morning. The Fire King watches it slither toward SWA. Abigor smiles a twisted smile.

Jamie is still asleep in the sanctuary. He seems to be having a bad dream. The people sitting with him get more forceful with their prayers.

Jamie is dreaming of a colossal snake wrapping around him, making it hard to breathe. He tries to call for help in the dream, but he is unable to. He finds himself in the very spot by the bonfire in the park. He sees markings on the snake, like those used in witchcraft. The snake squeezes him tighter and tighter around the chest where his cuts are.

Meanwhile, Jamie's parents in Minnesota feel the need to pray for him. They are pastors in a small town. They both get on their knees and begin to intercede for their son.

By now, Jamie is sweating and tossing in his sleep. The General stops to check on Jamie and sees his troubled sleep. He has to shake Jamie by the shoulder for him to wake up.

"Whoa, I am glad you woke me. A Spirit of Fear gripped me, and I couldn't move. A python, General . . . a huge python was squeezing me. A spirit of divination . . . Witchcraft . . . Python . . . idols . . ." Jamie says while trying to catch his breath.

"Oh, we need prayer and fasting. I will call a fast right away." The General pulls out his phone and walks off, giving orders to Yolanda. Jamie's prayer team gives him some water.

In just a few minutes, an announcement comes.

"The General has called a twenty-four-hour fast for Jamie, starting immediately. Please sign a commitment sheet in the dining hall so that the kitchen staff will know how many people will be eating."

Most of the students are out playing in the snow when the announcement comes. Jesse is walking a short hiking trail in the deep snow when he hears the speaker.

"There will be no classes today because of the students and families who left, as well as two from the teaching staff. All the courses will be reconfigured."

Ruby, Destiny, Jesse, and the rest of the gang go straight to the sanctuary where Jamie is to see the purpose of the fast. Jamie tells them of his dream.

"I thought a mountain lion/demon thingy attacked him," Manuel comments. "But I remember Jamie on the ground, not moving or talking when the attack came, and we all heard the hiss."

"Yeah, [34]Divination, spider webs, and other things, fasting is necessary. Jamie, almost everyone has signed up for the fast, over one hundred and forty kids and staff," Ruby reports.

"Wow, that is touching. Everybody will do that for me?" Jamie didn't realize how everyone loved him.

Jesse used to hate fasting because being hungry reminds him of being homeless. He would fast when the school called him to do so, but he would get grumpy and stay off by himself — this time, he expects to feel different.

They leave Jamie to rest and go back outside.

"I tried to fast; it lasted ten minutes," Alex admits to Manuel.

---

[34] **Isaiah 59:5 They hatch adders' eggs; they weave the spider's web; he who eats their eggs dies, and from one that is crushed a viper is hatched.**

"Yeah, me too. How do those guys do it?" Manuel wonders.

The two decide to go to the prayer tower to pray for Jamie. They will eventually learn all about fasting, as it is a common practice throughout the year on specific dates.

As they trudge up the Academic Tower East's spiral stairs, the view of the snowy mountain is beautiful.

By evening, the snow stops, and the campus is under a fresh layer of white snow. Boot tracks indicate the paths that lead from building to building. As usual, every year, several students are experiencing their first snow. Workers shovel paths between buildings.

Ruby has left Hope outside. She is hopping in the snow, now about six inches deep. The eagle is standing next to the heating unit of the sanctuary, attacking something in the snow. She pecks and then jumps back several times. The last time, Hope pops her head up out of the snow with a snake in her beak. The snake is dead, and Hope starts eating it. The young eagle wants to take her meal up on the dorm's steps, so Ruby keeps shooing her off the steps.

That night, Jamie returns to his cabin. Allen insists on staying with him, so Ira stays with Dana because Dana is afraid to sleep out in the "wilderness" alone, as she put it.

The General, Professor Alvey, Jesse, and Manuel are waiting for Jamie at his cabin to break the Python Spirit. The General and Professor Alvey have already fasted; they started fasting on October thirty-first.

The General has Jamie sit on the couch, and he lays his hand on his head and prays.

"By the blood covenant of[35] Yeshua Ha'Mashiach, we break the power of Python and command it to go to the desolate places where no man dwells."

Jamie begins to choke and cough, his eyes watering. Manuel and Jesse quote all the scriptures they can think of about the blood of Jesus.

Jesse feels himself going into the Spirit. He sees snake scales the size of dinner plates all around in front of him, writhing and turning. As he puts his hand out, the sword of the Lord appears in it.

Yeshua approaches Jesse and says, "Here, let Me show you how to do this."

Yeshua steps behind Jesse and takes hold of the sword also. Both, in tandem, begin to strike the massive snake creature. Jesse starts to swing effortlessly as the power of the Lord streams through the sword.

Manuel looks at Jesse, standing there, holding nothing, and swinging at nothing. Devin shrugs his shoulders and looks at Manuel's questioning face. He doesn't know what Jesse is doing, either.

---

[35] Hebrew for Jesus the Anointed One - Messiah

The General speaks with a loud voice, "Basilisk Strongman, the Lord rebukes you! Let your head be severed from you by the Son of Man Himself!"

Jesse and Yeshua make the final blow; the snake's body and severed head are gone. The spirit realm is clear again.

Jesse returns to the natural realm with his hand still in attack position; he brings his hand down to his side. Jamie takes a deep breath and drinks some water, wiping his eyes. Then he questions the General about the Basilisk.

"That anointing was the strongest I ever felt. General, how did you know about the Basilisk? I thought only witches knew about him," Jamie says, leaning up from the couch.

"I have run into it before; it is in the Bible," the General answers casually.

"Did you guys see the size of that thing?" Jesse asks, exhilarated by the battle.

"Nope, we just saw you swinging and stuff . . .," Manuel explains to him with a grin.

"Oh, well, it was huge, but the sword the Lord gave me sliced it like butter!"

"Like butter," Manuel repeats, "cool!"

Jamie isn't surprised at Jesse's exploits in the Spirit.

"Thank you, Jesus, for the work of the cross, thank you for the blood," Jamie begins to praise Yeshua.

He raises his hands and worships. Everyone else joins him in worship — Allen trembles in the presence of Yahweh.

"[36] **Great is the LORD, and greatly to be praised, and his greatness is unsearchable."** Allen whispers in awe. He just experienced a powerful event, a demonic entity attacking Jamie, and the power of Yeshua banishing it away.

The General knows Jamie still needs rest.

"Okay, you get some rest, Jamie," the General instructs.

"Thanks, guys, for praying; I am so glad you are in my life. Can we address this issue of idolatry now? Please!"

Jamie is getting emotional, and he is exhausted.

"You are a great asset to this campus, Jamie, and we love you," Professor Alvey tells Jamie. "Once again, this idol thing has to be put off."

"We are all leaving now so that you can rest," the General opens the cabin door to leave.

"Goodnight, Jamie," Manuel and Jesse call out as they leave.

Allen settles in on Jamie's couch as Jamie lies down in bed for the night. There is a residue of the power of God resting in the cabin.

---

[36] **Psalm 145:3**

Prophetess Ira and Dana are praying and worshipping in the Alvarez's cabin. The General calls Ira and tells her it's taken care of, and to get some rest.

There is a message on Jamie's phone. It is his parents. Jamie calls them up and assures them everything is fine. He tells them all that happened, and they encourage him to stay at SWA. They also tell him how proud they are of him.

As Jamie sleeps, the Lord tells him to wait and reveal the idols, "When the time is right." Jamie feels the urgency subside into silent alertness, knowing the enemy does not want the demigods revealed, and some people may not accept the revelation he has for them.

At King Abigor's cave, there is much yelling, and rocks are flying. The King has found out his Basilisk has been killed. In a fit of rage, he lashes out at any creature near him. He throws fireballs about the cave, and his angry voice echoes out into the air. The remaining eggs go dark, and the newborn snakes dry up, and only their skin remains. There is no more orange glow. Imps and demons crouch in fear as more yelling and violence emanate from Abigor's throne room. The dark king knows Baal will not be happy about this.

In Denver, several covens of witches also know the Basilisk is lifeless. They will have to start all over again. They all return to their homes scattered anonymously across the suburbs. Full of despair, a high priestess sits in her garden of gargoyles and crescent moons.

Back at the SWA campus, it is the next day, and the twenty-four-hour fast ends at noon. Jesse is feeling a little dizzy, but he sticks it out. Ruby and Destiny fast almost once a week, so they are fine. They drink a lot of water. Since Manuel has never fasted, he breaks the fast with a banana and a piece of cheese by breakfast time. He is instructed not to be too hard on himself and to try to skip lunch.

The snow remains, and the sun is blinding. Most everyone has ski goggles or sunglasses on. Jesse needs a new coat, so Ruby and Ruben plan to take him to town at the end of the day if the roads are clear of ice and snow. Jamie is up and walking, feeling pretty good. Many students have made him "Get Well" cards with notes inside, telling him how much they respect him.

Jesse runs up to Jamie to inquire about the idols. He has Ruby and Destiny with him.

"The Lord told me the time is not right . . . sorry guys. I must wait for His timing, yet a little while, and all will be revealed and will come into the light," Jamie explains.

"When the time is right . . . okay, yeah, we understand," Destiny assures him.

"We do?" Jesse says, wanting to deal with it already.

Classes are now smaller and more intimate; Manuel loves it. He is used to big schools. In Demonology 102, Professor Alvey's class, the topic is Basilisk, King of Snakes, and references to him in the Old and New Testaments.

At lunch, Jamie meets with a round of applause. He blushes slightly, not accustomed to the attention. Wanda and her gypsies have made him a tapestry. It is of an eagle holding a snake in its beak. Any thoughts of Jamie leaving are gone. (See "Types and Shadows" 13)

Manuel enjoyed detention with Jamie in August; now, he doesn't know how to fill his time. He dreads his spare time, knowing few people besides Jorge and Jesse. Manuel sees Alex, Ruby's newbie, playing guitar in the dorm lobby. He goes and sits by her, just listening. He doesn't say anything. Alex seems to like that and smiles as she keeps playing. Ruby sees Manuel with Alex. Her heart feels a little twinge; she is still crushing on him.

Ruby and Jesse meet at her dad's car. Ruben has a classic Corvette, but it will not handle the slick streets too well, so they take a school van. Their first stop is at the ski shop in Eastcliffe, just down the mountain from SWA. The salesclerk seems unfriendly. Finally, the clerk tells them that they aren't welcome in the store. There are rumors around town that strange things are happening at SWA.

Ruben takes them to the next store. Gabe's dad, Glenn, owns it.

Glenn meets them with open arms.

"Come in, come in! Glenn smiles warmly. "Anything you need is on the house. And look, no cane, and my arms are back to normal!"

"This is good news, to Yeshua be the glory. Now Jesse here needs a new coat," Prof. Alvey tells Glenn.

"Of course, everyone has heard of the demon attack. It made quite a stir around here, I assure you. The town has divided opinions of SWA; the mayor won't say anything one way or the other.

"It is mostly local townspeople who have taken their kids out of the academy," Ruben tells him.

Glenn acknowledges his comment with a nod.

Jesse finds a coat in his size.

"This coat is nice; how much is it?" Jesse doesn't want to pick anything too expensive.

"Here, let's have a look," Glenn pulls the tag off and puts it in his pants pocket. "It is free, my boy, free."

Glenn has a spark of joy in his eyes.

Gabe's brother Michael works at the cash register. He was fitted with an arm prosthesis and is learning to use it. He, too, appears to have a great deal of joy.

"Ruben, if there is anything that I can do for the academy, just ask," Glenn tells him, patting him on the back. "I am glad to have SWA in the power grid with my new wind turbine farm."

"Wow, Mr. Johnson, the turbines are quite a blessing for the campus," Ruben politely assures him.

Ruby heard that the wind turbines are dangerous to predatory birds; her heart twinges for all the eagles she is so fond of.

"Thank you for the coat; it is very nice," Jesse says, who isn't used to getting nice things from people.

"Thank you for your Healing Tent; it changed our lives," Glenn says with a tone of gratitude. "Tell Gabe we will see him Sunday."

They arrive back at the campus just before the roads ice up for the night.

The General decides to have an impromptu worship gathering the following night. Allen and Dana join the worship team as musicians, but they leave the vocals to the kids. Ruby joins the team also. They do slow and fast songs. The students worship in their own unique ways — jumping, dancing, hands up in the air. Aurora leads worship, and Ruby sings harmony. Two pros, Allen and Dana, polish the new sound. Allen plays guitar, and Dana is on keyboards. The Logans do not own much, but they have collected exceptional instruments through the years. They are happy to play them in the new SWA environment. Manuel is still thrilled to see so many kids worshipping even after several months at SWA. Back home, there are only twelve youths in his fellowship. Jorge also loves it.

CHAPTER NINE

IDOL TIME

Classes are resuming, and everyone is adapting to the new configurations. SWA is moving forward and preparing for winter.

For Thanksgiving, the General goes all out with decorations and a feast. Jamie seems tense as the Christmas decorations fully embellish the entire campus.

December arrives with brisk air and sporadic snow that never seems to melt completely.

The holiday season brings joy to the campus. As always, the campus gets decorated to the hilt — lights in all the trees on campus, decorations galore. Cars drive through all month to see the outdoor lights and buildings.

Evergreen garlands encircle the windows and drape the railings of all the facilities. Freshly fallen snow reflects the colored lights at night. Kristen wears her usual light-up hat and sweater, boots with bells, and a bag full of candy canes to pass out. And as usual, she must turn off her lights in class and lose the bells. The students decorate their dorm rooms, hoping to win a contest for the best-decorated dorm. The winners get a tray full of gourmet cookies, pies, and cakes, enough for the whole dorm to enjoy.

Today Kristen hands a candy cane to Jesse at breakfast; he freezes, looking at the candy cane, and then finally takes it from her. He lifts the candy cane and looks at Manuel; Manuel chokes up. Kristen decides the boys are nuts.

"It's just a candy cane!" Kristen doesn't understand boys; this is proof.

By the middle of December, all the Christmas lights are installed on the outside of the buildings. Christmas trees and garlands are throughout the dorms and structures. Many have Christmas cards taped on their doors.

Everyone gathers for lunch in the dining hall. A cluster of different-sized Christmas trees adorns opposite corners, lit with blue and white lights, silver balls, and an eight-pointed star on top of each.

Jamie comes in and stands in the middle of the room with a pained look on his face. Jesse notices it and begins to walk toward him.

Jamie suddenly runs toward the group of Christmas trees in the corner. He pulls down the tallest tree and pulls the star off.

"Sun-god, Baal . . . this is the idol for him!" Jamie throws the plastic star down with a crash.

A few shrieks of surprise follow. Everyone stops eating and stares in Jamie's direction.

"Jamie, what are you doing?" Jesse says, running up to him.

"Now is the time!" Jamie says tearfully, still holding on to the tree.

"This tree . . . this tree is Odin's and Ishtar's . . . idols from thousands of years of idol worship!" Jamie throws the tree on the floor; its lights go out.

By now, most of the cadets are alarmed and standing on their feet.

The General stands up and holds out his hands; he understands what Jamie is doing and tells everyone, "Now, everyone, don't be alarmed, we need to hear this. Jamie knows all about these things; we are uninformed, and now we must deal with the hidden idols of our ancestors."

Jamie bends over, weeping and repenting for the idols. [37]Ruach HaKodesh of the Lord is all over him.

---

[37] Hebrew for Holy Spirit

Over the fireplaces are boughs of evergreen. Jamie pulls it off, lifts it up, and says, "Offering to Ishtar." It crashes to the ground. Jamie is rushing around the room; he grabs Kristen's jingle bell headband.

"Yikes!" Kristen says as it slides off her head.

"Oden's imps, the Krampus, announced their arrival with bells to beat naughty kids. Jamie rattles the bells. Old Nick is another name for Satan!" Jamie gets winded. "December twenty-fifth is the birthday of a pagan god; this goes back thousands of years. Winter solstice, god of a thousand faces . . ."

Everyone gasps.

Jesse looks at Destiny and Ruby; this is not what they expected to learn about concerning idols.

Everyone watches Jamie as he picks up a candy cane and holds it up.

Jesse gasps, *Oh, no! Not the candy cane . . . not the candy cane too!*

"Not a shepherds' staff . . . a demonic staff of authority called a crosier. I should know; I used one on the roof last year!" Jamie sets it down; then, he drops to the floor.

"I don't have the strength to expose Easter to you . . . December twenty-fifth, as I said, is celebrated by witches all over the world as Baal's birthday. The sun god, Nimrod, Zeus, Bel, Dagon . . . all the same guy," says Jamie, his voice getting weak. (See "Types and Shadows" 9)

Silence comes over the room as Jamie sits on the floor, weeping and breathing heavily.

Kristen stands up.

"But it doesn't mean any of that stuff to us." Protests Kristen, in support of her favorite holiday.

"God sees idols, Kristen, old false religions going back to Genesis," Jamie replies gently.

The General has his hand over his mouth the whole time, just taking in the information.

Jesse stands, looking for permission to speak.

"Go ahead, Jesse," the General says.

"Over four months ago, we tried to bring down this demonic force, and it told us we were idolaters. It laughed with a 'HO, HO, HO' and disappeared. I think Jamie has exposed the hidden idols, and we need to remove this stuff from our affections! Why do we ignore Hanukkah, the Festival of Lights?" Jesse says, looking at everyone's confused faces. (See "Types and Shadows" 8)

"Yeah!" Yosef stands with a fist of enthusiasm. He suddenly gets embarrassed and sits down.

Then the General says, "It looks as though we need to see for ourselves in resource books. Each of us must deal with this in their own heart. We will discuss it two days from now in the assembly. Thank you, Jamie, for obeying the Lord at just the right time. I am ready to remove the trees and boughs; we must learn how to proceed," the General tells all the confused faces looking at him.

Jamie rests, still sitting on the floor with broken ornaments scattered about him. He can relax; he has revealed what the Lord told him. No one is angry with him as far as he knows.

"Ahh! Everything has gone blurry!" Gabe says as he stands up, looking around the room in a panic.

"Yeah, me too!" Kristen declares.

Others declare the same blurry vision. Everyone is stunned.

Jesse begins to laugh, "Take off your glasses and contacts! All of you! The Lord has confirmed Jamie's word by healing all vision problems!"

Gabe is the first to take off his glasses. "Oh, that's better!"

Kristen also removes her contacts and looks around.

"I don't need my contacts! I can see up close and across the room!" Kristen declares with joy.

A wave of joy and excitement sweeps across the dining room. Ruby and Destiny smile. Today brings a significant shift in the spirit realm. Jesse is excited that the idols' exposure has brought a new manifestation of the glory of Yeshua.

In the next few days, everyone looks up the information Jamie told them and finds out it is all true. The pagan history of many American holidays is clear.

Jamie spends several hours showing Aurora all the facts in books. They seem as though they are getting close — rumors of a potential romance float around.

"Obelisks are monuments to Baal? Wow, they are everywhere . . . and circles nearby are for Asherah, queen of heaven? That's crazy," Kristen remarks as the gang pours over the computer screen.

She has placed an order online for a bopper headband that has [38]Dreidels on springs in blue velvet and sunglasses that have nine candles across the top and mirrored words "[39]Hanukkah" on them. She will soon be able to start her holiday celebration again — this time with a new twist.

"Looks like Easter is out the window too," Devin states. "Instead, Resurrection Day, and Passover."

"The moon, stars, and sun are all worshipped. Israel angered God all through the Old Testament because of Baal and Asherah, clear back to Noah's great-grandson Nimrod," Destiny explains, looking up from her Bible concordance.

"I think a stronghold to Baal runs deeper than Christmas trees, in Jesse and Gloria. I can't explain it," Ruby tells the gang.

"Baal?" Gloria responds. "I don't have any history with Baal that I know of."

"The Lord promised to show us the darkness within if we would let him," Jesse tells her, knowing he still had some introspection to do. "The General is going to lead us in repentance tonight; we discussed it at the 'Gathering of

---

[38] Dreidel- four-sided spinning top used to play a children's game during Hanukkah.

[39] Hanukkah-**John 10:22** Feast of Dedication, started 700 BC

the Eagles' meeting. Maybe then we will learn more, as the Spirit moves."

All have assembled in Shekinah Sanctuary. Every Christmas tree gets removed along with the garland. However, there are multitudes of unmarked boxes piled up in every corner. Lights remain strung all over from the rafters, casting brilliant reflections. The General has Ira opening the repentance session.

"As we move forward and deal with the new things we just learned, I wish to mention how we should not scorn others who don't feel the need to remove certain items from their holidays. We prefer to err on the side of caution, which means taking no chances. Our focus is on drawing close to Yeshua and separating from Babylon. As we draw closer to the end, we will gain a deeper understanding of Mystery Babylon if we remain awake and in prayer. If others should have Christmas trees up, we should not shun them or rebuke them. We shouldn't act as though there is a demon in every Christmas wreath. We will celebrate Yeshua's birth, and give gifts if we wish. It is my conviction that Jesus was born during spring when all the lambs were born in Bethlehem for the temple sacrifices. That is when the shepherds would attend the flocks at night — during birthing time. Anyway . . . that was a rabbit trail."

"We are still the same group we were eight years ago. As we get revelation, we respond. In **Revelation 18:4,** it warns the people of God to come out of Babylon the

Great Harlot. So, if Babylon appears in our own lives, we choose to be free and separate from the spirit of this world.

"In conclusion, I say, let every man be fully persuaded in his or her own heart, but not condemn others who see it differently. Let's go forward with joy in our hearts and devotion to Adonai.

"Now I wish to announce our new dynamic duo, Jamie and Aurora. They are spiritual firebrands and highly advanced in the ways of Adonai. Come, you two, we are ready to get idols out of our lives in whatever form they may be."

Jamie and Aurora lead the repentance set. Jamie tells everyone about Gideon in the Old Testament.

"In chapter **six** of **Judges,** it mentions that Gideon pulled down his father's altar to Baal and his Asherah poles. They were idols in his own backyard. Gideon went on to be a great warrior for Adonai," Jamie says.

Aurora discusses deeper forms of idols that can grip souls and capture the affection and attention of people's hearts. The whole congregation lies on the floor and weeps, repenting for themselves and their forefathers.

Ruby and Destiny are now free from idolatry; Ruby can stop idolizing Jesse and see him in a more balanced light. Before, she thought he was some sort of super-prophet, and now she sees him as he truly is. She knows even she can have encounters like he does. Gloria still doesn't know how Baal got connected to her.

Eric repents for idolizing millionaires and movie stars. Kristen regrets idolizing the idea of fame; she spent hours daydreaming about it and now knows it was not a good idea.

"From now on, my purpose is to serve humanity and build the Kingdom of Adonai!" Kristen declares with passion.

Jesse was expecting more from the whole thing.

I didn't feel any emotion or revelation on idols for myself personally. I am afraid there is still some terrible thing lurking inside me. Something to do with that cave, but I can never look deeper. I always get scared and drop out of the trance or dream or whatever it is.

Destiny glances over at him.

"Hey, Jess . . . As long as you are dialoging with Yeshua and opening up to us, all things will come to light. In the fullness of time, Jess, in the fullness of time," Destiny tells him with a tender look in her eyes.

Ruby smiles and thinks: *They will make a great couple. So will Jamie and Aurora, but I don't even know if they like each other.*

After the repentance session, the General has boxes of eight-candle menorahs brought in.

"Okay, everyone, we have Hanukkah menorahs for all the dorm rooms. These large boxes are for everywhere else. Come on, everyone, and let's open the boxes and learn to celebrate Hanukkah!" the General declares with joy. "Oh yeah, we can also unpack these new decorations. I feel Yahweh wants us to celebrate Yeshua. Some scholars believe His birth was probably during the Feast of Tabernacles in September or August, but we will celebrate

Yeshua during Hanukkah also! Hanukkah, also known as the Feast of Dedication of the Temple, is centered around lights. It reminds us that Yeshua is the Light of the World."

Yosef begins to weep openly. He is overwhelmed with joy over the changes and all the Hanukkah decorations. Aurora puts on a Jewish celebration song; it is a disco/club style song in Hebrew. Everyone begins to dance to the beat, and the room fills with a celebratory mood. Yosef grabs Kristen's hands and begins to teach her a Jewish folk dance. She is quite delighted. They grin and move their hands together as he shows her the dance. Everyone is happy to see Yosef in good cheer; he has had a lonely time away from family. He is joyful and invigorated by the Hanukkah displays and music.

Several large floor-sized menorahs are assembled and taken to the dining hall, and two to the sanctuary. They are silver and feature a modern design. The General purchased various menorahs for the dorm rooms; everyone gets to choose from contemporary, traditional, and folk styles. Glitter-laden words that say, "Love," "Shalom," and "Joy" get placed around to replace boughs of evergreen. The metallic menorah's blue and white lights give new cheer on campus. Everyone has fun redecorating. Outside, the lights still outline the buildings. Whoever the mysterious benefactor to the academy is, he spent thousands of dollars on the new decorations. If the General is that millionaire, no one can prove it. Where the money comes from has been veiled in mystery all these years.

Jesse will spend his first Christmas with his parents. In the past, his family never celebrated the Christmas holidays. Dana, Allen, and Jesse would only have a lavish meal with Dana's Uncle Yishai (nicknamed Poppy, after Jesse) at a posh restaurant. That is Jesse's only Christmas memory. He remembers the encounter they had last year. He can't wait for the midnight candlelight service this year. Some parents come to SWA for the holidays, staying in Ox dorm in the last few spare rooms. Gabe's parents come for the Hanukkah feast, and so does his brother Michael. A few local families have children at SWA, although many left in October.

Devin, Eric, and some others go home for the Holiday break. They are so glad to see their family again.

On campus, it's time for the candlelighting service. The Hanukkah menorahs get lit each day, and this is the last day. These menorahs have nine candlesticks, whereas other menorahs have seven. In the sanctuary, some blue and white lights are on, and the worship band plays. Beautiful and fragrant blue and white floral arrangements adorn the corners. Candelabras get lit on the sides of the sanctuary. Worship and communion are next; they use beautiful crystal goblets. Like last year, two students play the harp and the violin during prayer. Jesse remembers his vision of his dad praying at the cross, how he was clean-shaven, and his mom with a new hairstyle. It had come true in less than a year. Jesse lies on the floor worshipping, grateful for his parents' salvation. His parents aren't sure what to think of that, but they enjoy the night. At the end of the meeting at sunset, everyone prays for the peace of Israel. Yosef says three special blessings in Hebrew. He uses the middle "servant" candle (symbol of Christ) to light the last one on both menorahs. The glory of the Lord settles thick like fog over a lake. Everyone knows Adonai is pleased with the changes. Aurora comes to close the gathering with a word from the Lord.

"And the Lord would say, well done. You have aligned with My times and seasons and cast off the Babylon system. Celebrate my Son! In all your activities, celebrate Him. I will pour out a blessing on you that will sustain you throughout the New Year. Darkness is coming; may people's eyes be open to find the light in you. I will purge this world of Babylon. Continue to pray for justice and Israel. After the fire comes My glory, look for My glory when the smoke clears; great things are in store for My separated ones," says Aurora with authority and dignity.

"We are free of Baal!" Jesse announces.

"Destiny and I are free, Jesse, but there is a dark secret that still gives Baal a place inside you. We have to wait for the Lord to reveal it," Ruby tells him. "And Gloria, she still needs to find how Baal got a stronghold in her."

"Aw, man . . . I guess I know it's true somehow," Jesse responds, with a hint of defeat.

"Don't worry, Jesse; when the time is right, it will all come to light," Destiny assures him again. "Gloria, you too, we need to be alert and not miss what this is all about."

Gloria nods deep in thought.

New worship flags, satins, and sheer, translucent fabrics of all kinds are passed out. Several white and blue flags on long poles are passed out to the students. All around the edge of the walls, people whirl the flags in celebration. It is a powerful scene. After the final song, everyone dismisses to go to the grand holiday feast.

The dining hall features lavish lighting, Hanukkah decorations, candles, a turkey, and an abundance of food at the feast. Goblets and fine China plates look elegant on the long wooden tables. Each tribe has a plate pattern at the banquet. The General addresses the students and families by reading from the Bible.

> **May grace and peace be multiplied to you in the knowledge of God and of Jesus our Lord. His divine power has granted to us all things that pertain to life and godliness, through the knowledge of him who called us to his own glory and excellence, by which he has granted to us his precious and very great promises, so that through them you may become partakers of the divine nature, having escaped from the corruption that is in the world because of sinful desire. For this very reason, make every effort to supplement your faith with virtue, and virtue**

with knowledge, and knowledge with self-control, and self-control with steadfastness, and steadfastness with godliness, and godliness with brotherly affection, and brotherly affection with love. For if these qualities are yours and are increasing, they keep you from being ineffective or unfruitful in the knowledge of our Lord Jesus Christ.

2 Peter 1:2-8

"Now Yosef will bless the feast," the General says as he motions to him.

The General hands him the microphone. Yosef is nervous but manages to say first in Hebrew, "Barukh atah Adonai, Eloheinu, Melekh ha'lom. Blessed are you, Lord, our God, sovereign of the universe. The blessing is longer, but I am too nervous to say it all!"

Everyone chuckles, and he feels more relaxed.

" [40] Abba, Yeshua, and Ruach HaKodesh, we acknowledge you as Lord of the feast. We honor You. We thank You, and we ask for Your blessing on this feast, this assembly, and this fellowship of warriors in Your army. Lead us into the next year with counsel, wisdom, and insight. In the name of Yeshua Ha'Mashiach, we ask all things. To You be glory in the ecclesia both now and in the

---

[40] Abba – Hebrew for Father, Yeshua- Jesus, and lastly Holy Spirit in Hebrew

age to come. Amen," says Yosef with more confidence growing by the end.

Pomegranates have been shipped in along with extravagant desserts and pastries, making the food and fellowship sweeter. Each tribe has its own specific place settings, featuring tribal emblems and colors. Candelabras also adorn the tables.

Yosef feels the most joy tonight since he left his family in Haifa for the U.S. He is finding that Adonai has placed him in a second family for now. Like Jesse, he is no longer an orphan. To his surprise, the cooks bring him a fully kosher feast, including lamb and Rugelach (pronounced ru-ga-lah, a cookie with a filling of chocolate, raisins, or fruit).

Afterward, everyone peacefully wanders to their dorms or cabins. Jesse stays in his parents' log cabin, and Ruby stays with hers. Several families have come in for the holiday, and their kids join them in OX dorm, with the gypsies.

As Jesse walks with his parents to their cabin, his heart is full. The snow glistens in the twinkling lights, and the air is crisp with no breeze, calm and peaceful.

"Allen . . . is Uncle Bill going to jail for drug abuse?" Jesse can't help but think about him from time to time.

"I don't know, Rocky, my boy. I guess they are waiting to see how he comes out of rehab." Allen, too, is thinking about his brother during the holidays. He wishes Jesse would call him dad, but knows he shouldn't push the issue. For now, he is content with their new life and the time they spend with their son.

Ruby is content walking to the Alvarez residence.

The New Year at SWA is going to be awesome, I just know it, Ruby thinks as their boots crunch in the pristine snow.

CHAPTER TEN

DAYS OF ELIJAH

January brings harsh weather to the Rocky Mountains. Classes are canceled several times due to blizzard conditions. On one such snow day, Jesse, Jamie, Manuel, and Eric gather for a prayer session to seek the Lord concerning the strategy needed for the "night is coming" warning. They meet in the commons area of Levi Lodge. The wind whistles through the pine trees outside.

Jesse relates his past vision of the Wedding Feast and then the war to banish the beast and Yeshua's reign for one thousand years.

Jamie comments, "There is a lot that is going to happen before the Wedding Feast."

Just then, Ruach HaKodesh's (Holy Spirit) presence manifests powerfully. Everyone falls to their knees or lies out on the floor, praying and worshipping.

Manuel is the first to get a word from the Lord. He hesitates to say anything, wishing someone else would go first. The room is quiet, with an expectation that Ruach HaKodesh wants to do something.

Finally, Jamie asks him, "Do you have a word?"

Manuel says, "Yes, yes, I do. Jesse, I feel I should tell you to guard your heart. Something will challenge you, and you need to guard against rage and resentment taking you over. I feel it very strongly; [41]guard your heart, for out of it flow the issues of life." (See "Types and Shadows" 10)

Jesse nods his head, taking it all in, wondering what challenge is coming his way.

Does it have to do with the Baal thing? Jesse wonders: *I am afraid of what I might learn about myself.*

Jamie puts his hand on Manual's chest.

"You need to be set free of the fear of man, so you will do God's will, regardless of what men might think."

Jamie feels Manuel yield to the Spirit. Manuel falls under the anointing, jerking, and twitching.

"Okay, that is different," Jesse says, seeing Manuel under the Spirit.

"Did anyone get any strategy from Adonai about the 'night is coming'?" Jamie asks.

---

41 **Proverbs 4:23**

“Who is Adonai?” Manuel asks, feeling inferior to the rest of the group, which seemed familiar with the word.

“Adonai is Hebrew for the Lord,” says Yosef, walking up.

“Oh,” Manuel replies.

“Anyway, all I heard was fire, bombs, and sounds like that, maybe a war or something?” Jesse tells them.

“Yeah, I heard sirens during prayer, but nothing specific,” Jamie adds.

“At the Hanukkah service last month, Aurora had mentioned glory after the fire . . . I think we have more questions than answers,” Jesse surmises.

“I guess we just stay alert and be ready for anything,” Jamie decides.

They all agree and get up from the prayer session.

The group walks toward the dining hall. The glare of the sun causes everyone to squint. Jesse realizes he is walking in new freedom from the dark clouds of shame and anger that once tormented him.

I’m not the same guy I was a year and a half ago. Being here has really helped me. Nothing can take away this good feeling, Jesse thinks to himself.

The Spirit prompts Jesse to meet with Professor White and discuss starting up Prayer Rock, as he did last year before the Great Crisis of April. They have already had some with just Gabe and Ray.

The news is on in the corner of the dining hall, where the staff eats.

"Across the nation, terrorists have contaminated large amounts of beef, poultry, and milk imported from other countries. There are many incidents where people fight over the remaining gallons of milk and meat in grocery stores. All shipping yards are currently receiving inspections. Food imports have slowed to a snail's pace. With new crises developing almost daily, this administration has had its hands full. The president's popularity rises or falls with each new challenge."

Eastcliffe is running low on food, so the General sends the small community more milk, eggs, and some canned goods. SWA has plenty due to their farming and livestock. More people live on campus than in the little town. Their economy is somewhat dependent on SWA.

A delivery truck manages to make its way up the slick road to the school. Allen and the General go out to meet it.

"That's odd; most trucks go to the back of the dining hall for deliveries," Ruby mentions, looking on.

Jesse is still wondering about the challenge Manuel mentioned at prayer, and he doesn't respond. Destiny shrugs her shoulders. Jesse gets lost in his thoughts all the time; she is used to it. Ruby is considering Baal's connection to Jesse and Gloria.

What could it be?

After lunch, the new worship team is meeting, but Allen is a "no-show." As a result, Aurora Oliver decides to hold a fellowship and prayer session as they wait for Allen and Dana.

Meanwhile, Allen goes and gets Jesse from the dining hall.

"Boy, I have something to show you."

Allen motions for Jesse to come outside. Jesse still doesn't like being called "boy," even after Allen explains how proud he is of his "boy."

Outside in the parking lot is a wooden crate, about the size of a refrigerator, lying on its side. The side panel is removed so that Jesse can see the contents; no one says a word. They just wait for Jesse to see the contents for himself. It is a 250cc dirt bike, new and expensive. Jesse swallows hard and asks, "Who is it from?"

Allen answers, "Your Uncle Bill."

Jesse steps back and shakes his head slowly, putting his hands out as if to protect himself.

"Allen, you know what he did to me. How could you let him send me this?"

Jesse is still backing away, and then he turns and runs into the forest behind the dining hall.

The General grabs Allen's arm.

"Better let him go for now. This gift is a hard thing to put him through right now. Maybe we should have told your brother William to wait," the General tells Allen.

"Yeah, but he said he is repentant and wants to make amends. I bought gasoline for it, and he spent a lot of money on this."

Allen desperately wants to believe his brother has changed his ways. He stands there with a gas can in his hand.

Jesse is running through the powdered snow, much like he used to do in New York. He runs till he gets exhausted, then falls in the snow. Jesse breaths hard and listens to his own breath and pounding heart. He rolls over in the snow and looks up. The forest is silent, with no wind or sound of birds.

"God, I was doing so well. Why did this have to come and stir up these terrible emotions?" Jesse says out loud.

He sits up and dusts the snow off his chest.

Jesse hears the Lord in his inner man: *"I am preparing you to go out into the world. I can't use you if you are not free of this bondage."*

"But I thought I *was* free."

Jesse examines his heart, checking for traces of bitterness.

"*It is more than just bitterness. Deep inside, you have darkness that you keep from Me. You have a room with the door shut. You must face this darkness. Together, We can go inside and deal with it. Do you not pray all the time, 'deliver us from evil'?"* the Lord reminds Jesse.

Jesse falls backward in the soft snow and looks up through the trees. A few snowflakes drift down around him. Jesse takes a deep breath and lies there, calming himself.

The General grows impatient waiting for Jesse to come back. He sees Eric, Destiny, and Ruby coming out of the dining hall. He tells them what happened and sends them to find him.

Allen feels terrible about the bike now, wishing he had asked the Lord before he told his brother he could send the gift. Allen is also trying to walk in love and not go and thrash his brother for the abuse of his "boy," knowing he had violent tendencies in the past as well. It is an ugliness he does not want to face.

It is easy to track Jesse's footprints in the fresh snow. Destiny spots him first and runs to him. She kneels down to him, and he leans up toward her. They embrace, and Jesse begins to cry in her arms. Eric and Ruby try to give them space, somehow, standing there in the forest. In what seems like an eternity to Ruby, Jesse stands up, and all four of them huddle in a group hug.

They break from the hug and stand there waiting for Jesse to gain his composure.

"Are you okay?" Ruby asks, with concern and worry.

"Yeah, I think so," Jesse says, dusting off the snow. His eyes are still red with emotion and sadness.

Eric, remembering the General's instruction to bring Jesse back, says, "The General is waiting for us."

The group begins to walk back to campus, mostly in silence, making only the sound of crunching snow.

Ruby, not being able to keep silent, finally asks Jesse, "So . . . what are you going to do about the dirt bike?"

Jesse sighs, "My flesh wants to beat it with a baseball bat and send it back, and my spirit is confused and cloudy. It's too cold to ride it till spring. Why now? Why did he send it now?"

Jesse wants to know his uncle's motivation, whether it is pure or not. He gets sick to his stomach and darts off behind a tree.

"Need any help?" asks Eric, wanting to do something.

"No, I can barf without you . . . thanks." Jesse tries to make light of his condition.

The four finally make it back to campus. The worship team gives up trying to have practice and reschedules for a later date. The General takes Jesse around the shoulders.

"Come with me," he tells him firmly. "Allen, we will return to you shortly."

Ruby feels a load of compassion and wonders how she could help Jesse. Destiny also wishes she could help him in some way. Allen stands in the cold air watching his son and the General walk away. He questions himself about whether he should have unpacked the bike and fueled it up.

The General leads Jesse toward his office. They walk into the administration building and take the stairs to his loft.

"Can't I deal with this on my own?" Jesse wants to save his pride and hide his dark emotions.

When they enter the office doorway, the General pulls out his cell phone and hands it to Jesse.

"Call him."

"No!" Jesse says quietly, feeling defeated. "What would I say?" Jesse wants to bolt, but has too much respect for the General. "I will . . . but tell me one thing. What is your real name?" Jesse is hoping to distract from the call.

"Eli, and you are not to share this with anyone, not even Destiny." The General lowers his voice and holds the phone out closer to Jesse.

Jesse feels his stomach turn.

"Let's get this over with," Jesse says with consternation.

He takes the phone and presses the call button (the number is already dialed).

Please don't answer! Please don't answer.

Jesse wishes his stomach didn't hurt.

"Hello?" It is his uncle.

"Uncle Bill?"

His voice wavers. His hands shake so violently that he can hardly keep the phone to his ear.

"The bike must've arrived. Do you like it?"

Bill tries to keep the conversation on a positive note.

Jesse disregards the question.

"Do you know how much you screwed me up? I was really messed up. You trashed me. You . . ." Jesse's voice is low and serious.

He slumps down in the big leather high-back chair next to the General's desk. The General puts his arm around Jesse and pulls him close, wishing he could calm Jesse's shaking.

Silence, just the sound of Jesse trembling and breathing hard.

"I . . . I wish it didn't happen, but it did. What can I do?" His uncle is getting honest for the first time.

"Repent and be forgiven, Bill, repent hard," Jesse had the clear mind to say with a touch of resentment in it.

"Will *you* forgive me, Jesse? Will you?" Bill sounds sincere.

"I need you to know what you did to me. Do you *even* remember? You got so plastered all the time!" Jesse waits for a response.

Tears are now streaming down Jesse's face. He is tired of crying and tired of all the emotions he is feeling today.

"I got self-destructive. I was a cutter." Jesse waited for it to sink in. "I was trash thrown out in the street. You can't undo what you did."

Jesse doesn't know what he wants his uncle to say to him at this point.

"Jesse, I don't want to burn in hell . . . I need to find forgiveness. I need to have *your* forgiveness. Is there forgiveness for someone . . . like me?"

Bill never talked like this before.

The General looks at Jesse with that "Do the right thing" look.

"It will take a while for my feelings to change toward you, but I will purpose in my heart to forgive you."

Jesse knows the consequences of unforgiveness (**Hebrews 12:15**). He leads his uncle in a prayer for salvation:

"Father God, I am a sinner and come short of the glory of God. I accept Jesus as my Lord and Savior. Let the blood of Christ cleanse me of all the bad things I did. Let Your Spirit fill me."

Jesse hands the phone to Eli.

The General takes the phone as Bill is not making sense.

"General . . . I have done a terrible thing, a secret too horrific to speak out loud . . .," Bill says with a tense voice and trembling.

"Okay, Bill, take it easy. Just ask for forgiveness; the blood of Jesus covers it."

The General advises Bill to find a local ecclesia and begin to study the Bible.

Jesse sits in the chair, feeling cold and indifferent to what just happened. Maybe he is simply too tired to feel anything. He looks at his hands. They are still shaking.

The General hangs up the phone and smiles at Jesse.

"You have a wounded spirit, Rock Man." He begins quoting **Isaiah 53:3-5.**

> **He was despised and rejected by men; a man of sorrows, and acquainted with grief; and as one from whom men hide their faces he was despised, and we esteemed him not. Surely he has borne our griefs and carried our sorrows; yet we esteemed him stricken, smitten by God, and afflicted. But he was pierced for our transgressions; he was crushed for our iniquities; upon him was the chastisement that brought us peace, and with his wounds we are healed.**

With each verse, Jesse feels waves of God's love wash over him. He leans back in the chair and closes his eyes.

"*Roll the pain over on Me,*" Yeshua tells Jesse.

Jesse remembers the encounter at the cross he had last year. It is beautiful and terrible at the same time. Jesse experiences light streaming toward him and warmth like sunshine; then, he feels the wounds of his soul begin to heal. Jesse doesn't know if it was minutes or days as he opens his eyes.

The General pulls Jesse up out of his chair.

"Ya know, Eli means 'My God.' Your name means 'God is.' In the Old Testament, Eli cared for a child prophet named Samuel, much like I care for you now. Soon you will graduate and move on."

The General doesn't like to think of saying goodbye to this exceptional kid.

"Let's go have another look at this dirt bike," the General suggests.

He opens his office door. Eric, Ruby, and Destiny are sitting on the couches by the receptionist's desk in the lobby.

"Did you hear everything?" Jesse is surprised to see them.

Eric tells him, "No, we didn't want to intrude; we were just worried."

The gang looks at Jesse, full of concern for him.

The General gives Destiny a hand up from the couch.

"I must caution you two to keep your relationship casual till you are older. I see how you two look at each other."

Jesse thinks: *Boy, I can't get away with anything around here.* They both blush, and Ruby grins.

Outside, Allen moved the dirt bike, and it is sitting in the snow by the street. It has a shiny red paint job with purple and lime green flames on the fenders and gas tank. Jesse goes out, sits down on it, kickstarts it, and takes off into the snow. He does wheelies in the parking lot and even jumps a few snow piles. People are coming out to see what the noise is. Jesse is enjoying himself.

Dana comes running out to the parking lot to give him the helmet that came with the bike. "Jesse Evan Logan, get on your helmet!"

The sound of the bike engine winds down from a roar to a gentle idle. Jesse pulls up to the curb, his face red from the cold air.

"I'm done, Mom. It's too cold; I can't feel my hands."

Jesse knows it isn't wise to ride anymore in these conditions. The small crowd that gathered applauds Jesse for his riding. Jesse smiles with a huge grin. Destiny melts, and Ruby glows with joy. Allen takes the bike to his cabin and parks it under the carport for his son. Jesse doesn't notice until the next day that the cycle is custom-made. The sides have the name "Redemption" airbrushed on them, and Jesse's name is on the fenders. His helmet is also customized. Inside is the inscription: "From Uncle William to Jesse Evan Logan." There is a note tucked inside the helmet.

"Where did you learn to ride like that?" Ruby asks, shivering in the cold air.

"I grew up around bikes. Even my dad rides."

Jesse tries to regain feeling in his fingers.

The next day, before classes resume, Jesse goes back to see the bike. He finds the note in the helmet and reads:

JESSE,

FOR THE PAST YEAR, YOUR FACE HAS HAUNTED ME. EVER SINCE YOU RAN AWAY, I HAVE FELT TERRIBLE DREAD. I LOOKED FOR YOU EVERY DAY WHEN YOU LEFT, AND I ENDED UP IN REHAB.

ANYWAY, I AM WRITING TO SAY I AM SORRY FOR WHAT I DID. I'M NOW DRIVING TO PAPA JOSÉ'S ECCLESIA, WHERE YOU GOT SAVED. PASTOR JOSÉ TOLD ME MY NAME, WILLIAM, MEANS "WILL, (DESIRE) + HELMET, (PROTECTION)."

I FAILED TO BE A PROTECTOR FOR YOU. THE ENEMY USED ME, AND I LET HIM. I NEED TO TELL YOU ABOUT THIS SECRET THING I DID WHEN YOU ARE READY TO HEAR.

MAY THE BIKE BRING A LITTLE JOY FOR THE PAIN I HAVE GIVEN YOU. I HOPE I CAN FIND FORGIVENESS AND GET SAVED. I WILL WAIT TO HEAR FROM YOU.

UNCLE WILLIAM

Jesse realizes his uncle was waiting to hear from him before giving his life to the Lord. He wondered if Eli knew that when he insisted on calling his uncle.

It is time for class. Jesse folds the note and heads off. He hopes to talk to Professor White today, after class.

All second-year students in the Levi tribe are in Ira's class on the book of Revelation and the Last Days. She writes a scripture on the whiteboard:

"Behold, I send my messenger, and he will prepare the way before me. And the Lord whom

you seek will suddenly come to his temple; and the messenger of the covenant in whom you delight, behold, he is coming, says the Lord of hosts. But who can endure the day of his coming, and who can stand when he appears? For he is like a refiner's fire and like fullers' soap. He will sit as a refiner and purifier of silver, and he will purify the sons of Levi and refine them like gold and silver, and they will bring offerings in righteousness to the Lord.

Malachi 3:1-3

Ira's topic for the day: getting refined and how uncomfortable it is to be purified. Jesse can attest to the painful process, but is glad that, thus far, he has been able to endure it. Everyone at SWA learns to pray for Israel to accept and believe in Yeshua as their long-expected Messiah. They get taught the term Yeshua Ha'Mashiach (Jesus the Messiah – the Anointed One).

Ruby looks at Jesse over during the lecture. His face is thin, and his clothes hang on him. She realizes he has lost some weight from yesterday's trauma.

Jesse drifts off to sleep in class. No one wakes him. Many snicker as they leave him sleeping when class is over. Professor White pokes her head into Ira's class and sees Jesse slumped over his desk, asleep. The professor shakes his shoulder to wake him.

"Rocky, Rock Man, wake up."

Professor White knows he had a rough day yesterday and goes easy on him.

"Oh, hello, Professor, I must have drifted off. It was a good lecture . . . till I drifted off."

Jesse rubs his face.

Ira smiles at Jesse from her whiteboard.

"It is time to start prayer rock again." She goes straight to the business at hand.

"Agreed. Where should we meet this year?" Jesse responds, with his eyes half-open.

"Your dorm lobby as long as you have under fifty; if it is more, use the sanctuary." Professor White remembers the considerable growth of the group last year. "I will have it announced if you don't mind," she tells him.

Jesse nods.

"So, Saturdays at four o'clock?" Jesse confirms.

She nods.

"Do you think you should take a sick day and rest?" Her motherly instinct is kicking in.

"Maybe."

Jesse has a hard time admitting to any form of weakness. The scripture in **2 Corinthians 12** echoes in his mind. He fingers the paper in his pocket, which contains the scripture.

"Can you give me a note? I hate to show up at the nurse's office again."

"Here you go."

Professor White scribbles out a quick excuse for him.

Ruby wanted to wake Jesse up so badly, but the Lord told her not to. She and Destiny sit down looking at his empty chair in third hour. They notice that Kristen and Yosef are sitting together in every class now.

Is Jesse gonna sleep through the day? Jacob is supposed to prophesy today. This class is getting interesting.

Ruby is looking forward to it.

Jesse looks at Hope in her cage as he drags himself to his dorm room.

"Hey, beautiful," he tells the eagle. Once in his room, he plops on his bed, kicks off his shoes, and rests comfortably.

Please, no cave in my sleep, just Jesus. . ..

The General teaches the next class — Law and the Prophets 102. (Ira and the General have taken over the classes the resigning teachers left empty.) He asks if anyone knows where Jesse is.

Jacob tells him, "Jesse is sleeping in Ira's class."

Everyone chuckles.

The General assigns Jamie to check on him and then goes on with class. Next, Jacob gets called to the front of the room. He is nervous; the prophetic is serious business.

The General puts his hand on Jacob's shoulder and prays, "Father, share Your heart with Jacob. Give him utterance and open his understanding in Jesus' name."

Jacob quickly gets the first part of his prophecy.

"I see Levi and Judah joined. I see music and the words, harp, and bowl. I see Jesse, Ruby, and Destiny. Jesse and Destiny bound at the wrists with a band of white flowers. Ruby is holding armor and a sword; plus, she has her own armor and a sword strapped across her back. It is Jesse's that she holds."

Ruby is disappointed that Jesse isn't there to hear what Jacob said. Destiny wrote it all down to make sure Jesse hears the whole thing.

It has been some time since Jesse saw demons in his sleep. They carry the same message they always have.

"You are a fake. You are good for nothing, worthless trash. You are fooling yourself and everyone else!" the voice snarls and accuses Jesse. "I am waiting for you in the cave, Jesse. Look into the darkness; what will you see?" it asks, with disdain and accusation.

Jesse's stomach begins to hurt. He rolls over on his side and holds his abdomen. Jesse is ready this time.

"Accuser of the brethren, be gone! In the name of Jesus, I take authority over you."

Jesse doesn't know if he said it out loud or in the spirit, but the enemy's oppression lifts like fog in the sun. Jesse's pain is gone, and he rests once more.

As he drifts off, Jesse tells Yeshua, "God, I think I have fallen in love with Destiny."

Jamie peeks in and sees Jesse sleeping comfortably, so he covers him with a blanket and leaves.

At suppertime, Jesse gets up, hungry and ready to eat. He goes to his parents' table and gives them a long hug. He tells Ruby he appreciates her. She is speechless. Then he sits and looks at Destiny with a silly grin on his face. The gang looks at Jesse differently. They sense a gentleness and a level of meekness that is new.

The next day in the second hour, Jesse is back in class as Ira writes on the whiteboard:

> **"Behold, I will send you Elijah the prophet before the great and awesome day of the Lord comes. And he will turn the hearts of fathers to their children and the hearts of children to their fathers, lest I come and strike the land with a decree of utter destruction."**
>
> **Malachi 4:5-6**

After attendance, Ira stands up to lecture. She begins feeling the anointing of Ruach HaKodesh and sets her notes on Elijah aside. She bends over as her body rocks up and down, as she often does when the anointing comes over her.

"Eric, read this scripture out loud, please," she points to the board as the anointing keeps her rocking gently back and forth.

As he reads, kids begin to cry out and groan to the Lord. Many did not know their dads because their dads had left their families. Other kids did not know their dads because their dads are emotionally distant from them. Ira instructs the kids to come up if they do not have the relationships with their fathers that they need. Eric, Jesse, and Devin lay hands on the boys, and Ruby, Destiny, and Milagros pray over the girls. Many weep bitterly, longing for the love of their fathers. The room erupts with crying and prayer. Many young warriors are set free of abandonment, rejection, and orphan spirits. Jesse shows real emotion, laying hands on his classmates and praying for deliverance. His transparency touches Eric and Devin, and they, too, weep more freely under the touch of God. Some, for the first time, experience the love of their heavenly Father. In the past, they had assumed God was like their earthly fathers, void of emotion and affection. As the class ends, kids get up off the floor. There are rare huddles of boys weeping and girls arm in arm, sobbing together. Ruby wonders if L and P class (Law and the Prophets) can top what just happened.

As everyone else shuffles out to go to third period, Jesse drops to his knees, covers his face with his bandana, and weeps. He knows that a year ago, he would not have been able to minister to anyone. He would have been in the line-up, bound up and hard-hearted. The Holy Spirit dances over him with rejoicing.

"I am sorry I grieved Ruach HaKodesh by not yielding to the weeping. I can get proud and carnal. Thank You for bringing my parents back to me."

Then he runs to the next class. The General has already called up Audrey to prophesy. The General does not get a chance to pray for her; she just begins.

"Adonai is bringing change . . . The warriors will go out as light into darkness, do not despise the refining fire. An army, He is raising up an army. I hear the clanking of swords and marching of boots." Audrey speaks with authority and confidence.

The General asks if there are any to confirm the word. The room falls silent while everyone seeks the Lord. Faith stands up, and the General nods for her to speak.

"I saw in the Spirit, chaos across the earth, people crying out in torment. Then I saw people in SWA shirts bringing peace to individuals, families, and entire villages. I saw smoke on this mountain."

Faith speaks her words clearly and sharply. Each is pronounced with emphasis.

"But what does smoke on the mountain mean?" Jesse is alarmed.

"Beloved, let not your heart be troubled. In this world, we have tribulation. But be of good cheer, I have overcome this world," the General tells his class.

He writes a scripture on the whiteboard:

> **Jesus answered them, "Do you now believe? Behold, the hour is coming, indeed it has come, when you will be scattered, each to his own home, and will leave me alone. Yet I am not alone, for the Father is with me. I have said these things to you, that in me you may have peace. In the world you will have tribulation. But take heart; I have overcome the world."**
>
> **John 16:31-33**

"Also . . . we do not yet know the time frame of this prophecy. It could be years," the General tells the class.

The General assures himself just as much as he does the anxious class. After the classroom empties, Eli puts his head on his desk and begins to weep.

"Lord, give me strength. You told me from the start that Spirit Wings Academy would go out in a blaze of glory, but all I see is the blaze. Show me the glory."

Eli's phone rings, and he goes on with the business of the day.

In Ira's next class, she gets another chance to lecture on Elijah. She shows them in the scriptures about John the Baptist:

> **From the days of John the Baptist until now the kingdom of heaven has suffered violence, and the violent take it by force. For all the Prophets and the Law prophesied until John, and if you are willing to accept it, he is Elijah who is to come.**
>
> **Matthew 11:12-14**

Then she tells them about the two witnesses in Revelation:

> **And I will grant authority to my two witnesses, and they will prophesy for 1,260 days, clothed in sackcloth."**
>
> **These are the two olive trees and the two lampstands that stand before the Lord of the**

earth.

Revelation 11:3-4

Lastly, she wrote the scripture from yesterday:

Behold, I will send you Elijah the prophet before the great and awesome day of the Lord comes.

And he will turn the hearts of fathers to their children and the hearts of children to their fathers, lest I come and strike the land with a decree of utter destruction."

Malachi 4:5-6

As the period ends, Ira wonders why everyone was so quiet in class. The classroom phone rings, and Ira answers it.

"Mom, are you free to come to my classroom?" Eli asks.

"Sure, is there something wrong?" Ira senses his tension.

"Just need to talk." Eli hangs up and waits for his mom.

Ira grabs Wanda and Jamie, and they head up the spiral stairs to her son's classroom.

"Eli needs strength and encouragement," she tells them as they walk to his classroom in a rush.

They see Eli at his desk, leaning down, head in his hands. He looks up; strain and weariness show on his face as he looks up at them.

"Dealing with Jesse and then the kids prophesying about fire on the mountain, I just feel worn down," Eli admits.

The three lay hands on Eli and pray for him. Jamie gets a word for him.

"You have been faithful and endured much. Your work with Jesse will yield much fruit. [42]The enemy desires to sift you as wheat, but I (Christ) have prayed for you. The strength I give you, pass on to those under you."

Jamie's hands shake under the anointing. Eli rarely cries in front of his staff, but these are also his dear friends. He gets up, hugs them all, and thanks them for their support.

Wanda, being loud and vibrant, lets out a "Glory" with her thick Slavic accent.

"I see a vessel of gold floating on a sea of glass. The vessel is under the altar of God!" Wanda waves her arms. Everyone has to move out of the way.

They all know martyrs are given a place of glory under the altar until they are avenged. (**Revelation 6:9**) Holy laughter breaks out in the classroom. People walking past the room just smile. It is normal to hear radical praying on campus.

The Holy Spirit is excited over martyrs. Jamie finds this interesting.

---

42 **Luke 22:31, 32** paraphrased

What we think of as horrible, the Lord finds priceless and joyful. Heavenly perspective is so different than ours, Jamie thinks. Then he quotes:

> **-let the wicked forsake his way, and the unrighteous man his thoughts; let him return to the Lord, that he may have compassion on him, and to our God, for he will abundantly pardon. For my thoughts are not your thoughts, neither are your ways my ways, declares the Lord. For as the heavens are higher than the earth, so are my ways higher than your ways and my thoughts than your thoughts.**
>
> **"For as the rain and the snow come down from heaven and do not return there but water the earth, making it bring forth and sprout, giving seed to the sower and bread to the eater, so shall my word be that goes out from my mouth; it shall not return to me empty, but it shall accomplish that which I purpose, and shall succeed in the thing for which I sent it.**
>
> **"For you shall go out in joy and be led forth in peace; the mountains and the hills before you shall break forth into singing, and all the trees of the field shall clap their hands.**
>
> **Isaiah 55:7-12**

"Even so, Lord Jesus, come," Ira says, ending their time seeking the Lord.

Everyone leaves with peace in their hearts.

CHAPTER ELEVEN

ASCENDING AND DESCENDING

By the end of February, the snowstorms are becoming tiresome, and everyone is looking forward to the spring thaw. The first-year students look forward to taking their hike to the summit and getting prophecy time with Ira in March. Jesse is thinking of his new dirt bike. The gang will graduate in May. None of them has plans for the future. All they know is they don't want to split up, as Ruby, Jesse, and Destiny have prophesies to fulfill.

Ruby prays, *Lord, would You give me an itinerary? I like things laid out. Jesse is seventeen, Destiny is nineteen; I'm just fifteen till next September. Please don't let Jesse and Destiny run off without me!*

Eli, Ira, Wanda, Jesse, and Jamie meet for their monthly prophetic discussion. Today, they are meeting at the top level of Academic Tower West. Aurora is added to the "Gathering of Eagles" now, and she joins them today.

General Eli Reports, "For now, the news is about the new superhighway built across the Great Breach of the earthquake region, and the touring music festival. It's called the Summer of Love. Top secular bands, dance troupes, and a huge light show comprise the festival. They are coming to Denver, and now that fuel is widely available, half of Eastcliffe is driving to Denver to see the show." He is not happy about the Summer of Love movement.

Jamie says, "Yeah, I hear they tour and sing of love and tolerance, preaching that love will bring all religions together. Peace will reign on the earth, they say. However, fights often break out at their gatherings, and violence is a problem wherever they go. They use the symbol of Kokopelli and images of the sun god Baal."

Aurora tells them, "Have you heard about the small group that travels ahead to publicize the event? They paint graffiti about it and walk through towns yelling the time and place of the next event. Their clothes are like those worn by heavy metal rock bands, but they mix them with Irish plaids. They dance in the streets and play songs with fiddles. Their dancing is fierce and precise; crowds gather to watch. They call themselves the Followers because they go wherever the festival goes."

As he paces in front of the windows, Eli says, "I have warned the cadets about a worship movement that will be the enemy's counterfeit and pull some believers out of true worship. These Followers carry an anti-Christ spirit. They are growing in numbers. In their abandoned frenzy, they leave towns littered and vandalized with messages of love and tolerance.

"They are very persuasive, and their message appeals to many. Some major ecclesiastical denominations changed their names to things like "Assembly of Love" or "House of Love." Other ecclesia buildings are getting burned to the ground, victims of arson. No one has been arrested for it yet," Ira reports.

The group dwells on what all this means. Jesse begins to process all the facts. "How far away is the 'night' that the Lord told us about?" Jesse asks.

"The great and terrible day of the Lord? No, not yet . . . we couldn't do any work for the Kingdom if night has fallen," Ira explains. "We can't know the day or the hour, but the season we can know. The signs are not all there yet, but we are most certainly at the beginning of the Great Tribulation."

"Jesse, I feel we are here for such an hour as this, and we will do great exploits," says Eli. "Things are going to get wild out there; we will have to rely on Yahweh for everything."

"Urgency, these are urgent times . . ." says Jesse.

"It is urgent; this is our time to work; advance the Kingdom of Light, bring in the harvest, and call for justice on the Earth," Ira declares.

"And . . . pray for Israel," adds Aurora.

"Of course!" Ira agrees. "And wake up those who slumber among us."

"So . . . I should stop looking for the 'night' and work while it is yet day, huh?" says Jesse, forming the idea in his mind as he says it.

"Yes, the Spirit of Slumber keeps many from their work; we need to be alert and about the Master's business," Aurora adds. "We have been quick to release several new worship albums. They are already going out to ministries and individuals. Many use the songs for dramas and dance routines," Aurora reports, "The new emphasis is on going out to the streets, not just expecting people to show up in our meetings."

The General nods and says, "You are getting well known, as are other worship leaders and songwriters from the academy. Allen and Dana are adding some real quality to our sound. They are happy to be part of the musicians involved in the projects. The mixing of the generations is Elohim's doing. It adds power that wouldn't be there otherwise."

Wanda stands at the window that faces the campus entrance. She points to a group of people walking up the road to the academy. "I think the Followers have come to our doorstep!"

The General tells Jamie, "Go get Professor Norman and his team, and Aurora, you gather your dancers and drummers."

Wanda tells the General, "The gypsy men will also go, just for back up. We know how to deal with conflict."

The General gives her the okay, "We might need them. Just as a precaution."

Ira puts her hand on Eli's shoulder, "Son, you are not to confront them yourself. Do you hear me? The Lord said to let your people do their job."

"But —" Eli stops his sentence when he sees the stern look on her face.

Jamie and Professor Norman gather with the guild members trained for security, along with Aurora's team of worshippers. Jesse runs to get Manuel and joins them. The gypsy men fill in the back. Professor Norman leads them as they walk toward the giant gate towers. The large metal grid (portcullis) is going down for the first time, blocking the SWA entrance; it squeaks and grinds its way to the pavement. The sound travels as far as the top of campus.

Walking down to the entrance, Professor Norman fills everyone in on what is happening as they approach the strangers.

"These are wild guys that dance and wear kilts and stuff. They are here to promote a new age festival. They enjoy brawling and causing upheaval. We need to send them away."

Norman's security guards and Aurora's dancers/musicians meet the Followers at the entrance gate. Ray and Gabe are there as part of the guilds of Gad and Benjamin. (Guilds of combat and security) Under the General's orders, the Followers are not allowed to enter. The rowdy travelers refuse to comply with the order to turn around and leave. It appears that a conflict may ensue despite the iron blockade. The travelers have a sniper hidden with the intention of taking General Eli out, but of course, he is nowhere in sight.

The leader of the Followers makes threats, "Where is yah General? He not good enough to speak to us himself — he has to send his lackeys? No — never mind. Yah cold dead religion is dying out. You think yah are safe behind yah walls and metal gate? Yah are not safe! Do us a favor and die quietly."

They shout curses and throw rocks through the iron grid. Many of them begin their fierce stomping dance while others accompany them on their fiddles.

Aurora tells all the drummers and dancers to proceed towards the gate, but to maintain a safe distance. She has the conga drummers and dancers walk in front of the gate tower's big rock arch toward the portcullis, drumming and dancing. The dancers stomp in rhythm, spinning and jumping around. Jesse and Manuel also arrive at the entrance. [43]The combat troupe is in readiness at the rear, the drums thunder in the open mountain air.

The Followers find that the high-altitude air takes the energy right out of them, and they cease their dancing. By the time Professor Norman's guards position themselves at the gate, the Followers' demonstration is over. They sit down at the gate, demanding to get in to talk to the General.

Professor Norman motions for the SWA drums to stop. Jamie, Jesse, and Manuel address the Followers. Jamie stands next to the gate and begins to read:

> **See, I have set before you today life and good, death and evil. If you obey the commandments of the Lord your God that I command you today, by loving the Lord your God, by walking in his ways, and by keeping his commandments and his statutes and his rules, then you shall live and multiply, and the Lord your God will bless you in the land that you are entering to take possession of it. But if your heart turns away, and you will not hear, but are drawn away to worship other gods and serve them, I declare to you today, that you shall surely perish.**
>
> **Deuteronomy 30:15-18a**

The Followers of the Summer of Love movement are silent. They all look to their leader for his reaction. He

---

[43] See **2 Chronicles 20:20-23**, Judah (praise) goes before the army.

is Scottish and fierce in his countenance. His accent is Scottish, and his intentions are straightforward.

He sees his group's confusion and walks up to Jamie and yells through the iron grid, "We renounce yur God of Abraham, Isaac, and Jacob, and Jesus. I would rather perish than have someone tell meh what is right and wrong. Passion is all we need. It dwells within us and moves us tah action. You are a black spot in our nation. Passion will prevail. We will prevail. You, me friends, are a dying breed!" The leader has tattoos with strange symbols on his arms and the side of his face.

His people cheer and pump their fists in the air. As he finishes, he motions for his group to leave. Turning to leave, he says, "Yah have not seen the last of us."

They don't dance or play anymore; they just walk in silence back down the road. Shortly after, the two policemen who were saved last year came up to see if everything is under control. The Followers move on peacefully, and Professor Norman talks to the police officers, Edwards, and Barnes as the iron grid raises again.

Officer Barnes tells the professor, "I believe these transients painted graffiti all over Glenn's store, but I can't prove it. I want them out of my town."

They watch as the Followers turn left toward the interstate instead of back toward Eastcliffe. They decide to close the portcullis for the night to ensure their safety. The lawmen ride their motorcycles back to town, and everyone walks back up to campus. Jesse sees a strange demon dancing over the Followers, playing the flute. He is dark like smoke and transparent. His eyes are fire.

That night, Jesse thinks about the day's affairs.

Antichrist forces are increasing. The ecclesia is under attack. The demon I saw is like the Pied Piper in fairy tales. He looks around the dorm. *The guys are doing their everyday things. No one seems aware of the changing climate in the Spirit. They need to be watching and praying more than ever before. I don't even know if my ties with Baal are broken or even how I got those ties.*

Ruby and Destiny don't give the rest of the girls in the dorm a choice. They get them sitting in a circle for evening prayers. Ruby opens with a familiar scripture:

> **Finally, be strong in the Lord and in the strength of his might. Put on the whole armor of God, that you may be able to stand against the schemes of the devil. For we do not wrestle against flesh and blood, but against the rulers, against the authorities, against the cosmic powers over this present darkness, against the spiritual forces of evil in the heavenly places. Therefore take up the whole armor of God, that you may be able to withstand in the evil day, and having done all, to stand firm. Stand therefore, having fastened on the belt of truth, and having put on the breastplate of righteousness, and, as shoes for your feet, having put on the readiness**

given by the gospel of peace. In all circumstances take up the shield of faith, with which you can extinguish all the flaming darts of the evil one; and take the helmet of salvation, and the sword of the Spirit, which is the word of God, praying at all times in the Spirit, with all prayer and supplication.

To that end keep alert with all perseverance, making supplication for all the saints,

Ephesians 6:10-18

Destiny starts, and they take turns praying out loud. They pray for the school's protection and its leaders, the ecclesia worldwide, and the Jewish people. They release peace to their hearts and cast out any fear.

Destiny prays using **Psalm 112:5-9:**

It is well with the man who deals generously and lends; who conducts his affairs with justice. For the righteous will never be moved; he will be remembered forever. He is not afraid of bad news; his heart is firm, trusting in the Lord. His heart is steady; he will not be afraid, until he looks in triumph on his adversaries. He has distributed freely; he has given to the poor; his righteousness endures forever his horn is exalted in honor.

Dr. Luz and Professor Norman assigned boys from Gad and Benjamin tribes for night watchmen duties. Each one taking a four-hour shift, they take the threats the

Followers made seriously. The perimeter stone wall is broad enough to walk on, so they pace on the wall all night. Jamie joins the [44]fourth watch; standing on the wall near the gates, he is literally a "watchman on the wall."

Angels on the roofs stand vigilant.

As Saturday morning arrives, songbirds sing out. The air is cold in early March, but that doesn't stop the birds.

Hope is happy to get out of her cage and get into the sunlight. Ruby leaves her to hunt while she goes for breakfast.

The news on TV promotes the arrival of the Summer of Love festival, which is being transported across the country by a caravan of trucks and buses.

"They are setting up in the Sports Stadium at Mile High, expecting fifty thousand to turn out," the anchorman says. "The Summer of Love message is, 'Together we can bring peace to the planet.'"

Footage of the Followers dancing in the streets is the main story. The logo for the festival is Kokopelli, a Native American deity, with a flute. Jesse recognizes it from yesterday.

Jesse nudges Eric, "Hey, I saw that Kokopelli dude, over the top of the Followers yesterday."

---

[44] Fourth watch –military watch from three to six in the morning. **Matthew 14:25**

"Weird . . . what does that mean?"

"Dunno," Jesse answers.

No mention of the graffiti or violence by the media. The news continues:

"More [45]Ecclesial buildings burned down in Texas and California. A small earthquake in Yellowstone Park caused the evacuation of the park. At the Great Breach, gas is still spewing in some areas, causing dangerous conditions, and a few closings on the superhighway. Tsunamis, floods, and mudslides are popping up all around the world."

Just before Eli turns off the TV, they mention a story on how the president has secretly made a deal to buy oil and gas from Israel. He does not want the world to know he is still a close ally of the Israelis.

As Ruby and the gang step out of the dining hall, the world seems at rest. The birds are singing, green grass peeking up, and the sun is warm on their skin. The gang walks out to find Hope.

"The newbies will soon take their hike to the summit. I think most people believe your warning that 'night is coming' is far off," Destiny tells Jesse.

"I know things are going to get chaotic, but I don't know more than that," Jesse says, looking around for Hope.

---

[45] Ecclesia – church – Called Out Ones.

"I feel a big change is coming, and Destiny heard the roar of fire. We don't know if it is spiritual fire, natural fire, or both," says Ruby.

"After the fire, My glory comes . . . that's what Aurora prophesied in December, remember?" says Jesse.

They walk a while thinking; then, Jesse stops and looks at Ruby.

Jesse gets up his nerve to ask again, "Ruby, do you think I still have ties with that Baal guy?"

Ruby stops and looks him in the eyes.

"Oh, Jesse, you still have some walls up, and you hide your pain, not just from us, but from God," Ruby says softly. "I saw a locked door."

Destiny seems a little alarmed, "And Jesse, I see a broken beer bottle. Does that mean anything to you?"

Jesse's face flushes with redness, and he breaks out in a sweat as he turns away from them and starts walking again.

"Sorry I asked . . .," is all he can say with sadness in his voice.

They know he is not ready to talk about it yet. Ruby's heart twinges: she worries about Jesse when he gets in his brooding mood. Destiny remains calm and simply gives him space.

After all this time, Jesse still hides things from us. What is he so ashamed of? Ruby wonders.

Destiny's thoughts are on the comment, "After the fire, My glory comes." She also remembers the prophetic words about refining fire and smoke on the mountain.

Hope is eating mice she caught behind the dining hall. That always disgusts Ruby, seeing Hope eat her catch. Ruby wants to put Hope up in her cage, but Hope doesn't want to go inside.

"Bird . . . get in your cage; the Followers might try to steal you or something." Ruby wrestles Hope back into her cage.

It is eleven-thirty in the morning when a tremor shakes the campus. Things fall off desks, and car alarms go off.

Three hours away in the mile-high city of Denver, the festival has started. The Summer of Love performers sing and dance in front of a big crowd. There are lights, fog effects, moving stages, and people swinging on high wires. An estimated fifty thousand have come to the festival. They feel the shaking there, too. The authorities say it is safe to continue the Summer of Love event. Thirty thousand cowbells get handed out to the crowd, and they are to ring for peace. At noon, everyone in the stadium is called on to ring their cowbells. The noise is heard for miles, causing small children to hold their ears, birds to scatter from the trees, and dogs to bark and howl.

Back at SWA, the shaking is over, and everyone continues with their day. Jesse sneaks back to his prayer rock. He never tires of the view. The deep rocky ravine is full of squirrels and chipmunks that scamper about, and birds in the trees. At four in the afternoon, the prayer rock group will meet in the sanctuary, and he needs some direction. The sun is shining, and the rocks are warm. However, cool breezes through the pines make it chilly outside. Jesse lies on the large granite boulder and thanks God for his parents' salvation and Manual being on campus this school year. He prays for General Eli; Jesse respects and admires him. A large number of noisy birds land in the trees nearby.

Jesse finds it odd.

Where did all these birds come from?

The crows are the loudest. Squawking, chattering, and fluttering sounds fill the air. Jesse sits up and looks around.

God, what is going on? He feels something is up, but what? No answer, then he hears, "*I desire My people to worship Me, not to get caught up in the noise of the moment. I want them to keep themselves deep in My presence,*" the Lord tells him, in a still, small voice in his head.

Jesse nods, thinking. He decides to get Ruby to play the keyboard and sing, and maybe Destiny could sing with her. He leaves his prayer rock and goes to get ready for the prayer session.

As Jesse walks in from the prayer rock, he finds over fifty students already in the sanctuary. Jesse is asking the Lord why he is put out in front to lead the meeting. He doesn't want to whine, but he is sure it sounds that way to the Lord. As more kids stream into the gathering, Jesse still doesn't have anything to say yet, so he has Ruby play a song she wrote last year. Her cords are simple, brooding, and gentle. She begins to sing:

Rise… Jesus is coming soon
Fi-gh-t…for what we know is right,
against the lies
Sh-ine… for we are the light, through the night
Pr-ay…for our faith stands in power,
not just words
Tell… of His wonders and glory
that they may believe
Da-n-ce…before His throne,
for He has made us worthy
Re-joice…for it won't be long,
till He makes earth His home
Rise… Jesus is coming soon

The second time through, Destiny blends her voice with Ruby's. As they softly sing, Jesse addresses the group.

"We have a season to enter into the secret place, to come into His garden. If you feel distant, if your heart is cold, if fear dominates your mind, come, and we will pray with you. Girls for girls, boys, pray for boys."

About one hundred kids come forward for prayer. *Where did they all come from?* Wonders Jesse.

More keep streaming in toward the front. Jamie is there to help, and so are Manuel, Eric, Devin, and the girls Gloria, Faith, Kristen, and Milagros. As they minister, some dance in the back of the room. Others worship and pray.

The General stands in the doorway, watching the prayer group. His eyes fill with tears.

This group is precious to me. Over the years, I have seen classes come and go through the academy, but these are the dearest to me, especially Jesse, Destiny, and Ruby.

General Eli knows that things are changing, and he is holding on to every last second.

Adonai, what part will I play in this New Era?

Ira comes up to him and puts her arm around her son.

Ira tells him, "I am leaving for the cabin. The hike is not far off, and I need some guidance from the Lord."

She gives her son a firm embrace and kisses him on the cheek.

"Listen to me, Eli, I am so proud of you and what you have done here. Don't worry about me for one second. The Lord has all things in order," she tells him as she turns for the door.

Eli feels a lump in his throat. He walks down and joins in the worship. The closer to the front the General gets, the more the power of the Lord affects him. Love, like warm liquid, flows over him; he feels himself drifting away.

General Eli is on the floor, his eyes shut, and tears stream down his face. He is in a vision of a field of wheat in the midday sun. The mature wheat sways in the breeze. Then he sees Jesse, Ruby, and Destiny swinging sickles. The wheat is popping up into bundles. Next, he sees angels marking credits on Eli's reward record.

One of the angelic bookkeepers comments to Eli, "It's going to be a good year."

Eli feels himself rise in the air. He sees more and more of his students harvesting the field, and the angels continually mark credits to Eli's record.

The sound of Ruby's singing becomes louder in his ear. The images he saw grows dim, and he opens his eyes. Jamie and Jesse are down on the floor, praying for him. Eli surprises the boys by grabbing them and hugging them. Jesse hears the crackle of a fire in his spirit as the General hugs him. He leans back to look at him. It grows louder. Jesse pulls back, and it stops. His heart pounds: the vision of fire shakes him up.

What does this mean? Jesse is taken aback.

Eli kisses the boys on their foreheads. Jesse has flashbacks to Italian movies where the families show affection like that.

Eli tells Jesse, "Look to the harvest, work while it is yet day." It is the scripture Jesse quoted a few months ago, **John 9:4-6**. Jesse feels tears welling up, and he doesn't know why. He wipes his face and shakes it off.

"General, I am sensing fire. Do you know what it means?" Jesse asks.

"Don't be concerned. The Lord has revealed something to me about a blaze of fire. I am sure we will be ready when it comes, whatever form of fire it is," Eli tells him with a grave tone.

"Okay . . . I . . . just wish I knew more," Jesse states.

"When the time is right," Destiny tells him.

More kids need prayer, so back to the business at hand. Jesse and Destiny pray for others as Ruby continues to sing by herself. Steven, Lee, Gabe, and Ray all need prayer.

The festival is ending in Denver, and people leave the stadium yelling, shouting, and stomping. The parking lots are congested as thousands of people return to their cars, honking and yelling at each other. There are numerous fender benders, and the police help direct traffic. The image of Kokopelli is everywhere — on t-shirts, bumper stickers, and posters. All the local news networks feature the festival on the evening news.

The large flocks of birds are still around the SWA campus. It is quite noisy. The prayer rock gathering is over after three hours. Jesse is still trying to make sense of the fire and Eli's words about the harvest.

Is the fire related to the harvest? Is it revival fire or something else?

Jesse will have to wait for the Lord to bring more understanding on the subject "when the time is right." That is Destiny's catchphrase. Tonight is a worship meeting, and Jesse can relax and just be part of the crowd.

Ruby is on the worship team, and she is tired from the prayer meeting. Supper will give her some energy. She also thinks about the days when she was part of the crowd and didn't have any responsibilities for meetings. She is glad about the commitment. The Lord has made her part of the music program, an answer to her prayer last year.

As usual, the General opens up the gathering with prayer. What is out of the norm is that he delivers a small message instead of going straight into the worship time.

The General stands before the school and looks over the student body.

"Beloved, if it were possible with my words, I desire to share my whole heart with you. I have never known such a great company of believers like you. Now is the beginning of a new era, and there are two things I desire to impart to you — a release from the fear of man and that the fear of the Lord will take its place. I decree and declare in the name of Jesus, be free of the fear of man. Holy grippings, the fear of God, which is the beginning of wisdom (**Proverbs 9:10**)."

The General puts his hands out, and a wave of glory runs through the crowd like a breeze.

At that very moment, in the throne room of Heaven, the seven golden lampstands begin to glow with more intensity. The seven colors of the rainbow are present in the flames of the seven lampstands. A blazing red flame shoots forth like a laser beam from the lampstand; it travels at the speed of light; the fire arrives at the sanctuary as the General continues to speak. The intense red stream of light glides across the room and lands on the chest of each person. Everyone begins to respond physically to this powerful touch of the Holy Spirit. Many tumble gently back to the ground. Some shake under this anointing of the Holy Spirit, as the fear of man and intimidation leave them. There is a soft, sweet weeping sweeping across the room.

The lampstand in heaven radiates the light and glory of Yeshua. It is the visible image of God's covenant with humankind found only in a relationship with Yeshua. Finally, the lampstand's colors resume their normal state of brilliance and consistency.

Although no one else is aware of the red light, Aurora and Jamie realize that SWA has received a touch from the very throne room of God. Many will feel the effects of this day for years to come, as they need to fear God above all else.

Ruby thinks to herself: *This is the General's farewell address. He is leaving . . . I just know it.*

She looks around to see if anyone else is thinking the same thing. Everyone seems caught up by the Spirit, so she will have to ask Destiny and Jesse later. It is time for worship. Ruby concentrates on her lyrics.

The worship band sings from:

Isaiah 43:1-2

But now thus says the Lord, he who created you,

O Jacob, he who formed you, O Israel: "Fear not, for I have redeemed you; I have called you by name, you are mine. When you pass through the waters, I will be with you; and through the rivers, they shall not overwhelm you; when you walk through fire you shall not be burned, and the flame shall not consume you.

Afterward, Destiny keeps wrinkling her nose and asking if anyone smells smoke. Jesse comments to the girls, "Did you pick up on the mention of fire and flames in the song? I heard fire crackling when we prayed for the General earlier. I still don't have a revelation of what it means. Eli talked about a 'blaze of glory.'"

Ruby asks, "Who or what is going out with a blaze of glory?

"When the time is right, you will know," she hears the Lord say.

Ruby asks the gang if anyone thought the General was giving his farewell speech. No one picked up on it. No one seems to know what it all means.

The next morning, Jesse wakes up in a thankful mood. He thanks God for the beautiful mountains, his parents' salvation, his friends, his new dirt bike, and everything else that comes to his mind. It is a chilly morning; spring hasn't arrived, and winter still makes its stand on the mountainside. The campus of Spirit Wings Academy, located in the Sangre de Cristo (Spanish for "Blood of Christ") mountain range, is one of the most extensive mountain chains on Earth. It stretches from Poncha Pass, Colorado, in the north to Glorieta Pass, New Mexico, in the south. There are ten peaks over 14,000' high, and more than two-dozen over 13,000'.

Four black wolves run through the campus; this is very unusual. They don't seem to notice where they are; the wild wolves just run as fast as they can. Everyone is talking about it.

At breakfast before the Sunday gathering, an announcement puts the campus in a frantic rush. A forest fire is burning that could threaten the campus. Everyone is to pack for an emergency evacuation that is scheduled to take place in one hour. The fire has consumed approximately one thousand acres to the north and is now moving down the eastern slope. It may be arson.

The usual fire evacuation site is not safe; they need to get farther away. The livestock at the academy mysteriously escapes at night and is gone, along with the chickens.

As the Logans begin to load their old VW van, Eli drives up in his sleek, dark blue, late-model BMW.

The General yells out, "I need to trade you vehicles."

Allen doesn't stop loading his old van with guitars. "No time for joking around, General."

Eli's face is serious.

"No joke. No time to argue; it's best if I drive your van today. Please, just load up and join the convoy out of here. Also, Jesse is on the first bus with his dirt bike. All students accounted for."

He trades keys with the mystified Allen, helps him remove all their possessions from the old van, and drives off in it to be the first in line for the convoy. Allen sees the pop-up GPS display on the BMW's dashboard. It is set for the Spirit Wings resort in Denver.

Dana just says, "Weird, why would he want to drive our junky van today?"

The wind is picking up, and the fire has increased its speed. The Rocky Mountain Area Coordination Center, located in Pueblo, is calling for the evacuation of the area. Eli wants to go up the mountain and get his mom from her cabin with every cell of his being, but he knows he has to lead the kids out. She had told him before she left the school not to worry for a second about her, because the Lord had everything in order. But he did worry; he worried greatly. He tries to call the authorities to tell them she is up on the mountain, but their line remains busy.

Jamie and Jesse have taken two rows of seats out in one of the buses to accommodate luggage, music equipment, and Jesse's fancy dirt bike. Jennifer, Eli's wife, rides on the first bus, calming some of the panicked girls.

Ruby needs help carrying Hope and her portable cage. Everyone's vehicles get lined up to leave, and they head down the road leading to the campground at the front of the Spirit Wings property. Birds and animals are now running south, away from the fire. Jamie drives the first bus. Ruby and the gang are together on that bus, and the

Alvarezes follow behind them. Four buses are behind the Logans. Eastcliffe is also being evacuated.

On the buses, all the GPS are set for Spirit Wings Resort, Denver. Eli instructs all drivers not to stop for anything. He gives his wife a long kiss and leads the convoy in the old VW van. Light snow begins to fall as they drive off the campus. Birds continue to fly, all sizes of birds. Eagles are flying at the highest levels, just dots in the smoky sky. The smell of fire is prevalent now. Jamie begins playing a song over the bus radio to calm the panicked group. It is a song called *The Song of Ascents* **(Psalm 121)**. Herds of elk dart across the road. Just outside the gate, about a thousand feet before the picnic area, several cars are parked on the roadside, and one white van is parked in the center of the road, blocking the passage out. Nathan Fox, the leader of the Followers, is blocking the road in the van. People are standing on the roadside. As the buses get closer, they see the people have wooden bows and arrows. It is a strange sight. The buses line up behind Eli in Logan's old VW van. Kids stand up from their seats and point at the road ahead.

"Get out of the way!" Jamie yells while driving, knowing something sinister is up.

All eyes turn to the van Eli is driving. He doesn't slow down. He speeds up.

Jesse stands up and yells, "The General isn't slowing down; he's going to ram the other van!"

Eli's van slams into the other van, knocking it off to the side. It slides into the ditch and bursts into flames, as does Eli's vehicle. The people on the road stand with their hands on their heads in surprise. The caravan drives through the spectacle, flames, and smoke engulfing Eli's vehicle and the white van.

Jesse cries out, "The General just got himself killed!"

Jamie yells for the kids to get down, worried that the people will shoot their arrows at them. Jamie tries to drive and wipe tears from his eyes.

Using his 2-way radio, he instructs the rest of the buses, "Don't slow down, keep going! Watch out for those people with bows and arrows!"

Birds are flying everywhere, snow is falling, and ashes are blowing; it is surreal. They feel as though everything is moving in slow motion. Overhead, helicopters are heading toward the fires with water and fire retardant. The nurse and Adora hold Jennifer as she cries out in grief.

Meanwhile, the song keeps playing, first in Hebrew and then in English:

> **I lift up my eyes to the hills. From where does my help come? My help comes from the Lord, who made heaven and earth. He will not let your foot be moved; he who keeps you will not slumber. Behold, he who keeps Israel will neither slumber nor sleep. The Lord is your keeper; the Lord is your shade on your right hand. The sun shall not strike you by day, nor the moon by night. The Lord will keep you from**

all evil; he will keep your life. The Lord will keep your going out and your coming in from this time forth and forevermore.

Psalm 121

Jesse doesn't crouch down in his front seat. He stands and watches the flames engulf his parents' old van, and he knows Eli is in it. From the driver's seat, Jamie finally grabs Jesse's shirttail and pulls him down. Everyone is crying and weeping. Jesse looks at his friends inside the bus, their faces full of pain. He grabs the 2-way radio and starts talking.

"Don't cry for the General. He is fine."

Ruby looks at him as if he is delirious.

Jesse continues, "I saw him leave, in a company of angels. They called him General Eli, and there is great joy in heaven. I saw it. He is not burned. He is now under the altar of the Father with all the martyrs. He is in glory now . . . cry because we miss him, or for his mom, who is missing her son. Cry for Jennifer being alone. I'm sorry, Jennifer . . . I'm sorry! I saw him leave. It was glorious. Another man died in the other van. He did not end well."

Back at the accident site, the people drop their bows and arrows and get in their vehicles and flee. The Followers have just lost their leader and much of their zeal for the Summer of Love movement. They were to shoot wooden arrows into the tires of the buses. However, the shock of the death of their leader caused their resolve to fail. Their leader had promised a glorious day of victory, and now he is dead. They begin to flee in defeat and fear of the fire.

When "Song of Ascent" ends, Jesse quotes **John 15:13**: **"Greater love has no one than this, that someone lay down his life for his friends."** Jesse sits next to Destiny, and she weeps in his arms. Ruby huddles with the girls. Everyone sits in their seats, numb, trying to take in what they have just seen. Yosef holds Kristen's hands from across the aisle. Jennifer's cries fill the bus. Snow, smoke, and birds all drift outside the bus's windows, as if in slow motion.

Inside King Abigor's cave, the dark fire king roars in disappointment. Smoke fills the cave, and the king's minions hunker down to escape the wrath of the Fire King.

"This is not at all what I wanted; this is worse! Now the light has gone to Denver."

The king knows his master will rail on him for his failure to bring devastation.

Back on bus one, Ruby changes expression and stands up, facing the direction of the demonic cave. She points her finger, and with bated breath, she declares, "You Fire King . . . Abigor . . . you have been uncovered, and you must leave this area now! Go back to the dry, desolate area where no man dwells, NOW!"

She drops to her seat and trembles.

"We are leaving, returning to Angel Fire, New Mexico," King Abigor announces abruptly.

The king flies out of the cave with his mass of unclean creatures behind him, leaving the dark lair empty, except for a few bats and two large eggs covered with spiders and webs. The eggs appear to have fossilized with no life in them.

The snow flurries begin to fade away as the caravan of SWA buses and cars moves down from the mountain. The sun is shining by the time they arrive in the foothills of Denver, near the resort. It took three hours to drive to Denver. The trip felt as though it would never end. Spirit Wings Resort, with stucco walls and stone edging running along the resort's perimeter, resembles a castle fortress. The outside walls got vandalized with graffiti from the Followers. Kokopelli was painted on them, and the date of the Kansas City tour is MARCH 17.

The resort doors open, and over two hundred souls enter the resort. Gabe's family is also there, as are all the families living on campus. The gypsies and all the academy staff arrive safely with the students.

"So . . . is the campus gone? How about the General's mom? Is she safe?" Jesse and the gang are trying to get some understanding of what just happened. They look around as they step off the bus.

The resort has the same style of construction Eli loved — timber frame and lavish. There are massive posts and beams, plaster walls, large rocks, and pines in the landscaping. The Spirit Wings resort features a half-octagonal shape, wrapping around the pool with a rock waterfall in the background. Eli's personality is evident everywhere in the buildings, which resemble transplants from the academy. The main things missing are the Shekinah Sanctuary and the Academic Towers.

Ira meets everyone on the palatial lawn at the entrance of the resort. A rescue helicopter had taken Ira from her mountain cabin to the Denver resort. No one knew Ira had been rescued until they saw her on the lawn. Jennifer runs to her, and they embrace. Everyone gathers around them. Ira heard all that happened on the helicopter's police radio.

Ira is pale but composed. She addresses the uprooted school. Choking back their tears, everyone huddles close to hear her.

"So here we are, the world goes on, and so do we. I don't have the luxury of throwing a fit and asking God, Why? Not today. This is a day like when the disciples saw their leader die on a cruel cross; they didn't know His resurrection was coming or that all things would be made new, like when Esther saw the threat that all her people could get wiped out. She didn't know her enemy would hang on his own gallows. We are in that place, waiting for all things to be made new, out of the ashes. Now is a time to get out our spots and wrinkles, a time of purifying and introspection, Pride and fear, desire to take charge where Christ should be in command. Thus, we take this time to deal with our pride and fear and allow the candle of God to search out the depth of our souls. We cannot heal others if our spirit is in shambles. Soon we will look outward to the harvest of souls, but today we look to the Christ who dwells in us. The prophecy is: after the fire comes the glory. Well, now we are in a place to receive that glory."

Ira has everyone sit on the lawn, and they pull a cello and a guitar off a bus. Aurora Oliver sings as the instruments play. A plume of smoke rises in the northwest.

She sings:

[46]There is one hope of our calling
One power to quicken our souls
One way unto the Father
Yeshua is the door

Come Lord, how us salvation
Our hearts long to know
Come Lord into our presence
Spirit take control

There is one place of refuge
One rest for our souls
By faith, we stand
Bibles in our hands

We choose to walk by faith

---

[46] Lyrics by Sandy Solis Jan 1996

No doubt can kill our dreams
This world is subject to change
Our God will remain

The sunshine on Ruby's skin is warm and calming. A slight breeze moves the newly grown grass. Everyone is open and real before the Lord. Hope sits on the grass, looking calm over the people.

After a moment of lingering in the grass, everyone goes into the resort with all their belongings. They all slowly check in at the front desk.

Dana and Wanda take Jennifer to a private room and sit with her. The flashing lights atop police cars soon dot the parking lot as the police come and take statements from the adults.

Eric and Jacob look over their new suite.

"We have six beds, laundry, living room, a small kitchen, a phone, and a large screen TV. It is quite nice, but it is not SWA," Eric comments, as the rest of the dorm mates bring in their bags. "Steven and Lee are gone, I guess. No one saw them leave the resort, but they were on the bus with us."

Sadness permeates the room like the smoke in the hills, as Jesse places Ana's quilt on a bed close to the window, and Yosef sets his menorah on his bedside table.

Jesse sits on one of the beds and thinks: *Everything has changed, suddenly without warning. I can't believe it.*

How can this be? How can this happen? Did Steven and Lee leave? Why?

Everyone ponders the same questions and tries to grasp what has just happened.

Gloria helps Ruby get Hope and the growing eagle's portable cage to the new suite. The raptor, restricted to the bathroom, is stripping lots of newspapers on the floor. Ruby can hear her ripping the paper. The TV is on with the news. Images of the fire and the academy burning gets shown without commercial breaks.

"Our beautiful school and the General are gone," says Ruby. "I can't believe it."

The other girls sit in silence except for an occasional sob. Gloria mentions, "Did you hear? Steven and Lee left without a word."

The girls are shocked and worried about them.

Now, in the boys' suite, Jesse is writing his vision down on the resort stationery. The rest of the boys lie on the beds, wiping their tears. Yosef is on the phone, talking to his mom in Israel. Soon, everyone will contact their families and let them know what happened.

Some people wander into the dining room in search of food. Most just drink water or a strong cup of coffee. Dana hands out lavender tea.

Allen is telling Jamie, "I need a cigarette! I really need a cigarette!"

"No, no, you don't, Allen. Just breathe in Jesus . . ." Jamie advises his friend. "That's it, just close your eyes and focus on Yeshua."

Allen closes his eyes and takes a deep breath.

"Okay, that's better, I'm better," Allen admits with relief.

That evening, Ira calls everyone into the large dining room. Large wooden beams angle on the ceiling, giving the room the feeling of a Viking banquet hall. The dining area connects to the lobby, which leads directly to the pool or the wings on either side, housing the suites. The rock waterfall and pool reflect sunshine into the spacious foyer. Eli's touch seems to be everywhere.

Ira tells them, "As you all know, Eli Dylan, my son, Jenifer's husband, the General died today. It seems the Followers had planned to flatten all the tires with wooden arrows, so we would die in the forest fire and leave no trace of their arrows. But God prevailed, and we are safe. Seven arrests were made, including the one who started the fire fifteen miles up the east slope. The campus is in shambles . . . I am sad to say, along with a few homes near Eastcliffe. This is evil at its purest form. Elohim has preserved us, and my Eli went out in a blaze of glory.

Everyone fills with emotion — from fear and rage to great grief.

"We are faced with the choice to love or hate. If we fail to forgive them, the image of our enemies gets formed in us. We will become like them. Love is stronger than hate; Yeshua will give us the grace we need to forgive.

"Now, we are forced to look forward. This is not night; it is still day, and we have work to do. The academy will finish out the school year here at Spirit Wings Resort. Those who wish to leave early can take their exams and go home. As a side note: if anyone knows where Steven and Lee are, let us know. The driver saw them getting off the bus here at the resort. Their parents say they haven't heard from them yet. We are all worried about them both.

"Some of Eli's old friends have contacted me, and we have decided to put on a memorial concert/outreach in one month. Will the following people please see me after we dismiss: Jamie Gerard, Jesse Logan, Ruby Alvarez, Destiny Morris, Devin Simmons, Manual Perez, Gloria Addison, Yosef Wiesel, Aurora Oliver, and Eric Sinclair. Tomorrow we will pick up the pieces."

They pray and disperse.

Ira has several manila envelopes in front of her. There are individual envelopes with names written on them.

As the ten people named approach her, Ira tells them, "I have envelopes from Eli here; he was going to give them out at graduation, but I want to give them out now."

She hands each person the envelope with their name written in Eli's handwriting.

No one opens their envelopes; they take them and hug Ira. It is too personal to open it now; they will need strength to look inside. Mourning for him demands all their energy. Everyone leaves to deal with the dismal prospect of trying to sleep. Steven and Lee are still missing.

Above the resort, the angels assigned to the school are at their new posts. The fire has flushed out all kinds of dark creatures, mainly various forms of fear and confusion; the angels, empowered by the worship earlier, have routed most of the remaining imps. Many angels get sent to the throne room for refreshing. Replacement angels bring with them grace and peace for the weary saints.

Anton is a seasoned angel, and he remains strong and vigilant over Jesse. He can strengthen Jesse and uphold him during this crisis. He looks out across the new territory; in the distance, a thunderstorm is brewing. Anton's partner, the warring angel Hightower, stands his vigil, swinging his sword in a dance of resistance with dignity and solemn composure.

Ruby takes Hope out of her bathroom prison.

How will she find her own food here in town? Ruby wonders.

In no time at all, Hope is eating rodents and a few small snakes from the grounds outside. Ruby wishes Hope's massive, ornate cage could be here. Ruby gets some quiet time watching Hope poke around in the scrubs and decides to open her letter from the General. She is afraid she will bawl like a baby. Inside is a checking account with her name on it, a gold coin, and a short note handwritten by the General.

Ruby,

Compassionate intercessor, insightful, focused, but a bit too fretful, Jesse's armor-bearer, Destiny is her other partner. She breaks up the ground for the seed with song and intercession.

Ruby realizes it is General Eli's notes from her file. Ira or someone must have put it all together. She wonders, *General gave me an account with a thousand dollars in it! What am I supposed to use it for? And the gold coin? How much is it worth?*

Around the coin is a cloth with a scripture printed on it:

> **…the fear of the Lord is clean, enduring forever; the rules of the Lord are true, and righteous altogether. More to be desired are they than gold, even much fine gold; sweeter also than honey and drippings of the honeycomb. Moreover, by them is your servant warned; in keeping them there is great reward.**
>
> **Psalm 19:9-11**

So many questions — *did all the others with envelopes get the same thing? I will ask Jesse and Destiny,* Ruby decides.

Hope and Ruby return to their suite; just the sight of the TV reminds her of the General. So many times, he had turned the TV on and off in the dining hall. Today, everyone is calling home. The phone in their room is ringing. Ruby answers it:

"Hello?"

"Ruby, it's Professor Norman. Are you girls doing okay?"

Ruby says, "Yes." It is an auto-response; she doesn't really know how anyone was doing, not even herself.

"Good. Well, just letting you know we found the guy who made Hope's lobby cage, and he will have another ready in a week. The academy is paying for it."

The professor is stammering a bit. He, too, is still in shock and adjusting to it all.

"That's good news, Professor." Ruby wishes she could say something that would benefit the professor's state of mind, but she has no clue what to say to him.

"Well, we have to get on with business as usual . . . I suppose so. Let me know if Hope needs a supplemental food supply. I am not sure I like her eating city rats."

The professor is worried about how Hope will do in the noisy city.

"Yeah, I guess we should ask those guys at the Wildlife Center for advice," Ruby suggests. "Have you heard from Steven or Lee yet?

"Nope, not a word, I'm sorry to say. We reported them as missing. Well . . . I will call the Wildlife Center tomorrow. Bye," Professor Norman hangs up.

Destiny steps in and looks their suite over.

"I miss the mountains. These foothills will have to do, I guess," she comments.

"How's Jesse taking it?" Ruby asks her.

"He seems obsessed with the vision he had. He needs to believe his own spiritual eyes, it's like he is conflicted within himself . . . Am I making sense?" Destiny asks her as she examines her red, puffy eyes in the mirror by the sink. "Hey, did you get a thousand bucks and a gold coin?" She asks Ruby and Gloria. They both nod solemnly.

The room is quiet. Everyone gets lost in thought. Images of the fire and Eli's crash are etched on their brains. Faith looks at her hands; they are still shaking. They will continue to tremble for several more days. Her mind struggles to make sense of the events of the day. It is just the shock of it all.

The Logans stand in the parking lot, looking at the beautiful car the General left them, and unload the trunk's remaining items. They find the title was signed over to them.

"I can't believe he is gone," Dana says. "He must have known something to give away his car like that."

"I know." Allen puts his arm around her. "I wish Jesse would stay in our suite," Allen admits.

"I'd better go check on Ira and Jennifer. Wanda and I should stay with them," says Dana, gazing at the front doors.

Dana leaves Allen standing, looking off into the distance. After a minute, he shakes himself out of the stupor, shuts the trunk, and goes to look for Jesse. He finds him out back by the pool.

"How are you holding up, Jesse? I know you were close to the General," Allen says, looking at his son's worn face.

"I'm okay, Allen, just trying to wrap my head around it all," Jesse tells him, not lingering for conversation.

Jesse needs time alone to think, realizes Allen.

Allen would like to pull Jesse close and hug him, but they are in an awkward place in their relationship right now, so he resists the urge.

As night falls, everyone finds themselves in their new surroundings. Jennifer requests to be left alone for the night; she wants some solitude to think and process Eli's loss. Everyone else struggles with the events of the day. It's so painful to let go of a great man they all dearly loved, and to let go of their beloved campus. One by one, the lights turned off in the suites as the tired flock of warriors seeks rest.

Clouds are moving in silently except for an occasional wind gust. The smoke from the fire remains off to the south.

Around three o'clock in the morning, a crack of thunder splits the still night. The wind picks up, and sporadic rain begins to fall over the resort. Again, thunder ripples through the night sky, etching a short, crooked line of lightning in the clouds. A bright blue glow flashes, illuminating the storm clouds for a moment, and then is gone.

The grief that still grips SWA has not waned; time's ebb and flow have not yet had their healing effect. Many can't help but wonder why the storm didn't come in time to put out the forest fire.

Jesse finds nature's display of power cruel, as an escape from the pain that sleep often brings is breached by the thunder and the flashes of lightning dancing in the darkness. Jesse looks at Ana's quilt, which lies at the foot of his bed. He grabs it and pulls it up to his chest like a pillow, thinking about the Perez family's loss of their little boy named Rudy. They survived the loss; knowing this, it encourages his spirit to give time its chance to ease the pain. He thinks of Manuel and hopes he is okay in the suite next door. He regrets being so caught up in his own thoughts and not checking on him.

Anton applies a blue light to Jesse's heart; it is a healing balm. Jesse feels a gentle, sleepy feeling that promises rest will soon come.

Ruby's eyes are wide open, and her mind is fully alert. She longs for the dullness sleep puts on the mind. Her spirit is weary as she seeks Ruach HaKodesh's presence in the stormy night.

All the SWA guardian angels seek to minister to their hurting clan. Angels lower down fuzzy blankets saturated with anointing from Ruach HaKodesh on the weary group. [47]**Comfort . . . comfort my people**.

Spring rain typically brings thoughts of warmth and the hope of summer. For this band of believers, the rain brings torment and strain. With songs of love, the Father dances over His little army of warriors. The flock didn't scatter, but remains huddled together in Denver's foothills, except for Steven and Lee.

Aurora feels the Father's love and smiles, "Let men speak of Your good works, Oh God . . ."

Jennifer gets out of bed and stands looking out at the stormy night sky.

"I feel I am going to be alright. Maybe not this instant, maybe not tomorrow, but in time my wrenched heart will know peace once more," Jennifer tells herself. She picks up a little t-shirt off her bed; it is an infant-sized SWA shirt. She holds it out and says, "I can't believe I am going to have a baby." Her voice wavers by the end of the sentence. She is happy and sad at the same time. "Oh Eli . . . I didn't get the chance to tell you the news. I didn't get to tell you . . ."

Jennifer found out that very morning, and she hadn't told anyone yet. Now she doesn't know how to break the news to everyone. For now, it will remain her secret.

---

[47] **Isaiah 40:1**

In the next suite, Ira covers SWA with protection by binding any unclean spirits that creep in the darkness. She sits at the small table by her window. In moments like these, she longs for her long-departed husband. That loss has left a silent longing. As she closes her eyes and leans back in her chair, Ruach HaKodesh begins to fill her emptiness with gentle love and tenderness. She continues with her prayers for the weary flock she now shepherds in her son's place. She realizes Eli and her husband are together now. Someday, they will all be reunited. But for now, she must continue with the good fight of faith without them both. She grieves that Steven and Lee left without saying goodbye. She is concerned they are in crisis somewhere.

Father God tells Ira, "*Eli is still one of My Generals; he sits at My war table. There is new life coming; it will spring forth in the appointed time.*"

Ira weeps . . . it is a bittersweet sorrow, but she finds strength in Yahweh's words.

New life . . . I wonder what He means.

As the morning sunlight warms the mountains' peaks and slowly reaches down to the hills, dampness from the rain lingers at the resort. The clouds have cleared, and birds sing as if everything is normal.

The songbirds wake Jamie up, and he contemplates how life goes on, relentless and steady. His thoughts turn to the others who are hurting. He rushes out to see how everyone is holding up.

Jesse finds himself out of his comfort zone. No prayer rock, no immense view, just pines and foothills, and the mountains to the west. He is wandering around the grounds when he bumps into Ira and Wanda in the lobby.

"Do I call you Prophetess or Professor or . . ." Jesse has more on his mind than he can juggle.

"Just Ira, Rock Man. What is on your mind?" Ira responds softly.

"I would like permission to do a graffiti-style mural over the vandalized front entrance. I don't have a sketch yet of what it will look like, but it will show Eli . . ." Jesse stops talking when Ira leans over and puts her hands on his shoulders.

"Jess, do all that is in your heart to do, for the Lord is with you," Ira says as Wanda and Dana approach them.

Dana hugs Jesse and inquires if he is sleeping okay, all the while balancing a teacup in her hand.

He says, "I'm fine, Mom, really."

She accepts his answer; for now, she is more worried about Ira and Jennifer. Dana greets her with a hug and then says to her, "Enough, Ira. Work will keep. You need to rest. Here I brought you some lavender tea; feel like eating anything?"

Ira drops her head as she takes the teacup.

"How is Jennifer holding up?" Dana asks.

"Jenny is in shock. I am concerned for her," Ira tells her dear friends. "You are right, though, I am *so* tired," Ira says, leaving her pile of papers with Ruben. He deals with the business at hand.

The women, arm in arm, take Ira to her suite and sit with her, comforting her and Jennifer as best they can. Jennifer's family is flying in from England and is due to arrive late tonight.

Jesse tries to pull the dirt bike out of the back of the bus. He is about to drop it when Eric shows up and helps him. Manuel and Jorge come out to the parking lot, and the boys find themselves huddled together and crying.

Jesse suddenly steps back and says, "I gotta go get some spray cans. Cover for me till I get back, okay?"

Jesse kick-starts the dirt bike and speeds off. The boys shake their heads.

"Oh, man, is he crazy?" Manuel looks around to see if anyone saw Jesse leaving.

The iron entry gates open for Jesse, and he turns down the street. The noisy dirt bike streaks illegally to the shopping center a few blocks away. Twenty minutes later, Jesse rings at the front entry gates to get back in.

"Please insert your resort pass in the slot," the voice says from the speaker at the entrance.

"Don't have it on me."

Jesse feels in his pockets.

The man in the front entrance tower steps out of his booth and looks at Jesse.

"Your name, young man?" He has a pen and a pad ready to write.

Jesse stands looking at the vandalized wall.

"YOUR NAME!" the man repeats himself louder.

"Oh, sorry, it's Jesse Logan." Jesse has multiple sacks of spray cans hanging from the handlebars of the bike.

The entry security guard steps into his booth and calls the main desk. After a minute, the gates swing open, and Jesse goes on in. He carries his sacks to his room, the cans clanging with every step. The boys see him come to the suite, drop his sack of cans, and dig for a sketchpad and pencil. He sits in the big chair by the window and gets lost in his work without a word. The guys figure it is his way of coping and leave him to his sketching.

Manuel drops off a sandwich and some fruit for Jesse since he didn't come out for supper.

"Your mom and dad send their love," Manuel tells him.

Jesse jumps up and gives him a bear hug.

"Manuel, you mean so much to me; I just want you to know . . . I . . . um appreciate you," Jesse says, returning to his table.

"Dude, your parents could use a hug right about now, you know?" Manuel suggests, remembering the expressions of worry on their faces from supper.

"I know, but we're not the 'huggy-kissy' type. Right now, I need to get this done. No word from Steven or Lee?"

Manuel shakes his head, "No."

Jesse gives a quick wave and bends over his pad. His resort ID sits on the bedside table, along with the rest of the guys' resort IDs.

Manuel leaves Jesse to his work and his brooding.

At eleven-thirty that night, Jesse is still sketching. All his roommates are in bed, exhausted. Jesse's eyes burn with fatigue. He gets a cold washcloth and wipes down his face.

It is late, but people still gather together. Ira and the women talk in hushed tones at the table by the enormous windows. Most of the men sit on the back deck of the resort by the kidney-shaped pool, surrounded by large boulders. They talk and weep. Wanda's clan grieves the loudest in their Slavic dialect. They cry out on occasion, comforting one another. The waterfall trickles down the rocks into the swimming pool. The sound is peaceful and beautiful, but it's not the same as the scenery of SWA. Blue and green lights change to purple and red in the waterfall and inside the pool as the night lingers.

Jennifer's family arrives at the resort around midnight. Ira and Jennifer greet Jennifer's mum and dad, as she calls them, in the lobby's entry. After hugs and comforting words, Jennifer holds up the tiny baby-sized SWA t-shirt. She starts to cry and laugh simultaneously.

Ira weeps and hugs Jennifer.

Ira realizes the Lord had told her yesterday, "New Life, new life!"

"Eli didn't know; I found out the day of the fire. I never got to tell him . . . I'm a month along," Jennifer tells them amidst her tears.

Her mother from England joins the embrace, "Just you never worry, my dear, Eli knows. Eli knows . . .."

The group goes to the dining room to sit and talk. When the gypsies hear the news about the baby, they inundate Jennifer and her family with kisses and well-wishes. The gypsy's warm sentiment touches the dignified British family and Jennifer.

Wanda shoos her clan away, "Let these people alone, now. They have much to talk about . . . We're going to have a new baby to play with!"

Wanda ushers her clan out.

Down the hall, Ruby dreams in her sleep of birds and ashes swirling around her, curving and dancing, making her feel weary and restless. Gloria wakes her up, "You were moaning," she tells her.

"Oh, glad to be out of that dream, thanks, Gloria."

Ruby looks out of the window at the moonlight. A few pines and a lamppost take the place of the mountain view from her old dorm room. Hope is calm but cramped in the wire dog kennel next to Ruby's bed. Ruby lets her out and sets her up on the bedspread. Hope lays her head down on Ruby's shoulder and gazes lovingly up at Ruby.

"Aw, you're a good bird," Ruby says as she strokes her head.

It will be more than a few years before Hope's head turns white. Ruby falls asleep with Hope, snuggled by her. Sleep comes quickly now. This time, she sees white snow falling elegantly, and the glitter of a thousand diamonds on the ground. Her angel makes sure her sleep is sweet. All he needed was for Ruby's thoughts to get off the fire. Gloria did well.

On the third morning, since the fire, the transplanted group continues to deal with the fact that it isn't a dream. Eli is gone, and so is the glorious campus. Classes resume in a week. Everyone stumbles over to the dining room as news of Jennifer's pregnancy reaches the entire SWA community.

The resort staff has a breakfast buffet ready, so even the SWA kitchen staff is free from responsibilities for now. Jennifer and her parents are eating, along with Ira and Ian. Wanda rushes up to the group, weeping.

"I see a red-headed son, fiery and brave. Call him Eliakim — the Lord rises. The honor of the father's house lies upon him. **Isaiah 22:22**."

All the room fills with her words.

Ruby repeats the name, "Baby Eliakim."

Destiny feels compassion for Jennifer: "Wow, I can't imagine how I would handle it if I were in her shoes."

"Lord willing, you will never be in her shoes," says Jesse.

Jesse stuffs some biscuits and a banana in a plastic sack and heads for the vandalized entrance. It's a little chilly outside, but the wall is exposed to the full sun, so it should be warm enough to work.

He starts painting fire at the bottom of his scene, yellows, oranges, and reds.

Manuel and Ruby are not happy with Jesse's distant ways. Destiny understands him and knows he is handling things his own way. Most conversations are about the Eli Dylan memorial concert.

One large meeting room at the resort gets set up for worship, and others for classes. Ira is on the phone a lot.

As it is their habit to watch world events and news together in the dining hall, a large-screen TV is rolled in and turned to the news channel. There is a feature on the forest fire and Eli.

"The forest fire is eighty-five percent contained on the east slope. The passing snow flurry did little to squelch the blaze. The entire town of Eastcliffe evacuates along with Spirit Wings Academy and surrounding homes and businesses. Unfortunately, the luxury campus is mostly devastated, costing millions. Two fatalities: Nathan Fox, reportedly a leader in the Followers of the Summer of Love movement, and Eli Dylan, the dean of Spirit Wings Academy. Both were lost in a vehicle collision just outside the gate of the academy. The Followers are not affiliated with the Summer of Love Festival. Festival officials made this known yesterday.

"Eli Dylan is known in the music business for his contribution to the Dylan Brothers Band, a heavy metal band popular almost a decade ago. Eli, the older of the Dylan brothers, quit suddenly and dropped out of sight. His brother Ian tried to continue without him but never made the charts as a solo act. Eli was reportedly quite wealthy, but his low profile left him a mysterious figure.

His wife, mother, and brother survive him. A memorial concert is scheduled to take place at Mile High Stadium next month. It is uncertain if it will be a rock concert or Ecclesia event since both his old friends and the academy are involved."

The students looked in amazement at the images of Eli as a heavy metal artist. It is so different from the General they knew. Ruby wishes Jesse were here to see it.

The news story continues:

"The academy Eli Dylan started has relocated for now to the resort he also built around the same time. It's located just twenty minutes from Denver in the foothills. The school was not without some controversy. Even Dylan's death is allegedly a result of Nathan Fox's white van being stopped in the middle of the road during the emergency evacuation yesterday. Witnesses claim Dylan's Volkswagen van rammed into the other van, clearing the road. Due to the fire that swept through the area minutes after the incident, authorities have had difficulty putting together an investigation. Nathan Fox had a reputation for being violent and extreme in his views. A native of Scotland, he had no police record here in the States. Watch for the documentary on Eli Dylan coming soon."

The anchorman goes on to other news.

"So, the General was a rock star, and he has a brother? He never talked about him." Ruby plays with her food as she talks.

"He never even asked for prayer for him or anything." Destiny finds it odd, too.

"Well, the General wouldn't even tell us his name. He was very private that way," Devin comments.

"Just imagine when the press learns about Jennifer expecting, it will be in all the tabloids. Eli would hate that!" says Kristen.

The group nods, their eyes gazing off into thought.

Ruby wishes the others would talk about their letters from the General, but no one offers any information on their envelopes. After breakfast, the gang decides to go out and watch Jesse paint. Grief counselors are now available for the students and staff.

Devin brings his "tunes," and they sit on the grass and watch Jesse's wall come alive. He has moved on from painting the fire, and they can make out part of a van and an outline of a person emerging from the fire. There are also three crosses in the background and a scroll set in the sky with no words on it yet. Jesse doesn't show them his sketch. He is making beautiful swirling clouds of white with pink and purple highlights.

Hope pokes around in the grass.

"Jesse, where did you learn how to paint like this?" Ruby speaks up.

"Aw, you know . . . New York. I watched taggers do it all the time. They showed me a lot."

Jesse barely bothers to answer, wanting to keep up his concentration. He shakes another can of white spray paint. The sound of the spray quickly follows the sound of the ball rattling inside the can. No one says much. Jesse's fingertips hurt, but he is driven and keeps going. Soon, he has the gang cutting stencils out of cardboard for him. They have to keep Hope from shredding the paper — her new favorite pastime.

The man stationed at the entry ignores them for the most part. He sits in his booth, doing word puzzles between opening the gates for people.

Next, Jesse fills in the words of the scroll: **"Greater love has no one than this, that someone lay down his life for his friends" John 15:13.**

Ruby bites her lip, and tears come to her eyes. Destiny wipes tears from her own eyes. The boys pull up grass and make little piles, as they don't want to cry anymore. Hope jumps around and puts her head in the grass piles, making the boys laugh. Jesse stops a minute, then puts his head back and closes his eyes. His arms hurt, his eyes burn, and he is tired of the bandana covering his nose and mouth. Cars start to honk in support as they drive past the entry and see Jesse's mural taking shape.

By noon, only Manuel remains with Jesse. Devin will bring them back some lunch. Several spiritual leaders who used to visit with Eli have arrived and are meeting with Ira. They seem to carry happy energy with them. They hug the kids and joke around with them. One of the men, known for his fasting and prayer vigils, is wearing bunny slippers around the resort.

Devin brings lunch to Jesse and Manuel at the front gates. Jesse chases them both off. He wants to finish the mural alone. Allen and Dana stop by the gates to check on him, and he asks them nicely to let him work privately.

It is four in the afternoon, and Jesse is eager to be done. He is painting Eli coming out of the flames and reaching up to Christ, who stands up from his throne to greet him. The bottom of Eli's clothes is brown and burnt; the top is white and shining. He paints two large silver angels escorting Eli up. At this point, Jesse wipes the tears out of his eyes as he paints. He paints Eli's hair pure white. Lastly, it is signed "Jess" with a little red heart with a cross in the middle. He gathers his empty supplies and heads for a shower.

When he finishes his shower, everyone seems to be somewhere else. Jesse goes to the lobby and sees, through the entrance doors, a crowd gathered at his freshly painted mural.

As Jesse walks down to the gates, he hears sobbing and quiet talking. Everyone is weeping as they look at the mural. People pat him on the back and say things like, "Beautiful, man."

Ira sees Jesse and smiles an emotional smile, tilting her head to the side. She walks over to him and puts her arm around him. He stands with his hands in his pockets.

He tells her, "I saw him go to the place of martyrs, under the altar in the throne room, ya know?" Jesse wishes she had seen it too.

"Jesse, did you see Christ's face?" Ira asks.

"No. It was too bright, just the scars on Jesus's hands and feet. They had jewels in them. He called him General Eli and said, 'Welcome, Heaven is happy to receive you.'"

"Jesse, Eli is also at times sitting at Yahweh's war table!"

"Wow, that must be a great honor," Jesse imagines.

Jennifer sits on the grass in front of the mural. She is weeping and holding tissues, and she begins to rock back and forth, her weeping mixed with laughter. Jesse goes and sits down by her. Everyone is fussing over her in her delicate condition.

Jennifer tells Jesse, "All I could see was my Eli in the fiery crash; it burned into my brain. Now I can see him with the Lord. I can move on from the crash; he is no longer in the fire. He is with the Lord. Thanks, Jesse, for painting your vision. I am free of that awful image at last. I don't want little Eliakim exposed to grief and horror; you have helped a great deal. A blaze of glory now takes the place of the accident."

She grabs Jesse and hugs him, holding him tight. He is frozen stiff in her arms; he finally puts his hand on her back.

Everyone's eyes fill with tears.

As she releases him from the hug, Jesse tells her, "I knew I had to get the images up . . . I couldn't rest until the story of his ascent to the throne room was told. I know it still hurts, but he is in a place of honor, in the middle of God's throne room."

As everyone returns to the resort, Destiny sees Jesse's fingertips are bleeding from being blistered by pushing the spray can triggers. She pulls him to a couch and puts bandages on the blisters. He sits in a stupor, exhausted and sad. Afterward, she pats his hands, and he gazes over at her and tries to smile. She leans toward him, and they kiss their first kiss. They embrace, and then Destiny sends him to get some rest.

The sun sets over the mountain ridge; the evening's coolness prompts everyone to return to the resort together, except for Ira, Wanda, Dana, and Jennifer. They keep looking at the mural and talking as the spotlights kick in for the night.

Jesse and the other students bed down for the night; Jesse's envelope from Eli tucked under his pillow.

The man in the entry booth leaves, and the night watchman takes his place. Steven and Lee are still not in touch with the SWA community.

CHAPTER TWELVE

SPRING FORTH

The next day is warm and sunny. For early March, the air is still crisp, and birds chirp in the budding trees. The Spirit Wings community remains in a state of shock, with no classes yet scheduled. The cadets have no chores other than cleaning their elegant rooms. The guilds are not even operating; everything is in a state of flux. There are some hiking trails behind the resort; many take to walking them in quiet reflection. Word has come from Steven and Lee's families that they are okay. Neither one will tell where they are or what they are doing, just that they are together — somewhere.

The students are scattered all over the place, sitting on rocks and enjoying the sunshine, while some are reading the Bible. Ruby eats breakfast with her family. She notices Jesse is not around. After asking all her friends, she finds Jamie.

"Jesse just called on his dad's cell. It seems he used some of his money from Eli to buy a used street bike and has gone up to see the campus, and he's in big trouble for leaving without a pass. Just because he will be eighteen in June doesn't mean he can run off like that," says Jamie, with worry. (See "Types and Shadows" 12)

"Oh, man, he can be a pain sometimes," says Ruby.

Ruby wants to panic and think of all the terrible things that could happen, but she controls her imagination and goes to find the new prayer room.

Jesse has been on the road for an hour and is feeling exhilarated by the speed. He hits a small rock on the highway, and the bike swerves a little. He can hear his heart pounding in his chest.

Okay, that was close. Better slow down and stay alert, Jesse tells himself.

Every hour or so, he pulls off and walks around. He doesn't want his hands to get too cold and become too stiff to respond quickly enough to drive well. If he has the sun on him, he is warm. He knows it will get colder the higher the elevation.

As he ascends into the mountains, he begins to see signs of the fire, patches of black and hints of smoke trailing off into the sky. The smell of burning grass is still very prevalent this close to the campus. Jesse sees a barricade that says, "Closed to Through Traffic." Jesse doesn't slow down. He goes off the shoulder and around the sign. He dodges fallen trees, but the road is passable. The spires used to hold the Spirit Wings Academy signs are blackened, and the metal eagle remains but is smoke-stained. Jesse stops and walks around. The stone sign with the words "Spirit Wings Academy" is mostly blackened, but it remains in its place. The metal eagle still gazes up at the sky. The four statues are smoke-stained but keep their vigilance on the outer entrance wall.

After all this time, the four creatures are still a mystery to Jesse.

He rides past the bridge gate and can make out the parking lot and parts of the buildings that remain as burned-out shells. All the roofs are ashes, and most windows have no glass. Like an ancient archeology site or the fallen rubble left after the destruction of some war-torn city, high, lonely stone walls remain. Bulldozers and large earth-moving equipment sit to the side where they were used to build a dirt barrier to stop the fire. Jesse takes the side road up to the middle level, parks, and takes off his helmet. He walks over to where the Levi Lodge stands. Below him, the stone stairs remain, connecting one level to the next. A large pile of fresh dirt stands next to it. Jesse sees his prayer rock and cliffs that are behind the campus. He drops to his knees on the dirt pile, grabs dirt in his hands, and begins to throw dirt clods. Tears well up, and Jesse begins yelling and throwing clumps of dirt. He watches the dirt clods burst on the ground, and little pieces scatter in a circle.

"WHY GOD, WHY? SWA was a powerful place. This school needs Eli; I need Eli! WHY DID YOU TAKE ELI AWAY FROM ME?" *This place was so beautiful; now it is a monument to sadness, just blackened stone walls and empty windows. It rained hours later, why didn't it rain in time to save the campus . . . in time to save Eli?*

Jesse lets his emotions go; he yells until his voice gives out, and his arms can no longer throw dirt. His rage turns to weeping.

He stumbles over to his prayer rock and lies face down on it, listening to the sound of his heavy breathing. The warmth of the boulder penetrates his skin, and he begins to feel calmer. A subtle breeze brushes the hair from his sweaty brow. In the gentle flow of wind, there rides a wave of the presence of God that washes over him, then another, and another rush of Father's love. The Spirit comforts Jesse with what feels like liquid love flowing over him. Jesse doesn't move but soaks it up.

Then Yeshua asks him, "*Will you glory in your weakness that the power of God may rest on you*?"

"Yes, Lord," Jesse manages to get out a response.

"*Remember, this world is not your home. You are only passing through. Your safety is in Me, My peace that passes all understanding is within you, as well. In this world, you will have trouble, but I have overcome this world,*" Yeshua tells him.

Jesse lies there on his rock listening and humbled in His presence.

"Now Jesse, get up and be about My business, announcing the Kingdom of Light is here and the good news," the Lord instructs him. *"Work while it is yet day . . . ."*

Jesse sits up and looks over by his bike. A black BMW, similar to Eli's, is parked next to it. Jesse figures his parents followed him up, but then he remembers the car is dark blue. One man stands alone in the parking lot, and his frame resembles Eli's. The man has a golden retriever with him.

Jesse's heart beats wildly. The man bears a strong resemblance to Eli, but with darker hair. Jesse wonders if he is hallucinating.

The guy calls out, "Are you alright?"

He even sounds like Eli.

"Yeah." Jesse manages to get an answer out. "Did you see the whole thing?" Jesse finds his pride violated again.

The man sits down on a fallen wall and nods his head. Jesse gets a chance to examine his face. The dog is friendly. He sits right by Jesse, looking at him and panting. Jesse pets the dog's head.

The man says, "You must have really been upset about losing Eli." The man is a younger version of Eli. It is eerie to Jesse.

"Are . . . you . . . his brother?" Jesse gets up the nerve to ask.

He nods, looking off across the blackened mountainside.

"If you ever need to make things right with people, do it. I said some awful things to Eli, and I never got to make it right," Eli's brother admits sorrowfully.

Jesse gathers his strength and begins to share with him his vision of Eli's death, the redemptive power of the cross, and how much Christ loves him. The man sits and listens quietly, occasionally asking a question, as Jesse shares his heart.

"Would you like to have the same relationship with Jesus, your brother Eli had?" asks Jesse.

"Yeah, I would. It's not too late, is it?" the man replies.

"It's never too late. Jesus is always ready for us to come to Him. Let me pray with you," says Jesse. "All you need to do is ask Jesus to forgive your sins and come and take over your life."

When they finish praying together, Jesse says, "Now you can be sure that one day you'll be with Eli again and both of you can spend forever in the joy of Jesus' presence."

Again, he nods. "I lost my dad also. I was ten."

"Oh, man, I am sorry. I expect your dad is with Eli?"

"Yeah, he got saved on his deathbed, I guess. By the way, my name is Ian. This fuzzball of energy is my dog, Goldie. I will follow you back to the resort if that's okay. But first, you look rather tired. I have a granola bar in the car."

In the parking lot, Ian grabs some snack bars from a bag, pulls a soda can out of a mini fridge from the back seat, and hands them to Jesse.

"I didn't get your name."

"Jesse, but you can call me Rock Man or Rocky, Eli did. I was the only student he allowed to know his real name. He helped me through some tough stuff."

Jesse's eyes well up, and so do Ian's.

"You know, I haven't talked to my mom in eight years," Ian admits.

Jesse has a look on his face that implies he wants to tell him something.

"Jesse, what is it?" asks Ian.

Jesse knows Jennifer should be the one to tell him he is going to be an uncle.

"It will have to keep for when we get to the resort; it's getting late, and my parents are going to be mad."

Ian would have liked to have asked Jesse more questions, but he doesn't want Jesse on the road after dark.

"There is this stone sign over there from Professor Alvey's class; can you put it in your trunk and take it to the resort?" Jesse asks.

"Sure; is it heavy?"

"Not too bad." Jesse points the way.

The Academic Towers are still up, black with smoke. They take the metal stairs, bring out the stone, and put it in Ian's trunk. It says, "For we do not wrestle against flesh and blood." (**Ephesians 6:12a**).

Jesse puts on his helmet, and they drive back down the mountain. They stop at the site where the accident took place. Both vehicles have been towed away. Then they travel the three hours to the resort. It is just getting dark as they drive up to the entry gates. Jesse is about to slide his ID card when Ian gets out of his BMW and stands in front of Jesse's scene painted on the entrance wall.

"Whoa," Ian says, shutting his door and walking onto the grass.

He drops to his knees and sits looking at the scene. The yard lights illuminate the mural, making it stand out.

Again, he says, "Whoa, this is what you saw? Did you paint this?" Ian asks Jesse, his voice strained with sorrow.

Jesse nods.

The guard at the entry says, "Are you guys coming in or not?"

Jesse slides his card through, and the two of them go into the resort. Together they park and walk to the lobby, Goldie trailing behind, panting happily. Jesse imagines the trouble he will be in and the embarrassment of getting chewed out in front of Ian.

The Logans and Ira are standing at the front doors, hands on their hips. When Ira sees Ian, she falls to her knees and just wails. Ian grabs her and holds her. She puts her hands on his face.

"Ian, my son, you look so good to my weary eyes," Ira whispers.

Jesse hands the phone back to his dad.

“We will talk in the morning, son, and you are not to leave the grounds.”

Jesse is disturbed by the worried look on his mom’s face. He thinks: *How selfish it was for me to run off like I did, but I couldn’t make myself say I was sorry. Sorry is a word that troubles me. Uncle Bill said sorry; did that make anything better?*

Dana kisses Jesse on the forehead and goes to Ira’s side. Wanda comes running.

“Ira, Sweetie, your other son has come!” Wanda waves her hands.

All three women and Ian sit on the floor as Ira weeps. Wanda loudly sobs as she is known to do. The sounds echo down the halls. Jennifer emerges from seclusion and sees Ian on the floor with his mother. She smiles tearfully at him. He looks so much like his brother.

Ian gets up off the floor and approaches her. He puts his hands in his pockets and lowers his head.

“I know . . . I said some awful things about you to the press and blamed you for the band's breakup. How can I make it up to you?” Her pain-filled face breaks Ian’s heart.

She responds, “Just stay with us, Ian. Stay with us. We need you here.”

“Okay, sure, if that is what you want. Did you know I found the Lord today on that burnt-up campus? Jesse here led me to Him.” Ian tells her, pointing at Jesse, who is covered in soot.

"That boy is something else," says Jennifer, half laughing, half crying.

Jennifer hugs her brother-in-law.

She then whispers in his ear.

Ian jumps up and down, "I'm gonna be an uncle; I'm gonna be an uncle!"

He hugs her again, and they weep together.

Everyone who sees Goldie wants to pet her. She is a kind dog and likes attention. She brings some much-needed cheer to the resort.

Just then, Hope and Goldie meet. Goldie does her sniffing, and Hope reacts by putting out her wings as best she can. Goldie hunkers down.

"Oh, so we see Hope is the alpha dog!" says Ian.

Ruby is relieved; she feared Goldie would chase Hope.

As evening falls, news spreads quickly that Jesse has visited the campus and brought back Ian, Eli's brother.

Ruby wants to ask Jesse all about his trip, but girls aren't allowed to call boys' rooms after hours. She will have to wait till morning. Hopefully, Jesse is back to his talkative self.

Jesse asks Devin to go over to get him some food; he is starving. Devin tells him, "While you were gone, a news crew came and interviewed some people. Eric was one of them, and they took footage of your mural without asking anyone about it. Hope was quite the hit. They spent a lot of time with her, Ruby, Jennifer, and her, expecting a baby. The news guy said it would be on the morning news."

Jesse tells him, "I don't want any attention for the mural. It is personal and emotional. I'm glad I wasn't around for the interviews. They better give Jennifer respect and not bother her."

"Yeah," agrees Devin.

As Jesse washes his hands and sees the water's blackness in the sink, he knows that a lot of the darkness has also left his heart. The bandages are ruined and need to be discarded.

"I need new bandages," Jesse grins, thinking of the kiss they shared.

The next morning, everyone wants to play with Ian's dog. Ian and Ruben take the carved stone out of Ian's car, wash it, and place it in the corner of the dining hall. Ruben is pleased and looks it over. He rubs his fingers over the lettering, remembering what it was like teaching for eight years at SWA.

Jesse finds that his peace is mostly back. He is eager to speak with Destiny and Ruby. After breakfast, they all go out back to the hiking trails. Students aren't allowed to hike in groups of fewer than three. Many kids are meeting Ian and his well-liked dog.

Jesse steps up to Ruby and puts his arm around her with a little hug.

Okay, this is unusual. Jesse hadn't hugged her but a few rare times. He gives Destiny a tender-eyed look that melts her heart, and they embrace.

"I have to have a meeting with my parents and Ira to see what my punishment is for running off without permission," Jesse tells the girls.

They sit under a large pine tree until the meeting, out behind the boulders of the pool with the waterfall, where some large stones protrude from the hillside. Hope is with them, getting some time out of her cage.

"What did the campus look like?" Ruby wishes he had taken pictures with the cell phone.

"Oh, it is all black. The huge dorms' roofs and windows are mostly gone. There are empty stone shells with window frames, but no glass. Smoke stains jut out the window tops. It is dreary. Shekinah Sanctuary and Levi Lodge suffered the least damage there in the center, with all the cement surrounding it. I saw lots of stone walls standing lonely in the sun, miles of blackened forest floor, with burnt stumps. Did you know Ian has a car just like Eli's?" Jesse wants to stay upbeat.

"I can't believe your mom and dad have Eli's car now," Destiny says with a smile. She wants to get away from the morbid talk, too.

"Why did you run off anyway?" Ruby is the one to ask the piercing questions.

"I just needed to get it all out with God. I was mad, and that's the only way I know how to handle it." Jesse shrugs his shoulders.

Jesse looks at his blistered fingertips and blushes. Destiny smiles and looks away momentarily.

"Didn't your vision of Eli give you peace?" Destiny questions him.

"You would think so, but my emotions don't match up with my mind. Oh, I gotta go." Jesse gets up and dusts off his pants. "I hope I don't get kitchen duty!" Jesse yells back at the girls, and he jogs back into the resort.

Inside, Allen is waiting for Jesse and ushers him into a side room where Ira now has an office. Ira hasn't gone to Eli's office at the resort; she doesn't have the strength right now. She and Dana are waiting for him.

"So, what have you to say for yourself?" Ira asks him, leaning forward on her desk.

Jesse takes a deep breath. "I was selfish, inconsiderate, and irresponsible. I'm sorry if I worried you. And I am still mad that Eli isn't here to keep me in line."

Jesse wanted to keep things casual and wished he hadn't mentioned Eli.

"I know, I know," Ira says, nodding her head. "You led Ian to the Lord. That is something, for sure. I prayed for ten years, and it took you one afternoon, but that's not the point."

She can't help but focus on the miracle of his salvation. She is still somewhat rattled and tends to ramble on in her British way.

Jesse's parents are mostly awkward with parenting and don't know how to handle the situation. They just want

Jesse not to be so unpredictable. However, Allen wants to try and deal with Jesse.

"We have decided you need more structure in your day; consequently, you can help out in the kitchen two hours a day for three months," Allen announces.

"Okay." Jesse drops his head.

"This is not to make you feel shame, Rock Man. It is to remind you that we are a team, and you can't go rogue on us," Ira admonishes him.

"I just don't know the guys that work here at the resort," Jesse protests slightly.

"Sounds like you will get to know them soon. The kitchen staff is expecting you." Ira points to the dining area.

Jesse sees everyone outside in the sun. He imagines himself in a hairnet when he steps into the large kitchen area. Everyone speaks only Spanish, except the head chef, Mr. Sanchez. He introduces himself and assigns Jesse to mop floors.

Okay, God, this isn't funny.

Devin and Eric catch a glimpse of Jesse with a mop. They snicker.

Out in the parking lot, several vehicles arrive with trailers in tow. Ten young men arrive at the resort. They all have British or Scottish accents and know Ira and Ian. Ira and Ian are discussing the upcoming concert with them in a month. They are all friends from their rock and roll days. They are roadies, sound technicians, set designers, stage managers, lighting experts, and special effects technicians. They are the "best in the business." They have come to donate their skills for Eli's memorial concert. Soon they will meet with the worship band and others to start planning the event. They bring flowers for Jennifer. They are loud and laugh a lot. They all react loudly to the news that Jennifer is expecting.

"Oh, Jen-Jen, we are going to be the best step-uncles. We will teach little Eli all we know. We will buy him toys and fast cars and —" says Elton.

"Okay, okay, boys, one day at a time," says Jennifer.

The ten tough guys tear up and give "macho" hugs to each other, softening their voices and getting emotional.

It is quite a spectacle. Wanda and her gypsies chuckle.

Wanda comments, "These are our kind of people, travelers . . ." The other gypsies smile and agree.

Ira has Professor Alvey announce an assembly for that evening to introduce the ten men to the students and staff. They are set up for worship now and can have their first real gathering since the fire.

At lunchtime, Jesse is still on kitchen duty. He has to deal with his pride. Everyone is going through the buffet line, and he is washing dishes. It is lonely with no one who speaks English. The kitchen staff's young ladies laugh a lot, and Jesse is sure it is about him. All the workers smile and are friendly enough. Jesse wonders about the ten guys with accents sitting with the adults. Allen and Dana seem to get a kick out of talking with them. He wonders if they are more of Jennifer's family from England.

Finally, at one o'clock, Jesse is dismissed from the kitchen. "Hasta luego, Jesse," Mr. Sanchez tells him. Jesse gives a feeble smile and runs off to find the guys.

Manuel is waiting for him in the hall.

"Jesse, if I'd known, I would have gone to the kitchen with you. It is only fair. I will get permission to go tomorrow." Manuel pats Jesse on the shoulder.

"Oh man, that would be good! I can't make out anything they say. I know you will really rock a hair net."

"Man, if I have to wear a hairnet, deals off, dude. That's where I draw the line."

Jesse laughs, "No, man, I didn't have to wear one; I'm just kidding."

Jesse feels some relief about working in the kitchen tomorrow.

Ian brings one of the ten men up to meet Jesse. "Rocky, these dudes were our roadies back in the day . . . This grubby guy here is Elton. Everybody calls him 'Weasel,' because he is always weaseling out of things," Ian says with a grin.

Elton has coal-black hair back in a ponytail and a t-shirt that says "Lights, camera, action, -me" on it.

"Ello, mate," Elton greets him with a cockney accent. A fat gold chain about his neck flashes in the light.

Jesse shakes his hand.

"This is my friend Manuel; he is from New York," Jesse says, pointing to him.

"New York, my kind of town," Elton replies with a smile. "Rocky, we saw your artwork on the entry. It made us bawl like babies. Took us a while to get our dignity back; seriously, mate, that is 'eavy-duty stuff. We are quite moved by it. Eli was our mate. We miss 'im terribly."

"Yeah, I miss him too," Jesse tells him.

Jesse is surprised by the man's kindness and candidness in contrast to his rough appearance.

Elton calls out to his mates, "'ey, come meet the guy that made us cry!"

They are a rough-looking crew; most of them have tattoos visible under their long-sleeved shirts.

They shake Jesse's hand and call him "Rocky." Everyone has to have a nickname. Some of them are Porkchop, Pretty boy, Stormy, and of course, Weasel.

Elton tells the boys, "The Dylan boys (Ian and Eli) made us pretty wealthy, they did. Eli led us all to the Lord except for Ian, Grayson, and Brody, here. Brody is a hardheaded Scotsman."

Elton slaps Brody on the back and chuckles. Brody, a bearded redhead, shrugs his shoulders and smiles.

They are all in their early thirties. Brody asks Jesse, "Are you the main speaker at this shindig we are throwing?"

Jesse laughs, "Who me? Huh, uh." He shakes his head and waves his hands back and forth.

Brody seems confused.

"Well, we gotta get Brody ready for the gathering tonight. May take us 'ours to clean him up!" Elton says.

They joke as they walk down the hall, laughing and carrying on. Goldie is with them. Her paws click on the hardwood floors.

The young men have cheered Ian up considerably. There are moments when he will break down, though. Ira, too, has her moments. The whole SWA community is emotional. It has only been five days. Jennifer doesn't come out of her room much, and her face looks worn.

That evening feels strange for everyone to be in a large conference room with steel-framed chairs. The worship team is on the elevated platform with their equipment. Professor Alvey takes the microphone and opens the meeting in prayer. Then Jamie gets up to say a few words.

"Beloved, we are still together. We are a family that doesn't mourn as others with no hope. We will see General Eli again. You may wonder why he kept his name from us; remember, he always said, 'The Lord must increase, and I must decrease.' Maybe he didn't want us to know about his past. I don't have an answer. His friends have come to be with us during this time of loss, to share in this difficult time. Everyone, I want to introduce you to Ian, Eli's younger brother. You know his dog, Goldie."

Jamie introduces the ten guys and explains that they will be the leading force in directing the memorial concert. Everyone gives them applause.

Next, Aurora and the worship band begin, and SWA loses themselves in worship. Ian and the young men look around with wide eyes; this is not what they expected to see at a religious service. Sure, hands in the air are typical for a concert, but kids jerk under the anointing, weep, kneel, and then jump and yell during the fast songs. The guys get a kick out of it. Brody especially looks around, not knowing what to think. Together, everyone worships, including staff, teachers, the young, and the old.

As the last song ends, Ira stands up to talk. Everyone gives her a standing ovation and weeps. She bites her lip and wipes her eyes. Jennifer is now out and attending meetings, with her parents by her side for now.

"Beloved, you have been so supportive of Jennifer and me. I thank God for you. I feel the need to get us focused once again on the eternal. We have an excellent opportunity to share the good news of our good God with the people of Denver. Every Friday night, we will meet to intercede until we have the concert, and the prayer room is open twenty-four hours a day. I recommend everyone make use of it. I need to have a meeting with the worship team, Jamie, Jesse, Professor Alvarez, and, of course, the Ten Horsemen, as they call themselves.

"Classes will resume in just a day or two, and we will get this year finished early. Then Spirit Wings Academy will be closed."

A gasp comes from everyone, and the room turns gloomy. Ira doesn't blink but continues.

"Don't be sad; we are changing due to the urgency of the hour. Jesse told us last summer that the Lord wanted to bring change. We are just now coming to understand. Eli told us this is a new era. Those who wish to remain for the summer and participate in mission work should fill out an application and receive their assignments later in the summer. This resort is now Spirit Wing's home. Many youths will be returning to their own homes and families after graduation. First-year cadets can stay for a little more training, but Spirit Wings is changing paradigms. From now on, this is **S**pirit **W**ings **O**ut**R**each **D**ivision, S.W.O.R.D. for short. Wanda and her clan are now a permanent part of Spirit Wings. They are looking to the Lord for direction and purpose, and where they fit in this new paradigm. I invite each one of you to do the same. I wish to remind everyone again that Aurora prophesied 'after the fire comes the glory.' We will align ourselves to be carriers of that glory, in whatever form that may take."

Jesse looks over at Ruby and then at Destiny. There is a sense of surprise.

All these changes are so fast, Ruby realizes.

"These are the last days, and we must be sober and alert, as Jamie spoke of last fall: '[48]**Servants who wait for their master.**' To avoid anyone else running off unaccounted for, we have planned a trip back to see the campus after the concert is over."

---

[48] **Luke 12:36**

Jesse shrinks lower, but everyone knows she is talking about him.

Ira continues, "I would like to thank all the parents for not being fearful and taking everyone out of school. Eli said the remnant would be true and faithful . . . I am counting on the grace of God and your prayers. Make our ten guests and Ian feel at home, and I will see you all in the morning."

Ira dismisses everyone except those she called to the meeting.

During the meeting, Elton provides everyone with the details of the event. To Jesse's alarm, he gets scheduled as a speaker, along with Jamie. Ian is to be the emcee (master of ceremonies). Elton explains their plans for fireworks, pyrotechnics, lasers, and moving platforms, as well as a balloon release and giant beach balls. They are donating almost everything. Others donated the cost of the stadium and advertising. An Ecclesial TV network is going to televise it live all over the world. Jesse is strangely calm. When Eli prayed for the fear of man to leave, it had worked for Jesse, and he isn't nervous, just concerned that he will say the right thing. Rehearsals start in a week.

After the meeting, Allen is waiting for Jesse.

"Son, let's go for a hike tomorrow so that we can talk," he says, with the kindest of eyes. Jesse remembers when Allen's eyes were always angry.

"Okay, Allen . . . I mean Dad. Sounds good, after kitchen duty, about one-thirty."

After hearing how Ian regretted not making things right, Jesse decided to call Allen dad again. Jesse wonders what his dad wants. He wants to spend some time alone with God tomorrow and wash the street bike he bought to remove the black soot from it.

"See you then, Jesse," Allen says as he and Dana go to have coffee with most of the adults. Allen almost fell over when Jesse called him dad. It is a good step in healing their strained relationship.

That night, Ruby and Destiny discuss which songs would be suitable for the concert and wonder what Aurora will choose. Alex walks up without a greeting and hands them a paper full of song suggestions.

"I don't have the nerve to walk up to Aurora and give these. Would you guys give this to her?" Alex asks, still walking.

The girls nod their heads in surprise.

At lights out, Jesse tells the guys he can't show them his new bike tomorrow because his dad wants to go for a hike and talk.

Manuel remarks, "You have been sort of distant recently. I hope we can spend some time together."

"Yeah, if you want to seek God with me, I have to find out what to say at the concert. They gave me twenty minutes to fill. I can use your prayer support," Jesse tells his dear friends.

"You got it," they all tell him.

The next day is warm and sunny again. Hope is happy to get outside. Ruby walks her around the hiking trails, and Gloria and Faith keep them company. Yosef is teaching Kristen Hebrew by the pool. They are close now.

Manuel gets permission to go with Jesse to kitchen duty. In the kitchen, he chats in Spanish with everyone, and there is a lot of joking going on. Jesse looks over at Manuel, waiting to get clued into the conversation.

Manuel finally does.

"Okay, Jess. They love your piece on the entry wall. Corazon, the chef's assistant, has a brother who is a graffiti artist. Your mural blows him away. Allegra wants to know if you have a girlfriend. I told her Yes, you do. Then they wanted to know what you did to get in trouble. That's about it," Manuel says matter-of-factly.

"Wow, all that in such a short time," Jesse responds with a shy smile as he mops the floor.

An older lady with a hairnet and apron on pats Jesse on the back, and she says in broken English, "Jou are a good boy."

The morning goes a lot smoother with Manuel around.

Soon, Jesse meets Allen out back for their hike.

"Where is Mom?" Jesse asks.

"It's just us guys today, Jesse," Allen says as he puts his arm around him as they start on the trail.

It features rolling hills, not deep forests, but plenty of pines and rocks along the trail.

Allen breaks the silence.

"I feel the need to remind you that we are here for you now. We could have taken you up to the campus if we had known, and you wouldn't have had to spend all your money from Eli." Allen looks him in the eye.

Jesse responds, "I know . . . it was kind of a compulsive thing. I was emotional. I know I'm used to worrying about myself, on my own, and old habits. I didn't want you to see me lose it up there. It was a private kind of thing."

Jesse stops walking and looks up at his dad.

"Dad, I am so glad you are here during this difficult time. There were times when I longed for you two, so bad." Jesse grabs him, and they hug.

Allen is relieved. He feared that Jesse would always be distant from them. They resume their walk.

"It was all I could do to keep your mom from calling the police when you took off. She thought she was going to lose you like Ira lost Eli," Allen explains.

"I called after I left and let you know."

Jesse is surprised at his mom's anxiety.

"Now I know why you borrowed the phone," Allen tells him.

"I will have to make it up to her somehow," Jesse promises his dad.

"Just spend some time with her. Let her know you still need her, that you aren't too old. You are almost eighteen, on the cusp of adulthood. She missed almost five years of your life." Allen's concern for his wife is a new development. Before they got saved, he rarely showed her any consideration.

During the rest of the trail, they talk about what the campus looked like after the fire.

Jesse gets back from the hike in time to wash his bike and show it to his buddies. Then they go in search of a suitable place to pray together. Jesse sees Destiny with the girls on the back deck by the pool. He keeps his eyes on Destiny till they pass the swimming pool, and she stares back. He trips over a potted plant, and everyone laughs. It is good to laugh again.

Just then, they hear someone yell, "Aaaahhhh!" Elton and his friends have just thrown Ian into the pool. By the time it is over, all eleven of them are dripping wet. Everyone gathers around and laughs at their shenanigans. Goldie has joined them in the pool also.

"I missed you guys!" Ian tells them, and then they all start crying and hugging. People just smile and shake their heads. These guys are really something to have around.

"Do we act like that?" Devin asks the gang.

"No, but it looks like fun," answers Eric.

"Ian is nice, but he is not Eli," Manuel comments.

"Yeah, he's not Eli," Jesse chimed in. "I am glad to know him, though, and he needs us to pray that shame will not drag him down."

The boys find a rocky spot with plenty of trees around and settle in to pray. Devin brings the "tunes" like always, and they get down to business. They lay hands on Jesse and ask for revelation and insight.

"Give him utterance," Devin prays.

The mood changes, and prayers turn to spiritual warfare. The boys rebuke the enemy and speak protection over Jesse. Devin rebukes condemnation, which Jesse thinks is odd. He hasn't felt condemnation for quite a while.

Eric sees in the spirit and tells the guys, "I saw a dark cloud. It's small, but it's spinning over Jesse's head. I think it is to hinder you from speaking at the concert."

"Hmmm, that is odd." Jesse doesn't get a revelation of what it is.

It is getting late, and Jesse has promised to eat with his mom at supper, so they go back inside the resort.

Dana is beaming with joy as Jesse sits down next to her at the volunteers' table. She kisses him on the forehead.

"You seem thin, Jesse. Are you eating enough? Are you off your iron pills?"

"The nurse said I don't need iron anymore. She said to have it checked every six months for a year."

"I have some great essential oils here in my purse for you, dear." Dana starts digging in her purse.

"Mom, that's okay. I am fine," Jesse urges her. Allen glances over at his son.

"But if you think I need it." Jesse changes his tone.

"Here it is!" Dana holds up a small brown bottle with a label on it. Jesse takes the bottle and reads it, "Frankincense."

He looks at his mom and twists his head. "Like frankincense, gold, and myrrh? What does it do?"

"It is an old remedy from ancient times. Just drop some on your pillow at night. See here; it has the Jewish word for HOLY on it, 'Kadosh.'" Dana points to the Hebrew word.

Jesse sniffs, "Smells okay." He puts it in his pocket. Jesse figures it is a "hippie" thing. She also likes organic food.

Allen informs him that it is anointing oil from Israel.

"Cool." Jesse feels better about it.

That night Jesse forgets to anoint his pillow with the oil and leaves it in his shirt pocket.

The boys can hear the ten young men running down the hall with Goldie and Ian.

Ruby and Destiny get the rest of the girls together for a quick prayer session.

"Let's pray for Ira, Jennifer, and Ian," Gloria suggests.

Ruby feels the Lord wash over her.

The Spirit tells her, "*Tell Jesse it is not his fault.*" Ruby wonders, *WHAT'S not his fault?*

She waits, but no answer. They finish praying and go to bed. Sleepiness overcomes Ruby. She is the last one to go to bed. The lights are to go off at ten p.m., just like on campus. Ruby doesn't wait. She turns them off because everyone is telling her to turn off the lights and go to sleep. Milagros has already fallen asleep. All the girls seem to be frazzled lately. Ruby attributes it to the trauma of losing Eli and the campus.

Jesse's room is dark already. Devin's earbuds are loud, and Jesse can hear a faint "bump, bump" of a bass beat from his bed. He prays till sleep overtakes him.

In his dreams, a shadowy snake-like figure comes up to his face. It has red eyes and talks with a hissing sound.

"It is your fault, you know . . . Eli would be alive if you had prayed. The hot flame and crackling sound you sensed that day was a call to prayer. You missed God. You are a miserable excuse for a prophet. Failure, fool, faker! Eli could still be alive if you were a good servant. [49] Unprofitable servants like you get cast into utter darkness for the millennia. You are worthless . . ."

The figure starts wrapping around Jesse's leg, then Jesse wakes up.

Jesse sits up in his bed; his heart is pounding. He remembers the fire he sensed in the Spirit that day. Jesse falls back down and pulls his pillow over his face and weeps bitterly.

---

[49] **Matthew 22:13**

What if the snake was right? Did I miss God? Could I have made a difference?

Eric stirs from his sleep and hears Jesse.

"Are you alright?" He leans up on one arm.

Jesse stops weeping and tries to get his composure.

". . . just mourning over Eli, I'm okay now."

Jesse hopes his voice doesn't sound too strained.

"Okay, man. Just think about your vision. Everyone else finds comfort in it."

Eric wonders why Jesse doesn't find solace in his own vision.

After everyone else leaves the suite for breakfast, Jesse gets up. He stares in the bathroom mirror at his reflection and almost sticks his tongue out at himself, but refrains. In his mind, he looks awful, with bags under his eyes.

"I have to talk to Jamie," he tells his reflection.

He walks out the door.

Manuel is waiting for him, but Jesse doesn't let him speak and walks by him, then Jesse turns back.

"Gotta go, I will see you in the kitchen later, okay?" Jesse mumbles.

Manuel shrugs his shoulders. He knows there is something definitely wrong, but he can't put his finger on it. The Lord tells Manuel not to push the issue and just to let Jesse go on. Manuel sighs and walks into the dining room for breakfast. He sees Jesse and Jamie leave out the back by the pool.

Jamie and Jesse don't talk. They walk out to the trails and sit down on a park bench behind a group of thick pines.

Jesse starts to shake. He leans over to Jamie and cries on his chest.

Jamie puts his arms around him and pats him on the back.

"What's up, Jess?" Jamie knows it is more than sorrow over Eli's passing.

Jesse tries to tell him, but the guilt grips him, and he cries too hard to speak. He is mad at himself, angry at the emotion pouring out of him, and mad that he didn't have the foresight to know to pray for Eli concerning the fire he sensed in the Spirit.

Jamie tries to seek the Lord to hear what he should do to help Jesse. Images of Eli driving into the white van and catching fire flash through his mind. He, too, begins to weep. The two remain there, huddled together, crying.

"We are a sad sight." Jamie laughs, half crying.

Jesse nods, doing the same.

"I am sorry to stir up all this emotion for you, Jamie. I am just dragging you down with me."

Jesse is trying to get a grip on his sorrow.

Jamie leans back and looks into Jesse's eyes.

"All I know is the enemy doesn't want you and me to speak at the concert. God is faithful. He will get us through this."

Jamie is reminding himself as well as Jesse.

Jesse takes a deep breath and wipes his face with his shirt collar. He looks at Jamie with the saddest eyes. He didn't expect things to go the way they did, and he doesn't know what to do. The two rest there on a bench, gazing sullenly off into the distance.

Jesse and Jamie turn their heads to see Ruby and Destiny coming down the path toward them. Ruby has a determined look on her face. The girls walk as though they are on a mission. Jesse and Jamie just remain there, engulfed in gloom, watching the girls approach.

Ruby steps up to Jesse, lays her hand on his chest, and says with forcefulness, "It is not your fault."

Jesse's eyes get big. He takes a quick breath and looks in her eyes. She begins to pray and rebuke demonic forces. Destiny does the same to Jamie. Waves of glory wash over the guys.

"Whoa," Jamie responds as a strong touch of the Spirit hits him like electricity.

Jesse feels a force on his face like a shield of protection. It runs over his head and then down his body. His feet begin to get hot, and he shakes them.

In the Spirit, Ruby is pulling the shadowy snake off Jesse's feet. Hope has been following the girls and just catches up with them, then the eagle squawks and flings her wings, jumping and carrying on. Jesse hears a terrible hiss and holds his ears. The shadowy snake jerks violently, and he sees an eagle in the Spirit fly off with it in its beak.

Jesse has his eyes closed and his hands still over his ears. Destiny shakes his shoulder.

"Oh," Jesse looks up and smiles sheepishly at her.

"I heard the snake-like thingy scream too, but it is gone now," says Destiny, looking tenderly at him.

"An eagle —" Jesse says, pointing up with his thumb.

"I know Jess, I know." Destiny keeps her hand on his shoulder.

Manuel arrives and sees the group gathered under the trees. He walks up to Jesse and gives him a hand up from the bench. He begins to give Jesse a word in the Spirit.

"Arise, be strong, and have good courage. Trust Me with your whole heart and [50]lean not on your own understanding. [51]My ways are higher. My thoughts are higher than yours; look for the joy that awaits you. I still see the warrior and the prophet. It was good for you to go to the mountain and work out your anger. Even in your rage, I was with you. The fire has come; glory is coming, look for My glory." (See "Types and Shadows" 12)

He turns on his heels and addresses Jamie.

---

[50] **Proverbs 3:5-6. Trust in the Lord with all your heart, and do not lean on your own understanding. In all your ways acknowledge him, and he will make straight your paths.**

[51] **Isaiah 55:9 For as the heavens are higher than the earth, so are my ways higher than your ways and my thoughts than your thoughts.**

"Beloved, the Lord would say: I am your counselor and guide. I will not leave you desolate or in want. I am your provider. I will never leave you or forsake you; be of good cheer. Your prayers have more power than you know. Do not draw back. I enjoy Our time together. The glory is coming; I will release glory upon the earth."

Manuel's voice is strong and forceful. He reaches his hand and pulls Jamie up to his feet.

"Thanks, guys," both Jesse and Jamie say at the same time.

Everyone chuckles at their combined response as they all return to the resort.

Dana is standing at the entrance to the pool. "Jesse, you need to eat."

Jesse looks at the time. He has to report to the kitchen for duty. "Okay, Mom. I will grab something in the kitchen, promise."

Allen pokes his head in the kitchen, where Jesse is putting on a chef's smock.

"Did you remember to anoint your pillow with the oil?" Allen asks his son, looking at the bags under his eyes.

"Oh, man, I forgot." Jesse reaches into his pocket and pulls out the anointing oil.

"Well, it works better on your skin and mixed with prayer; also, it represents Ruach HaKodesh, you know. I just learned that this week," Allen says, feeling Jesse and Manuel know more than him.

Allen waves and steps back out of the kitchen's swinging door so Jesse and Manuel can get back to work.

The boys are looking for the chef as one of the older ladies sees Jesse. "Jou need to eat. I get jou good food."

The hefty Spanish woman gets out her own lunch and opens it for him.

"Tortillas, frijoles, e pollo (beans and chicken), eat . . . eat." She holds it out to him.

"Oh, man, homemade tortillas. I am homesick." Manuel bends his head back and looks up with emotion.

Another woman goes back and gets her lunch, pulling out tortillas for Manuel.

"Here, mijo." (My little boy, Mi+Hijo, my son, slang in Spanish, pronounced: "me hoe")

Professor Alvarez steps into the kitchen to check on the boys and sees them sitting and eating all the Mexican food. He begins to chat in Spanish with everyone. They all laugh and talk cheerfully. Manuel tries to translate for Jesse, but there is too much to keep up with, so the boys just sit and enjoy the food.

The mood of the conversation changes as Eli's name is mentioned. The women wipe tears from their eyes. Eli was their employer, but he was also revered and loved by the staff at the resort. Jesse sees they have the same passion as the gypsies.

The chef comes from the large freezer and sees everyone talking to Ruben. He smiles and sets down a tray of frozen vegetables.

Ruben discusses having a Mexican meal for Resurrection Sunday.

"Four hundred homemade tortillas will need to be made. You will need to hit up every Spanish market in town," says Ruben to the chef as he pats the boys on their shoulders and then leaves them to their kitchen duties.

At lunch break, Ruben returns with pizza for the kitchen staff.

"Since you gave away your lunches to the boys, I thought I would return the favor and feed you!" he tells them in Spanish. They are quite happy with the pizza, saying it is something Eli would have done.

Manuel and Jesse thank them for their kindness and put their aprons on the hooks.

"Freedom!" the boys say as they leave the kitchen for the day. Manuel wants to be outside, and Jesse needs to start his notes for his speech. They both sit out on the park benches behind the big rock fountain that surrounds part of the swimming pool. Almost everyone is out there. The grass is growing now, and spring bulbs are in bloom, with the jonquils and daffodils — little clumps of yellow and white — contrasting with the bright green grass. Hikers can often see deer in the foothills behind the resort. Birds chirp, and the mosquitoes are out.

"*Life goes on,*" thinks Ian, as he sips his tea on the pool deck.

By now, everyone refers to General Eli's old friends as the "Ten Horsemen." They are all in Ira's office, along with Wanda. They come to her office to see if there's anything they can do for her.

Wanda and Ira begin to prophesy over them and minister to them.

"Elton, you were mistreated by your classmates, and you are still looking for approval. God loves you and accepts you," Ira tells him.

"Brody, you think you must work for God to love you. He loves unconditionally. He wants you to draw close and know Him; go boldly to the throne of grace," Wanda exhorts Brody.

Elohim touches the young men, but Grayson (nicknamed Pretty Boy) remains unemotional. Some have visions, others — encounters. They spill out of Ira's office, sniffing and tender-hearted, and hug everyone they see, staff included.

They see Ian and grab him.

"Aye, mate, you need to feel God's presence, too," Elton tells him.

Ian is resistant. He is uncomfortable with his mom being a prophetess, and it scares him.

Grayson tells Ian, "They will make you cry, dude. I don't want to cry."

Elton finally convinces Ian, and they all flood back into Ira's office. The power of God hits him, and he melts with emotion. He receives healing over the death of his father from when he was ten. Grayson, for now, has kept his composure and stays aloof.

They call Ira Mum with respect. It will help fill the void of losing Eli just a little.

Ian finally experienced what his brother tried to explain to him.

"It's a relationship, not a religion," Eli used to tell him.

"I have spent all these years resenting Eli leaving the music business and the band for God. Now I get it."

Ian and the Ten Horsemen walk out into the evening air to sit on the pool deck and talk about the Lord. Jamie joins them, along with Allen.

Jesse, looking on, says, "And that makes thirteen horsemen!"

"They sure have a lot in common," Ruby adds as she walks by, taking Hope back to her cage in the suite.

Hope's new cage is due to be installed in the main lobby tomorrow. Ruby worries that Hope may not feel happy in the new enclosure.

Devin, Eric, Manuel, Destiny, Gloria, and Faith join Jesse in the lobby for some small talk. They hadn't talked much since the campus fire.

Manuel, Jorge, Alex, and Trisha all have cell group meetings with the rest of the newbies. Some things are getting up and running again.

Classes will start in the morning.

Many wake up to the sound of metal and power tools. Hope's new cage is getting installed. It is just as impressive as her old one, with wrought iron craftsmanship at its finest, very ornate and decorative. It has some real branches for her to perch on and plenty of paper to tear up and make a nest. The sound of the waterfall now greets everyone in the main entrance.

Jesse will not have kitchen duty till after classes at three p.m.; Ira made the change so that he wouldn't miss class.

Concert rehearsals start at six o'clock in the evening; they have one week until the memorial concert. The Ten Horsemen recruit students for their crews.

Elton (Weasel) - lighting effects
Grayson (Pretty Boy) - pyrotechnics
Liam (Porkchop) - hydraulic stage lifts and moving platforms
Percy (Brody) - sound
Geoffrey (Stormy) - stadium screen displays, videos
Winston (Churchill) - security
Nigel - parking lot guides
Hugh - (Ugh) moving equipment for bands
Sean - t-shirts and CD sales
Austin - publicity and advertising

Between all these groups, everyone has a part in the concert. It's like having the guilds again, with everyone putting all their energy into the work.

That evening, everyone sees Austin's TV ad on local Denver networks. It shows images of General Eli from old concert footage and pictures of him as the school's dean. Worship bands will play, along with two secular bands. The secular bands are both Called Out Ones but not known as worship bands. "Free to the public." The ads are state-of-the-art with 3D animation and effects. Everyone gives Austin applause; he stands, grins, and bows.

Jesse looks at Jamie, and Jamie looks back. Jesse wonders if they are ready to speak to thousands of rock and roll fans about Christ, not to mention live TV.

Hope scratches around in her new cage, enjoying the fresh newspaper and perching on the branches. The stone water feature trickles off to one side.

CHAPTER THIRTEEN

MILE HIGH

The morning of the memorial service rolls around all too soon. The weather is pleasant enough, in the sixties and sunny, with no wind. Every team receives its corresponding t-shirts and ID passes as the secular bands arrive and start rehearsals and sound checks.

Ruby has butterflies in her stomach, but Jesse is calm. He is just concerned that the Lord will make him weep in front of the crowd.

That morning, everyone gathers in the lobby where Professor Alvey leads a brief prayer to ask Yahweh to bless the day. Hope is happy to look out of her new cage at everyone standing there among the plush couches, a grand piano, and a stone fireplace.

"Adonai, we align ourselves with your plans and purposes for this day. Give us the strength to perform Your good pleasure. Help us to walk in love, and may Christ be seen in us today. As we honor General Eli, may You be honored most of all," prays Ruben.

Certain groups, wearing matching t-shirts, board the bus and will spend the day in preparation. Others will not go to the stadium till later in the day. Spirit Wing's buses shuttle everyone back and forth from the stadium.

By five p.m., Ruby and the gang step off the bus, looking around; many others are already at their posts. Gloria and Kristen are at a table selling t-shirts by one of the interior doors leading to the seating area.

Sean, a dignified Brit, has set up the tables on the perimeter of the inside, and they are ready to sell T-shirts, albums, glow sticks, and other items. One of the t-shirts features Eli's picture, along with his birth and death dates. Another shows the school's logo, which depicts wings with praying hands underneath. The text says, "Got Wings?" Another one has **W**arriors **IN** **G**ods' **S**ervice on it. On the back are scriptures on prayer. Proceeds go to a new fund – **S**pirit **W**ings **O**ut**R**each **D**ivision. (S.W.O.R.D)

"We can hear you guys from here, so we are pulling for you," Gloria tells Ruby and Jesse.

"Yeah, don't embarrass us!" Kristen says in jest. She is adorned with every neon glow item they have for sale.

Ruby grins at her; her stomach is still in knots.

As Destiny, Ruby, and Jesse look inside the seating area, they notice TV cameras with long booms set up to record the concert. Outside, media buses park in front of the stadium.

By six p.m., the Bronco Stadium is filling with people. It is an open-air stadium that replaced Mile High Stadium in 2001; it has undergone several name changes.

Ruby finds herself on stage with Aurora and the worship band. She glances out from the three-level platform. A digital light panel runs across the back of the stage, resembling a TV made up of individual lights. Stadium Jumbotrons display "**S**pirit **W**ings **O**ut**R**each **D**ivision presents Eli Dylan Memorial concert." She looks out at the full house of the three sections of seating. It is filled with noisy chatter and clamoring from the crowd.

The worship band begins and ends the concert. Jesse and Jamie will speak between the headlining bands.

Ian's voice echoes as he announces, "Welcome to the Eli Dylan Memorial concert, here at Bronco Stadium at Mile High!"

Jesse hears the crowd roar as they stand to their feet.

"Some introductions are in order. I am Ian Dylan, your humble announcer for this event." He bows with a grin. "I wish to thank you for coming to honor my brother, Eli."

The crowd whoops and yells from their seats.

"Now, I wish to give respect to my mother, Eli's widow, Ira Dylan, and Jennifer Dylan," Ian points them out.

They both hesitate to stand but get to their feet and smile feebly.

The crowd jumps to its feet to give a standing ovation to them. Ira and Jennifer try to smile, feeling the crowd's respect; it was a special moment for all of them.

As the great stadium settles, Ian continues. “Now, my peeps, let’s settle in to hear the mellow sounds of Aurora Oliver and the SWA worship band.”

Aurora is calm and collected, as are her musicians. Ruby’s hands shake as she sings, but her voice is clear and in control. They sing a song about life as a shadow.

The crowd raises their hands and swings them back and forth to the music. The song’s words are displayed on the Jumbotrons and video boards dotted around the stadium. It appears that about half the crowd are lovers of Yeshua.

After the first set of worship songs, the footage of Eli and a short biography are shown. The crowd screams with delight at the footage of his concerts. His face is animated and playful on stage. He sang of being disillusioned with life and regrets. The songs were mournful and moody, topping the charts for five years straight in the past. They then show how the band never regained prominence and how Eli dropped out of the public eye. Next, footage of Spirit Wings Academy being built is shown. Lastly, photos of Eli with students, laughing, and being silly are shown. The last footage is of his school staff photo, and the dates of his birth and death.

The screen fades to black as the simple sound of a bell echoes. Lights dim on stage. Then, the low tones of stringed instruments play a moody melody. A single spotlight expands to reveal Aurora at a grand piano. She plays a simple piece and begins to sing; the strings and bell continue as part of the song. (See "Types and Shadows" 13)

She sings a tribute to General Eli:

"How long has it been since,
You have been gone?
Can't remember you not being here
Just out of reach, your face lingers in my mind
See you on the other side
Next time we meet, there will be no tears to cry
This is not goodbye
You were good, and you were kind
You never said, "I don't have time."
You took us in and showed us the way
You showed us what is good and what is right
You taught us to fight
This is not goodbye; see you on the other side
See you on the other side

Aurora plays a simple melody, and the music fades out. She looks up from the piano and gazes up. The entire crowd and the SWA community choke with emotion.

A massive balloon release sends thousands of white balloons into the evening sky. Silence lingers for a moment, and then the event continues, as they press on as the last few balloons disappear out of sight.

Ian emcees the rest of the concert with superb professionalism. He enjoys the spotlight, but it doesn't go to his head. The Ten Horsemen make sure of that from their many positions in the stadium. Next, a headline band comes out. Ruby sees the famous singers pass by her casually to get on stage.

From where Ruby stands behind the stage, she can see the fireworks, puffs of smoke, and columns of fire shooting up. Electronic synthesizer music breaks the silence with a heavy bass beat. The crowd screams with delight when the special effects go off, synced with the sounds. It is a refreshing spectacle. The band sings about being ready for the afterlife.

Images of Eli appear on the giant video screens and video boards between sets, along with footage of his life that Geoffrey has compiled. Next, the worship band returns to play softly without vocals, as Ian introduces Jesse.

With his long hair and t-shirt, Ian is casual as he announces to the crowd, "You are in for a treat. The speaker who is coming out to address you is a dynamic young man. He paints murals, rides dirt bikes, spent several months on the streets of New York, and lived to tell about it. He knew my brother well, and he is a godly firecracker, to say the least. Denver, I give Jesse Logan, the Rock Man."

Jesse walks out and stands in the middle of the stage. He reaches into his pocket and pulls out the gold coin Eli gave him. He flips it in the air and catches it. The massive video screens display a close-up of the coin spinning in mid-air; the sound of a bell ringing reverberates on the sound system. Jesse stands on stage alone wearing a plain white t-shirt, jeans, and motorcycle boots. He starts his speech.

"Let me tell you about this gold coin. When Eli's mom left for her cabin before the fire, he gave her his notes on all one hundred seventy students at the academy and the gold coins he was in the habit of giving out to a select few who were graduating. She took them, prayed over them, and anointed them all. As she got airlifted out during the fire, she had a clear enough head to grab the files and coins, and she took them out with her. If you have never met a prophet, you should meet her."

Jesse talks in a casual voice. The crowd screams at the mention of a prophet. Then they are quiet and still, listening to this young man standing alone on stage.

Jesse holds out the coin.

"I know you want to hear about my time homeless on the streets of New York. I can only say no matter how deep the pit you dig for yourself, Yeshua can pull you out. General Eli helped pull some deep junk out of my soul. He was there for me, and I trusted him. Eli wanted —" he gets choked up, and you can hear a pin drop. He tries again.

"Eli wanted me to have this coin. It is one ounce of pure gold. I have yet to learn its value. He gave me something more valuable. He was instrumental in leading me out of bondage. Through the power of Jesus Christ, he delivered me from rejection, depression, rage, self-hatred, and more than I care to list here tonight. I serve the living God. Our frailties touch him."

The crowd whoops and hollers in agreement. Jesse waits for them to get quiet again.

"At the end of this event, Jamie will allow everyone to lay down their lives to Christ. Jesus can clean up your foul mouth or dirty mind, stabilize your emotions, and get you off drugs, pornography, and even video games!"

The entire stadium chuckles.

"He can heal your torn-up heart, calm your raging anger, give you peace, and rain on your dry places. Even change you on the inside so that you like yourself. He can preserve you blameless before Him at His coming. Darkness is coming, and we need to connect to Yeshua in a real heart-to-heart connection. Religion will not give you peace when your world falls apart under your feet. His sheep know His voice; do you know it? Can you hear His voice? This world yells at us every waking hour. What do you have in your life that crowds out His voice? He is speaking; are we listening? He is speaking of His love for us!"

"This is His earth, and He will reign forever. Israel is His people, the glory is His, and the honor, dominion, and all power of Heaven and earth are His."

The people clap, standing in praise.

Jesse finishes his speech.

"The blood of Jesus, the redemptive power of the cross, and His resurrection on the third day all speak of one fact. God, the Father, the Son, and Holy Spirit love you with an everlasting love. Night is falling, beloved, and we will all be questioned about one thing: what did we do with the love of Christ?"

Jesse flips his coin up in the air again. The video boards show a coin flipping slowly through the air; the ringing sound effect echoes as the coin's slow-motion image appears on the massive screens all over the room. It is very dramatic and moving.

Jesse catches the coin. His last words to the crowd are, "**For what does it profit a man, to gain the whole world, and forfeit his soul?**" **(Mark 8:36)** He turns and waves to the crowd and walks off stage.

Destiny and Ruby are waiting for him. They hug him as the crowd applauds enthusiastically.

Ian tells him, "Well done, Jesse the prophet . . . well done."

As Ian goes back out and introduces the last headlining band, he high-fives Jesse. Soon, Jamie will wrap up the concert. Prayer warriors are placed down in front of the stage, ready for the call for salvation. As the lights dim, the band sings about looking for angels. The last of the special effects is released. The lead singer stands on a platform that rises straight up. He grabs a zip line, steps out on it, and flies off the platform. The line brings him down to the floor while he sings the whole time. The people in the stands go wild. When the band finishes, the crowd applauds loudly with whooping and yelling. The lights remain dark, and the stadium becomes quiet.

The video wall displays a scene of the cross, and the video boards replay the coin toss as Ian introduces Jamie. The sound effect of the coin ringing plays again.

Ian tells the crowd, "This guy you are about to meet is an ex-cult member. He came to Spirit Wings Academy to cast spells and instead became totally given over to Adonai. Jesse and others led him to the Lord, and now he serves the Living God. This . . . is Jamie Gerard."

Jamie walks boldly to the center stage runway. He paces as he talks, using his hands. The worship band plays in the background. Ruby stands ready to sing at her cue.

"There is no doubt that these are the last days." Jamie begins with fire in his eyes.

The worship band plays a moody, dramatic instrumental. The electric guitars are playing a soulful melody. In the background, the ring of the coin-flipping gets heard all over the stadium.

Jamie continues. "Our eyes must be open to discern the times and seasons, or we will be found unworthy. Yahweh desires a people who have on their wedding garments, their lamps lit, and they have their swords in their hands. Watching and waiting for their Master."

Ruby sings, "[52]**For the creation waits with eager longing for the revealing of the sons of God**." A violin joins the song, and then a drumbeat of war.

Jamie walks to the edge of the stage, and cameras zoom in on his face. The video boards show Jamie's face all over the stadium.

He looks serious and says, " 53 We need to be people who abide under the shadow of the Almighty, who are engaged with heaven, gazing on the face of Yeshua. As in Noah's day, there is a place of safety. That place is a habitation of watching and prayer."

The beat picks up, and Ruby sings, "Whoa, whoa, whoa."

Many in the crowd are weeping. Others close their eyes and raise their hands. Jamie quotes a scripture:

> **"... [54]that the creation itself will be set free from its bondage to corruption and obtain the freedom of the glory of the children of God. For we know that the whole creation has been groaning together in the pains of childbirth until now. And not only the creation, but we ourselves, who have the first fruits of the Spirit, groan inwardly as we wait eagerly for adoption as sons, the redemption of our bodies. For in this hope we were saved. Now hope that is seen is not**

---

[52] **Romans 8:19**
53 **Psalm 91:1**
[54] **Romans 8:21-25**

hope. For who hopes for what he sees? But if we hope for what we do not see, we wait for it with patience.

Ruby sings his words, "We wait . . ."

Jamie continues. "The great question is: who has stored up the word of God, and His Spirit in their belly and knows the Living God on a personal basis?

"Luke 21:34-36 says,

But watch yourselves lest your hearts be weighed down with dissipation and drunkenness and cares of this life, and that day come upon you suddenly like a trap. For it will come upon all who dwell on the face of the whole earth. But stay awake at all times, praying that you may have strength to escape all these things that are going to take place, and to stand before the Son of Man."

"In our nation, we need a wake-up call. We need to know God sincerely, not just know about God. It's time to get real and lay down our plans and agendas and take up Yeshua's.

"I Peter 4:7-11 is my conclusion; heed it well for it is the power of God unto salvation.

"The end of all things is at hand; therefore be self-controlled and sober-minded for the sake of your prayers. Above all, keep loving one another earnestly, since love covers a multitude of sins. Show hospitality to one another without grumbling. As each has received a gift, use it to

serve one another, as good stewards of God's varied grace: whoever speaks, as one who speaks oracles of God; whoever serves, as one who serves by the strength that God supplies—in order that in everything God may be glorified through Jesus Christ.

To him belong glory and dominion forever and ever. Amen."

The sound of a bell ringing is played, like the sound of Jesse's coin.

Jesse walks out and joins Jamie. They are both wired with wireless microphones now. Jesse addresses the crowd:

"[55]We are fake. The world says we need worldly products to be beautiful, but I say we need God to like the reflection in the mirror. The world says we must be ourselves, but I say we need to be more like Jesus. Everyone is being beaten down in this world but isn't saying a word. Life is more than money, clothing, and other worldly things. It's a test, a journey, and even a battle. But it's not something you can sleep through, which is something most people are doing. Sadly, people don't recognize that life is a gift. That life could end in a second. We must realize we are here to bring God glory, not ourselves. I see such wonderful talents wasted on people who use them to bring themselves money or fame. Talents

[55] Jordan Solis-Barnes March 2010

are gifts given by God. They were given to us to bring Him glory. So stop, everyone! Stop wasting your breath on yourselves. You should breathe for God. He is the One who made you; He's the One that felt your pain. He's cried your every tear. But you choose the world over the most beautiful thing in the universe! What kind of fool are you? So why would you choose to live a worldly life; because it's easier? We have been like a foolish child disobeying its parent. Only a fool despises a parent's discipline. Whoever learns from correction is wise. So reach for God's hand, for He's the only one that always stands and never falls. The way of the Lord is a stronghold to those with integrity, but it destroys the wicked."

Jamie urges people to come forward and seek the Lord. The front security barricades get moved, and people now have room to meet the prayer warriors in the front. The worship band stops playing for a moment as everyone who wants to come up for prayer makes their way up.

Jesse and Jamie have everyone stand quietly before the Lord. At that moment, you can hear a gentle breeze. Then Jamie says, "Cry out, cry out to the Lord."

First, you can hear a few girls going, "Aaaah!" Then everyone cries out, and the Spirit moves across the stadium. As the crying out to the Lord mellows, Ruby feels it is the right time to start her song.

A simple piano chord progression plays, and Ruby begins.

I know your pain

I know your grief
I also know just how it feels
When love runs deep

I'll take your pain
I'll take your grief
I died that you might have life
Cast your cares on Me
Just one more step
And you'll be home
See how the Father
Leans from His throne
All that you need is coming down to you
So take it now; I'm here for you
You have My love,
Now go in peace, go in strength

Just one more step
And you'll be home
See how the Father
Leans from His throne
All that you need is coming down to you
So take Me now; I am here for you

Ruby's voice is soft and quiet at the end. It echoes through the stadium but feels intimate.

Ten thousand are led to discover the Lord personally. Others get a new intimacy with Him. Still, others go into intercession for the first time. It is almost midnight before all the people have cleared from the building, and the cleanup crews take over.

As Jesse and the gang get on the bus to go back to the resort, Devin comments, “Do you think anything will top this in our lives?”

Destiny has an answer.

“Let’s see; how about signs and wonders, miracles, the rapture, the marriage supper of the Lamb, the triumphant return — Need I say more?”

Devin replies, “I stand corrected.”

He grins, knowing all of that. He just got caught up in the grandeur of the evening. The stars are brilliant back at the resort, where there are fewer lights, and the gang stands outside the resort, looking up at the night sky.

Faith breaks the silence with, “Even so, Lord Jesus, come.”

Aurora walks up to the group and tells them, “I think the glory after the fire is coming soon, in the least expected place. I am sure it will manifest in all of us. The glory of God contains all we need for the last days. You all are to be carriers of that glory.”

The gang stands, taking in her words; it impacts their very cells. There is another shift in the spirit realm.

Jesse manages to say, “After the fire comes the glory.”

“Yeah, the fire purified us, and now we can be glory carriers,” declares Destiny.

“I just wish Eli were still here,” laments Jesse.

They all agree. Steven and Lee have mysteriously left the fellowship, and no one knows their whereabouts. Everyone feels sadness for them, too.

"The memorial service was a powerful expression of the Kingdom of Light. In the future, I think things will continue to grow in intensity, both the wheat and the tares all together till the end," Ruby finds the boldness to speculate.

Jesse flashes on the name "Nimrod" and sees a fallen angel with downturned horns on his head. Jesse's face shows his confusion.

The gang lingers, thoughtfully reflecting on the day's events.

Ruby tells the Lord; *I don't even know who the 'tares' are.*

Ruach HaKodesh tells her, *"All in good time, My bright and shining one . . . all in good time.*

Wheat and tares, the term presents a new mystery to uncover. A deep and delightful game the Spirit plays, teaching the secrets of the Kingdom to those who have the heart to run after Him.

Ruben comes up and says, "It's been a long day; why don't you all retire to your rooms for the night?"

He hugs his little girl and tells her, "I am so proud of your singing in front of an estimated forty-eight thousand people tonight."

"I got lost in the Lord, and I was fine. The anointing was thick, like no other; I have felt before," Ruby says, being invigorated by the night's events.

Her mom kisses her, and the tired group meanders to their suites.

Jesse comments to the guys, "Eli's death brought the salvation of ten thousand, not counting the ones who are watching by TV and the internet."

Devin responds, "Yeah, Truly, truly, I say to you, unless a grain of wheat falls into the earth and dies, it remains alone; but if it dies, it bears much fruit **(John 12:24).** I miss him."

"Me too." Jesse still has a deep pain in his heart.

Jesse knows the ache will reduce in time, and he will see Eli in eternity. However, at this moment, sadness fills his core.

The weight of General Eli's loss, combined with the reality that their beautiful campus has been destroyed, impacts all of SWA, even on this night. With mixed feelings, everyone deals with the pain in their own way.

Jennifer is alone in her suite in a rocking chair. She sings to her unborn child, "You are strong, you are gentle; you are all that Yahweh designed you to be."

As the gang walks through the lobby, someone is playing the "Song of Ascents" (**Psalm 121**) on their violin. Ruby thinks of the Holocaust survivors and how they mourned for their lost loved ones.

"Save Israel, Lord, remember Your people," she whispers as she steps into her suite. The rest of the girls are preparing for bed as Ruby hears the Lord tell her, "*Look in the book you are reading by your nightstand.*"

It was a book Ira had them read for class. She loved the book's imagery and insight, so she will reread it to keep her mind occupied. She opens up randomly and reads: [56]"But remember; love is My greatest weapon. Love will never fail. Love will be the power that destroys the works of the devil. And love will be what brings My kingdom. [57]Love is the banner of My army, and under that banner you must now fight."

---

56 *THE FINAL QUEST* by Rick Joyner, 1996, page 58 http://www.morningstarministries.org/ (used by permission)

57 **Song of Solomon 2:4 He brought me to the banqueting house, and his banner over me was love.**

CHAPTER FOURTEEN

A NEW SONG

The next morning, Jesse is waiting for Destiny and Ruby before breakfast. He is in an exceptionally good mood.

"Let's go for a walk!" Jesse grabs Destiny and Ruby both by the hands and heads for the front door.

"Before we eat? The trails are in the back?" Destiny says, pointing to the other way.

"The Lord said to come out here this morning. He said He would meet us here; that's all I know," says Jesse, with a spark in his eye.

It is nine o'clock in the morning, and they have just missed breakfast, and worship is starting inside the resort. Ruby is anxious that they will be in trouble for standing out on the street. Jesse doesn't want to leave. He feels the Lord standing there. They end up sitting in front of the mural and seeking Adonai. Destiny is relaxed and seeking God, but Ruby is looking back at the resort where the gathering is about to start.

Are they having trouble without her backup vocals? We are missing Resurrection Sunday service! Concentrate . . . Jamie is walking toward us. Is he sent to make them return and go to service? Are we in trouble? Being out here is all out of my comfort zone.

Ruby gives up praying and waits for Jamie to walk out the front gate.

The man at the front gate seems to ignore them, neither asking for their ID cards nor looking their way. He opens the street gate for Jamie without even an acknowledgment. Jamie smiles and sits down with them, and brushes Ruby's red-brown hair out of her eyes. A passing car honks.

"Aw, Ruby, much is on your heart. You are the watcher and protector. Jesse is the driving fire, Destiny is the wind, and you are the earth," Jamie tells them.

"Dirt?" Ruby doesn't like the analogy.

"Earth," Jamie continues, "refers to the soil, the soil of the hearts that you tenderize with prayer and song before Jesse ever gets to them. You go before with prayer, as an armor-bearer. Destiny stirs up his fire, and the three of you go hand in hand. [58]The threefold cord is not easily broken," says Jamie, watching the cars drive by. (See "Types and Shadows" 14)

More cars honk as they drive by on the street. Many people have the habit of walking on Sunday mornings. Now people are stopping and gathering around the mural. Soon, many people gathered at the resort's front entrance. Before they know it, Jesse and Jamie introduce people to Yeshua, and Ruby and Destiny are praying for others.

At noon, Ira stands on the other side of the gate, watching what is going on. She motions, and the man in the booth opens the gate.

"Oh, this gate business is not needed. You can just leave the gate open. Go on home, Joe; I see your nametag there. I dismiss you from this post."

"But boss . . . I need this job!" the man replies.

"How about something in mall security? I will give you a reference," Ira suggests.

The man grabs his lunchbox and puzzle book and walks home, complaining all the while.

Ira smiles at everyone standing outside the gate and invites them all in for lunch. She tells Jamie and the gang, "You have been about the Master's business, I see."

---

[58] **Ecclesiastes 4:12**

About twenty neighborhood people follow Jesse and the gang up the sidewalk to the resort. The newcomers join everyone in the dining hall. It's Resurrection Sunday, and a meal with homemade tortillas is on the menu.

Gloria asks Ruby, "Where have you guys been? You missed the whole meeting!"

Ruben leads everyone in Communion before the meal begins; there is no time to answer her: a violin and a harp play in the dining room.

"We had a memorial service for Eli yesterday; today, we remember Yeshua's suffering on the cross with bread and grape juice. If you have not made Yeshua Jesus your savior, please pass on taking communion."

He instructs one person from each table to take the long loaf of bread and hold it over their head.

"[59]This represents Yeshua's body broken for us; do this in remembrance of Him." Ruben addresses the SWA community and their guests.

At each table, a person breaks the bread in half and takes a piece for himself, then passes it for others to take a Piece until everyone has a portion.

Ruben announces that Yosef has his Communion declaration in Hebrew. Yosef stands with his loaf of bread and splits it, saying, "Baruch Atah Adonai, Eloheinu Melech ha'olam, Sh'hecheyanu, V'Kiyemanu, V'Higianu LaZman HaZeh.

---

[59] **1 Corinthians 11:24,25**

Ruben has the translation written on paper, and he reads, "Praised are You, the Eternal One our God, Ruler of the Cosmos, who has kept us alive, sustained us, and enabled us to reach this moment."

Then Ruben says of the grape juice, "[60]This cup is the new testament of His blood; we drink this in remembrance of Yeshua." He holds up his beautiful goblet.

After everyone has a piece of bread, they begin to eat the bread and drink from the goblet.

Wanda stands and says, "I remember what You did, Jesus, how You got rejected by Your own people and suffered outside the gate."

Dana stands and says, "I remember You, Jesus, how Your thirty-nine stripes were for our healing."

Ruben invites everyone to remember the work of the cross and thank Jesus personally.

The room fills with prayers of thanksgiving to Christ.

After the Communion, the head chef, Mr. Sanchez, informs everyone about the Mexican dishes they are serving. The kitchen staff are very proud of their culture and happy to share it on this distinctive Sunday. He also tells them that there are hot and mild versions of the dishes. The kitchen staff has the day off to spend time together and fellowship with the Spirit Wings community. SWA

---

60 **1 Corinthians 11:24,25**

kitchen staff take their places for the rest of the day.

Manuel, Jorge, Ruby, and Milagros especially enjoy the great flour tortillas. "Just like mom makes," Manuel says in between bites.

The spicy hot food makes Ruben sweat. He wipes his brow and keeps on eating. Ruben's sister, Adora White, has to laugh, seeing her brother eat like he did back home when they were kids. Manuel comments that his dad and all his uncles sweat the same way when eating spicy food.

Ira is eating with Ian and the Ten Horsemen. An empty seat is left in memory of Eli. Next to them sit Jennifer and her parents. Yosef remembers how his family always leaves an unoccupied seat at Passover. Allen and Dana sit with Jesse, Ruby, and her family. Jesse is looking over at the empty seat when Ruby sees him choke up a little. He shakes it off and goes on with his meal. Ira decides to make it so that everyone can sit together, rather than having twenty-five small tables, but instead, one large round banquet table. She is making changes; she feels Eli would approve of them. It brings her strength to carry on.

After the meal, Ira takes Jesse and Jamie for a walk. They are curious about what she wants from them. She leads them down a path that is closed to the public. It is a narrow path that leads down to a small canyon area, featuring a wall of rocks and a small natural waterfall.

Ira motions for Jesse to sit by her on the rocks and talk.

"I know how you loved SWA and your prayer rock and Eli. This spot is where I go for solitude. I hope you will make this your prayer rock as well. I will leave you two boys so that you can have some quiet time with the Lord."

Ira smiles and climbs back up the small trail. Jesse admires her so much; she is tough, kind, and wise.

Jamie drops to his knees and begins to cry to the Lord.

"Abba, (modern Hebrew for dad) I need You, I need Your guidance and clarity. I let things steal my peace. I get in fear, and I am not as strong as I thought I was. I fear the future; I have no direction. Losing General Eli is just so hard."

Jesse spreads his arms out in the beautiful place Ira showed them.

"Jesus, I feel empty inside. Our lives have no direction; I have no strength to help anyone else. Jamie and I realize how much we need You."

Jesse joins Jamie on the ground. He feels the warm rocks and hears the gentle sound of the waterfall. They spend several hours alone with the Lord getting refreshed.

As Jesse and Jamie start to walk back to the resort, they hear the sound of a guitar playing and singing. They shut the small barricade that says, "No public admittance." Everyone is around the pool singing. Some talk; others pray together. The mountain range to the west has a bluish hue with patches of snow on the upper peaks, and to the east are Denver's skylines, high-rises, and buildings. Jesse finds it odd to always see both the Front Range and the skyscrapers of the big city. The weather is warm, but snow can still show up.

Hope is happy to be out of her cage. The locals from dinner come to watch her jump around in the grass and eat the fresh fish Professor Norman got for her holiday meal. Goldie comes to smell her fish. Hope screeches and flares out her wings. Goldie yelps and runs backward. Everyone laughs. Hope continues to eat her salmon with piercing eyes. Goldie sits close by Hope and takes a nap.

That night, Ruby looks out her window that faces west toward the Front Range. The night sky is brilliant with stars. She used to look at the stars all the time when she was little.

She has a lot on her mind.

Just a few more weeks of classes, and everyone will graduate. I'm only fifteen; I won't turn sixteen for four months. Destiny is nineteen, and Jesse will be eighteen in June. Manuel is older than me, but Alex is younger than him too.

She was homeschooled before joining the academy and is ahead of most kids her age in public school.

I'm worried that Destiny and Jesse will run off and have adventures without me. Destiny's family is coming for graduation from South Dakota. I wonder what they are like, missionaries for India.

Ruby feels sleepiness sweep over her, so she crawls into her bed. Everyone else is already in bed. She looks at her nightstand. The worship album from the Eli Memorial Concert is there. She flips it over and tilts it to see in the little light from her clock. There is her name and the song she wrote and sang, *Just One More Step.* She is a published singer and songwriter — *Cool.*

Sleep is generally sweet. Some students still have bad dreams of the fire and Eli's accident. Others watch for wildfire alerts on TV and radio before they go to sleep.

Ira no longer has the luxury of solitude in her cabin on the mountain. She has a youth ministry to run, ten English men who need mentoring, and an expecting daughter-in-law. Her plate is full, and Prophetess Ira feels satisfied with her new state of affairs. Although she weeps for her son Eli, she consoles herself that it is, "See ya later," not "Goodbye." She has Ian back in her life, and he is now a disciple of Yeshua.

Jennifer is getting her strength back and is ready to put a nursery together. She smiles on occasion and leans a lot on Ian and Ira. Jennifer's parents promise to return in December for the birth of baby Eli. The Ten Horsemen are making a unique handmade crib for the baby. It promises to be oversized and ornate. "But very functional," Elton assures her.

A grand piano and a harp are in the main entrance past "Hope's Landing," where Hope can greet people if she chooses. **S**pirit **W**ings **O**ut**R**each **D**ivision will have someone playing all hours of the day and night at the resort, just off to the side of the check-in desk. Anyone can sit and pray or read in this unique lobby. They call it "The Soaking Room." Ruby thinks she will try to memorize enough songs to do a two-hour set someday.

Destiny and Jesse are signing up for assignments at S.W.O.R.D. after graduation. Ruby has yet to sign up.

Two buses will take students back to see the burnt campus today. Some do not want to go, and they stay at the resort. The others take the three-hour drive up to the mountains. Ira asks Jesse and Jamie to join the trip and counsel students, helping them deal with the campus's sad state. Jesse dreads the trip but promises Ira he will go.

Jamie isn't driving today, and he sits with the gang on the bus. Ruben is driving.

Jamie tells the gang, "I think the cadets will cry and say goodbye to a life they've come to love at Spirit Wings Academy. We lived for several months without electricity or fuel; yet, we transformed into a thriving, productive community with a marketplace, learned to trust the Lord for the basics of survival, and grew together as a body of believers. It was a special place, like no other in the world."

"Yeah, we learned real survival skills. We have formed friendships that will last throughout our lives, I think," Jesse adds. "I remember the first day I saw the campus; it blew me away. I heard Yeshua speak to me like a casual reply! It was life-changing."

Eric and Devin sit, grasping the notes in their envelopes from Eli; they have never read them yet. They are going to wait till they get back up on the mountain. Destiny and Ruby go just to support Jesse. Ruby did not especially want to see the campus in its burned condition. She wants to remember it the way it was. But for Jesse, she will go and deal with the ruins.

Boys sit on one side of the bus, girls on the other. Jesse is in a quiet mood now.

Destiny is thinking: *It is going to be a long three hours if Jesse isn't talking.*

Ruby sees his expression and gets his attention.

"Rocky, what's on your mind?" She can be blunt with him. Destiny still can't talk to him like that.

"Last July, in the dorms, when I yelled about night coming, work while it is yet day. I still don't know how we can wake up multitudes of people, and what exactly our work is. Jesse needs reassurance that he is on track with the Lord's will.

"Jesse," Destiny tilts her head and speaks kindly to him. "When the time is right, you will know . . . The Lord doesn't reveal everything in your timing. Just wait and let Him tell you in *His* time."

Jesse looks down at the bus floor, thinking. The rumble of the engine is loud, and the ride is bumpy.

Ruby reaches across the aisle and taps him on the shoulder.

"You know the time is short. You are not asleep, as some are. You are ready for the Master."

Jesse nods, but his face still expresses tension.

"Yeah, I know. I just don't want to waste time on things that have no eternal value, you know? Jesse looks at the girls with a serious expression.

"Jesse, you are so intense at times. Relax and mellow out a little," Destiny advises him.

"I'll try."

Jesse leans back and looks out the window of the bus. He remembers hitchhiking to get to SWA almost two years ago. Jesse should be glad about how much he's grown in the Lord, but instead, he feels the need to strive for more. He still has unknown darkness to unearth. It is starting to wear him down. Jesse looks over at Jamie, who is weeping openly and causing others to cry. Ruben keeps patting him on the back and comforting him from behind the wheel.

Eric tells Devin, "Jamie is not going to be much help on this trip; he is crying more than anyone else."

"At least he doesn't cry in his sleep like *someone* I know."

"I do not!" Eric defends himself.

Devin just smiles and gestures with his hands, "I'm just saying . . ."

Eric kicks him, "Okay, just give a guy a break."

"Owe! Okay, okay, sorry," says Devin, rubbing his shin.

They drive past the picnic area and then the accident site, and everyone gets quiet. The bus stops at the portcullis. The spires on the side have been washed by rain and are grey again; however, the brass eagle on the sign is smoke-stained and hanging sideways. After a short moment, they head on up to the main campus. The road was cleared of fallen trees; the blackened mountainside is just burnt tree trunks lying over in various directions. The parking lot still has debris on the sides and piles of dirt where firefighter equipment had been used to create barriers to stop the fire from spreading. The equipment Jesse saw on his visit has been loaded up and moved.

Ruben cuts the engine off. Everyone stands up and looks around. One by one, they step out and wander about the parking lot. The dining hall and dorms are roofless, with stone walls and glassless windows. A few burnt-out car bodies and metal structures are recognized. Ruby feels her hands start to shake a little, and Destiny leans over on Jesse's shoulder. Ruben begins to tell Destiny, "No public displays of affection with boys," but changes his mind. They are almost adults and graduating, after all.

No one is allowed to walk in the blackened places. There are already strips of grass starting to grow back, with some wildflowers poking through the black earth. Devin takes pictures, including a close-up of the flowers blooming in the burnt soil.

Manuel says, "I remember the smell of fire. You can still smell it here."

Jesse looks for anyone who needs prayer. Everyone seems calm and walks around sadly, except Jamie. He has a bandana over his mouth, and tears run down his face. He shakes his head and murmurs, "No, no."

"Let it go, man, just let it go," Jesse tells him, expecting Jamie to be like him and go into a raging, angry fit or something. But Jamie is not wired like Jesse; he is affected differently. Ruby and Destiny lay their hands on his back and pray for him.

"I remember the spells I used against this school before I got saved, Jesse. Prayers of destruction." Jamie's eyes fill with concern.

"Oh, you pulled me through this phase already, Jamie. You are not responsible for this fire; you did not do this. You confessed it; you moved on. You renounced your old life, and the blood covers it, Jamie. Don't lose sight of the power of Christ's blood." Jesse holds Jamie's shoulders and shakes him gently.

The demonic attack is over. The smoky demons of condemnation ran at the mention of Christ's blood. The love of God washes over Jamie, and he jerks slightly as the power of God hits him. It is as though he were in a dream, and he just woke up.

"Wow, that was a heavy attack. I didn't expect it," comments Jamie. "I'm glad I talked to you about it and didn't keep it bottled up inside."

"Yeah, the enemy did me the same way, out of the blue." Jesse takes his hands off his shoulders. *I still keep things bottled up; it's better to bring stuff out, but I even fail to talk things out with my friends.*

Destiny and Ruby are so busy praying for Jamie that they don't notice he is okay. Jesse taps them on their shoulders, and they look up.

"Oh, okay then," says Ruby, looking up. They begin to worship the Lord for freedom from bondage. Soon everyone on the trip feels praise in their hearts. Jamie gets his guitar off the back of the bus and sits down to write a song.

Everyone sits around him and listens. Ruby echoes his words on his chorus, and she blends with him on his verses when he finishes writing.

They sing his new song:

[61]When I look into your eyes, I see Your glory.
And when I see Your face
The past just fades away
No matter what they say
You'll always stay the same
    You are beautiful
    You are beautiful
Oh Father of the Heavens look down
upon Your children
We are hungry for Your glory
    Your beauty fills the air and
    Everywhere I stare
        You are beautiful
        You are beautiful
    Oh, and when I feel scared
    Your comfort overwhelms my heart

---

[61]You are Beautiful, Jordan Solis-Barnes 2010.

And when I don't know where You are,
Your comfort is still over me
Oh, my Glorious King,
Come rain down on me
Let the world fade away,
Because You're all I want to see
Let myself decrease, and You increase
That's how I want it to be
Become more real to me,
My beloved King
Let Your love consume my heart
and soul
Let myself fade away and
You come into view
    You are beautiful
    You are beautiful
And though the world may say
You cannot live this way,
I will always live for You
This world means nothing now,
Because I have seen Your crown,
My beloved King.
    You are beautiful

Destiny and Jesse are gazing into each other's eyes intently. Some of the kids intercede on behalf of the people of Eastcliffe. Manuel is feeling grieved and interrupts the singing.

"How can you sing that? Your beauty fills the air, and everywhere I stare. We are totally surrounded by blackness and destruction, right now.

He is surprised by his own anger.

Jamie puts down his guitar.

"Manny, all around is blackened forest, but in my heart, the little flowers are popping out of that blackness. I feel newness and hope and peace." Jamie pats his chest as he talks.

"I just — got overwhelmed by the destruction of it all. This place was so special, so beautiful, now it's gone," Manuel says, looking around, his voice wavering with emotion. "It's like the Devil is throwing it up in my face. 'Look what I did; I destroyed this place.'"

Jesse and the boys lay hands on him and pray that he can see past the devastation around him. The wind changes direction, and the smell of smoke blows away from them. Drops of gentle rain begin to fall in the parking lot. Manuel has his eyes closed; he begins to smile and raise his hands.

A cool breeze comes up, and it begins to rain.

Everyone lumbers onto the bus; some have handfuls of wildflowers. Devin takes pictures of people holding flowers in their hands. Eric teases him that he is obsessed with flowers. The rain is gentle, almost cleansing. The lightning in the distance only flashes occasionally. It rains for the entire three hours back to Denver.

As they enter the resort, the sound of the piano and a singer greet them. Hope is content in her cage, watching them pass by into the lobby. Several people give Ira and Jennifer the wildflowers they picked. Jennifer is going to press them in a book to preserve them. (See "Types and Shadows" 11)

At the end of April, the Ten Horsemen are still around; they will soon be off to do concerts all over the world, but they decide Spirit Wings will be their home base. They adopt Ira and Jennifer as their extended family. They finish the unique crib for baby Eli, carved from oak with a canopy, reminiscent of Viking design. It must be put together inside her suite and is quite heavy. The wood is varnished smooth as glass, and the side opens without a sound. Doctor Luz approved it as baby safe.

Ian also stays by his mom's side and is there for Jennifer and the coming baby.

Everyone thinks of last April when the Great Terrorist Crisis happened, and then about the earthquake. The time has gone so fast. Graduation in May will not be the same at the resort as it would have been on the mountain, but it is graduation, nonetheless.

During the summer, Jamie will be taking a group of workers to help build houses for a few weeks in the earthquake zone, also called the Great Breach. Others are doing inner-city outreaches.

Destiny and Jesse seem to be busy being in love.

Ruby feels dull inside. She watches Manuel and Alex hanging out together and feels a sense of jealousy. Her thoughts turn to a happier subject. She has a thousand dollars to spend, and Ruby feels she should spend it on something meaningful, not just clothes or a down payment on a car. Her dad wants to put her gold coin in a safety deposit box, but she wants to have it to look at and think of the General.

The newbies did not get to hike the summit and have Ira prophesy over them, as is the academy's tradition. Instead, Ira is getting S.W.O.R.D. set up. She sets up a prophecy room at the resort, where people can sign up and receive a prophecy. She is also setting up dream interpretation and healing rooms. The resort part of Spirit Wings remains in business as well, so it is a bustle of activity.

Gabe's family is relocating from Eastcliffe to the resort; they love the SWA community and don't want to part fellowship. He is relocating all his businesses to the foothills as well.

Hope is a year old. Her plumage is a mix of black and white, her beak is becoming lighter, and her eyes are brown. She won't have the white head for several more years.

CHAPTER FIFTEEN

DREAMING AT THE GATE

The time has finally come for the SWA graduation service. There are only about fifty graduates. Over half of the school is first-year cadets. Ruby is graduating from the academy. She is, of course, younger than her friends. Most of the SWA cadets will leave Spirit Wings and return to their families. They will take with them the dedication and passion of the academy. It will spread all over the country. Some will go overseas to live and minister. Others may return later as adults and serve at the **S**pirit **W**ings **O**ut**R**each **D**ivision. The resort doubles its functions, being a resort and a mission base for S.W.O.R.D. (See "Types and Shadows" 15)

Yosef has been appointed as the Hebrew instructor at the base. His years in Hebrew school in Israel are paying off. There is a large Jewish community in the Mile High area. Jacob loves Denver and is considering auditioning at the local comedy club. Ira offers all the students lodging for the summer so they can seek the Lord and know what to do.

They set up the graduation ceremony outside, in the back of the resort, where the gardens and hiking trails are located. It is a beautiful setting, with blooming shrubs and potted plants, pine trees, and wandering trails. The chairs are set up in the flattest area they can find.

Aurora Oliver sings:

[62]There is one hope of our calling
One power to quicken our souls
One way to the Father, Jesus is the door

Come Lord show us salvation
Our hearts long to know
Come Lord into our presence, Spirit take control

There is one place of refuge
One rest for our souls
By faith we stand, sword and Bible in our hands

---

[62] *One Hope of Our Calling* written by Sandy Solis Jan of 1996

We choose to walk by faith
No doubt can kill our dreams
This world is subject to change
Our God will remain

The gang sits by tribe and looks around the graduation ceremony. The graduating class is in blue and white graduation gowns and caps. Everyone hopes Steven and Lee will show up today. But so far, they are still mysteriously gone, only phone calls to their parents; lets everyone know they are alive . . . somewhere.

Ira stands and announces, "Beloved, we are a family with eternal ties. We have a bridal dinner to attend one day. I look forward to seeing all of you there. **'Weeping may tarry for the night, but joy *comes* with the morning (Psalm 30:5b).** I know General Eli is so very proud of you all.

"General Eli always handed out the certificates and diplomas, but this year Professor Alvey will take his place."

A brief comment is made about each student as their name is called, and they walk forward to get their diploma.

Professor Ruben Alvarez calls out, "The tribe of Judah goes first!"

Jesse asks Destiny quietly, "Why? Why does Judah always go first?"

Destiny leans toward him, "We can't go into it now; it just has to do with **2 Chronicles chapter twenty**, okay? Now hush up!"

Jesse makes a face of frustration.

Professor Alvey continues, "From the tribe of Levi. . . ..

"Gloria Leslie Addison. A spitfire prayer warrior that can knock about thirty pounds right off you."

"Ruby Yolanda Alvarez. Most likely to be found in the prayer room and the best daughter a father could ever have."

"Faith Alison Andover. Has beautiful visions and is beautiful to view."

"Steven Michael Daniels. Voted most likely to get his foot stuck under a boulder (there is a chuckle)."

Steven did not show up. Everyone looks around, wondering what is going on with him and Lee.

Professor Alvey asks, "Has anyone heard from him or Lee?"

Everyone looks at each other, no one has heard or seen them since arriving at the resort on the day of the fire.

"Well, Steven and Lee . . . our prayers go out for you."

Professor Alvey moves on.

"Jesse Evan 'Rocky' Logan —"

The group stands and applauds.

"—The best pain in the neck student we ever had."

Dana stands up and yells, "That's my boy!"

"Destiny Kathryn Morris. Knows the word as well as Jamie, I would say. And that is saying something."

"Jacob Jedidiah Morris. Funny guy, serious future in comedy."

"Audrey Elizabeth Moss. One smart cookie."

"Kristen Marie Rutherford. Voted most cheerful and most likely to have a fit, all in the same day."

"Milagros Maria Salazar. Now celebrating the removal of her braces also. I don't know which makes her happier, graduating or no more braces. Congrats Millie. She is the bright and shining face that greets visitors now at the main desk!"

"Devin Robert Simmons. Future businessman of the year and a scholar of Revelation."

"Eric James Sinclair. A real powerhouse of a godly man, what can I say?"

"Yosef Adiv Wiesel. I hope I pronounced all that correctly, our Messianic Jew from Israel. He knows how to bless you in two languages. He has an inner strength that only Yeshua could put in him."

All the tribes are called, including Gabe and Ray. The graduates throw their caps in the air. Destiny and Jesse have a lengthy kiss.

Destiny and Jacob's parents from South Dakota (On a long sabbatical from the India mission field) have dinner with her and Jesse after the ceremony. They had heard a lot about Jesse and are not sure what to think of their daughter's boyfriend yet. Jacob tells them about the prophecy that Jesse and Destiny will marry in the future;

they seem to accept his prophecy with a small level of trepidation. Jesse feels nervous around them, but Destiny delights in his awkwardness, knowing it is because he loves her.

As always, Spirit Wings Academy gives a huge feast. It is the last thing the academy does before it turns into the mission base for good. Afterwards, Destiny and Jacob's parents return to South Dakota. Their parents are currently unable to return to the mission field due to political upheaval. After seeing the Morris's off, they talk about the future. Jesse grabs Ruby when Destiny is not around to tell her what he is up to.

I'm thinking of selling my street bike to buy an engagement ring for Destiny. I'm pretty excited."

"I'm so glad you guys are finally getting engaged," says Ruby.

"Yeah, and I have a big mural job lined up on the edge of town," Jesse adds. "Destiny has college offers but wants to do missions instead. Eli said we are in a new era . . . Things are going to be quite different. Will we get jobs and houses with white picket fences? Yahweh is pulling us out into the world to bring the Kingdom down," Jesse says in an invigorated tone.

His countenance changes, "That stupid darkness thing still hangs over my head. I am sick of it."

"You know how God has everything lined up in its time," Ruby reminds him. "I want a nice list from Adonai, like where to be and when, and for what purpose. I don't like the unknown so much. I am excited to see what the

Lord has in store for us, as a team of three; I hope Jamie is in the picture. We are lucky our families are backing us up and to have Ira and the Spirit Wings Base for headquarters," Ruby is filled with hope and optimism.

As the days continue, Aurora Oliver sings in the Soaking Room quite often, and people crowd in her sessions. The Prophetic, Healing, and Dream Interpretation rooms are now operational. Of course, there is a prayer room open twenty-four hours a day, where people pray for the nation, Israel, and justice throughout the world.

Over the next few days, many young warriors say "Goodbye" and return to their families. Ira knows they are seeds going out and will produce a harvest of souls and disciples for Christ. The newbies didn't get their full two years at the academy, but times have changed, and the academy is now a mission base. Additionally, S.W.O.R.D. will provide educational and spiritual resources to the community and anyone who wishes to participate. All of the members of the Levi tribe remain at S.W.O.R.D., with the sad exception of Steven and Lee. Ira will soon assign mission teams to go all over the world to further the Kingdom of Light. Jesse and Destiny are signed up; Ruby still needs to complete her paperwork.

As S.W.O.R.D. gets in full swing, there is a flurry of activity at the resort. This includes new signs being installed that say, "Home of **S**pirit **W**ings **O**ut**R**each

Division and resort." In the front lobby entrance, across from Hope's giant cage, is a portrait of Eli along with a large plaque talking about his contribution to Spirit Wings Academy. The Soaking Room is popular in the central lobby where the piano and harp are. As a result, more leather couches are put in. Signs showing locations of Healing Rooms, Dream Interpretation, and Prophecy rooms are being posted.

It is late May. The resort seems empty with the Ten Horsemen out on jobs, and most of the newbies returned home, except Alex and Manuel. Milagros smiles a lot now that her braces are off. She is happy working at the front desk as the receptionist. Dana and Allen are on staff in the new music studio, where S.W.O.R.D. will soon record worship albums and teaching albums. Ruby's parents are Ira's assistants. Jennifer is back to wearing her fashionable heels despite everyone's protests. She tells them they are being overprotective and intends to wear them to the delivery room.

Jamie left on his mission to the earthquake zone right after the graduation ceremony. Ira tells all who sign up for mission work that the summer will be spent seeking God before they are sent out. Additionally, she feels the need to cultivate extensive gardens and maintain some livestock. The resort has over fifty acres, including the trails, so S.W.O.R.D. Base members find plenty to keep them busy, even some embroidery work, just like "the good old days". Wanda and her gypsies all find positions to fill and settle in.

Shirts will soon have S.W.O.R.D. emblems embroidered on them.

CHAPTER SIXTEEN

SUMMER OF TRAVAIL

Ruby, Alex, Jorge, Trisha, and Manuel are hanging out in the lobby, listening to Aurora's set. They are all filling out their mission applications. Destiny and Jesse did theirs some time back. Ruby is nervous that she will not get assigned to them, and worried Manuel would feel the need to return to New York. She glances over at Alex. *Alex used to like him in the past. I wonder if they are still interested in each other.*

Ruby's thoughts are interrupted by the sound of planes overhead. She is ready to turn in her paperwork. It's two-thirty in the afternoon, and it's going to be a long day. She looks over at Manuel and smiles. He smiles back and keeps writing.

Destiny spends the afternoon in the vegetable garden. Jamie won't return for two weeks. Jesse is done with kitchen duty and goes over to the new prayer rock. He will be praying for Ruby for a change. He knows she feels unsettled about the future. Professor Norman takes Hope out to the garden for Ruby. It's the first day of June, and it's warm outside.

Destiny keeps noticing small planes in the air. She doesn't know if crop dusting is going on or why there are so many small planes out today. The Great Crisis of April happened with a small army of planes; is something happening again? Jesse also sees all the light aircraft from the secluded prayer spot. He wants to check the news for answers and heads back to the resort. He finds the news channels discussing ordinary topics, such as weather, sports, and political events.

Ruben has just talked to Jamie on the phone. He, too, feels something is up.

Jesse feels a stirring in the pit of his stomach. He grabs everyone he can and pulls them into the prayer room.

Devin is helping Allen set up a new soundboard.

"Jess, what's going on? I was busy," he complains.

Jesse tells them, "I just feel an urgency in my spirit; something is going to happen."

"That's all you know; something is going to happen?" Destiny wants some direction on how to pray.

No more talk. Jesse is on the floor in the prayer room in fervent prayer; everyone follows. Jesse thinks of

Jamie*; is he safe?* He prays harder. The room is filled with groaning and supplication. Adora, Ruben's sister, leads the prayer set; she assigns people to assist those in travail. She calls Ruben on her cell after about an hour.

"Something is happening. I need you to come to the prayer room." She hangs up.

By the time Ruby and the others follow Ruben in the prayer room, it is four-thirty in the afternoon. A few small planes are still streaming across the sky. Ruby wants to drink pop and eat a candy bar, but everyone is in the prayer room, so she goes in. She sees Jesse doubled over on the floor. She recognizes the travailing spirit and goes to pray over him. He is crying for mercy. Devin is also on his face on the floor, weeping, his hands covering his face. Only his chest heaves as he cries out to the Lord. She is always the one to travail; this is a switch. They tarry in prayer for two whole hours when sirens pierce the air.

"There isn't a cloud in the sky. It can't be weather-related," Adora remarks, looking upward.

Next, the power goes out. In the prayer room, the acoustic guitar and drums are the only instruments to make sounds. Then the music stops altogether, and everyone listens to the sirens.

Jesse stops sobbing and sits up to hear the sirens.

"Bombs," Jesse says. "Bombs," he repeats louder. He lies on his back and listens, his hands over his face.

Jennifer steps into the room with a candle and reports, "All the large cities are getting bombed, so nobody should go outside. Denver is the twenty-first largest city in the nation."

Ruby gasps, "Hope, is Hope outside?" She doesn't remember if Hope was in her cage or not.

Ruben tells her, "Professor Norman brought Hope in before lunch, and she is okay."

Just then, Professor Norman brings Hope into the prayer room for safety.

"Jamie is okay in Arkansas when I talked to him a few minutes ago. Yolanda and Arlo are on their way to the prayer room now." Ruben tells Ruby.

Everyone huddles together and prays in hushed tones. Allen and Dana enter the prayer room, and then all the kitchen staff join them. Norman turns on the news, and everyone listens to the news feed. Sporadic bombings are happening, mostly back east.

It is now six-thirty in the afternoon, but no one leaves for supper. Jesse huddles with Destiny and Ruby, and Ruben puts his arm around Ruby, too. Her mom and Arlo join the huddle. Soon, everyone is silent, listening for something to happen. The sirens continue. In the distance, they hear a 'KAWUNK' sound like a resounding thud. They hear another booming sound; this time, it is closer. Everyone's eyes get big.

"Was that a bomb?" Kristen asks.

Yosef sits in the center of the prayer room. His face is without expression, just one tear running down his face. Eric goes and sits by him.

"My parents sent me, um, to the States to get away from bombing; now here I am. I don't want them to live in fear for my life here," Yosef tells Devin.

For over an hour, everyone sits and listens to the occasional rumble. The uncertainty of what is happening is too much for Jesse; he jumps up and runs out.

Destiny yells to him, "No, Jesse, they said no one outside!" Her plea doesn't slow him down.

He runs to the covered parking lot and starts his street bike. By now, fire trucks and EMT vehicles are on the roads, their lights flashing and sirens blaring. Some military jets streak through the air, chasing small planes that are low and slow, hard to hit from a fast jet.

No one is in the front security gate booth, so Jesse drives on through the open gates. He speeds toward the loud 'KAWUNK' he had heard. The streets are empty except for emergency vehicles. Jesse's bike is heard clear down the neighborhood. From the lobby doors, Destiny and Ruby see him fly out of the resort on his motorcycle. The girls run back to the safety of the prayer room.

It is getting dark now, as there are no streetlights. It is an odd feeling for Jesse. He sees the glow of flames and drives toward it. Looking up, he sees one of the small planes; it is flying very low. It is right over his head; he can see the numbers on the bottom of it. It has small tanks attached to each side. The plane banks to the right, and the tanks are released. It is going to hit near Jesse. He turns a hard left into a park and drives as fast as he can away from it. It hits a middle school — little pieces of cement and shards of metal fly everywhere. Jesse feels a sting on his right leg; he reaches down to touch it and feels blood on his fingers. His heart is pounding in his chest; I *have had enough! I'm going back.* A row of police cars rush toward the bombed school area. Jesse pulls into a driveway while they pass. He hears a rifle shot; it hits the plane's fuel tank, and it explodes over the park and crashes. Now Jesse drives back to the base, full speed, before the police ask him about being out on his bike. He flies past the iron gates and drives up to the pool in the back. Hiding his bike in the bushes, Jesse goes through the back door. Everyone hears him drive in and meets him at the pool doors.

"Jesse, you are bleeding!" Destiny sees his hand and leg.

"Oh, please don't make a big deal. It's just little holes." Jesse doesn't want everyone to get upset.

"Are you alright?" asks Ira.

"Yeah — these small planes are dropping homemade bombs. One landed in the middle school," Jesse breathlessly tells everyone. "Someone shot the plane with bombs; it crashed in a park!"

Everyone gasps.

"So, how did you get hurt? By the bomb?" Dana finds her voice getting louder with alarm.

"I got a little too close," Jesse admits as the pain begins to course through him now.

"Jesse, sit down here and let me look at your leg," Doctor Luz tells Jesse.

He rips open Jesse's pant leg and looks at his injuries. Everyone gasps at the sight of many streaks of blood running down his leg. The doctor realizes he needs to do this privately.

"Ouch!" Jesse pulls his leg back from where Doctor Luz pinches to see the metal fragments in his leg.

"Come on, Jesse, we are going to have to pull out these pieces of shrapnel," Doctor Luz points to the kitchen. "Eric, you know where my new office is?"

Eric nods anxiously.

"Go get the black satchel by the door and bring it to the kitchen," says the doctor to Eric.

Eric is off like a shot.

Ruben instructs everyone else to go back to the prayer room, where there are no windows. It will be safer.

Dana, Destiny, and Ruby want to go with Jesse, but Jesse doesn't want them to.

In the kitchen, the doctor asks him if he left anything out of his story.

"There were jets all going toward the east. They couldn't hit the small planes. I expect those planes will hit the power grid when they are through with their bombs."

Eric returns out of breath with the black leather bag.

"Thank you, Eric, you may return to the others," Doctor Luz waves him on.

Eric hesitates and then leaves.

Jesse winces as Doctor Luz uses surgical needle-nose pliers to remove the metal from his leg.

"This is ground-up metal from the bomb, Jesse, not debris from the school. How close were you to the bombing?"

"I ended up right under the one by the middle school. Had to ride through a park to get away." Jesse is still breathing hard, the adrenaline and pain coursing through him.

"Do you need something for the pain?" Doctor Luz asks, looking up at his face.

"No, it's not that bad." Jesse doesn't want to get doped up with all that is going on. He squeezes his knee to keep the pain down while the doctor digs in the wounds for metal. There are about twenty pieces of metal on the counter; shrapnel pulled out of his leg. Some are like tiny metal ball bearings; others are metal shavings, curled and sharp.

"Okay, let's get you cleaned up." Doctor Luz sets down the pliers and gets a clean cloth and hot water. He scrubs Jesse's leg to prevent infection.

"Ah, that hurts more than the metal extraction!" Jesse is starting to feel ill. He is glad the girls aren't in the kitchen looking all worried and upset.

"Wash your face. You have blood from your hands smeared on it," Doctor Luz instructs. "You're good to go, but Jesse, don't go rogue on us again. You hear me?"

Jesse looks him in the eye, "I hear you."

Jesse tries not to limp as they return to everyone in the prayer room. The doctor pulls Ira and the leaders aside to inform them of what Jesse had told him.

Jesse sits down, his leg wrapped in bandages, the stripped jean leg dangling down. Destiny holds his hand. Dana is trying not to overwhelm him with questions or demands to examine his leg. Ruby gives him a look of understanding and simply sits by him, saying nothing. The sirens have ended, and it is creepily quiet. The power is still out. With only candles in the room, it gives off an eerie atmosphere.

Ruben gets through to Jamie on the phone. Everyone tries to hear what Ruben and Jamie are saying. He puts it on speakerphone; Jamie's voice sounds tense.

"Yeah, we are all okay here. We saw numerous small planes, followed by jets. We heard the battle in the air and some distant bombs, but none here. I hope the roads are intact so we can come home on schedule."

"Okay. Love you guys, the Lord keep you safe. Bye."

Ruben ends the call.

"We are lucky to get through on the cell phone," says Ruben.

All the emergency radio says is, "This is an emergency. Stay indoors away from windows and doors. A curfew is in effect," over and over.

Dana goes to the kitchen and gets Jesse some milk and a sandwich. He is glad to eat, not realizing how tired he is. Travail alone took a lot out of him.

"It's late. We should all eat something, and perhaps we should all stay in the prayer room for the night until we know what is happening. I know we all wish Eli were here to help us through this. But we have the Lord, and He will see us through," Ira tells her band of believers, packed into the windowless prayer room.

As everyone streams into the dining hall, a policeman enters and instructs them to check if anyone has rifles or guns and to load them, just in case. Gasps and exclamations go throughout the room.

Gerald Norman tells them, "I have a hunting rifle, but that is about all the weapons we have at the base. A few students from the Gad and Benjamin tribes received some degree of combat training. We will organize and take watches."

"Okay, that will have to do. Stay inside, away from windows and doors." The officers leave in a full run.

Kristen takes the first watch with Gabe and Ray. They position themselves in the lobby where they can see the front and the back.

Candles are limited; they are lit and placed around the prayer room. Groups go and get bedding to make pallets to sleep on the floor. It is quiet outside, except for the occasional sound of a car or ambulance.

Aurora and a few others, on guitar, begin to play and sing softly on stage. Others take their place in prayer.

Jesse's head is still racing with the carnage he saw earlier. His stomach aches, and his leg throbs. Doctor Luz comes to check on him.

"You feeling okay?" he looks in Jesse's eyes with a flashlight.

"Yeah, just kinda sick to my stomach," Jesse says, putting his hand on his stomach.

"I think we all are feeling upset," the doctor replies. "You don't have a fever. That is good. How is the pain level?"

"I'm okay, *really*." Jesse tries to assure him, but his voice gives him away.

"I want you to take just a couple of ibuprofens so that you can sleep, okay?" he hands him two pills.

Jesse swallows them.

Everyone is making pallets and lying down for the night. Jesse gets up and walks to the men's room. He throws water on his face and looks in the mirror. A streak of blood runs down his temple. When he pulls back his hair, he sees a shrapnel hole on the side of his head. Dried blood is in his hair. He holds paper towels over it until the bleeding stops. He realizes it is painful to apply pressure there.

"All I need is to have blood running down my face. My mom will come unglued."

Devin comes in.

"Did you say something, Jesse?"

"No, man, nothing." Jesse throws the towel away before Devin can see the blood.

"You really gave us a scare today, running off like that. Your mom cried the whole time you were gone. They had to take her off to a room and calm her down," says Devin, as though it were an everyday conversation.

Jesse looks out at the group huddled in the prayer room. His mom is sitting next to Destiny, looking for him to return to his place on the floor.

Allen meets him on his way back. "Jess," Allen begins to speak.

"I know, Dad. I am sorry." Jesse looks up at him.

"It is your mom who suffers when you run off," Allen responds.

Jesse thinks of his own suffering when they ran off for almost five years, but he doesn't say anything. He lies down by where his mom and Destiny are about to fall asleep, waiting for him. Dana stirs and looks at her boy lying there, and runs her hand through his hair. After a minute, she lifts her hand and feels dampness on the tip of her fingers. Jesse's mom has broken the small scab on his temple, and it begins to bleed again. She lets out a blood-curdling scream that brings everyone to their feet in alarm.

Jesse sits up in alarm.

"What's the matter?" Jesse asks as a small stream of blood runs down his chin and neck. He sees his mom looking at his face and realizes what happened.

"It is just a little hole, Mom. It's okay."

Jesse calms her down and gets her to sit back down; her hands are shaking. Jesse feels terrible for his mom.

The doctor shows up with the medical pliers and cocks his head toward the kitchen.

"You know the drill, Jesse, let's go."

The doctor pulls Jesse up off the floor. Jesse stumbles a little, still half asleep. He must press on the cut on his temple to stop it from bleeding. Dana gets up to follow. Jesse knows she needs to come, so he lets her.

"Just give me a Band-Aid, and I will be all fixed," Jesse suggests, wanting to defuse the tension.

In the dark kitchen, they take the brightest flashlight in the resort and set it on the worktable. The doctor takes out his medical bag and retrieves his pliers and some gauze.

"Okay, let's have a look here." Putting on some sterile rubber gloves, the doctor pulls Jesse's hair back. "Put your head on your mother's lap so that I can get a clear view and work," he tells Jesse.

Dana sits down on a bench, and Jesse sits down, laying his head on her lap. Dr. Luz has her hold the flashlight on the area of Jesse's head wound.

"Ow," Jesse says as he squints his eyes. The doctor pulls out a small piece of metal.

It is another coiled metal shaving. The doctor pours some antibiotics over the tiny wound while Dana holds a towel to keep it out of Jesse's eyes.

"Think two stitches will do it. The head bleeds so much more than other places."

Doctor Luz digs around in his bag for more items. He pulls out a syringe and a small vial with a clear liquid.

"You have to be joking, stitches?" Jesse doesn't think it is necessary.

The doctor holds up a small syringe to eye level and gently expels the air from the needle.

"Just a little to numb it . . ." The doctor looks at Dana. She is not having any trouble watching him work. He injects a numbing agent next to the wound. The needle hurts Jesse's temple area; Jesse squirms while the Doctor injects the numbing solution. Jesse grits his teeth and groans anxiously for him to get done with the syringe. Dana squeezes his shoulder.

"Hang in there, Jesse; he is almost finished." She is much calmer than before, still holding the light.

Doctor Luz finishes the stitches on Jesse's temple. "There. Please stand up so I can check. Did we miss any more?"

Doctor Luz has him turn around with his arms out, looking for more wounds. He thoroughly checks his head, and they return to the prayer room.

Dana and Destiny are fussing over Jesse. Ruby gives him a slight smile. She knows he is uncomfortable with people worrying over him. Dana wants to reprimand Jesse for going out without a helmet, but she holds back.

Soon, the room is quiet. Prayer vigils continue, and everyone else gets some sleep. The Gad and Benjamin tribes continue the night watch.

At about four in the morning, the power comes back on. Many get up to see the news in the dining area.

Dana is sleeping between Jesse and Destiny. When she leaves, Jesse reaches over to hold Destiny's hand.

The news has been running all night, where there is power. There is footage of the small planes and their bombs and jets shooting a few down. Only ten planes managed to reach and hit power stations. Four hundred small planes were stolen, rented, and chartered for this attack all over the nation. The damage is minimal, but the fear it causes is enormous. They call it "Night of Terror." Some anti-Israeli terrorists take credit for it. No specific nation to declare war on. Different agencies get criticized for not catching the warning signs of the unusual number of plane charters. A Summer of Love spokesman urges everyone to "Think Peace."

In contrast, a jihadist group wears prayer shawls that say in Arabic, "Jerusalem is ours; there is no Israel."

Professor Norman finds Jesse's bike, which he had hidden in the bushes; it has shrapnel holes all over it. The professor is amazed that the tires are all up. He rolls it up on the pool deck.

When Jesse finally wakes up that morning, everyone has gone to eat and watch the news. Jesse walks by to see his bike by the pool, full of holes. He sits down next to his mom at breakfast.

She looks at his bike outside and says, "Where was your helmet, young man?"

Dana had rebuked him only a few times in his life. He tends not to take authority well. He just looks down at the table and waits for the conversation to change.

"You are —" Dana stops herself.

She wants to tell him all the things a mother would tell her son. But they aren't a typical family yet, and Jesse is all too distant most of the time.

Jesse asks Ruby and Destiny as they come to sit down, “Are you both still ready to go out there and save the world?”

They both nod at Jesse; Jesse sees the doctor coming; he tries to hide by hunching down at the table. Dr. Luz grins and walks up to Jesse’s chair.

Jesse looks over at the girls, “Is he gone?”

The girls giggle, and Jesse turns red and faces the physician.

Jokingly, the doc says, “Let’s go, bucko!”

“Aw, come on, Doc. I will tell you if it gets infected.”

“Just like you told me, you had an entry wound on your temple.”

The doctor wants to see for himself.

Jesse limps to the kitchen. He needs a smaller bandage anyway so that he can change into some clean clothes.

“You could have had damage to larger arteries. The Lord was watching over you last night,” Doctor Luz tells him as he removes the bandage and checks for infection. He feels the leg for fever. “You realize if shrapnel penetrated your fuel tank, it would have exploded. Try to keep your head wound dry one more day.” Doctor Luz looks him in the eyes sternly.

Jesse swallows hard and drops eye contact.

“Yeah, that came to mind . . . well, thanks, Doc.”

Jesse is thankful he is around. He shakes off the gripping comment and decides he should put his bike away to keep everyone from seeing the shrapnel damage. He is about to roll his bike back to the covered parking lot when his dad walks up. Allen puts his finger through one hole on the fender and then looks over at Jesse.

"Please, Dad, don't say anything."

Jesse isn't ready to be corrected by him yet. His mom's screaming last night was bad enough, and he doesn't want any more drama right now.

"I am sorry, okay?" Jesse puts his hand in his pockets and looks up at him, expecting those angry eyes he knows so well.

Allen grabs him and holds him tight.

"We just couldn't stand to lose you, Jesse, we couldn't."

Allen is weeping. Jesse is shocked and puts his arms around his dad.

Ruby sees them from where she is eating. She just looks back down at her cereal. Jesse is such a private person; she wants to protect him somehow. Dana and Destiny sit down with their plates of food. They don't notice Jesse and his dad outside the window.

By lunchtime, the news is still doing live coverage of the "Night of Terror." Jesse grabs Destiny and Ruby and starts walking out the front doors. He leads them past the iron gates out to the street. He tells them, "Let's do this thing."

A word about the darkness and light, fear, and faith:

> **Again Jesus spoke to them, saying, "I am the light of the world. Whoever follows me will not walk in darkness, but will have the light of life."**
>
> **John 8:12**

> **In their case the god of this world has blinded the minds of the unbelievers, to keep them from seeing the light of the gospel of the glory of Christ, who is the image of God. For what we proclaim is not ourselves, but Jesus Christ as Lord, with ourselves as your servants for Jesus' sake. For God, who said, "Let light shine out of darkness," has shone in our hearts to give the light of the knowledge of the glory of God in the face of Jesus Christ.**
>
> **2 Corinthians 4:4-6**

Prayer of Salvation: I accept Jesus Christ as Lord and Savior. I believe that He is the Son of God, born of a virgin, died on a cross for the sins of the world, and rose on the third day. I ask for forgiveness, as I forgive others. I pray for the peace of Israel.

Peace I leave with you; my peace I give to you. Not as the world gives do I give to you. Let not your hearts be troubled, neither let them be afraid.

John 14:27

Sandy Solis's playlist for *The Cave of Abigor*

1. Cory Russell's "End of the Age" from *Ancient Paths* album. His words and mood fit perfectly in Jamie's speech in chapter one.
2. Laura Hackett's "I put on Christ" from the single -*I put on Christ*. This is perfect for the worship song that plays when the power comes on in chapter one.
3. Michael Card's "Psalm 121" is the song Jamie plays on the bus fleeing the fire.
4. Misty Edwards' "Only a Shadow" fits well in the opening song during the memorial for Eli.
5. Skillet's "Looking for Angels" also fits for the concert part of the Memorial.
6. Corey Russell's "Urgency of the Hour" from *Days of Noah* album is great for Jamie's speech at Invesco Field at Mile High.
7. Switchfoot's "AfterLife" fits well after Aurora's tribute song.
8. Misty Edwards' "Surrender" from her *Relentless* album. This song Aurora could sing at graduation

1

NIGHT IS COMING

If Yeshua is the light of the world, and we are of that light. It goes to reason that we would be out of the world for it to be dark. Obviously we can't work if we are removed from the planet. But don't forget we will be back!

A PURE BRIDE

The symbolism of a warrior bride is found in The Song of Solomon. A book just now coming into clairity.

SLEEPING AND THE SOUND OF ALARM -

Our spirit-man can remain in a state of dormancy if it is not brought forward and allowed to get strong and rule over our will and emotions.

~See Page 2~

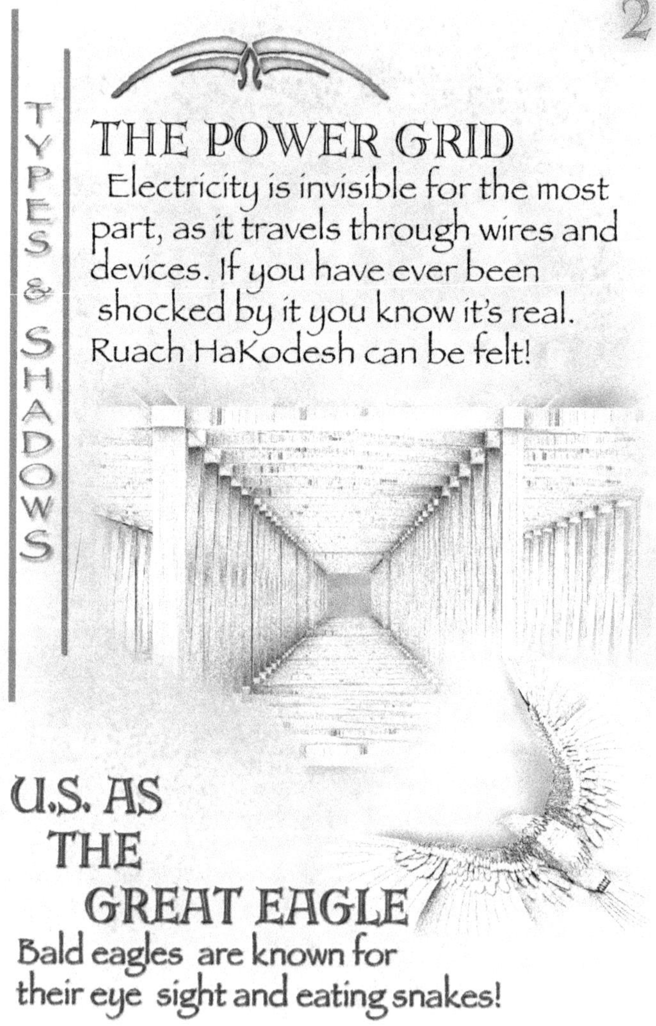

THE POWER GRID

Electricity is invisible for the most part, as it travels through wires and devices. If you have ever been shocked by it you know it's real. Ruach HaKodesh can be felt!

U.S. AS THE GREAT EAGLE

Bald eagles are known for their eye sight and eating snakes!

~See page 71~

3

TYPES & SHADOWS

SHAKING FRACTURES AND DIVISION -

A shift in society can bring good or ill favor. As public opinion shifts, people may change the side they are on.

See Matthew 10:16-39

Creatures from the Crevasse - The earth is cursed by the fall of man Genesis 3:17. What manner of evil lies under the crust? JRR Tolkein wrote of all manner of creatures from inside the earth, orcs for example.

~See page 81~

4

BABYLON

Babylon reprsents the corrupted world system, and HaSatan's headquarters. The word is associated with chaos. Chaos had its start in Genisis 1:2. Babylon's end is discussed. in Revelation 18:21:

Then a mighty angel took up a stone like a great millstone and threw it into the sea, saying, "So will Babylon the great city be thrown down with violence, and will be found no more;

ORPHAN SPIRIT

When the connection with an earthly father is severed, one may find it hard to connect with Abba Father.

ANCHOR OF THE SOUL

Soul- our mind, will, and emotions. If our soul has no anchor we are all over the place. . .

~See page 101~

5

TYPES & SHADOWS

PILLAR IN THE TEMPLE

Psalm 144:12 May our sons in their youth be like plants full grown, our daughters like corner pillars cut for the structure of a palace;

COBWEBS

Spiders and their webs often are associalted with evil. Isaiah 15:1-8

~See page 135~

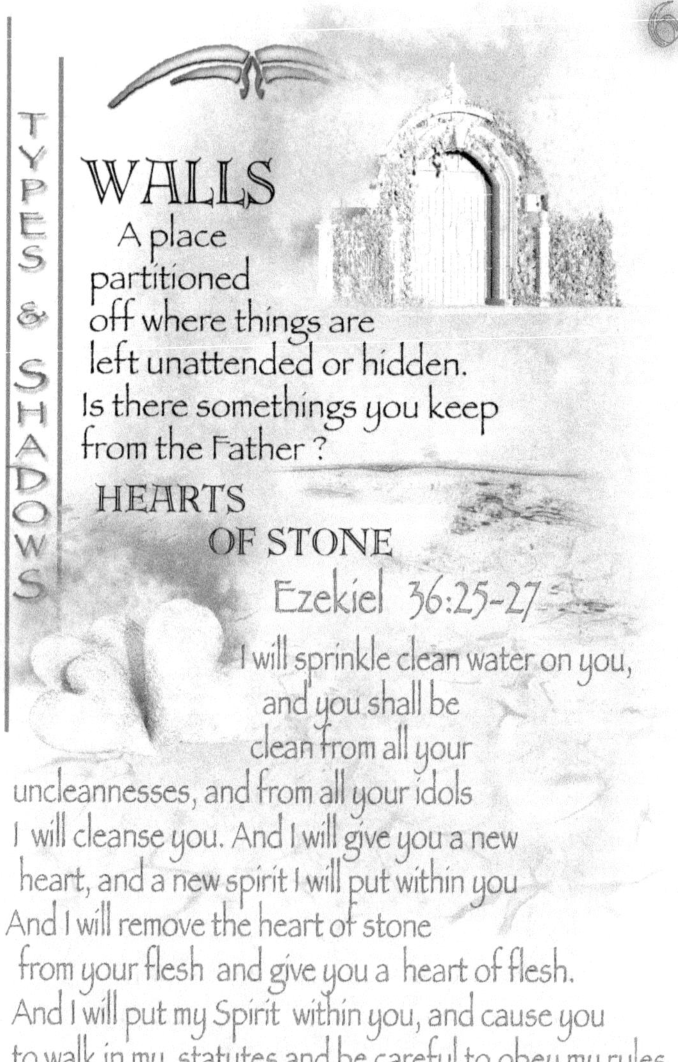

WALLS

A place partitioned off where things are left unattended or hidden. Is there somethings you keep from the Father ?

HEARTS OF STONE

Ezekiel 36:25-27

I will sprinkle clean water on you, and you shall be clean from all your uncleannesses, and from all your idols I will cleanse you. And I will give you a new heart, and a new spirit I will put within you And I will remove the heart of stone from your flesh and give you a heart of flesh. And I will put my Spirit within you, and cause you to walk in my statutes and be careful to obey my rules.

~See page 167~

7

TYPES & SHADOWS

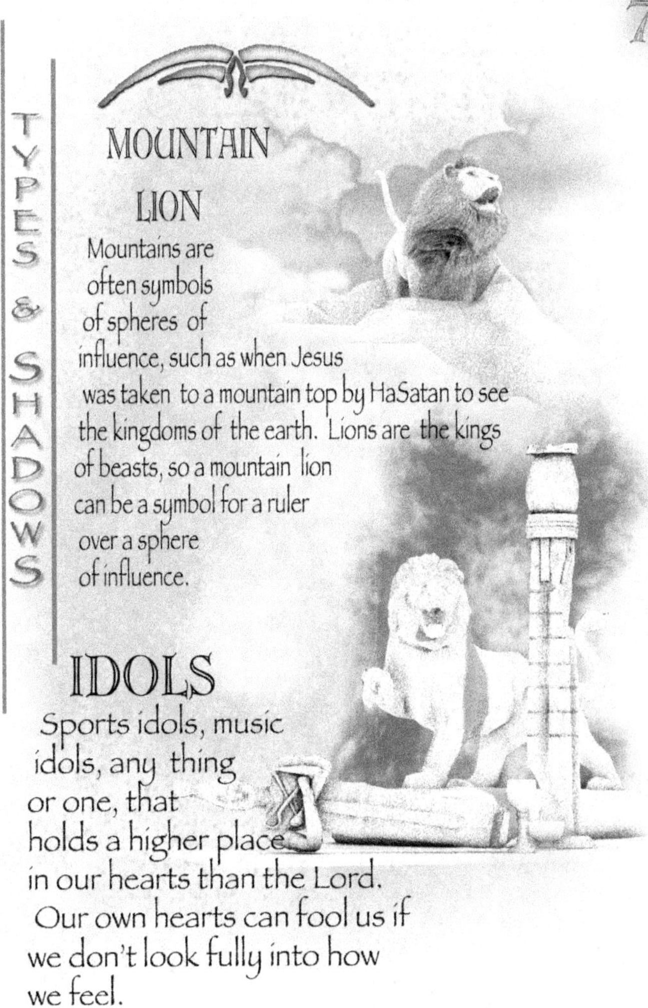

MOUNTAIN LION

Mountains are often symbols of spheres of influence, such as when Jesus was taken to a mountain top by HaSatan to see the kingdoms of the earth. Lions are the kings of beasts, so a mountain lion can be a symbol for a ruler over a sphere of influence.

IDOLS

Sports idols, music idols, any thing or one, that holds a higher place in our hearts than the Lord. Our own hearts can fool us if we don't look fully into how we feel.

~See page 184~

8

HIDDEN IN PLAIN SIGHT

Days of the week- IDOLS.
Sunday- day of the sun
Monday- day of the moon
Tuesday- day of Mars, (god of war)
Wednesday -day of Odin or Mercury
Thursday- day of Thor
Friday- day of Venus
Saturday- day of Roman god Saturn

Did you find the sun and the moon?

ANNIVERSARY SPIRIT

Some days are marked forever in our minds by tragedy. When those dates have a repeating misfortune it could be this spirit. Some premature deaths in families often occur on certain dates or interval of years, maybe a curse is involved. Examples are "The Ides of March", Adar 9 for Israel, Check out this Jewish date!
Idols are mentioned Exodus 10.

~See page 229~

9

TYPES & SHADOWS

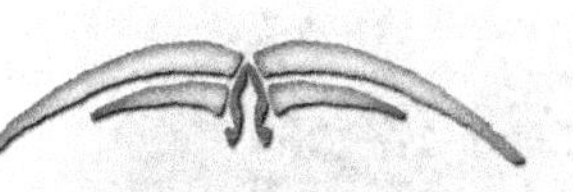

U.S. HISTORY WITH SPOTS OF PAGANISM.

Check out obelisks, Ashera poles, Free Masonry, Easter origins, Halloween, Statue of Liberty's real symbolism. Look for 8 pointed stars, sun gods, crescent moons, curved swords, pyramids with an eye in it.

ALIGNED WITH YAHWEH'S TIME

Yahweh's Feasts were lost to the church over time. All the feasts mark Elohim's time line for earth, 3 feasts are yet to be fulfilled.

COME OUT FROM AMONG THEM
Revelation 18:4

Don't forget our Jewish root!s! In book three a major character finds out about roots that were hidden

~See page 228~

TYPES & SHADOWS

10

GUARD YOUR HEART

The heart ia a place of emotions and attitudes. Our heart can surprise us sometimes. The heart is where Yahweh invests the most. Integrity and valor nest in the heart.

REFINED LIKE SILVER AND GOLD

Intense heat. dross burns off. In a melted state metals can change shape. What matterial would reflect your self image? Plastic can shatter, rubber bounces back.

I Corinthians 3:10-15

According to the grace of God given to me, like
a skilled master builder I laid a foundation,
and someone else is building upon it.
Let each one take care how he builds upon it.
For no one can lay a foundation other than that
which is laid, which is Jesus Christ.
Now if anyone builds on the foundation with gold,
silver, precious stones, wood, hay, straw—
each one's work will become manifest,
for the Day will disclose it, because it will be revealed
by fire, and the fire will test what sort of work
each one has done. If the work that anyone has built on the
foundation survives, he will receive a reward.
If anyone's work is burned up, he will suffer loss,
though he himself will be saved, but only as through fire.

~See page 243~

SPIRIT OF SLUMBER

Romans 11:7

GREAT BREACH

Psalm 60:2 You have made
the land to quake; you have torn it open;
repair its breaches, for it totters.
Baal-perazim, is a term of Yahweh -
II Samuel 5:20
And David came to Baal-perazim, and
David defeated them there.
And he said, "The Lord has broken
through my enemies before me like
a breaking flood." Therefore
the name of that place is called
Baal-perazim.

HOPE IN HER CAGE

Eagles are symbols of prophets. In the past prophets were "caged" and not given a voice in culture.

~See page 140, 399~

~See pages 325, 355~

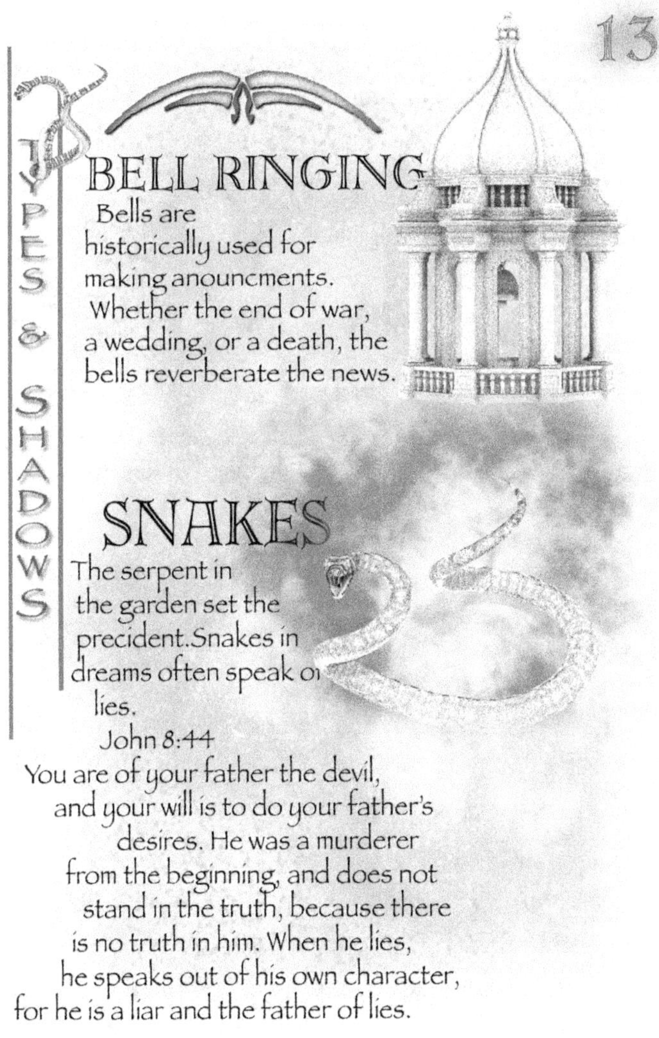

BELL RINGING

Bells are historically used for making anouncments. Whether the end of war, a wedding, or a death, the bells reverberate the news.

SNAKES

The serpent in the garden set the precident.Snakes in dreams often speak of lies.

John 8:44

You are of your father the devil, and your will is to do your father's desires. He was a murderer from the beginning, and does not stand in the truth, because there is no truth in him. When he lies, he speaks out of his own character, for he is a liar and the father of lies.

~See pages 222, 367~

EARTH

This can be an analogy of the heart. Hosea 10:12, also the parable of the sower Matthew 13

WIND

Ruach HaKodesh is Hebrew for Holy Wind or breath.

John 3:8

The wind blows where it wishes, and you hear its sound, but you do not know where it comes from or where it goes. So it is with everyone who is born of the Spirit."

FIRE

Fire can stand for passion, change agent, purifier, rage, ect. The fire of God burns in Jesse. He is a flame that does not bring ruin, but hope and intimacy with Yahweh.

~See page 384~

15

TYPES & SHADOWS

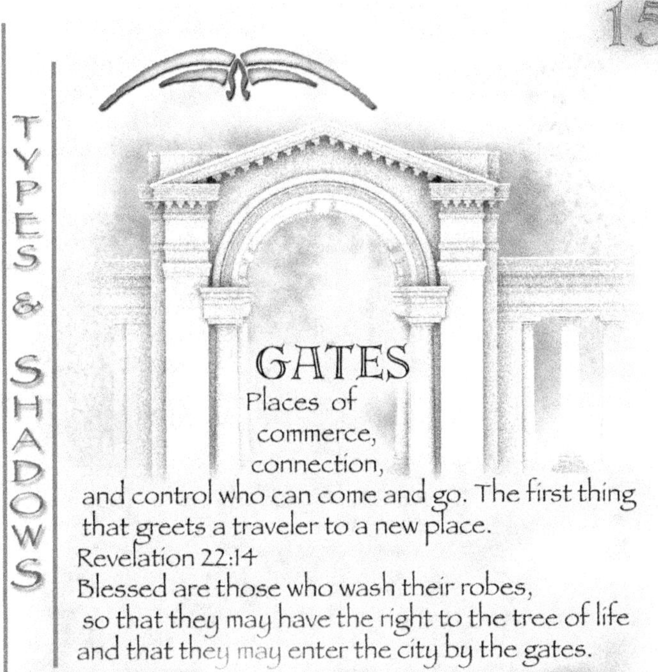

GATES

Places of commerce, connection, and control who can come and go. The first thing that greets a traveler to a new place.

Revelation 22:14
Blessed are those who wash their robes,
so that they may have the right to the tree of life
and that they may enter the city by the gates.

GRADUATION

Life has many growing levels. As we go along we gain favor, influence and other benefits of graduations.

~See page 401~

16

TYPES & SHADOWS

BATTLES WITHIN

II Corinthians 10:3-5

For though we walk in the flesh, we are not waging war according to the flesh. For the weapons of our warfare are not of the flesh but have divine power to destroy strongholds. We destroy arguments and every lofty opinion raised against the knowledge of God, and take every thought captive to obey Christ,

BATTLES WITHOUT

Romans 16:4

For they are demonic spirits, performing signs, who go abroad to the kings of the whole world, to assemble them for battle on the great day of God the Almighty

~See page 428~

About the Author:

Sandy Solis is a native of Colorado, now living in Green Country, Oklahoma. She is a 3D computer artist and lives on the family ranch. You can see her videos on YouTube under the channel name Biblerock.

In her spare time, she enjoys home remodeling, stained glass, and shopping for silver jewelry.

The author's website is www.SpiritWingsOnline.com

CHECK OUT THE COMPANION ANIME-STYLE COLOR BOOKS FOR EACH BOOK IN THE SERIES. AGES 13+

SPIRIT WINGS BOOK SERIES

Look for:

Book One –
The Academy

Book Two –
The Cave of Abigor

Book Three–
The House of Asher

Book Four –
The Scepters of the Kings

Book Five –
The Landing Strip

Book Six –
The Jade Seal

Book Seven –
The Sound of Heaven

Book Eight
The Great Threshing Floor

MORE BOOKS IN THE SERIES
COMING SOON

www.ingramcontent.com/pod-product-compliance
Lightning Source LLC
Chambersburg PA
CBHW070829260626
47170CB00007B/2313

* 9 7 8 0 6 1 5 9 0 1 6 4 0 *